Praise for the novels of *USA TODAY* bestselling author Stefanie London

"Funny and sweet... I devoured this book in one sitting!"
—*New York Times* bestselling author Jennifer Probst
on *The Dachshund Wears Prada*

"This is the romcom Carrie Bradshaw would have written if she were a dog person, and I'm obsessed!"
—*USA TODAY* bestselling author Teri Wilson
on *The Dachshund Wears Prada*

"One of the year's most delightful rom-coms. Ms. London pens a sparkling confection of all the feels and I devoured it."
—*New York Times* bestselling author Julia London
on *The Dachshund Wears Prada*

"Heartwarming, charming, and adorably sexy, *The Dachshund Wears Prada* made my dog-loving heart smile."
—*USA TODAY* bestselling author Tawna Fenske

"At turns both witty and tender, *The Dachshund Wears Prada* is a delightful treat of a novel, guaranteed to give you the warm fuzzies."
—*USA TODAY* bestselling author Melonie Johnson

"In a sea of 'hot guys in suits,' London's sharp writing helps this sweet and sexy story stand out."
—*New York Times* bestselling author Lauren Layne
on *Bad Bachelor*

"A wonderful escapist treat."   —*Booklist* on *Bad Reputation*

The Dachshund *Wears* Prada

STEFANIE LONDON

HQN

Recycling programs
for this product may
not exist in your area.

ISBN-13: 978-1-335-63983-7

The Dachshund Wears Prada

Copyright © 2022 by Stefanie Little

For questions and comments about the quality of this book, please contact us at
CustomerService@Harlequin.com.

HQN
22 Adelaide St. West, 41st Floor
Toronto, Ontario M5H 4E3, Canada
www.Harlequin.com

Printed in U.S.A.

To all the dogs who've held a special place in my heart:
Jasmine, Cici, Zorro, Lady, Maggie and Harry.

The Dachshund *Wears* Prada

1

Theo Garrison had never felt so uncomfortable in a suit in all his life, which was saying something, given an ex-girlfriend had once asked him if he exited the womb wearing a three-piece. But today it felt like his signature outfit was suffocating him, despite being tailored to his exact measurements. He reached up to his shirt collar and hooked his finger over the edge, tugging in a desperate attempt to find relief. But none came.

Maybe it wasn't the suit at all.

Maybe it was being surrounded by two hundred people. *Too* many people, for such an event. Theo avoided large gatherings where possible. But not today. Today, he was here to honor his grandmother, and she never did anything without a crowd.

Not even dying.

He tugged at his collar again. The sun beat down relentlessly and agitation prickled along his skin as the priest talked about his grandmother's life. The weight of curious eyes made him antsy. He hated being watched. Hated that people looked at him as they might a reptile in an enclosure, tapping on the glass to see how he'd react. Thankfully, Etna Francois-Garrison had been commanding most of the attention today, which Theo was sure had been her goal.

Otherwise why choose to be buried in a Valentino ball gown?

The casket—now closed after a viewing period earlier that morning—was pure white, lined with pale pink silk and studded with glinting stones that Theo was pretty sure were real diamonds. Frankly, as executor of his grandmother's estate, he'd barely even looked at the list of requests when it had come time to sign off. Whatever his grandmother wanted, she would have. No request too outrageous. It was the last time he'd ever get to say yes to her. The last time he'd ever get to show her how important she was to him.

After all, when his parents had died, leaving him orphaned at the tender age of ten, she'd taken him in. She'd been his mother, father, grandparent, confidant. His whole family. Only *she* could have filled so many roles, with personality left over for more.

Theo swallowed. A lump was firmly lodged in the back of his throat and a yawning sense of loss roared like an open cavity in his chest. But he stood tall, with shoulders back and squared, and eyes drilling a line straight ahead.

"If the family could please come forward to pay a final tribute," the priest said, gesturing to Theo.

The family. It was a word that belonged to a group. But he was the only person who stepped forward. This was it, the entire Garrison family reduced to a single person. A Manhattan legacy hanging by a thread.

Theo walked toward the priest, who stood next to a small portable table. It was piled with roses. Not red, because his grandmother hated a cliché. Not white or yellow, because those seemed too sad. But a hot pink so bright they seemed artificial. Theo took one, noting how the thorns had been carefully removed. His thumb skated over a spot of raw green where the sharp edge had been sliced off.

"Goodbye, Gram," he said as he tossed it into the open space where the casket had been lowered into the ground. The rose landed softly on the shuttered white lid. "Say hi to everyone for me."

He reached for another rose, and then another, tossing one in for each of the people who should have been by his side—his mother, father and grandfather, all taken too soon. All gone before they'd lived a full life.

Theo stepped back, thankful he'd remembered to wear a pair of sunglasses. He liked having a shield between him and the world at the best of times, but he needed it now more than ever.

When the service concluded, people came to pay their respects. His hand was pumped over and over, cheeks kissed in sweeping, perfumed grazes. Theo had spotted plenty of familiar faces today. The funeral was a who's-who of New York society—fashion designers, politicians, blue bloods—which was exactly how his extroverted, attention-loving grandmother would have wanted it.

It didn't matter that he would rather be alone to say his goodbyes. Today was about her. Letting out a long breath, he stuffed his hands into the pockets of his suit pants as he waited for the gravesite to empty.

"She was a magnificent woman," Father Ahern said, walking over and laying a comforting hand on Theo's shoulder. "Incomparable. Truly one of a kind."

"I know." He nodded.

"She used to come to my service every Sunday and sit in the front row. Nobody dared to take her spot, even if she was late." The older man chuckled and folded his hands in front of his robes. "The one time a few kids *did* sit there, she shooed them away with her purse. It was like watching someone scatter a flock of seagulls. Nobody tried again after that."

Theo smiled. He could easily picture it. She was like that— a woman who commanded others. A powerhouse, even back when women were rarely in charge. And recently, a Goliath as she battled illness until her last breath.

"You never attended with her," Father Ahern commented.

"I don't like crowds."

"Think of it as more of a community."

Theo watched the last few people trickle down to the town cars lining the road that wound through the cemetery. He caught a glimpse of the media further back, only stopped from getting closer because of the burly security guards he'd hired for the day. The vultures waited with cameras poised, cementing Theo's belief that there was one thing in the world that sold better than sex.

Grief.

"I don't really like communities, either," Theo replied.

That was putting it mildly. Barring today, he couldn't remember the last time he'd been in a room with more than three people—outside work. And it wasn't by accident.

The priest frowned. "I know losing your parents the way you did must have been hard."

"It was a long time ago." And he still woke with night terrors about it, even now, a quarter of a century later. He'd never get the image out of his head—the mangled car, blood splattered against the windows. Every news outlet had plastered it with bold headlines and people reacted with shocked faces like nobody had seen it coming.

Hollywood sweetheart and New York royalty pronounced dead at the scene.

His heart clenched. His mother and father *had* seen it coming. They'd taken preventive measures to avoid the paparazzi and their increasingly intrusive, aggressive behavior. Decoy cars, unfamiliar routes, evasive driving…right into the side of a bridge.

So yeah, Theo had a bit of a problem with the media. He also had a problem with people poking their noses into his private life. He discouraged that by keeping to himself. It wasn't personal, though. It was protection.

"It's okay to grieve," the priest said. "God gave us emotions for a reason and sadness is natural."

Before he had a chance to say anything further, Frank Ferretti appeared beside them. He was dressed in all black, which was appropriate for a funeral but also completely on-brand for the older Italian man. He'd been a longtime family friend, initially a bodyguard to Theo's mother and then a right-hand man and confidant to his grandmother.

"Ready?" Frank asked. "I've got a car waiting for you."

Theo stuck his hand out to the priest. "Thank you, Father. It was a wonderful service. You did her memory proud."

"If you change your views on community, I'd love to have you as part of ours."

Theo nodded, though he knew deep down nothing would change. Ever since he was a child, he drew a circus wherever he went. Today was no different. Next week would be no different. It would never be different until he was the one closed inside a casket and buried six feet under.

It was easier to keep to himself.

"This way." Frank led Theo through the family plot, where his grandmother had been laid to rest with her husband and Theo's parents. They moved away from the road, cutting through a section of manicured garden and slipping into a gap in a hedge. Sunlight streamed down, warming the back of Theo's neck and shoulders. Reminding him that even on his darkest days, the world still turned.

Behind them came the annoyed cries of the media as they realized they weren't going to get their scoop. Frank and Theo hurried to the waiting car and slipped inside as a few photographers made it through the hedge behind them. Flashes went off, but they peeled away, causing Theo to white-knuckle the door handle.

Usually, his drivers were under strict instruction to *not* go fast. But these weren't usual circumstances. The car navigated the road out of Green-Wood's main entrance and soon they were leaving Brooklyn in the rearview mirror as they crossed the bridge back into Manhattan. Mercifully, it seemed as though the press hadn't kept up. Not that it stopped Theo looking over his shoulder.

He *always* looked over his shoulder.

"They only do this shit because you insist on being such a mystery," Frank muttered. "The quieter you are, the more desperate they are to get information."

"Let them be desperate. I'm not going to give them a damn thing."

Frank let out a raspy laugh. He had a voice as rough as alligator skin. "You know, I read an article about you the other day."

"Really?" Theo raised a brow. "Are they still rehashing the same old shit? Because I certainly haven't given them anything new to talk about."

"They called you the Hermit of Fifth Avenue."

"It has quite a ring to it." He glanced at Frank. "I also liked Most Mysterious Man in Manhattan. They're turning me into an urban legend."

"Don't let it go to your head."

"Never." Theo watched Manhattan roll slowly past them. There were times when this place felt like a shoebox, which would sound ridiculous to any normal person. But there was something about the way the towers reached up to the sky that reminded Theo of bars on a cage. "I'm really going to miss her."

"I know." Frank laid a heavy hand on Theo's shoulder. "Me too."

The car continued to work its way through the city, and as the Upper East Side got closer, Theo leaned his head back against the headrest. The weight of the past few weeks crushed down on him and brought a sense of exhaustion and finality that penetrated his bones.

It was over now. She was really gone.

"It won't take long to go through the final bits and pieces," Frank promised, as if sensing Theo's thoughts. "I found a few more old photos and some letters in a drawer. I thought you might want them."

"Honestly, I'm beat. I'll come by tomorrow after work to sort through the last of it."

"Sure, but you still have to pick up the dog."

Theo snapped his head toward the other man. Clearly his lack of sleep was getting to him even more than he realized. "The dog?"

"Yeah, the dog." Frank looked at him like he'd sprouted a second head and started speaking Elvish. "Camilla? You know, little torpedo of fluff with the disposition of a belligerent drunk in a bar fight. Teeth as sharp as needles. Invisible horns and devil tail...any of this ringing a bell?"

"I'm familiar," he said, shuddering. His grandmother's dog was as notorious for her bad attitude as Theo was for his privacy. "But why do I need to pick her up?"

Frank was still giving him that look. The look that said he could see Theo's lips moving but he didn't understand a word coming out of his mouth.

"Because," the older man said, stretching the word out like he was speaking to a small child. "You are now the proud owner of one pampered devil princess."

"What?" Theo blinked and shook his head. "Since when?"

"Since you signed off on all the paperwork for the estate. Remember, the lawyers went through your grandmother's will and all the donations she wanted to make and—"

"Yes, yes." Theo waved a hand. "I remember that meeting. But I *don't* remember anything about the dog."

To be fair, he'd been in such a daze that day. His grandmother had updated her will right before she passed, since Theo was adamant that a good portion of her money go to the charities she supported. He was wealthy in his own right, these days, and he didn't need more from her. But it had been hard to concentrate, the grief already freezing him before she died. It had been like trying to think through thick fog and all he really remembered was saying "yes, of course" over and over and over.

But adopting that tiny hellhound? Surely, he would have remembered *that*.

"It was under the list of heirloom possessions to remain in the family." Frank scrubbed a hand along his jaw.

"Heirloom possessions?" Theo sucked in a quick breath through his teeth. "Are you fucking kidding me? Heirlooms are things like antique watches and family photo albums and embroidered goddamn table linens. Not pets."

And definitely not *this* pet. Heirloom, his ass.

"She was on the list," Frank said stubbornly. "Do you make a habit of signing things without reading the fine print? Your grandfather would have something to say about that."

No, Theo never signed a thing without first using his eagle eye to parse the terms. But these had been unusual circumstances—he'd wanted to give his grandmother every-thing before she left this earth. He'd wanted to make her as happy and comfortable and appreciated in her final days as possible. He wanted to be the perfect grandson one last time. But he damn well *should* have noticed if she was trying to foist that awful animal on him, even with the mental fog.

Yet she hadn't said a word about it to Theo directly.

Which meant his sweet, yet cunning grandmother had purposefully hidden her pampered pooch in the fine print so Theo wouldn't notice. Because as much as he wanted to make her happy, there's no way he would have agreed to this. No way in hell.

Theo's life ran like clockwork, because he stuck to a very strict set of rules:

1. No interviews.
2. No surprises.
3. No relationships.
4. No exceptions.

The last point on that list was especially important. Which was going to pose a problem. A four-legged, glossy-maned, foul-tempered problem.

"I can't believe this," Theo said, shaking his head.

Frank sighed. "Let's see what happens when we get to her place, okay?"

"Fine."

By the time Theo and Frank made it into his grandmother's brownstone on the Upper East Side, Theo felt like his head was going to explode. The place was almost empty now, since an army of staff had spent the last week packing up her impressive art collection and all the antique furniture. Most items were being donated to museums or charity auctions, although some close friends had been allocated special pieces in the will. Her extensive wardrobe of couture clothing had been curated for a display at the Fashion Institute of Technology, and the jewels were going to the Metropolitan Museum of Art.

Well, all except her wedding ring. That one was tucked away in Theo's private safe along with the one worn by his mother for sentimental reasons *only*. Neither of them would ever again grace a woman's finger.

Everything else was checked and accounted for. Boxes were neatly labeled and piled into stacks depending on who would come to collect them. The office had been locked up, awaiting a final sweep by Theo to make sure all the important paperwork went to him.

Everything had been going according to plan...until now.

Theo's footsteps echoed through the mostly empty space, the sound bouncing off the high ceilings. The place looked cavernous without her. It was a shell, with no life and no light and no joy.

"You're early!" A woman emerged from the sitting room. "I wasn't expecting you back for another hour."

Theo didn't recognize her, but Frank was quick to make an introduction. "This is Marcie. She's been looking after Camilla for the last few weeks, ever since your grandmother went into hospital."

"I'm very sorry for your loss." Marcie bowed her head. "And I'm sorry that I had to insist on dropping Camilla off today. I know it's a difficult time. But I...can't do this anymore."

At that moment, as if summoned by a sound no human could hear, or perhaps by the devil himself, Camilla entered the room. The Dachshund was less than a ruler's length in height, with stumpy little legs that made her waddle with each step. Despite that, you would have thought the Queen of England had entered the room.

In fact, for a minute Theo was sure he'd heard trumpets announcing her arrival. Or was that simply warning sirens going off in his brain?

Her long champagne-colored fur was brushed and gleaming, and a pink collar sat around her neck, a silver C-shaped charm dangling from the loop at the front. On first glance, one might call her cute. Or even sweet. But more fool anyone who assumed Camilla was some passive little lap dweller ready to cuddle and beg for belly scratches.

Oh no, this tiny beast was a dictator on four legs.

"Everything you need is in the other room," Marcie said, the pitch of her voice climbing. "I've marked off where we are in her daily routine and I've packed all her things so you can take her straight home. On that note, I really need to get going. Actually, right now."

And with that, Marcie scurried from the room as though fearful someone might try to stop her. The woman clearly had an exit plan. After the sound of the front door closing echoed through the room, Theo stared at the dog.

Camilla stared back.

"Well, then…" Frank cleared his throat. "What do you want to do? I can call a shelter and have her picked up. Or I can call around Etna's friends and see if anyone will take her."

Camilla's head swung to Frank, and Theo would swear he saw the little dog's eyes narrow in fury.

In his heart of hearts, he knew he couldn't dump the dog. Not now. His grandmother had meant the world to him, and while he would absolutely have argued the point when she was alive…that was no longer an option. Which meant he only had two choices: honor her wish, or not.

"I *know* I'm going to regret this," Theo said, with a shake of his head. "But I'll take her."

"You sure?" Frank asked with a grimace. "What does it matter now? Your grandmother won't know the difference."

"Yes, but *I* will." He sighed. "Gram obviously wanted me to have her for a reason."

Both men looked at the small, sausage-shaped dog and for a moment, no one made a move. Then Camilla marched over to Theo and tipped her face up, two beady black eyes looking right into his soul as if telepathically communicating how much she hated him. Why did Theo have the feeling that this wasn't going to end well? It wasn't until a few seconds later, when the dog trotted back into the other room, nose and tail in the air, that he realized she'd peed all over his shoe.

2

If Isla Thompson had known she was staring down the barrel of the end of her career, she might have dressed differently. Stilettos didn't make for a quick getaway. Neither did bandage dresses or ridiculously small clutches that required professional-level Tetris skills to pack.

Unfortunately, she'd worn all three.

"And that's why I chose Sahara Vanderkamp to dress me for this year's Met Gala." Amanda Harte, Disney princess and America's teen sweetheart, shone her trademark beaming smile into the tiny camera in Isla's phone. "We wanted to explore this year's theme of *flora and fauna: fashion in nature* by drawing inspiration from my hometown of…"

Isla zoned out as her client explained the inspiration behind her dress. The poufy monstrosity was a retina-searing mix of gold and lime-green, with tulle and satin and sequins and beading. What had the designer said? The intersection of powerful femininity and the avant-garde?

Avant-garde nothing.

The dress looked like a couture version of a kindergarten craft project gone horribly wrong. But Amanda had wanted to stand out in the crowd of fashion icons, Hollywood royalty and design industry movers and shakers.

And apparently lime-green was the Pantone color of the year, so what Isla thought was beside the point.

She monitored her phone, following the interactions from users watching the live Instagram video. Hearts bubbled up the side of the screen and comments scrolled to the right, littered with emojis and cries of "I love you, Amanda!" Of course, as with every young female star online, there were lewd comments, but part of Isla's job was shielding Amanda from all that.

"This is my first year attending the Met Gala," Amanda said, smiling at the camera as she gave her dress a swish in the luxe hotel room they'd camped out in, a block away from the Metropolitan Museum of Art. In the background, Manhattan glittered through a large open window, the perfect backdrop for this glamorous occasion. "Actually, I'm a little nervous…"

Isla's head snapped up. They'd talked about this. Rule number one: no showing nerves on-screen. Aspirational, aspirational, aspirational—that was the motto. They wanted Amanda to come across as confident and warm. Verging on relatable, but not quite. Their strategy was to make her appear so beautiful and talented that her fans could only *hope* to achieve a grain of her success.

Aka the T-Swift publicity model.

"Who are you most excited to meet tonight?" Isla asked, prompting her client to talk about her latest celebrity crush.

Crushes were good; they made her seem close to the millions of fans logging on to watch her. But instead of making goo-goo eyes over a cute boy in calculus, Amanda crushed on the handsome stars who graced the posters inside her fans' school lockers. There was that word again: aspirational!

Amanda's tight expression morphed into pure teenage joy— pink cheeks, sparkling eyes and a full smile. "Tom Holland, of course. Who *doesn't* have a crush on Spiderman?"

The comments exploded on the live video, and hearts flooded the side of the screen. Isla gave Amanda a thumbs-up and motioned for her to wrap up the livestream. They had about ten minutes before it would be time to take the private elevator down to the hotel's back entrance and slip into a waiting limousine.

"Thank you so much for watching." Amanda blew a kiss to the camera. "I love you all so much. Don't forget to check out my film debut, *Return to Heaven*, coming out next month. See you on the red carpet!"

Isla tapped the screen to end the live video, but her phone chugged for a minute. The Wi-Fi in this hotel was appalling. How could they be in the middle of the Upper East Side and have such shitty reception? Amanda was still waving at the screen, her eyes darting over to Isla for a signal that she could relax. The phone went blank.

"Crap." Isla twisted the device, which was nestled in a sturdy but small tripod, and tapped the screen again. The rest of Amanda's posse was hovering nearby, anxious to put the finishing touches on the young star for her Met Gala debut.

"Can we get this show on the road?" Amanda's manager, Manny, clapped his hands together. "We have to leave in five."

"One more touch-up." The makeup artist came closer, holding a compact and a fluffy facial puff. "She's glowing under all these lights."

"Glowing." Amanda rolled her eyes. "I'm not glowing, I'm *sweating*. Everywhere."

"Okay, okay," Isla muttered, still tapping the screen. Her phone had completely crapped out. Oh well, it would mean they probably wouldn't save the live video to Amanda's Instagram profile but at least the session went well. "My phone died. I'll plug in my battery pack—"

"We don't have any more time to fuck around." Manny loomed over her, the smell of his cigarette-infused breath making Isla's stomach curl. "We need to get Amanda downstairs. Now."

"I need a minute." Amanda fanned herself. The poor girl had gone pale, nerves clearly taking ahold of her. Tonight was a big night. An opportunity for her to grab the attention of the public right before her first movie came out.

"We had more people watching this live session than *any* other video you've done before," Isla said, trying to get Amanda to focus on something positive. They needed her in fine form tonight. Aside from the movie, she'd recently signed a deal with a major cosmetics house to be the face of the youth line they were about to launch.

At seventeen, she was on the verge of great things.

But the internet could be as cruel as it was adoring, and if Amanda didn't perform tonight...well, then she could end up turning into a meme. And *nobody* wanted that.

"The fans think you look beautiful," Isla added.

"I look like something a cat choked up." Amanda's chest started heaving, her bust straining against the tight bodice of her dress. "What even *is* this dress? I would never have chosen this ugly piece of crap if any other designer had wanted to dress me. But oh no. They're all saving themselves for the Kardashians."

Shit. Her client was about to enter full-blown panic mode— Isla knew the signs well. Her skin was sweating faster than the

makeup artist could blot the moisture away and her hands fluttered uselessly by her sides. If she went downstairs and anyone
snapped a picture of her looking like this...

"Amanda, it's fine." Isla left her phone sitting in its tripod
and went to the young star. "The Met Gala is the one event
where you *should* go over the top. It's the whole point. Trust
me, when you're trending on Twitter tomorrow for this amazing gown, you'll be happy about it."

"And if I'm a joke?" Amanda shot a steely-eyed glare at
her stylist, who looked like she was about to burst into tears.
"This is my one chance. Oh God, what if people make fun
of me? What if I end up on some gross, pimple-faced blog-
ger's worst dressed list?"

Think, dammit. We do not *need a teenage meltdown right now.*

"I can't do this." Amanda shook her head, almost dislodg-
ing the carefully pinned hairpiece. The hairstylist shrieked
and rushed over, forcing the young star to stay still while she
reinforced her handiwork.

"Everything will be fine," Isla said, soothingly. She looked
over at Manny, but he was tapping away at his phone, brows
furrowed.

"Can someone pour me a drink?" Amanda said, pressing a
hand to her chest. "I need to calm down."

No shit.

Isla glanced around the room, her eyes darting to the open
champagne bottle nestled in a bucket of ice. It didn't feel
right giving alcohol to a minor. Even though alcohol seemed
the least of anyone's concerns when it came to young stars in
Hollywood. If they weren't snorting coke off a bathroom van-
ity, then everything would be okay, apparently.

But still...

"Am, baby, look at me." Isla touched her client's arm, ignoring the request. "You have a whole bunch of people here

who think you're amazing. We wouldn't lead you astray. You know that, right?"

Amanda looked at her, blue eyes wide and tear-filled. But she nodded. Isla had a chance to take everything down a notch. So many people thought her job was only about finding the perfect hashtags and securing brand partnerships and understanding Facebook's ever-changing algorithms. But with a young star like Amanda, it was also about providing support and guidance in a terrifyingly critical and public world.

"Let's take a moment," Isla suggested, shooting Manny a nasty look when he glanced at his watch. The gala could wait a few minutes. Besides, the red carpet lasted forever at those damn things. "To appreciate what an amazing year you have ahead of you."

Amanda reached for a glass and the bottle of Dom. "Great idea. Let's toast."

"Maybe you shouldn't..." Isla looked at Manny for support, but now he was talking on the phone, moving away from the group. Nobody else seemed to be concerned about Amanda drinking. Was she being a prude? Probably. "Just a little bit, okay? You don't want to be woozy on the red carpet."

The fizzing liquid tipped into the glass and rushed up in a wave of bubbles, almost spilling over the edge.

"To me," Amanda said, raising her glass.

"To you, a woman on the verge of an incredible career. We're all here for you," Isla said. Finally, Amanda seemed to be calming down. "Slay that red carpet, girl!"

Amanda took a sip. Wait, no...a gulp. Shit. The girl downed the entire thing in one swoop like it was a glass of water on a hundred-degree day.

"Pace yourself," Isla said with a nervous laugh, coaxing the glass out of her client's hand. Teenagers. They thought they were invincible.

Wait until you're twenty-six and the hangovers feel like there's a competitive bongo-drum squad in your head.

"You've got this, okay?" Isla said, picking up Amanda's gem-encrusted clutch and handing it to her. "Do your thing. Look beautiful, smile for the cameras, and then go and enjoy the rest of the night."

Amanda took a deep breath and nodded, and for the briefest moment Isla thought that everything would turn out okay. That was, until Amanda clamped a hand over her mouth and promptly vomited all down the front of her couture gown. The chunky fluid splattered across the floor and there was a collective gasp in the room as everyone jumped out of the splash zone. The acrid stench turned Isla's stomach.

"Oh my God." She could only stare at her client, open-mouthed and frozen with shock, while her mind spun over and over like that beachball that appeared when her Mac-Book crashed.

What the hell were they going to do now?

Amanda started to cry and everyone in the room panicked. The flurry of voices wasn't going to fix anything, nor was Manny's bellowing growl of frustration. It only made Amanda cry harder.

"We can fix this," Isla said, flipping through options in her head. A ruined dress could be replaced, and they could touch up her makeup. If they acted fast, it could all be saved. "Mel, you've got a backup dress right? That pink one with the ruffle hem. I'll call downstairs for extra towels and…"

Isla's words died on her lips as she reached for her phone, still nestled in the black tripod, the screen suddenly alive and well. There were no hearts this time. Only a steady stream of crying-laughing emojis and exclamation marks, as Isla accidentally broadcast this colossal failure to over one million people.

3

ONE MONTH LATER...

Isla trudged along the hallway toward her apartment, high heels swinging from her finger. Usually she wouldn't dare go barefoot on public carpet—especially not in a building of questionable standards, like this one. But after walking six blocks to get home in the pretty, stiletto-heeled death traps, her feet had officially given up the ghost.

Besides, foot hygiene was the least of her problems. With another rejected job application—this one coming through *before* she'd even made it home from the interview—she had bigger things to worry about.

Isla unlocked her front door and stepped inside, her lips quirking at the familiar sight. Her little sister, Dani, was standing next to the wall, one hand resting on a makeshift barre crafted from a shower curtain rod and some wall brackets they'd found at the dollar store. She was dressed in a plain black leotard and a pair of pink ballet tights with a hole in the knee. Her battered pointe shoes were frayed around the toes, though the ribbons were glossy and new, stitched on with the utmost care.

Classical music blared from the stereo and Isla hit the pause button. "What have I said about disturbing the neighbors?"

Dani paused mid-plié. "If you're going to do it, do it properly."

"That's *not* what I said." She shot her sister a look, trying to ignore how her leotard was digging into her shoulders. It was clearly a size too small because the damn girl was growing like a weed. At fourteen, she'd already surpassed Isla in height.

"Oh, that's right." Dani grinned. "You said that about schoolwork. But, to be fair, ballet is even more important than schoolwork, so…"

"We'll agree on that when you can pay the bills with pliés." Isla hung her keys on the hook by the door and dumped her purse onto the kitchen counter.

"Working on it." Dani continued warming up, her pointe shoes knocking against the floorboards. "How was your day?"

Ugh. You mean, how were the three dozen rejection letters and this last interview, which was clearly only for curiosity's sake because the recruiter straight up laughed the second I left the interview room?

"It was…fine," she said, without much commitment.

In reality, it was anything but fine. What had her old boss called her? Oh, that's right: Instagram poison.

"You told me once that saying something is 'fine' is no better than saying it's 'purple pineapples.'" Dani dropped down from her *relevé* and frowned. "What happened?"

What *hadn't* happened?

Isla pulled a bottle of wine out of the fridge and poured herself a glass. She'd been rationing it, since the only stuff that was left after this was a box wine of unknown origin. "Amanda lost her contract with that makeup company *and* her movie is flopping. She sent me an angry email today."

"Whatever happened to all publicity is good publicity?"

"It's a myth. Turns out some things *are* career killers." Isla took a gulp of the wine. "And now I'm *that* woman who filmed a Disney princess vomiting all over herself."

After the live video had been splashed across the internet and featured on network television, Isla had swiftly been fired from her job as a senior social media consultant with the Gateway Agency. All her freelance clients had dropped her like a hot potato, too. Now, anyone who searched Isla's name got page after page of the same thing: *vomit girl and the person who was too dumb to stop recording.*

Hence the growing pile of rejected job applications.

"I take it the interview didn't go well?"

Isla cringed at the concern in her sister's voice. Most fourteen-year-olds were worrying about frivolous things, like which shade of lip gloss was the most on trend or how to craft the perfect TikTok dance routine. Hell, she would argue that's the stuff they *should* be worrying about. Not whether they were going to have a roof over their heads.

"No, it didn't," Isla admitted. "But honestly, I'm not sure I would have wanted to work there anyway."

It was a total lie.

Isla was ready to take anything at this point. It was humiliating to be begging for jobs she could have done ten years ago with her eyes closed, only to be rejected because the recruiters had found someone "with more experience." Umm, what?

In other words, she'd been officially barred from the social media industry.

"How come?" Dani walked over to the kitchen, her arms

swinging gracefully by her sides. Her dark hair was in a neat bun on top of her head, tied with a piece of leftover ribbon from her pointe shoes. "Were they not very nice?"

"Not really."

Dani came up to Isla and put an arm around her, stooping so she could lean her head against her big sister's shoulder. Some days it felt like it was them against the world. Given they didn't actually know where their mother was these days—and they hadn't seen either one of their dads in God only knew how long—they really *did* have to stick together.

Isla remembered the day it all happened—the eve of her twentieth birthday. Their mother had announced she was eloping overseas with a boyfriend she'd known less than a month, and they hadn't seen her since. Apparently motherhood was a temporary commitment, in her eyes. That left Isla responsible for the well-being of another human, and more terrified of the future than she'd ever been.

Six years later, Isla had built a life for them both. She'd fostered and financed her half sister's dreams, built up her own dream career and done it all while hiding how often the numbers weren't in their favor. But the older Dani got, the more keenly she observed what was going on.

"Maybe you can ask the ballet school for our money back," Dani suggested quietly.

Her spot had been secured for the summer intensive ballet camp months ago, before Isla's job situation had fallen apart.

"I know it was really expensive," she added.

Isla felt tears prick the backs of her eyes, but she refused to let her sister see even a sliver of her emotion. It was her job to be a pillar. To be the strong one. To be the positive mother figure neither of them ever had.

"Dani, I would sell my right kidney if it meant you could go to ballet camp."

"I'm pretty sure that's illegal."

Isla snorted and wrapped her sister into a big hug. Like always, she smelled of oversweet vanilla perfume and mango-scented shampoo. She would do anything for this kid. Anything to make sure Dani grew up knowing that dreams were worth chasing, and that family came first no matter what.

"And how do you know so much about black market organ sales?" Isla raised a brow and Dani laughed.

"*CSI.*"

"Ah, of course." She laughed. But when Dani pulled back, Isla noticed her sister's characteristically carefree attitude was hidden under the worry swimming in her blue eyes. Isla hated seeing that. "Why don't we go to Central Park, huh? We'll take your phone and I can get a few shots of you for your Instagram account."

"Really?" Dani's eyes lit up.

"Sure. Just let me get changed."

"I promise not to make you take a hundred photos this time." Dani grinned and did a little *pirouette* in the kitchen. "Not even half that!"

"Don't make promises you can't keep," Isla shot over her shoulder as she headed into her bedroom. "Trust me, I know where you get those perfectionistic tendencies."

The second Isla closed her bedroom door behind her, she slumped against it and deflated like a balloon the day after a birthday party. Outside, the city roared with life. Sirens and horns, music blaring from the open window of another apartment, the shrieking laughter of people enjoying the early evening. She gazed out of the window, her eyes catching on the usual things that faced their cozy (read: cramped) place. There was a glimmer of light as the sun reflected off glass panes, and the zigzag of a fire escape from the building opposite them.

The same three apartments always had their blinds wide open—either inviting voyeurism or not caring enough to prevent it.

Sometimes she wondered about their lives. Had they been stuck and struggling at some point like her? Had they lost faith in themselves and the world?

After she got fired, Isla had assumed it would all blow over if she kept a low profile and didn't make matters worse. But then Amanda's movie tanked and all her sponsorships fell through, and people stopped taking Isla's calls. Even when she'd tried to laugh the whole thing off as a "Miley Cyrus exercise" her contacts had frozen harder than an Upper East Sider's Botoxed face.

New York could be like that—when you were successful it felt as though the sun was made of gold. And when you fell from grace, you hit the concrete so hard you shattered every bone in your body.

How much longer was she going to be able to keep faking that everything would be fine? Rent was due next week and the final payment for Dani's elite ballet camp had come out of her account a few days ago. Isla's eyes had watered at the amount. But Dani had worked so hard, practicing every day and pushing herself to the limit to beat out the rich kids with their prestigious coaches and private lessons and their lifetimes of opportunity.

How could Isla pull the rug out from under Dani like that? What kind of lesson would that be teaching her?

"You'll figure this out," she said to herself. "*Someone* will hire you."

After all, she *had* to make it work. Because letting her sister down was not an option.

4

It wasn't often that Theo could say he'd witnessed actual carnage. Most days he saw the same places: his penthouse, the back seat of his town car, and his corner office at the publishing house his great-grandfather started before the Second World War. That was it.

Two buildings with private elevators and one vehicle. Not much room for change or surprise, which was exactly how he liked it. As far as he was concerned, a life with minimal variables was a life you could depend on.

Unfortunately, chaos had *also* become something he could depend on of late.

He stood at the door to his bedroom, blinking at the wreckage. A drawer was open next to his bed and his collection of business socks—usually arranged by color—was strewn across the floor. A single sock hung limply from the drawer handle, bereft of its mate. Silk ties had been torn from the hanger inside his wardrobe, threads pulled and their pristine, gleaming surfaces ruined by small, needlelike teeth.

And all of that paled into insignificance next to the dry-cleaning bag that had been carefully laid across his bed, which was now in a heap on the floor, shredded and torn...like the bespoke suit inside it.

"That's the third suit this month." He raked a hand through his hair, stifling a cry of frustration.

Camilla sat in the middle of the room, front paws crossed like da Vinci himself was about to paint her portrait. He never caught her *in* the act, of course. She was smarter than that. So much for silence being golden. Theo was starting to learn that when it came to dogs, silence was very, *very* suspicious.

A scrap of Zegna Italian wool lay on the ground right near Camilla's paw. She dropped her face down to look at it and then looked back up at Theo as if to say: *checkmate, asshole.*

"Hailey!" He turned and stormed through the house. Where was the dog sitter now? She should have prevented this. Apparently the agency he was using had sent yet another dud.

This was ridiculous. It couldn't be *that* hard to get good help.

He found the woman standing in the foyer, tapping at her phone with one hand and slipping a scarf around her neck with the other. Her ponytail was barely hanging on, and she had an angry-looking scratch on her arm.

"Hailey. What the hell is going on? I found Camilla in my bedroom and it looks like Godzilla has torn through there."

"I'm not Hailey." The woman straightened and glared at him. Her pink lipstick was smudged across one cheek and her glasses sat lopsided on her nose. "*Hailey* was the girl who came here last week and didn't even survive the day."

That would explain why he couldn't seem to keep up with their names.

"Monica?" he tried. Hmm, that didn't seem right, either.

"Monica was the first girl you hired, the one who texted to tell me *not* to take this job after she quit. But did I listen? Oh no. I was lured in by the Fifth Avenue address and the promise of a lucrative contract." She threw her phone into her purse and snapped it shut. "Then came June, who ended up in emergency after Camilla purposefully tripped her."

"I really don't think a dog would—"

"*Then* it was Hailey." The woman was on a tirade and there was no stopping her. "Then Belinda, who'd worked for her previous client for fifteen years without incident. After her came Portia, then Amy, then Fran and *then* me... Lucinda."

Had he really been through that many dog sitters already? It had only been four weeks.

"Right, Lucinda." It didn't ring a bell, not even a little bit. "Look, I really don't have time—"

"No, *I* don't have time, Mr. Garrison." She slipped her purse over her shoulder and stared up at Theo with fire simmering in her eyes. "I love animals, but that small creature can only have come from evil itself. And you—" she jabbed her finger in his direction "—are no better."

Theo blinked. What the hell was happening right now?

"Rich people," she muttered. "You think anyone who works for you is nothing more than a figure on a spreadsheet."

"Now, hold on a minute," he said. "The terms of this contract were clearly laid out. I needed a dog sitter, that was it. You turn up, you look after the dog, you get paid. End of story."

"That would be fine, *if* you had a dog. But you don't. What you have is a Stephen King novel—Cujo himself could have been inspired by her. And I have better things to do with my life than degrade myself for the sake of a job."

Degrade herself? Okay, so maybe Camilla's daily to-do list was a little more intensive than the average pet's—even Theo had raised an eyebrow at some of the items on the list his grandmother had left him. But that's what she'd wanted for her dog, so who was he to question it? Besides, he'd gone to one of the top agencies in the city and they'd *assured* him that no dog's needs were too big or too outrageous, even when he'd warned them about Camilla's pampered life.

"You might be used to people doing your bidding simply because you wave a few zeros in their face," Lucinda said, shaking her head. "But some things are more important than money. My dignity is one of them."

With that, Lucinda yanked the front door open and exited, letting it slam shut behind her. A second later the elevator pinged from the hallway and Theo tilted his face up to the ceiling. He really didn't have time for this. Work was heinous, since yet another member of his management team had quit, *and* he'd been dodging calls from the media all week about a proposed acquisition that was supposed to be top secret.

Growling in frustration, he pulled his phone out of his pocket and called the pet sitting agency. The receptionist answered on the third ring, but before he could even get a word in there was a click, meaning he'd been transferred to another line.

"Mr. Garrison, this is Elaine Goldsmith. I guess you're calling for yet *another* replacement." Her voice had a clipped edge to it, an educated tone that was probably acquired at some Ivy League school. "I'm afraid that we are no longer able to service you or your pet's needs."

"Why not?"

"Because the safety and well-being of my employees is my primary concern. I've had one end up with her leg in a cast, another who almost lost a finger, and another who is refusing to come back to work."

"Are you seriously telling me that all your 'highly trained professionals' haven't been able to handle a dog who's barely the size of a loaf of bread?" He paced across the foyer of his penthouse apartment, raking a hand through his hair. Okay, so maybe the loaf of bread comment was a bit of an exaggeration, but seriously. These women were acting like Camilla was a deadly predator, not a dog that looked like she belonged in a fancy purse. "I was assured that you could handle any dog."

"Not *that* dog, I'm afraid. You'll need to find another agency to help you." A click on the other end of the line signaled that the call was over.

Theo stared at his phone. This was not what he'd signed on for.

"Well, technically you *did* sign on for it," he said to himself. "Literally."

Curse his wily grandmother for knowing that he was a bleeding heart. Well, only when it came to her. As far as the rest of the world was concerned, Theo Garrison had a lump of coal where his heart was supposed to be.

The familiar clack of toenails against marble tile made the hairs on the back of Theo's neck stand up. What now?

When he turned, Camilla was standing in the arch between the foyer and the open living area, a Louis Vuitton leash in her mouth. Apparently, this was the universal signal that it was time for a toilet break. Couldn't the sitter have at least done *that* before she stormed out?

Scrubbing a hand over his face, Theo let out a long sigh. "Fine, I'll take you outside."

Ten minutes later, Theo was crossing the street into Central Park. Camilla trotted ahead of him, tail wagging and looking like butter wouldn't melt in her mouth. That was until a small kid tried to pet her while they waited for the lights to change and she almost took his hand off.

"Do you have to be such a..." Camilla threw him a look over her shoulder that dared him to use the *B* word. "Never mind."

Central Park was bustling, as usual. It was one of the reasons he chose to run on his treadmill with a view overlooking the park rather than running *in* the park. Being outside these days required so much effort, especially after his grandmother's death was covered in the *New Yorker* and a photo of them had been plastered all over the front page.

But Theo had perfected his disguise and, so far, had a flawless record. The aim was to look like a visitor, rather than a resident. Not a full-blown tourist, though. More of a bridge-and-tunnel kind of visitor. Which was why he wore a Mets baseball cap, despite the fact that it'd hurt his Yankees-loving soul to hand over thirty bucks for the blue-and-orange monstrosity. Not to mention it was probably making his father turn in his grave.

He also wore a pair of wraparound shades that fully concealed his eyes and a T-shirt with the logo of some little pizzeria in Williamsburg, which some might have called a useless, esoteric detail. But Theo knew that caring for the details was what separated the men from the boys. It wasn't good enough to cover just your face—anybody could do that. You had to turn yourself into a different person. Which, given he was walking a pretentious little dog with a gaudy custom-monogrammed LV leash, was exactly how Theo felt.

Camilla led the way, tugging left and then right as she navigated to her usual spot. Apparently the damn creature could only pee on one particular bush, which seemed so on brand for her that Theo could only roll his eyes.

He checked his email while the dog did her business. It was apparent that she couldn't simply squat and get it over with. Oh no, she had to scratch and circle and sniff until she'd found the *exact* spot worthy of her furry little ass.

Fortunately—or unfortunately, depending on how you

looked at it—Theo's email had plenty to keep him occupied while the princess did her thing. His inbox was clogged with yet more inquiries about the acquisition, reporters wanting statements and so many meeting requests it almost made his eyes go square. No wonder he was always barking at his people to get shit done—how was *anyone* supposed to do their actual job if they spent all day in pointless meetings? Theo would have been quite happy to put a lock on his office door and tape up a No Trespassing sign if it would get people to leave him alone.

But apparently, according to his office manager, that made him "unapproachable."

Like being approachable was something to aim for. Maybe if people spent a little more time focusing on their own business and a little less time worrying about others, they'd get further ahead in life.

"Uh, excuse me?" An unfamiliar voice and a flash of movement caught Theo's attention. "I think your dog is…escaping."

Theo's head snapped up in time to see Camilla's wiggling backside hightail it across the park, right past the Alice in Wonderland statue. How in the heck…? That's when Theo realized he was still holding on to her leash. *And* her collar was still attached to the end of it. She'd pulled a Houdini!

"Camilla!" He raced off after the dog, who was moving at a shocking speed. Every morning she plodded across the apartment doing her best tortoise impersonation and now suddenly she was Usain Bolt?

"Shit, shit, shit." He picked up speed, dodging a woman with a stroller who yelled something at him as he flew past, squeezing between her and another park-goer. The Conservatory Water pond was up ahead and the *last* thing he needed was to fish Camilla out, should she go over the edge.

What did you do to deserve this?

"Camilla, stop right now!"

Camilla's ears and tail flapped as she ran, her fur shimmering in the late afternoon sun. She barreled past a toddler, making the kid stumble and topple over onto his well-padded backside. An indignant piercing wail shattered the air. More people were looking now, but not a single one stepped in to help. They all got out of Camilla's way, clearing a path right around the edge of the pond.

"Stay away from the water," he called out, knowing it was useless. The dog didn't listen to anyone.

He gained some ground and made a swipe for her, but she dodged his grip, darting to the side with a professional-grade evasion tactic. She had an unfair advantage being so low to the ground. Theo's six-foot-two frame was not made to bend in half *and* move at the same time. The dog scampered away from the pond and toward the Hans Christian Andersen monument, where a teenage girl in a ballerina outfit was posing.

The dog bolted straight for the girl, who was standing on one leg, the other extended behind her. Another woman was crouched in front of the girl, holding her phone up to take a picture.

"Camilla! Stop!"

The monument of the great Danish storyteller had him sitting on a bench, book open in his hands. There was also a sculpture of a little duck on the ground. The ballerina posed next to the statue, in perfect ballet form, peering over as if reading the book.

"Okay, ready?" the woman on the ground called out to the teen. "Three, two, one…"

Camilla raced into the shot, bypassed the girl and went straight for the duck statue, and began…humping it.

"Camilla, no!"

The dog wiggled up the back of the unsuspecting duck, and threw her paws over it, hinging her little hips back and forth.. Her mouth was open, tongue out, and she looked like the happiest canine on planet earth. An older woman grabbed her small child and covered his eyes, gasping at the lurid scene. Angry eyes followed Theo as he ran over. But the young ballerina burst into laughter and came out of her pose, heading straight for the dog.

"Wait, don't touch her!" Theo finally caught up and had his hand outstretched. "She can be vicious."

The ballerina froze, startled by Theo's warning, her hand hovering over Camilla's body. Usually this would be the point where Camilla would bare her teeth and make the kind of growl that sounded as though it belonged to a creature four times her size. But instead, probably because today was the day the dog decided to well and truly fuck with him, Camilla paused her sexual interlude and flopped onto her back, legs in the air.

Theo stopped dead in his tracks. He'd literally never seen her do that with anyone before.

"Yeah, she looks *real* vicious." The woman who'd been taking the photo stood and smiled. "You should put a muzzle on her before she hurts somebody."

"More like a condom." Theo shook his head. "That poor duck."

All the people around the monument had paused, watching the scene with every expression ranging from prudish disgust to intense amusement. Some even had their phones out to take pictures. But since it was clear that the peep show was over, the crowd began to dissipate.

"Oh, Isla, she's so cute!" The teen girl was crouched beside Camilla, tentatively stroking her belly. A huge smile blossomed on the girl's face. "We should get a dog."

"Now you've got me in trouble," the woman said, looking at Theo with a rueful expression. "I'm going to be hearing about how we need to get a dog constantly."

"You're welcome to take this one. Free to good home," Theo joked.

The woman laughed and the sound was like church bells and snowflakes and sunshine. She had wide blue eyes and glossy brown hair, and her figure was perfectly enhanced by one of those dresses that tied at the waist. The fabric was pale blue and dotted with white flowers and she reminded him of some Brigitte Bardot–esque silver screen siren.

"We could do a trade. I'll take the dog and you take the teenager."

"I heard that," the girl said, looking up and narrowing her eyes, but the lure of playing with Camilla kept her from saying anything else. She cooed at the dog and Camilla seemed perfectly content to lie on her back and lap up the attention.

"I'm Isla." The woman stuck her hand out and he took it without thinking. Something crackled as his palm slid against hers, a strange sensation that was warm and pleasant and totally unfamiliar.

"Theo."

Shit. What happened to the bridge-and-tunnel cover? He even had a fake name, should he need it: Martin Russo. But pretty Isla with her thick eyelashes and sky-colored eyes and magical-sounding laughter had immediately tripped him up.

"Well, Theo. It's very nice to meet you."

"Sorry we interrupted your photo shoot." He rubbed a hand at the back of his neck and held up Camilla's leash. "I took my eyes off her for one second and she pulled a disappearing act."

"Totally okay. I'm sure this video is going to get even more likes now."

Isla turned the phone to him and showed him the video, which captured the whole incident so perfectly one might assume it had been planned. He thought about asking her not to post it online. In his mind, social media was one of the worst things to happen to society, but right now he didn't feel like wiping away Isla's sunshine smile. Besides, there was nothing that might identify the dog, since she wasn't wearing her distinctive pink collar or monogrammed leash.

So maybe, for one day, he could pretend not to be a grumpy bastard.

"I know social media can be tough for teens but it's part of their world now," Isla said. "I'd rather help her with it, and teach her how to use it safely, than have her do it behind my back."

Theo could tell from her tone that she'd been criticized before. "I'm not judging your parenting."

"Sistering," she corrected with a smile. "Although I'm the closest thing she has to a mom, so I guess you *could* say parenting as well."

For some reason, the words reached into Theo's chest and squeezed. Which was odd. He wasn't one to take on other people's problems or get wrapped up in their stories. In fact, one of his assistants had told him that he had as much empathy as a pet rock. But something about Isla and her sister called to him.

Maybe because he knew what it was like to be alone in the world, forced to grow up quicker than his peers and having to learn about things no child should need to understand. Words like *manslaughter* and *negligence* and *dead on arrival.*

That's your story, not hers. Stop projecting.

"Just the two of you?" he asked.

"Yeah, it has been for years. I wouldn't have it any other way. Although if I could get a damn job that would make it easier to sleep at night." She shook her head and pressed a hand to her cheek. "Please ignore that. I swear, I don't usually spill my sob story to complete strangers. It's been…a helluva day."

Didn't he feel that down to his bones?

At that moment, the teenager stood and brushed her hands down the front of her stomach. She was wearing a pink dress and those special ballet shoes that allowed dancers to go right up onto their toes. Ribbons were tied around her slender ankles and she moved with the grace of someone who'd studied dance all their life.

Camilla trotted back over to Theo, nose in the air like always. But her tail was wagging and she looked…happy..That was a freaking first. In the entire month since he'd taken ownership of the Dachshund, not once had she seemed even remotely satisfied. Let alone happy.

"Aren't you a good girl?" Isla leaned forward to scratch behind her ears. "Sit."

Camilla plopped her furry little butt onto the ground and Theo almost fell over in shock. He'd been convinced that she didn't know any commands at all.

"What else can you do?" Isla crouched down and held her hand out. "Shake?"

Camilla daintily raised one paw into Isla's hand and looked up at Theo, as if to make sure he was watching. That sneaky little—

"Good girl!" Isla gave her a scratch. "What about this one? Drop."

She pointed to the ground and Camilla lay down flat and then rolled over without even being asked.

"I used to dog sit on weekends for a neighbor who had Dachshunds back in high school. I helped to teach them all the commands," Isla explained as she scratched Camilla's belly before standing up. Theo took that moment to slip the dog's collar back on and tighten it by one notch. No way was she wriggling free this time. "Your girl is so well trained."

"I swear, she's never done *any* of that for me," he said, shaking his head. "You're a miracle worker."

"Ha, thanks. Maybe I should look for a job as a dog trainer instead of what I'm doing now." She rolled her eyes. "I might have more luck."

"Come work for me." He blurted the words out before having a chance to think them through. Offering a job to a stranger on the street was so *not* his style. In fact, he'd been known to drag candidates for the publishing house through fourth and fifth rounds of interviews to make sure he was absolutely certain they were right for the role.

But Theo was desperate.

And it sounded like Isla was, too.

"Are you serious?" She blinked.

"Deadly serious. My dog sitter quit today and…well, she left me in the lurch. Plus, you mentioned that you used to do some dog sitting." He gestured down to Camilla. "I didn't even know she could shake hands until now."

"Really?"

"She's, uh…adopted."

Isla made an *aww* face that stirred something in Theo's chest, but he frowned behind his sunglasses and quickly shook the feeling off. This wasn't about emotions, this was business. He needed a dog sitter and Isla needed a job. This was a simple solution.

"It's very kind of you to offer, but…" She laughed and shook her head.

"But?"

"I'm pretty sure a wise person once said you shouldn't accept a job offer from a stranger on the street." She laughed, her eyes searching his face.

"She doesn't want to end up like those people on *CSI*," the teenager piped up. "Like, you meet a cute guy on the street and the next thing you know he has your liver in a blender."

"Dani!" Isla shook her head. "Please excuse my sister. Clearly I need to monitor what TV shows she watches from now on."

"Just sayin'." Dani shrugged.

"How about a one-month trial?" he offered. "Four weeks for you to see if the job is a good fit and if it's not, you can walk away. I'll give you all my details so you can look me up in advance."

This would take care of everything. It would save him having to find another agency for at least a month and it was clear that Camilla liked Isla. Hell, she *listened* to her, which was nothing short of an honest-to-God miracle. And Theo prided himself on being a good judge of character...which was why he could count his entire social circle on one hand with several fingers to spare.

Isla was one of the good ones.

And if she wasn't...well, he had insurance up to the teeth. Right now, he needed someone to take care of the dog so he could get back to focusing on his work. Back to his normal routine and well-organized life.

"What have you got to lose?" he asked, fishing out a business card from his wallet and handing it over.

Isla's eyes flicked over his information and she bit her lip. He could see the cogs turning in her brain, though he wasn't sure if that was because of his offer or because she recognized his name. "Four weeks?"

"And not a day more unless you say so."

"This is crazy but..." She bobbed her head. "I'll give you a month."

Theo let out a sigh of relief. Life might keep throwing things at him, but he was still swinging. Still dodging. Resiliency was a core skill he'd been cultivating ever since he was a kid. Nothing would stop him. Not even a dog who seemed determined to test him.

He had four weeks to convince Isla that this was her dream job, and then maybe his life would finally be back to normal.

5

Isla decided to walk to her new, temporary job for a few reasons. One, it was free, which made it a better option than both a cab and the subway. Two, it was probably a good idea to get the lay of the land since she figured a large part of her job would be taking Camilla out and about in the neighborhood. Three, it would give her extra time to think about backing out of this ridiculous scenario.

The trip from her tiny glorified cupboard of an apartment on East 104th Street was about one and a half miles to Theo Garrison's penthouse. In event season, she could cover twice that in trips around a starlet's hotel room trying to make everything perfect for an Instagram story.

Those days are over, girl. It's doggy day care for you now.

Well, doggy day care for Upper East Side royalty. Theo freaking Garrison. Something had chugged in Isla's brain when he'd handed over his business card, because she knew the name. *Everybody* in Manhattan knew the name. Garrison was synonymous with wealth and power, and only a person with their head in the sand for the last couple of decades wouldn't have heard about the tragic demise of America's most beloved couple.

Isla had only been a little girl at the time, but she remembered her mother crying in front of the television with a wad of tissues in her fist, her other hand pressed to her mouth. Grace Porter-Garrison had been her mother's favorite actress. She'd even styled her hair and makeup like Grace did after the eponymous documentary, *Graceful*, had come out.

But *Theo* Garrison. At first Isla had wondered if he was a distant relative, or someone who shared the name but bore no blood relation. After he'd left her in Central Park, she'd Googled him.

Theodore Clifford Garrison, also known as the Hermit of Fifth Avenue. Orphaned son of parents rumored to have been murdered by paparazzi. Conspiracy theories abounded—a contract hit, a revenge plot, an inside job. An investigation had cleared the photographers involved of any wrongdoing, but questions persisted. Theo himself was a ghost, according to the web. A business tyrant. An urban legend.

Wealthy beyond comprehension.

Surely this whole job offer was a joke.

Isla walked along Fifth Avenue, past the Guggenheim, her mind whirring like an overworked laptop. What if this was an elaborate scam? Or a cruel joke? What if the guy was actually a rabid fan of Amanda Harte's and this was a misguided form of revenge for ruining Amanda's career?

Crazier things had happened.

She stopped at the edge of the sidewalk and paused for a moment, sucking in a deep breath and forcing herself to calm down.

"You're alive, you have a roof over your head, you have options," she said to herself.

A man in a suit looked at her as though she'd sprouted a second head. New York was *not* the city for positive affirmations. Isla wasn't sure if she believed in any of it either. Mantras, personal talismans, mind over matter…stuff New Yorkers would roll their eyes at, if they didn't spit at it first.

But desperate times called for examining every option, even the woo-woo ones.

Scrubbing a hand over her face, Isla pulled her phone out of the black leather purse with a shiny gold clasp slung over her shoulder. The leather was a little stiff since the bag had spent more time looking pretty on her dresser than it had being useful. The clasp was fiddly, and fashioned into the initials YSL. Yes, *that* YSL.

And no, it wasn't a knockoff from Canal Street.

It had been a gift from a former client, a very generous gift that Isla had almost pawned on at least three occasions in the last month. Frankly, the value of the bag would have been better spent by taking care of a month's rent. But something had stopped her from taking it to the consignment store and this morning, when she'd had an awful sense of impostor syndrome about working for a man like Theo Garrison—even if it *was* only to look after his dog—she'd slung it over one shoulder in the hopes it might boost her confidence.

So far, no such luck.

Isla turned the phone over in her hands. To cancel or not to cancel, that was the eternal question. Seriously, if Shakespeare lived in current times he wouldn't have been quite so existential. Who had time to be worrying about the essence of a person? Managing one's schedule was hard enough.

Ugh, Isla was *definitely* spiraling. That meant it was time for a final opinion. She swiped her thumb over the screen and called her best friend, Scout.

On the third ring, the call was answered with a sleepy *hmmello*.

"It's eight thirty," Isla chided. "What are you still doing in bed?"

"Sleeping," Scout grumbled. "Like a normal person. What are you doing?"

Isla continued her walk down Fifth Avenue, wedging the phone between her ear and her shoulder because she needed both hands to close the fancy purse. It was stupid to pretend she fit in on the Upper East Side.

"I'm walking to my new job," she said.

"Oh!" Scout suddenly sounded more awake. "That's today?"

"Uh-huh."

"Still think he's going to Liam Neeson you?"

Isla snorted. "If you remember rightly, Liam Neeson does the rescuing, not the taking."

"Right." Something clattered in the background, followed by a soft thump and curse from Scout. Knowing her friend, she'd probably stubbed her toe on the same potted plant she always did, because she never remembered to move it to a more suitable spot.

"Should I turn up to this thing? Am I a fool taking a job from a guy off the street?" Isla looked around. "I mean, granted, if I'm going to take a job from a guy on the street then Fifth Avenue is probably the street to do it on, but still…"

"Are you really concerned about your safety?" Scout asked. Water rushed in the background and taps squeaked. Then something mechanical sounded—a coffee machine. "Because if you are then you have a few options. One, record every-thing on your phone and send it to the cloud so if he *does* ab-duct you then there's evidence. Two, you could create a poison body lotion, so that if he touches you then he'll die a swift and painful death."

Isla couldn't help but laugh and she felt some of the tension evaporate out of her body. "But wouldn't the poison body lo-tion *also* kill me?"

"I didn't say it was perfect. Personally, I'd go with the cloud thing."

"Great advice, thanks. So glad I called." Isla shook her head. Scout was one of her oldest friends and while she wasn't some-one you'd think to ask the advice of—on account of being a self-confessed hot mess, something which was backed up by a reasonable amount of evidence—she *did* know how to take Isla's type-A overthinking down a notch.

"You texted me the address, right?" Scout asked, her tone turning serious.

"Yeah, I did."

"And you've got a personal alarm on you?"

"Yep."

"And you have emails from him setting up the details for today?"

"Yeah, from him and his assistant." Isla bit down on the inside of her cheek.

"Okay, so what are you *really* worried about?"

She let out a breath. The truth of it was that her personal security wasn't the thing really bugging her—she'd felt no warning bells nor seen any red flags. His assistant had sent her a contract to cover the month and an NDA, which might appear excessive for a dog sitting job but that felt totally on brand for what she knew about Theo. And rich people in general, since she'd signed her fair share of non-disclosure agreements in the past.

"Part of me is worried that this is nothing but a huge joke. That Ashton Kutcher is going to jump out from behind a fancy, tufted couch and shove a camera in my face while he screams that I've been Punk'd."

"Babe, that show hasn't aired for like a decade. Probably more than that. Ashton is all Mr. Silicon Valley now." Scout tutted like Isla was a great disappointment. "You of all people should know that."

"You know what I mean," Isla groused.

"I know your confidence has been dented and you're still feeling guilty about what happened to Amanda," Scout said. "I know the internet is full of shitheads who've said some pretty nasty stuff to you and about you. I know you're worried about taking care of Dani…think any of this stuff might be messing with your head a little?"

Isla rolled her eyes. "I hate it when you're logical."

"Luckily for you, that doesn't happen very often."

Isla toyed with the strap on her bag, watching the gold links twist and catch the morning sunlight. "I need this to be real. My bank account is looking leaner than Tom Hanks in *Cast Away* right now."

"Do you need help?"

Isla sighed. She knew Scout wasn't in a much better position than she was on account of bouncing around with her employment and having no family support of her own. "If this job works out we'll be okay."

"Then don't cancel," Scout replied. "Nothing that's happened so far should give you any cause to believe it's not a legitimate opportunity."

It was true and Isla had *looked*. She'd checked that the domain name from the email she'd received matched the Garrison & Sons publishing house website. It did. Pictures of Theo matched the guy whom she'd spoken with in the park as much as she could tell, given he'd been wearing a baseball cap and sunglasses. But that sharp jaw had the same lines, and he had a single, small mole on his neck that appeared to be in the right place.

Hell, she'd even figured out that the Dachshund belonged to his late grandmother and had found a picture to prove the dogs looked the same.

If this was a ruse, it was an elaborate one.

"I'm being paranoid," she admitted.

"Yeah, you are."

"Can you blame me?"

"Not at all," Scout said. "Hell, I know strong people who would have crumpled after what you've been through. You've got tenacity to be putting yourself out there now, but that doesn't mean you avoided getting any scars."

"Big ones." She still had nightmares about that night, still woke up experiencing that same hot, gut-clenching flash of fear as the moment she'd realized what she'd done. Still felt guilty as hell for what had become of Amanda's career.

Still believed there was a grain of truth to the hate emails she received.

"Stop being so hard on yourself, Isla. News flash, you're human and you made a mistake. That's all it is."

"You say mistake, I say giant, colossal, epic career-ending screwup."

"Tomato, tom-ah-to."

Isla shook her head. That was Scout in a nutshell—she got on with things, no matter how difficult they were. It was something she really admired about her friend. Hot mess or not, Scout *always* dusted herself off.

"Okay, I'm doing this."

"Excellent. Call me by dinnertime or else I'll report you missing." Scout paused. "Seriously."

"I will, but you're right. I did my homework and there's no red flags."

Just the sense that after everything that's happened an opportunity falling out of the sky seems more like a trap than a relief.

Isla ended the call and smoothed her hands down the front of her simple black pants and silky blue wrap top that was probably a bit overdressed for the gig. She caught a glimpse of herself in the reflection of a window—chunky black sunglasses gave her an air of mystery and her red lipstick was a nod to who she used to be before a phone glitch ruined everything. Okay, she was *definitely* overdressed. No doubt by the end of the day she'd need to make sweet, sweet love to a lint roller on account of Camilla's champagne-colored fur, but professional impressions were important.

"Let's hope he hasn't Googled you in the meantime and changed his mind," she muttered to herself.

Isla approached the address Theo had given her. It was quarter to nine and she was early. She glanced around the street, watching the well-heeled people coming and going. A woman breezed out of the building, an Hermès Kelly tote slung casually over one arm and a flash of red at her soles punctuating each step. There was a point in time when those things had started to feel comfortable to Isla—she'd been around success long enough that it felt like it belonged to her.

Now it felt like a flashing neon sign above her head. *Impostor. Impostor. Impostor.*

"You're doing this for Dani."

Sucking in a breath, she strode toward the entrance of Theo's building. Inside the foyer looked like something out of a painting—high ceilings, an actual freaking chandelier, lightly textured wallpaper and marble. The tones were muted.

Cream, bone, silver, a light ash gray. A hint of velvet, the modern dazzle of chrome. It was like someone had been asked to create a picture to accompany the word *luxurious* in the dictionary.

A man in a uniform stood behind the front desk. Isla expected him to look at her with suspicion, but he didn't. Apparently Theo Garrison was expecting her.

Isla's stomach flipped as the elevator whisked her up to the penthouse. She caught herself in one of the mirrored panels chewing her lip—which was not a good move. The old habit, something she thought she'd kicked after her early days of taking care of Dani, had started creeping back in.

"You can do this," she said to her reflection, checking the outline of her lipstick and swiping her nail along one edge to neaten it. "It's dog sitting. Literally the easiest job in the world."

Lord knew it would get her into less trouble than her old job. How hard could it be? Clip a leash on Camilla and take her for a walk. Spoon some dog food into a bowl. Pick up her crap.

Sure, it wasn't glamorous. But it was easy money and easy money was exactly what Isla needed right now.

To calm her nerves, she did a few breathing exercises, but the fluttering in her stomach persisted. The whole "incident" had really shaken her confidence, making her question every decision she made. Making her triple-check everything she did, as though she could no longer trust her own actions. Hell, even packing her purse that morning had taken three times longer than normal because she didn't want to come across ill-prepared.

Ping!

The elevator opened and Isla blinked. Instead of finding herself in a corridor or elevator bay, she was staring at the most beautiful apartment she'd ever seen. How was she inside already?

It was white as far as the eye could see—white marble tiles leading to snowy white carpet, white plush couches and gauzy white drapes. The crispness of the room was warmed by gold accents and shimmering glass items that seemed to capture the light in a special and beautiful way. There were several paintings on the walls, depicting lush green scenery of forests and rolling hills.

It should have felt cold and impersonal, but it didn't. Instead, it felt like...a sanctuary.

Despite her not wanting to touch anything for fear of making it dirty, the room had a surprisingly calm feel to it. The all-white backdrop let the art take center stage, and whoever had decorated this room had clearly wanted the paintings to stand out.

What the hell was she supposed to do now? There was no door to knock on, no bell to ring. Did she call out? Did she wait for someone to come fetch her? Was this one of those places where a surveillance camera was trained on people twenty-four seven, giving that creepy vibe of portraits whose eyes followed you around the room?

Isla didn't dare breathe for a moment, while every possibility of how this could go wrong swirled in her head.

"Isla?"

She heard his voice before she saw him, but the anticipation was like a swarm of something winged and desperate in her stomach. The sensation was fizzy. Exciting. And reality didn't fail to deliver.

Theo walked around the corner, looking vastly different than the day in the park. Gone were the cap and the sunglasses and the graphic tee. In their place was a charcoal suit cut to accentuate broad shoulders and a trim waist, a crisp white shirt and a gleaming silk tie in pale silver. His hair was loosely styled, slightly longer on the top and a dark espresso brown that bordered on black. But it was his eyes that made Isla falter—warm, glowing amber, like his mother's. They were an unusual family trait and if there'd been any doubt in her mind about who Theo was, those eyes would erase it.

Her stomach vaulted. Mesmerizing eyes, her ultimate weakness.

"Mr. Garrison," she said, sounding almost breathless, as if she'd climbed up to the penthouse instead of riding in an elevator. "So, uh, the elevator comes right into your living room."

He raised an eyebrow.

Thanks, Captain Obvious. Anything else you want to point out that he already knows? Hey, Theo, did you know you're hotter than apple pie straight out of the oven?

The quicker she got hold of the dog and got out of here, the better.

"Yes, it does," he replied. "You came up in the private elevator."

"Is that secure?" The question jumped out of her before she had the chance to think about whether it was prudent to quiz her new employer about his personal security.

"Nobody can access it unless the concierge lets them through." He was difficult to read—was he amused? Annoyed? Bored? "And then I receive an alert that someone is coming. Most people use the regular elevator that goes to the hallway outside, though. But I figured there was no need to send you the long way around."

This version of Theo seemed worlds away from the frazzled and charmingly self-deprecating man she'd met in the park. Here, surrounded by eleven-foot ceilings and precious artwork and wearing a suit that probably cost more than every flight Isla had ever taken combined, he was…something else.

"Good." Isla nodded, her brain whirring as she tried to get her head back into the game. "It would be awkward to walk into your living room and find someone in here. Imagine that, finding that someone had wandered in off the street!"

Theo looked like he was stifling a shudder.

Great, talk to your boss—who is notorious about privacy—about strangers wandering into his home. Wonderful first impression. Why don't you bring up the murder rate in New York while you're at it?

"If we're done discussing my home security, I need to get to work," Theo said, and Isla was grateful that he was moving the conversation along.

"Of course."

"Camilla's itinerary is on the kitchen counter. There's a folder with all her appointments and the details for the events you'll need to take her to," he said.

Itinerary? Events? What kind of dog-sitting job was this?

"Everything that Camilla needs is kept in the first closet in the hallway. Her leash, food, toys, grooming things…it's all there."

"Okay." Isla nodded.

"If you have any problems, please call my assistant. Irina is much easier to get ahold of than I am. She can relay any messages." Theo's amber eyes flicked over Isla's face, as though he was looking for something. But what, she had no idea. "I know you signed the NDA already, but I wanted to clarify a few things about you working here."

Isla sucked in a breath. There was a tension in Theo's tone, in the aura around him. The way he radiated power made her feel as if she were looking at an ancient carved stone door—impressive, resolute and impenetrable. The barrier between him and the world was as palpable as if he had a physical wall around himself.

"Sure," Isla replied.

"People who work with me have certain rules to follow." He slipped his phone back into the pocket on the inside of his jacket. "Nobody comes here to my home unless I vet them personally, not even for Camilla's appointments."

That seemed reasonable. "Of course."

"You're not to repeat anything that you may hear while working in my home. If you're approached by any media while coming or going from the building, you're not to talk to them. In fact, it would be preferable if you didn't tell anyone that you were working for me at all."

Isla blinked. "O…okay."

"I'm a very private man, Isla. I'm sure you did your homework before coming here."

He paused long enough that Isla got the impression he wanted to hear her answer and wasn't asking a rhetorical question. "Uh, yes, I did. You, well…you were a man in the street who offered me a job. I wanted to make sure it was legitimate."

He nodded. "Then you've probably seen a lot of unflattering things written about me."

She had. Words like *recluse*, *hermit*, *misanthrope*, *ascetic*. One article went so far as to call him a martyr, which seemed particularly callous after all he'd been through. Was it the man himself who'd inspired such speculation, or was it speculation that had turned him into this man?

"I…" Oh God, how the hell was she supposed to respond to that? "I didn't read any of the gossipy stuff. I only wanted to verify the information you gave me."

Theo didn't look convinced.

"I won't let you down," Isla added, pasting on a confident smile that felt as brittle as old plastic.

She had to make this work. She *had* to get back on her feet financially so that Dani didn't suffer from her mistakes. And that meant she would be the best darn dog sitter Manhattan had ever seen. She was going to rock this, because there was no other option.

Mollified, Theo nodded. "I'll be home late, but Camilla hasn't been doing so well without supervision. Would you mind staying back a bit? You can bill me for the overtime."

"Of course." Dani had ballet class tonight anyway, so Isla didn't have to rush home. "Is there anything else I need to know?"

"I guess we'll find out."

The response struck Isla as a bit cryptic, but Theo was already making his way toward the elevator door. Now that she looked at it from inside the apartment, the door was seamlessly hidden into the wall. There was paneling across the room that cleverly disguised the door's frame.

It was lucky the room was painted white, Isla thought, or else this whole situation would have some strong Batman vibes. Reclusive billionaire, dead parents, a fixation with privacy...

At this point, it wouldn't totally shock her to find out that Theo had a secret identity. Well, a *second* secret identity anyway. She'd already seen the one he used to walk around Central Park unnoticed.

With a soft *ping*, Theo disappeared and Isla found herself rooted to the spot, her gaze swinging around the big apartment. He'd just...left her there. Unsupervised. She wondered how she'd instilled him with the confidence to do that.

"He's probably got cameras everywhere," she said under her breath, fighting a shudder.

The whole situation was more than a little bizarre. And if Isla wasn't hovering above rock bottom, she might be inclined to analyze things more closely. But the fact was, she needed this job and when Theo's assistant had sent across the contract with the hourly rate triple what she could have hoped for, there was no way she could refuse.

Hell, working for Theo she could make more money than with most low-to-mid-level social media jobs. Sure, she didn't want to be a dog sitter for the rest of her life. But this was a lifeline that she desperately needed right now and who was she to look a gift horse in the mouth?

Isla wandered through the apartment, still feeling like she wasn't supposed to be there. It struck her that while the penthouse was stunningly beautiful—seriously, it was an *Architectural Digest* spread waiting to happen—it was so devoid of personal touches that literally anybody could have lived there.

"Anybody with a whole lotta cash," Isla said as she walked into the kitchen.

A leather folder the color of cognac sat in the middle of the counter, as promised. It was bound with thin strips of leather and Isla carefully unwound them so she could see what was inside. There was more paper than should have been necessary, with a host of business cards tucked neatly into the slots inside the front cover.

An itinerary labeled Monday was sitting on top, with an hourly schedule dictating everything Camilla would be doing that day.

9:00 a.m.—breakfast and morning grooming session.

10:00 a.m.—walk around Central Park.

11:00 a.m.—playdate.

Aww, she had weekly playdates with her friends? Okay, that was kind of cute. But as Isla's eyes drifted farther down the page, she blinked. Then she flipped to Tuesday. Then Wednesday.

Grooming and playdates were not the only sort of activities that Camilla was expected to partake in. Not by a long shot.

The itinerary for Thursday included:

10:00 a.m.—day spa appointment: keratin hair treatment, blowout and nails.

12:00 p.m.—appointment with pet psychic.

And when Isla continued flipping forward she saw an entry that said: *photo shoot for Vogue.*

What the hell was going on right now?

Despite what Scout said earlier about Ashton Kutcher going all "Silicon Valley," Isla was quite sure she was in the middle of a giant practical joke. What else could possibly explain taking a Dachshund to a psychic? As for the *Vogue* photo shoot…

Isla shook her head.

Exactly what kind of mess had she gotten herself into?

6

Theo leaned back in his office chair and looked out of the enormous floor-to-ceiling windows. Manhattan was stretched out in front of him, like a beautiful sacrifice to some ancient god. Early-evening light bounced off all the glass and steel and water, making everything shimmer in gold.

His grandmother had loved New York.

A year after his parents' deaths, he'd begged her to move somewhere else—anywhere else. Boston, maybe. California, though he was sure he'd hate the relentless optimism their sunshine encouraged. Better yet, why not Antarctica? Or a remote village somewhere. Maybe the outback of Australia.

Somewhere he could disappear.

She'd never let him, of course, because Garrisons didn't

run away in the face of hardship. Terrible things built character, in her mind. Theo was never sure he agreed with that, but he *had* stayed in Manhattan and by her side. For a moment at her funeral, Theo had wondered if maybe now was the time to move.

He had no family left. No ties. He could sell the company and finally escape the city that had always felt like a prison to him. A beautiful, gilt prison.

He could be free.

But the thought of leaving now didn't hold the same appeal as it did back then, because he'd structured his life to provide the privacy and solitude he craved. And now he'd become settled into it like a piece of clay fired in a kiln.

He could not be changed without first breaking.

A soft knock at his door caught Theo's attention and he swiveled away from the window. "Yes?"

His assistant, Irina, pushed the door open and stepped inside, closing it immediately behind her as she'd been instructed. Theo didn't like the idea of anyone overhearing his conversations, even if they were banal ones about the type of catering he wanted for the company board meeting.

Besides, an open door invited people to disturb him. And he hated being disturbed.

"We need to talk about your grandmother's charity gala," she said, dropping into one of the twin leather chairs that sat on the other side of his desk. Irina had a thick Russian accent, a stare that could turn grown men into petrified wood and a total lack of tolerance for bullshit.

Theo might have considered marrying her if she wasn't old enough to be his mother *and* if the idea of marriage didn't make his skin crawl.

"Why do we need to talk about it?" he asked, his eyes drifting back to his laptop. He had work to do. "I don't care about the details. Just make sure it's something she would have liked."

Irina sighed in that way that said she was tempted to go all No BS Baba on him. "At some point you'll need to pay attention to the details, Theo. You need to give a speech and—"

"No." The word had an ice-cold edge, like a blade that had sliced through the surface of a frozen lake.

"What do you mean, no?"

"I'm not giving a speech."

Irina narrowed her gray eyes at him over the top of thick, tortoiseshell glasses. "We need someone to talk about the work your grandmother has done and to introduce the people who will be taking over."

"I completely agree, it's important that we make a smooth transition." But that did *not* mean he would be getting up in front of a room full of people and making a speech.

Truth be told, public speaking repulsed Theo as much as crowded rooms and small talk and questions about his family. Actually, that wasn't quite the truth. Public speaking *terrified* Theo...but he'd been taught at an early age that men shouldn't be afraid of things. Or, at the very least, they shouldn't admit to it.

The idea of fronting three hundred of the country's most influential people sent a shudder through him, and he let Irina interpret it as derision. Better she think him an asshole than a coward.

"Have the current director of operations do it," he said, waving his hand as if shooing a fly. "He's been there the longest and Gram always respected his take on things."

"That message should come from you," Irina argued. "This is as much to honor her memory as it is to honor her work."

"And I'll honor her work by doing the thing she did best... delegating."

She sighed and looked at him in a way that only she could get away with. There were certain privileges for people who'd been with the publishing company from back when his father still sat in the corner office, but it was a short list. Most had come and gone. Theo knew he wasn't an easy man to work for, with his exacting standards and brusque manner.

Brusque might be generous. What did your last CFO call you? The human embodiment of a cactus?

The problem was that people wanted to do things the easy way, rather than the right way. That didn't fly with him. Irina, however, had mastered her job. She managed his inbox and his calls with ease, she shielded him from the constant barrage of requests, allowing only the most critical or important things through. Seriously, there was something almost Tolkien about her. Give her a large stick and a bridge to guard and *nobody* would get past without her approval.

Which meant that Theo put up with her occasional meddling, though he didn't like it.

"You can look at me like that all you want," he said with a shrug. "It's not going to happen. So, either you organize someone else to do it, or there won't be a speech."

"Fine." She pushed back on her chair and smoothed her hands down the front of her gray tweed pencil skirt.

"Fine, a decision has been made?" he asked. "Or fine, you're biding your time until you're going to push again?"

An amused smile flitted across her lips, which were painted in a shade of deep purple that matched the plum-colored streaks in her short, spiky hair. "Don't worry, I know who's the boss around here."

She left his office, her sensible block-heeled shoes clacking against the polished boards in a way that reminded him of a horse clip-clopping around Central Park. A memory stirred— his grandmother and mother, a carriage ride. Cameras flashing.

He sucked in a breath and fought against the uncomfortable feeling crawling along his skin like an army of beetles. They'd gotten worse, the memories. It was the shake-up of his routine, a disturbance in the calm, blue surface of his life like ripples across a pond. They'd ease soon.

In the meantime, he had to deal with another disruption to his life: Camilla.

Curse his grandmother. If there was such a thing as heaven, then she'd be up there smoking a cigarette, diamonds dripping from her ears and her wrists as she watched him, cackling in that distinctive way of hers that she only allowed herself to indulge in behind closed doors.

Theo pushed up from his chair and steeled himself to head home. All he could do was hope that the devil dog hadn't scared Isla away on day number one. That was, if the ridiculous itinerary hadn't done it already. But the way Theo saw it, he was due some luck.

And Isla Thompson was the closest he'd come to having the perfect solution to a problem dropped into his lap in a long time.

By the time Theo made it home, he'd conjured up all kinds of things that could have gone wrong in the course of the day. Maybe Camilla had bitten Isla and she'd ended up in the doctor's office. Maybe Isla had taken one look at the itinerary and decided to GTFO. Maybe Camilla had slipped out of her leash again and run into oncoming traffic.

Gram would never forgive you.

He was almost at his wits' end with this damn dog, and yet stubbornness wouldn't allow him to quit. A promise was a promise...even when it was hidden in fine print.

The doors of his private elevator whooshed open and he stepped into his living room. It was almost 7:00 p.m. and the place had a warm dreamlike quality at this time of day. The sun was getting lower in the sky, casting rich orange light through the room and glittering off the simple touches of gold on some of the furniture.

Theo listened.

He could have checked his security system on the way up, to see if Isla and Camilla were in the house. He'd often done that whenever staff were around, so he knew how long to wait before coming home to avoid the false pleasantries and small talk. God how he hated that stuff.

But for some reason he didn't have that same desire to avoid Isla like he did with other people on his payroll. There was something…calming about her. Something easy and genuine. It wasn't often that he met a new person without his hackles raised and his defensive shields on high alert, but she didn't trigger those responses in him.

"Oof! Will you please hold still?"

Isla's voice carried through the silent apartment, any response from Camilla drowned out by the whine of something electrical. Was that…a hair dryer?

Frowning, he walked through the living room and into the hallway, his dress shoes sounding against the marble-tiled floor. The bathroom door was ajar, and he found Isla wrestling with Camilla. She had a round brush in one hand and a small hair dryer in the other, and the dog was wriggling in her lap.

"What are you doing?"

Isla yelped in surprise, releasing her hold on Camilla. The dog shot out of her arms, skidding out of the bathroom like she was an extra in *Fast and the Furious: Tokyo Drift*. The sound of her canine nails skittering across the tiles faded as the dog disappeared into the far end of the penthouse apartment.

"I was giving her a blowout," Isla said with a weak laugh.

Champagne-colored dog fur dusted her black pants and her brown hair had started escaping the clip holding it back.

"A blowout?" Theo had seen it written on the itinerary, but he'd been completely clueless as to what it meant.

"Yeah." Isla held up the hair dryer. "A blowout. On low temperature, of course."

"Oh, it's a hair thing." Okay right, that made sense.

"How did you put something on her to-do list without knowing what it is?" Isla got to her feet and tried to dust the dog fur from her pants, but it didn't help much.

"I didn't make that list."

"That makes sense," she replied. "You didn't strike me as the type who would want their pet to see a psychic."

He made a soft snorting sound. "Uh, no."

"Did that all come from your grandmother?"

Theo's shoulders tensed. Not because he thought Isla was prying for information—he didn't get that vibe from her—but because Theo hated the way his grandmother was always portrayed as one of those overly eccentric, more-money-than-sense people. And yeah, she was a little indulgent when it came to her dog…okay, *ridiculously* indulgent. But she'd been a good woman with her head screwed on properly and way more intelligence than anyone ever gave her credit for.

"It did," he said stiffly.

"I can tell she really loved Camilla."

Isla's soft voice surprised Theo and he took a step back as though the kindness of her words was so confronting to him that he wasn't quite sure how to deal with it. "She…had a lot of love in her."

Where had *that* come from? He didn't talk about his family. Ever.

"I read a bit about her as I was getting prepared for today. She seemed like a very interesting and accomplished woman."

"I'm surprised you got that from anything online," he said drily.

Lord knew the media had mixed feelings about his family—they loved to talk about them, whether saying something positive or negative. Having his parents die so young and in such a tragic way had mostly protected them from the shit-slinging, but for everyone else who was left alive it was game on.

"Her charity work was incredible." Isla steadily packed up the tools from the aborted blowout. "And I think you can tell a lot about a person by how they treat animals, actually."

"I've never thought about that before." But it struck him as true, although he wasn't sure he wanted to ponder too deeply on what it said about him. He'd wanted to foist the creature off onto someone else as soon as she'd come home with him because the thought of taking care of anyone but himself was daunting, to say the least. "Camilla's previous dog sitters… struggled with her."

That was putting it mildly.

"I can *also* understand that," Isla replied, getting to her feet. "She's got a strong personality."

The laugh that shot out of Theo took him totally by surprise. "She and my grandmother had that in common."

Who was he right now, standing around and chatting with an employee? Laughing? Sharing tidbits about his family?

Had Irina slipped something into his afternoon espresso?

"So," he said, clearing his throat. It was time to wrap this up. He had a long night of work ahead of him and Isla surely had family to get home to. "You'll be back tomorrow?"

She blinked, an adorable line forming between her brows. "Of course. Unless you're not happy with something?"

He held up a hand. "No, no. Everything is fine."

"I mean, I didn't quite get the blowout finished." She bit down on her lip. "But I can practice, I'll get better."

The tight note of desperation in her voice tugged at Theo's heartstrings—heartstrings which he'd thought were permanently severed. It was a strange reaction. A strange sensation.

He didn't care about people outside a very exclusionary circle of one—his grandmother. Now she was gone and Theo was *not* looking to fill her spot. He was quite happy living up to his lone-wolf reputation, caring only about his work and protecting the impenetrable bubble that encircled his world.

Which meant he knew better than to be fooled by Isla's sweet disposition and the surprising, caring comments that came out of her mouth. At best, she was saying what she thought Theo wanted to hear. At worst…well, he'd fallen prey to people who said they cared about him before. Turned out they only ever wanted to use him for their own personal gain.

And that would never happen again.

7

Isla learned from the mistakes she made on day one. No more black pants, because Camilla shed like an army of chinchillas. Seriously, if Isla collected all the hair that dog shed in a couple of days she would be able to build herself a brand-new dog.

Secondly, she knew to expect the unexpected.

The Camilla she'd met in Central Park on the day Theo offered her a job was *not* the normal Camilla, it turned out. Oh no. The adorable, playful, charming little canine of that first day was apparently the Jekyll part of her personality. Unfortunately for Isla, it appeared Camilla preferred to play the role of Hyde more often than not. Isla hadn't thought it possible for a dog to have a capital *R* reputation…but she did.

"You know the staff here have tried to ban Camilla like *ten* times." One of the other dog sitters, a woman named Michaela who talked as if she was permanently rolling her eyes, plopped down next to Isla. "Your boss must be forking it out to keep her here."

Itinerary item number two for the day was a "group playdate" at what appeared to be a super high-end version of a day care facility...only for dogs. Camilla's schedule showed that she came three times per week, always during the same morning slot. Isla sat on a tufted couch—one of several that lined the room—while a small group of dogs played in the middle. There were fancy coffee facilities, an attendant who ran fun activities for the dogs, *and* a professional groomer for anyone who wanted their pooch to go home with a new haircut.

Hmm, from now on she would be palming off the blowout duties to someone who knew what they were doing.

"Why would they try to ban her?" Isla asked.

"No offense, but she's kind of a bitch." Michaela shrugged in a way that said *sorry, not sorry* loud and clear. "And I don't mean in the technical sense."

Isla bristled. Sure, it wasn't *her* dog. And yeah, Camilla was proving to be a little difficult what with almost biting Isla's wrist that morning when she'd tried to do her daily brushing... but the dog *had* lost her owner. Maybe she was grieving.

Did dogs grieve?

"She's not that bad," Isla argued.

Michaela snorted. "I've seen her pee on someone's purse. Twice. And the second time it was a Chanel 2.55 and not the basic lambskin ones that you could wipe down, either. It was one of the fancy ones with tweed and sequins. No way is that smell coming out. It's going to smell like pee *forever.*"

"A dog wouldn't know the difference."

"She *knew.* Belinda took her out to do her business not five minutes before it happened and that sneaky beast saved some for the purse. And not just any purse, *that* specific purse," Michaela said solemnly. "The most expensive one in the room."

Isla raised her eyebrow. On one hand, she'd been grateful for the other dog sitters making her feel welcome earlier that morning when she'd turned up for the playdate. But, on the other hand, it seemed like the hatred of Camilla was pretty universal.

The woman next to her, Wei, nodded and made a sound of agreement. Her hair was cut into a sharp black bob and her makeup was so perfect, it looked like a professional had applied it. "There's a reason she's had so many dog sitters."

"How many has she had?" Isla wrinkled her nose. Theo had given her the impression she wasn't the first, but the women here made it seem a little more extreme than that.

Wei laughed. "I've lost count."

"Must be over ten in the last month. Maybe more," Michaela said.

Isla blinked. "Ten?"

"At least." Wei tapped a perfectly manicured nail to her cheek, an engagement ring glittering in the light. "Might be closer to fifteen. There was one week that we saw three different sitters."

Isla watched Camilla trotting around the middle of the room. Her champagne-colored fur gleamed and she seemed… like a normal dog. Certainly not troublesome enough to warrant a parade of sitters to walk out on her and Theo.

Or maybe people aren't as desperate for work as you are.

That was entirely possible.

"Well, *I'm* not going anywhere," Isla said stubbornly. "I need this job."

"We'll see," Wei replied with a snort. "That's what the last girl said."

"Unless you're personally connected to Camilla's owner?" Michaela asked.

Both women stared at Isla expectantly, like they were waiting for a tidbit of juicy gossip. But yesterday's conversation with Theo floated around in her head: *it would be preferable if you didn't tell anyone that you were working for me.*

And by preferable, Isla was pretty sure it was a condition of employment.

As far as she could tell, none of the dogs' owners were in attendance. Most of the people there were young women, like her, who were more likely on the payroll than the one footing the bill. And there seemed to be some secrecy about who the dogs belonged to. All that was obvious to her was that they were stinking rich.

"Fine, keep it a secret," Michaela huffed when Isla didn't answer. "Doesn't matter. Half the fun is trying to figure out who belongs to who anyway."

"I'd bet the Chihuahuas belong to a certain former boy-band singer." Wei leaned forward and narrowed her eyes as if studying them intently. "One who might say bye, bye, bye."

"No way." Michaela snorted. "He does not strike me as a little dog man."

"You know what they say about men with small dogs…" Wei grinned.

Isla sipped her coffee. "They're not his dogs."

Both of the women turned to her with varying levels of disbelief. Michaela made a scoffing noise. "Excuse me, Miss I've Been Here One Day, how do you know that?"

How would she know that? Oh, only because she'd worked with the wife of this "certain former boy-band singer" six months ago on an "at home with" social media campaign for an international fashion magazine. So she'd *been* to the Tribeca penthouse where they both lived. It had been one of those "pinch me" moments when she'd finally seen how far her career might go.

But all that was old news now.

"Just a feeling," she lied with a shrug.

A sudden commotion in the middle of the room caught Isla's attention. A small white Bichon Frise named Sascha had a stuffed bear between her teeth, while another dog fiercely gripped the bear's leg. Both of them growled and yanked on the stuffed animal in a game of tug-of-war. As Isla looked on, she could see the bear was tan, but its paws were the exact shade of blue as a Tiffany box and it wore one of the brand's famous silver charms around its neck.

Seriously, who gave dogs a toy that cost that much? Ridiculous.

But as she looked around the room, she noticed all the food bowls were the same blue, and Isla would bet her bottom dollar they were designer, too. Hell, in the forty-five minutes she'd sat here watching the animals play, she'd spotted almost every major French, Italian and American designer brand. Louis Vuitton, Chanel, Prada, Dior, Ralph Lauren.

Enough to fill the shelves at Saks.

Nobody else seemed perturbed by this fact, except her. Michaela scrolled on her phone and Wei stared into space as if willing herself to be transported to somewhere more interesting.

You're out of your depth here.

Who would have thought a world of luxury and celebrity name-dropping would feel so foreign, when not too long ago that was the crux of her job. Back then designer dog bowls and Fifth Avenue pet playdates wouldn't have seemed unusual at all. But now it all felt so...excessive.

Sneakily, she held up her phone and snapped a picture of the dogs fighting over the stuffed bear. Right in the bottom corner of the photo, was the back of Camilla's head as she looked on. Isla texted it to Scout.

ISLA: Ugh, there they go again, fighting over the Tiffany.

She knew her friend would have a laugh at that. Scout was the most down-to-earth person ever, and they'd both come from the kind of homes where brands of any kind were *not* the norm.

SCOUT: Tell me the dog has an Instagram account. I need to live vicariously. I'll never earn enough to afford a little blue box.

Hey, maybe that wasn't the worst idea in the world. Since Isla had put her own Instagram account on private due to the barrage of nasty messages and comments she'd been receiving, she'd missed the fun of posting pictures during her day and coming up with captions she knew would make people laugh.

Her goal had always been to make social media a more positive place by bringing some humor and levity into what could be a very negative and critical environment. She believed the internet could connect people and provide quality entertainment, and it fed her creative side.

Frankly, she missed her old job. It was the only thing she'd ever been good at.

Biting down on her lip, she checked the time. Another forty-five minutes? Isla sighed and tapped her foot. Well, maybe something to keep her occupied wouldn't be the worst thing in the world. She opened the Instagram app on her phone and created a new account. What should she call it?

She watched Camilla trot haughtily around the room, her nose in the air and her fluffy tail sweeping back and forth with each short-legged step. A black dog came over, tongue lolling out of its mouth, but when it tried to sniff around her, Camilla snapped at the other dog and it slunk away with its tail between its legs. Then she plopped down onto the floor as if bored by the whole thing and lazily scratched at her collar.

Her Prada collar.

That was it! *The Dachshund Wears Prada*. It was totally fitting, not only because it was accurate, but Camilla definitely had a Miranda Priestly slash Anna Wintour vibe going on. Seriously, if they ever decided to do a canine remake of the film, Camilla was a shoe-in.

Or is that paw-in?

Chuckling to herself, Isla selected the photo of the dogs fighting over the teddy bear and typed out a caption.

Last week it was Manolos, this week it's the Tiffany. Is nothing sacred anymore? xoxo C.

This was a silly distraction, but at least it was something to keep her amused. And Scout would love it. Besides, she wouldn't take any pictures inside Theo's house or do anything else that might reveal his identity. To be on the safe side, she wouldn't even post pictures of Camilla face-on. She would never betray Theo's trust.

And it wasn't like anyone would even find the damn account. Organic reach was in the toilet these days and nobody accidentally went viral...well, unless you filmed a Disney princess vomiting all over herself.

Right now, having something that made her smile was important. She might even say it was *necessary*. Ever since The Incident Isla's life had been balancing on a knife edge, anxiety and stress creeping up on her day after day as she tried to figure out how the heck she was going to keep all her plates spinning.

It felt like for the first time in over a month she could... breathe.

"What are you laughing at?" Michaela asked, leaning over to see Isla's screen. But Isla quickly tucked her phone away, and shook her head.

"Absolutely nothing at all."

★ ★ ★

"Come on, Camilla, please." Isla sucked in a big breath and looked up to the sky as though she might find answers there. "You have to eat something. It says so right here on the itinerary, see? 6:00 p.m., dinner. No exceptions."

But the precious Dachshund simply stared at Isla, her furry ass planted to the ground as the bowl of food remained untouched. She wouldn't even glance in the direction of her dinner. Yesterday Camilla had been reluctant, but she'd at least taken a few nibbles.

And now today…nada.

Camilla looked at her as if to say: *if you think I'm going to eat that, you're as stupid as you look.*

Isla fetched the fork she used to dish the food out of its tin and speared a piece, holding it toward Camilla's nose. Maybe hand-feeding would work? Talk about a fall from grace. A month ago, she was sharing air space with Chrissy Teigen and John Legend…and now she was trying to fork-feed a dog.

"Look, it's delicious." Isla moved the fork back and forth and made airplane noises like she'd seen mothers do on television. "Here comes the tasty airplane!"

But Camilla continued to look at Isla like she was something stuck to the bottom of her paw. At least she hadn't walked away, or tried to pee on her. Apparently that was Camilla's go-to power move, or so Isla had heard from at least three separate people.

"Come on, girl. Aren't you hungry?" Isla sighed and nudged the fork toward Camilla once again. "Okay, so I'll admit this doesn't smell amazing. And yeah, it looks a little slimy…okay, fine. It's definitely gross. But you have to eat."

Camilla was unmoved by Isla's attempt to connect with her. Nor was she tempted by the tasty food airplane. Huffing in frustration, Isla abandoned the fork in the laundry sink.

Could she really blame the dog for not wanting to eat something that looked like ground-up roadkill? Not really. And despite what the fancy design on the tin said—complete with a fluffy white poodle spokesmodel—this meal looked neither nutritionally optimized nor sublimely satisfying.

"Let's see if we can find you something in the kitchen." Isla pushed up to her feet and headed out of the laundry room, which appeared to only exist for show. Or at least, to house Camilla's unwanted tins of dog food and other canine paraphernalia. "You think a man like that does his own laundry? Yeah right."

She walked into the kitchen to see what she could cook up for the dog. No way was she going to leave until that stubborn little creature had something in her belly. As it was, she looked a bit on the lean side. Camilla had snubbed the snacks at doggy day care too, so dinner was very important.

"My next-door neighbor used to give her dog leftover pasta with plain chicken and she really liked it," Isla said. "Maybe you'll like it, too."

Theo's kitchen was easily as big as Isla's entire apartment—and everything gleamed. The marble countertops, the arty light-piece hanging overhead, the coffee machine that looked like it required an engineering degree to operate.

"I bet he doesn't even use all this, does he?" Isla shook her head. "Not that I'm a great cook, mind you. But maybe I would be if I had a kitchen like this."

Camilla trotted behind her, toenails making a sharp clicking sound against the tiled floor. She watched Isla, as though curious about what she was doing.

Isla went to a long cupboard door, which she assumed was the pantry, and pulled it open. Huh. Old Mother Hubbard had *nothing* on this cupboard. She couldn't claim it was totally bare, on account of the few bags of coffee beans sitting on one shelf.

But that was it. Coffee beans.

Frowning, she closed those doors and opened the next set. That one contained some protein powder, and the next set housed a few bottles of expensive-looking wine. Shaking her head, Isla pulled the refrigerator door open and blinked. A jug of milk and a container of spinach.

Did the man not eat?

"Your owner is ridiculous, you know that right?" Isla said to the dog, shaking her head. Camilla huffed as if to say *tell me about it*. "Well, I'm going to fix this. You sit right here and I'll go get some groceries."

The second the elevator doors opened Theo knew something was amiss. There were noises coming from his house that he hadn't heard since he was a child—the clatter of pots and pans, rushing water in the kitchen and the sound of… chopping. Unless his apartment had suddenly become haunted by a ghost with culinary skills, then it sounded a hell of a lot like Isla was cooking in his kitchen.

Sure enough, the second he walked into the big open-plan kitchen area, he saw her. Music floated up from her phone, which was sitting screen up on the countertop. Pop music played from the tinny speakers. It sounded…pink. He wasn't exactly sure how a song could sound like a color, but that's the only way he could describe it. It was bright and positive and pink.

Isla was dressed in a pair of blue jeans with a pretty gray sweater, which was perfectly in-between being tight and loose. It showed off her slender shoulders and hinted at curves beneath, but it looked soft and comfortable and…touchable. Her dark ponytail bounced as she half walked, half danced over to the stove and that's when Theo caught a glimpse of her sock-covered feet.

The socks were yellow and covered in bright green frogs

with big, buggy eyes. They were so playful and silly that he couldn't help a smirk tugging at his lips.

"What on earth are you doing?" he asked.

Isla jumped, a shriek rushing out of her as she startled, almost knocking over the pot of boiling water on the stove. Some sloshed over the edge and hissed on contact with the cooktop. Camilla, who'd been half dozing on the floor, was suddenly up on her paws, barking like she'd spied an intruder climbing in through the window. Or maybe she was telling him off for ruining her nap.

"My God." Isla pressed a hand to her chest. "You scared the crap out of me. You can't sneak up on a girl while she's in the zone."

"I wasn't sneaking." Theo raised an eyebrow. "And I can walk anywhere in this house, especially since I hired you as a dog sitter and not a cook."

Isla reached for her phone and tapped the pause button, cutting the music off. Camilla was planted at Theo's feet, still barking. He couldn't remember the last time he'd gotten such an earful.

"Oh, Camilla, hush." Isla crouched and patted her knee. Camilla didn't exactly go running to her, but at least she stopped barking. Her furry head swung from Isla to Theo and back again, and then she walked over to the corner and plonked her butt down, giving them both an epic case of side-eye. "Oh, she's a cranky one today."

"Today?" Theo snorted. "Try every day of every week until the beginning of time."

"Dramatic much." Isla shot a cheeky smirk in his direction.

"What on earth are you doing in my kitchen?"

It was weird to see someone here—because Theo had always felt the kitchen was the most useless part of the apartment. It was simply a space for him to blend his morning smoothie or make coffee. Most nights he had his dinner delivered to the office—a nearby corporate catering business he used specialized in healthy meals that he could easily eat at his desk. They called it the CEO special.

On the off chance he ate dinner at home, it was usually a treat from one of his favorite restaurants. Truffle oil pasta or the incredible duck risotto from a French restaurant which didn't deliver...except to him.

He wasn't even sure the oven had been used in the past year. Maybe two.

Now he was looking at a picture he never thought he would see in his own life—a gorgeous woman walking around the place like she owned it, the smell of food being cooked, a warm feeling stirring in his chest.

Don't get attached. This is about as far from your future as you can possibly get.

"I know you didn't hire me as a cook, so it's a good thing I'm not cooking for you." She waded a wooden spoon through a pot of water with something bobbing inside. Pasta and little bits of chopped-up carrot.

"You're cooking for Camilla?" He frowned. "I don't remember home-cooked meals being on the itinerary."

"They're not. However, Little Miss Fussypants decided she didn't want to eat her regular old dog food and so I'm making her something special. Apparently mixing some cooked pasta and carrots into dog food is a great way to get a dog to eat." Isla scooped out a single piece of pasta with the wooden spoon and blew on the curling tendrils of steam. Then she popped it into her mouth and chewed. "Not quite ready."

Theo glanced around the kitchen and saw three bags of shopping sitting on his countertop. A carton of milk, a hunk of cheese and a loaf of bread were out, several more items packed inside. A cutting board that Theo didn't even remember owning was out as well, along with a knife and a neat pile of carrot skin peelings.

"What's the rest of the stuff for?"

He must have looked so confused that Isla let out a little laugh. "Well, two bags are for me because I needed to get some groceries tonight. But the other one is for you. I went looking for something to feed Camilla aside from the dog food and..."

"Didn't have much luck?"

"Not exactly."

He wasn't sure why, but a touch of shame crept through him. His bare cupboards felt symbolic somehow, like the emptiness of his life was on display. The lack of food showed how little time he spent at home, and how few visitors he had. To someone like Isla, it probably looked strange. Sad, even. Pathetic.

Poor little orphan Theodore.

He'd resented that. Resented the pity that seemed to come without empathy. He'd resented the way the media seemed to feed off his sadness, like they were a monster from one of his books.

He wasn't poor little anything and he didn't want *anybody* feeling sorry for him.

"I don't need you to stock my shelves," he said coolly, pressing down on the bad feelings gathering steam inside him. "You're here to look after the dog, not me. I don't need a caretaker."

"I know what my job is." Isla blinked, as if surprised by his reaction. "I just thought that since I was going to the store anyway..."

"Everything you need to do is clearly laid out in Camilla's itinerary, as we discussed on day one."

Her big blue eyes looked at him, brows furrowing slightly as though she wasn't sure why he was having a negative reaction. But instead of arguing, she simply nodded and *that* made him feel like an even bigger jerk. Isla didn't have a nasty bone in her body—and as someone who'd spent his formative years feeling like a mouse in a snake pit, he knew how to read people's motives. Isla was goodness, through and through.

Firstly, you don't know that for certain because intuition is not truth. Secondly, if you are right that's all the more reason to keep as far away from her as possible.

"I didn't mean to overstep," Isla said. "I'm sorry."

Words danced on Theo's tongue, the need to apologize climbing up the back of his throat. But there was no point. Besides, it was better that he didn't get used to the feeling of anyone doing something good for him. It was one thing to pay a catering company, and a whole other thing entirely for a beautiful woman to be flitting about his kitchen, showing him what he would never have.

With a nod, Theo turned and walked out, ignoring both the prickling sensation of Isla's gaze on his back and the sharp glare that Camilla was shooting in his direction.

You're an asshole.

True. But being an asshole was a whole lot easier and less complicated than trying to untangle the dark web of fractured parts and memories that made up who he was. It was better for Isla not to do things for him, better for her to see him as the jerk who signed her paycheck and nothing more. Because any time Theo even thought about trusting another person outside his family, they betrayed him.

The lure of five minutes of fame or the big payout of a scandalous story was always more compelling than Theo himself. He'd learned that lesson several times over.

And Isla might be sunshine and light, but that didn't mean he could trust her.

8

Later that night, Isla slumped onto the couch with a glass of wine in one hand. And, more importantly, it was *not* the box wine of dubious origin. It was an actual bottle of wine.

"That last post you made totally cracked me up." Scout took a seat next to Isla, also holding a glass of wine. Across the room, Dani practiced a barre routine with earbuds lodged in her ears and the sound of her pointe shoes brushing against the floor as she completed a set of *rond de jambes*. "The captions are pure gold."

Isla laughed. She'd taken a photo for the Dachshund Wears Prada Instagram account of Camilla's dinner with the pasta and carrots mixed in.

The human tried to feed me plain dog food. Not. Going. To. Happen. What is this, business class? How insulting...

"Call it frustrated creativity." Isla took a sip from her wineglass. "You know, I can't even remember the last time I used social media for fun. After spending years working on finding the perfect captions and pleasing the algorithm and trying to figure out how to make sponsored posts sound authentic, it's kind of refreshing."

"Too bad doggy social media assistant isn't a job."

"I doubt I could even get *that* job right now," Isla replied with a sigh. "But at least being a dog sitter is helping to pay the bills."

"And by bills you mean expensive ballet tuition?"

Isla watched her sister. She often joked that when they eventually moved out of this place, Isla would have to replace the floor where Dani's daily practice had worn a groove into it. But the girl worked her ass off. Every day after school until dinnertime, she did her barre exercises. Then, while completing her homework after dinner, she'd sit on the floor and stretch.

She lived, breathed and dreamed ballet.

"If I was half as talented at anything as Dani is at ballet, then I hope I'd have the opportunity to pursue it," Isla replied. "I don't care how much it costs. I'm going to make sure she understands the importance of chasing a dream."

"You're plenty talented." Scout dug her elbow into Isla's rib cage. "One mistake doesn't erase everything you've done. You climbed your way up from nothing to work with celebrities—that doesn't happen by accident. You've got to stop being so damn hard on yourself."

"I'm realistic." Isla sipped her wine. *Oh yes, mediocre wine, how I've missed thee.* "Dani can do something with her ballet if we get her access to the right opportunities. She works twice as hard as everyone else and I don't want to see it all go down the drain because *I* made a mistake."

Scout looked at her and then nodded. Clearly she knew when to back down in the face of Isla's stubbornness. That was the best thing about a long-standing friendship—they'd tested these limits before.

Scout and Isla had been BFFs since day one of high school, when Scout was the new kid and she'd gotten picked on for her handmade clothing and bowl-cut hair. Granted, Scout's mother *had* put her in some hideous sweaters that looked like they belonged in a cat lady costume rather than on a preteen, but that wasn't a reason for anyone to get bullied. Never one to let the bad guys win, Isla had stood up for Scout and they'd been thick as thieves ever since.

Isla was the steady, responsible one and Scout made sure they had fun. It was a good pairing.

"So tell me, what's the Hermit of Fifth Avenue like in the flesh?" Scout burrowed back into the corner of the couch, drawing her knees up to her chest and getting comfy. She wore a pair of hot-pink leggings with silver lightning bolts on them and a black hoodie that contrasted against her long, blond hair. "Have your murder fears abated?"

"No more murder fears," Isla replied. "He's...well, I can't say he's a normal guy, because he's not."

"Nobody with that much money is normal," Scout said, sipping her wine and leaning forward to grab a handful of potato chips from the coffee table. "How could your life possibly be normal when you've been in the spotlight since you were a kid?"

"And for all the wrong reasons, too." Isla shook her head. "The way his parents died is so tragic. It's clearly left a mark, though, because he asked me not to tell anyone I was working for him."

Scout raised an eyebrow. "That's a bit weird."

"I think it was more of a 'don't talk about me' kind of thing. Like, he knew that if I told people who I was working for then there would be questions that he didn't necessarily want me to answer."

"Of *course* there would be questions. I mean, there's famous and then there's the Garrison family. We're not talking about some schmuck who managed to get himself on a long-running sitcom, ya know?"

Isla nodded. "It's like stepping into a whole other world and yet, there *is* something normal about him. He's just a guy trying to live his life with a misbehaving dog and…"

"More money than God."

Snorting, Isla rolled her eyes. "Okay, yeah. Definitely not normal."

But despite all that, Isla saw glimpses of the real man behind the glamorous mask. A guy who was weirded out by cooking and who said sweet things about his grandmother and who, when he smiled, lit up the whole room.

"Maybe it's the aura of the urban legend," Isla said. "But he's very…magnetic."

Magnetic was putting it lightly. When Isla had caught Theo watching her in the kitchen tonight, it was like her whole body had been infused with sparkling electricity. There was something about the way he looked at her, those warm eyes smoldering, that had every part of her tingling.

But he was so damaged. So walled off from the world. *So* not her type.

"What do you mean?" Scout asked.

"He's got a presence. When he walks into a room you *know*. It's like the air changes."

Scout snorted. "Okay teenybopper, you're sounding a little bit Bella Swan right now."

"Shut up."

"Does his magnetism include a glittery sheen whenever he walks into the sunlight?" she teased. "Does he look at you like he's hungry for your virgin blood?"

"You're such a goof." Isla couldn't help but cackle. "And I may not have had a boyfriend in what feels like six billion years, but I'm no virgin."

"Ugh, who needs men anyway?" A dark shadow passed over Scout's face and for a moment, her usually jovial, class clown attitude vanished. "More trouble than they're worth."

"It's all irrelevant. I don't have room for any relationships outside the ones in this room." Isla let her gaze drift across her tiny apartment. "I've got you ladies and that's all I need."

"Back at ya." Scout leaned over and slung an arm around Isla's shoulders, their heads resting together. "We'll figure out your next steps, don't you worry. It won't be doggy day care forever."

Not forever, but doggy day care was what she had now and Isla was going to make the most of it. As for Theo, she wouldn't overstep that line again. He'd made it very clear that she was the hired help for Camilla and that *didn't* involve doing anything for him. Isla wasn't annoyed, because a line in the sand was exactly what she needed.

Clear boundaries. Separation.

That way she could focus on what mattered—hers and Dani's future.

The next morning, Theo was gone by the time Isla got to work. It was probably for the best. Things would likely have gotten awkward between them and Isla didn't want to do anything else to piss off her mysterious boss.

Which meant she followed the itinerary to the letter.

Today that included a morning at the doggy day spa, where

Camilla had her toenails clipped and painted a classic cherry red. Her fur was brushed and trimmed and she had some kind of treatment that made her gleam like she was made of pure gold. Isla's eyes almost bugged out of her head when she saw the bill, not to mention that by the time you added tax and a tip she could have bought Dani at least five new pairs of pointe shoes!

If this was how much Upper East Siders spent on their dogs, Isla could only *imagine* what their personal beauty routines looked like. Maybe that whole long-standing rumor of '90s supermodels bathing in a tub full of *Crème de la Mer* wasn't so unrealistic after all.

But a crazy expensive haircut *wasn't* the most outrageous thing on Camilla's itinerary today. Oh no. That honor would go to an appointment with Ms. Sylvana Adonay, pet psychic.

"I can't wait to tell Scout all about this," Isla said as she bent down to clip Camilla into her harness for the walk to the psychic appointment. She could hear the horrified gasp of the pet beautician behind her, no doubt because the harness was going to ruin the perfectly silky strands of Camilla's fur.

But the little dog pulled way too hard on a regular leash and Isla refused to carry her around in one of those obnoxious tote bags.

Once they were outside the salon—which had an entrance detailed with bits of blush marble and gold, and a chic white flowerpot filled with dozens of pink roses—Isla stopped to snap a picture for the Instagram account, catching the tail of another dog entering the building right on the edge of the phone.

Then she hooked Camilla's leash around her wrist and slid it down to her elbow so she could use both hands to type her caption as they walked.

Another wonderful appointment at Le Paws. Getting my hair and nails done makes me feel like a brand new woman… I mean, dog.

Camilla trotted happily in front of Isla, her tail swishing back and forth. Every so often, she would look over her shoulder at Isla, tongue lolling out of her mouth, and for a moment Isla wondered why Theo had gone through so many dog sitters. Camilla wasn't *that* bad.

But then she remembered how the little dog had almost taken the hand off the groomer who'd gotten a brush stuck in a knot.

While the little princess was in a good mood, Isla would enjoy it. It was almost too easy to imagine this was her life—strolling down Madison Avenue, a cute dog at her heels, credit card not even close to being maxed, a handsome man waiting at home.

"Ha. This is the peak of your delusions," Isla said to herself. "Set your sights on something more realistic…like making next month's rent."

Isla's phone pinged with a notification. It was a text message.

SCOUT: Holy bananas! Have you checked Instagram?

ISLA: You mean the dog account? I just posted a picture.

SCOUT: Go look at the profile.

Frowning, Isla opened the Instagram app and brought up the profile for The Dachshund Wears Prada. Then she blinked…and blinked again. Then she stopped so suddenly poor Camilla almost tripped from the change of pace.

"Sorry, sorry." Isla pulled them to the edge of the sidewalk so she could make sure her eyes weren't fooling her.

How on earth did the account have over a thousand followers already? Weird.

She'd barely even posted half a dozen photos so far. Not to mention that she hadn't done anything much to optimize the account. The photos were an okay quality but nothing amazing. The reel she'd posted was fun but nothing wildly innovative. She didn't even have a strategy for her hashtags.

Hell, she didn't have *any* kind of strategy!

This was supposed to have been a little in-joke between her and Scout, a way to blow off some stress from her failed career. Fun and nothing more. Isla hadn't even been checking the comments or the number of likes, since that wasn't why she was doing it. Really, in the grand scheme of things a thousand followers was nothing. That was barely even cracking the threshold to be considered a micro influencer.

ISLA: I have no idea how that happened.

SCOUT: If you needed any proof that you're good at what you do, despite a minor setback, this is it. You got more than a thousand followers without trying.

Isla wasn't so sure she'd call The Incident a "minor setback" but Scout had a point. Isla had always had a keen intuition when it came to what would interest people. Call it having a finger on the pulse or whatever, but in some weird way this felt like the universe telling her something. That she shouldn't give up. That she *could* find a way back into her old career and her old life, if only she kept trying.

But right now, she had a paying job to do.

"Come on, Camilla," Isla said as she led the dog back into the busy street. "We've got an appointment to make. Let's see what your future has in store for you."

The pet psychic's office was only a few blocks from the salon. Isla was surprised to find it located in an office building, with a frosted glass door bearing the words *Adonay Pet Communication Consulting*. It looked like they were about to enter a recruitment office or an accounting firm. She pushed open the door and found lots of calming white, green and blue, a frosted glass coffee table and some pictures on the wall of famous people and their pets. There was Tori Spelling and some fabulous-looking fluffy chicken, Tippi Hedren and her tiger, Kirstie Alley and her lemur.

"Camilla?" A woman poked her head out of one of the doors. She had long dark hair, startlingly bright green eyes.

"Yes. Well, I'm Isla and this is Camilla." She gestured to the dog.

The woman came out to greet her. She wore a long white dress in some gauzy fabric that seemed to swirl like clouds around her feet as she walked.

White seemed like a bold choice.

Oh God, if Camilla pees on her...

"Lovely to meet you. I'm Sylvana." She extended her hand.

"Oh." Isla blinked and then covered her surprise with a smile. "Nice to meet you, too."

She'd been expecting something a little more crushed velvet and rose quartz and burning incense. Maybe some strands of tinkling beads as she entered the office. A crystal ball, perhaps. But the reception area looked like an advertisement for an interior design firm and Sylvana herself had the vibe of a retired fashion model.

"Come into my office."

Isla walked Camilla through the doorway and the dog immediately spotted a big potted plant. Uh-oh. She tugged on her lead, swinging her head back over her shoulder to glare at Isla when she refused to let her near it.

"Don't you *dare*," Isla whispered. "No peeing on things."

"Now," Sylvana said, closing the office door and coming up behind them. "Why don't we get Camilla out of her harness?"

She crouched down, her long white dress billowing around her feet, which must have startled Camilla, who immediately bared her teeth and growled, snapping at Sylvana's hand when she tried to touch her.

Didn't see that one coming, huh, psychic?

"Who's a grumpy lady?" Sylvana said, pulling her hand back. "She's got trust issues."

"Doesn't take a psychic to see that." The words left Isla's mouth before she could stop them. "I'm sorry, I didn't mean that as a comment on your profession."

"It's quite alright." Sylvana smiled serenely. "And you have a point, Camilla does *not* wear her heart on her sleeve. Anyone can see that. It's the best defense mechanism, isn't it? Letting people think you're horrible."

For some reason the comment made her think about Theo. He didn't do anything to disprove the world's assessment of him. Given Isla had spent a good portion of her adulthood trying to do the opposite—working hard to *make* people likeable—the fact that Theo seemed quite happy to hide behind his reputation as a brutish recluse struck her as unusual.

But Sylvana was right, that *was* a great defense mechanism.

"How about you get her out of the harness?" Sylvana said. "It looks like you have a good trust bond with her."

Isla snorted. "I don't know if I'd go that far."

"She's not your dog, correct?"

"That's right." Isla crouched down and held her hand out for a second, giving Camilla notice that she was going to be touched. She'd figured out that sudden movements seemed to startle the dog and had taken to signaling her actions so she didn't get snapped at. "I'm just the dog sitter."

"You're more than a dog sitter to her."

Isla unclipped the harness and Camilla stayed still, ducking her head as it was slipped off her body. Then she gave a happy little shake and started trotting around the perimeter of the room, sniffing away as though wanting to figure out the new environment.

Isla bundled up the harness and popped it into the bag of things she carried around for Camilla. Sylvana motioned for her to take a seat.

"Can you go into this with an open mind?" she asked.

Isla smoothed her palms down her thighs. "Does it really matter what I think? This appointment is for Camilla, not me."

"Yes, but you're the sole person in her life right now and she takes her cues from you." The psychic leaned back in her chair and knotted her hands in her lap. She looked serene, almost too serene.

Isla blinked. "I'm not the only person in her life."

"That's the vibe I get from Camilla. It's not a bad thing, many pets like to have their human soul mate and prefer it when it's a one-to-one relationship." She smiled. "Camilla might not show her feelings, but I could tell as soon as you walked in that there was a bond between you."

Maybe because I'm the only person willing to cook her pasta from scratch.

Wasn't that the way to animals' hearts, through their stomachs? Isla was pretty sure this whole thing was some kind of scam—a grand an hour scam. Did people really have nothing better to do with their money? It got under her skin, the frivolity of it. The excess, while others had so little.

"I guess I'm a practical person," Isla said, choosing her words carefully. She didn't want to offend the woman, but the chances of her pretending that any of this woo-woo bullshit was believable...eh, her poker face wasn't *that* good. "I'm here because my employer wanted to keep this appointment and so I assure you, it really doesn't matter what I think."

Sylvana cocked her head and looked at Isla like she was the subject of the meeting, rather than Camilla. Then her gaze drifted to the dog. Camilla was still inspecting the area, careful to sniff out every section of the room with an almost methodical precision. Funny, Isla had never noticed her doing that before.

"She lost her owner recently," Sylvana said. Did she know about Theo's grandmother's death? It would be easy enough, if the person who'd booked the appointment—presumably the woman's assistant, since it had been made months ago—had provided the Garrison family name.

Wasn't that how most psychics worked? They gathered information and had a deep sense of perception. Isla had seen that old show, *The Mentalist*. They had special tricks to convince people. What did they call it? Hot reading.

"She's grieving deeply." Sylvana pressed her fingertips to her temple as though tuning in with some higher force. Isla tried not to roll her eyes. "She's concerned her owner didn't know how much she loved her. But Camilla's past prevents her from showing her love, because she was treated badly for it."

Isla kept her eyes on the dog, making sure she didn't suddenly want to relieve herself on any part of the pristine white office.

"Camilla originally came from a bad home. She was abused. Neglected."

Was that true? The dog suddenly stopped and looked at Isla in such a way that she could almost see what the psychic was saying. Like she wanted Isla to believe.

Okay, now you sound crazysauce. The dog is not communicating with you.

"When her owner found her, Camilla thought all humans

would harm her. She had developed defense mechanisms—she snaps and bites so that people know she's not a punching bag. She feels like it's hard to trust." Sylvana paused. "But she trusts you."

Despite thinking the entire thing was a load of garbage, Isla couldn't help but feel a warm glow in her chest. She held her hand out and Camilla came willingly, her pink tongue swiping across Isla's fingertips.

"The other people who've been with Camilla have not taken the time to earn her trust. They grow frustrated with her and she's still frightened. Losing her owner was the saddest day of her life because she had finally found someone to love."

Tears pricked the backs of Isla's eyes but she blinked them away. This was what they did, playing on fundamental human emotions, picking common scenarios that anybody could connect with. Sylvana *must* know about Theo's grandmother.

But these were human emotions. Human stories.

Isla looked down at the dog, whose glossy eyes stared right back up at her. She seemed relaxed, open.

"Sometimes the beings who seem the most closed off have the biggest capacity for love. But that capacity has been exploited in the past. That softness has been taken advantage of, and so they adapt. They harden their shells." Sylvana released a long breath. "It's those who are slow to trust who can be the most giving, loving people when they finally find their person."

Was she even talking about animals anymore?

That thought resonated with Isla—she shut everything out of her life that wasn't work and family, and Scout was included in the second category. She didn't trust anyone else, not since the person she should have been able to trust most of all abandoned her.

But inside she had a lot of love to give.

"Maybe we're not so different, you and I," she said quietly to the dog.

Sylvana seemed to still be in her state of "connection" with whatever power she supposedly tapped into. Later, if Theo wasn't in one of his beastly moods, she may even ask him if he knew about Camilla's origin story.

Why do you want to know? This is a job. A means to an end.

Only that didn't explain why she was so intrigued by her mysterious boss, his glittering world and finding out whether there was a heart of gold hiding away behind his iron exterior.

9

Isla took her time walking Camilla back to Theo's place, stopping to snap another covert picture for the Instagram account and writing a snappy caption to go along with it. She'd gained more followers over the course of the day, and that number was creeping toward fifteen hundred. *Somebody* must have found the account and shared it. That was the only explanation.

But it triggered something inside her, a little part of her ambitious, fighting spirit that wanted to see that number grow. Maybe it was because she was wired for progress—after all, that was how she'd kept herself motivated working long hours for little pay while taking care of Dani in the early days. Every tiny shuffle forward was worth cheering for.

But maybe it was more than that—an opportunity for redemption. To prove she wasn't a screwup like people said. To prove she knew what she was doing.

Feeling a little unsettled by the day's proceedings, she took Camilla into the apartment building and up the elevator toward the penthouse. Most days she didn't use the private elevator, because she enjoyed seeing who else would step into the carriage with her. Isla was pretty sure there was a rock star living in this building somewhere.

When they got to the top, Isla headed down the hallway with Camilla tugging the whole way.

"Hungry?" she asked as they got to the door and the dog looked up at her, as if to say *hurry the hell up!* "Okay, okay. No need to give me the stink-eye."

She unlocked the door and headed inside. A strange whirring sound was coming from the depths of the house and Camilla suddenly went nuts. She yanked so hard on her harness that it caught Isla off guard and she lost her grip on the leash. The dog tore through the house, barking like they were being robbed.

Were they being robbed?

"Camilla! Crap." Isla let the door swing shut behind her and dumped her stuff on the ground so she could go chasing after the animal.

Lord. The last thing she needed was for Camilla to hurt herself or tear the apartment to shreds by getting her leash caught on something. Following the sound of the barking, Isla found herself in the back part of the apartment, where she hadn't been before. She could see the dog had wriggled through the gap of an ajar door and was barking at something.

Isla pushed the door open and halted suddenly.

The whirring sound was a treadmill and Theo was in the process of running on it, shirtless. He had a pair of those fancy noise-canceling headphones on and hadn't noticed the dog barking behind him. Camilla seemed angry at the treadmill and was doing her best to tell it off.

Sweat clung to Theo's skin. He was lean and his body tapered to a trim waist above a pair of running shorts. The muscles in his shoulders and back rippled as he pumped his arms in time with each stride, his body working like a perfectly tuned machine. For a moment, Isla was rooted to the ground, mesmerized.

But then sense finally overcame her baser instincts and she shook her head. It was so *not* cool to check your boss out while he was exercising, especially when he didn't even know you were standing there.

"Camilla." Isla crouched down and reached for the dog, who snarled at her, neat rows of pointy white teeth bared in a clear *stay back, evil human* message. "Come here, now!"

So much for Sylvana's whole thing about the dog trusting her. See, it was a load of garbage.

"The treadmill won't hurt you, now come *on*." She stayed crouched and inched forward, trying to snag the leash with her hand so she could get the dog out of Theo's workout room and slink back into the house like she hadn't been practically drooling over his hot half-naked body.

But Camilla continued to bark, dancing around the machine like she was about to go all Muhammad Ali on it. And then...

Then.

It all happened in a flash. Camilla lunged forward, trying to nip at Theo's heels. She must have gotten a piece of him, because he let out a yelp, and one of his feet scuffed against the rotating band. He fell and slammed his knee into the base of the machine before being rocketed off the back and almost bowling Camilla over. His headphones came off and smashed against the wall, bouncing onto the carpet in two pieces.

"What the ever loving—"

Bark! Bark, bark, bark!

"Oh my gosh." Isla rushed forward and grabbed Camilla's leash, deftly getting her hand out of the way of snapping teeth. "Theo, are you okay? I'm so sorry. She rushed in and—"

"Can you turn it off? The treadmill." He was still on the floor, one hand pressed to the back of his head. "I can't stand the barking."

"Of course." Keeping a tight hold on Camilla, Isla went to the treadmill and looked at the control panel. More than a dozen flashing buttons and gauges stared back at her. "Is this an exercise machine or a fighter pilot cockpit?"

"Bottom left-hand corner. It's the red button that says *stop*," Theo replied drily. "I know, so ambiguous."

"Hardy har."

Okay, so he had a right to be annoyed. She'd been too busy ogling him to get Little Miss Trouble out of the room and now he'd hurt himself. She pressed the button and the treadmill slowed to a stop. Thankfully, so did Camilla's barking. Now that the room had calmed down a little, Isla looked back at Theo. His knee was red and he winced when he tried to move his foot. Uh-oh.

"Do I need to call an ambulance?" she asked, biting down on her lip. Was she about to get fired?

"Don't you dare," he said darkly. "I wouldn't ride in one of those things if you paid me."

"Pretty sure that's not a career option." She frowned. "Are you going to bite my head off if I try to help?"

Theo looked up warily, his warm amber eyes reminding her of a lion with a thorn in its paw. Was she going to be the helpful mouse who braved the beast, or a naive gazelle about to get eaten for dinner?

"You know me so well, already," he drawled. "Clever girl."

"Yeah, yeah, you're a big bad, scary hermit. I'm shaking in my boots." She rolled her eyes. "Stay there. I'm going to get Camilla out of her harness and then I'll come back and help you. You can fire me later."

Without waiting for a response, she marched the dog out of the room and took Camilla to her favorite place—the little nook in the living room where her dog bed was kept. She unclipped the harness and the dog immediately scampered into her bed, snuggling into the soft base and glaring up at Isla like it was all her fault.

"I don't have the energy to deal with you right now. I'll feed you in a minute."

Hanging the harness by the front door, Isla made her way back into Theo's workout room. He was still sitting on the floor, but he'd taken the sneaker off one foot. His ankle already looked like it was puffing up.

This was *not* good.

"We should get you out to the living room so you can get it elevated and iced." Isla took a step closer, bracing herself for Theo's reaction.

"Are you a first aid expert?" he asked, a stormy expression on his face.

"Sort of. My sister has had her share of ballet-related injuries and I know how to do the RICE thing."

"RICE?"

"Rest, Ice, Compression, Elevation." She tried not to notice how his stomach remained flat even when he was sitting. Seriously? Was the guy training to be a fitness model or something?

It wasn't like Isla hadn't seen beautiful men before. Working in social media, she'd spent plenty of time around models and actors and other people who were paid to look a certain way. And yet it wasn't Theo's hard body and steely disposition that made her heart flutter like a butterfly trapped under a glass dome. It was the edge of him—sharp and real and raw—that appealed to her.

Maybe because he was the antithesis of her old life. Maybe it was because there was an honesty about him. He didn't pretend, didn't bend himself for others. Didn't put on a face so that you couldn't know if he was real or not.

"Look, you've got two options. Let me help you or let me call someone who will come and check you out."

"No. I don't want anyone seeing me like this." He attempted to push up on his own, but the second he tried to put any pressure on his ankle, he bit back a groan. "Fuck."

"You're as bad as that goddamn dog," Isla muttered, deciding to take matters into her own hands. "Come on, let's get this over with."

She grabbed Theo's wrist and hauled his arm around her shoulders. He smelled like sweat and residual cologne and his body was warm and hard. Slowly, she eased them both to standing. It must have looked ridiculous, because Theo was well over six feet tall and Isla was lucky if she reached five-six with good posture and thick-soled sneakers, but she was strong and she wasn't about to leave the man to look after himself.

Theo limped beside her as she helped him out to the living room, ignoring his request to go straight into the kitchen.

"Sit your ass down and I'll get you some ice." She grabbed a fancy-looking cushion that she was sure the designer had *not* intended to be a footrest and fluffed it up at the end of the couch. "Put your ankle on this."

"You're bossy," Theo grumbled, but he did as he was told. Isla helped him lower down onto the couch and she waited until he propped his foot up before she went to get some supplies.

The refrigerator had an ice machine, so she collected a generous amount in a hand towel. Then she fetched the emergency Tylenol from her purse, figuring that was quicker than trying to navigate the vast, barren kitchen, and filled a glass with water.

"Here." She held out the water and the pill.

Theo didn't argue with her. He downed the Tylenol in one long gulp, the muscles in his throat working in a way that had Isla's mouth running dry, and then plunked the glass on the coffee table. When he reached for the makeshift bundle of ice, she handed it over.

"What happened exactly?" he asked as he leaned forward and pressed the ice to his ankle, a breath hissing out between his teeth.

"I didn't know you were home and when we came in, Camilla heard the treadmill and went nuts." Isla sighed. "The leash slipped out of my hand and she ran into your room. Then she tried to attack your feet."

Let's leave out the part where I was dumbstruck by the whole shirtless thing, shall we?

"Right." Theo looked rightfully unimpressed.

Isla gnawed on the inside of her lip. Was this it? The perfect solution ruined by a simple lack of grip strength? By a moment of weakness? She hadn't even received her first paycheck yet, since that was due to come tomorrow, at the end of her first week. Losing that money was *not* an option.

"Look, I'm really sorry about what happened." She gestured to Theo's foot. "But I'm doing my best with this job and I think it would be a mistake to fire me over a single incident."

Go big or go home, right?

Theo raised an eyebrow. "I thought you said before that I could fire you later?"

"It was a figure of speech. The fact is, I've lasted longer than your previous dog sitters *and* the psychic told me today that Camilla trusts me. So really, I think it's in your best interests to—"

"You don't know what my best interests are," Theo said, his amber eyes boring right into hers. There wasn't any malice in his tone, just a clearly drawn line in the sand that warned her not to overstep. "Only *I* know that."

Theo watched Isla's mouth open and close like a goldfish. Like a pretty, shiny goldfish. And he didn't mean shiny like sparkly, because Isla was dressed practically in jeans and flat shoes and a lightweight blue sweater which complemented her eyes.

But shiny more in the sense of…angelic, perhaps? There was a goodness in Isla that beamed out of her like sunshine. The way she didn't hesitate to help someone in need, the way she took action even if she felt she might be punished for it.

Wholesome didn't sound right, though, because there was *nothing* wholesome about the way Theo felt looking at her. Her glossy dark hair was half up and half down, the lengths cascading over her shoulders. Her lips were slicked with pink gloss and her cheeks were the color of cotton candy.

So shiny it was.

"Right." She sucked in a shaky breath. "But I'm doing a good job with Camilla and—"

"I know." He nodded. "I'm not going to fire you."

She opened her mouth as if to retort before realizing that Theo had agreed with her. "Really?"

"I don't know many people who would do the grocery shopping and cook a meal to appease a fussy dog." A hint of a smile ghosted over his lips. "My grandmother would be happy knowing Camilla was in such good hands."

"Oh," she said, blinking. "Well, thanks."

"Although let me give you a tip, never lead off with the words 'and the psychic told me' if you want me to take anything you say seriously, okay?"

That was one thing he'd never understood about his grandmother—she put stock in so many of those things. Tarot readings and psychics and palm lines and the spirit world. It was a secret of course, because if the media knew they would have had a field day. There was a fine line between eccentric and cuckoo.

But Theo suspected it was more about her searching for certainty in an uncertain world. And really, he knew a thing or two about that.

He might not use magical cards or mediums, but he found certainty with routine and passwords and locks. With making sure that he never ended up like his mother and father, running from people. Hiding was safer than running.

"She had some interesting things to say." Isla lowered herself onto a round pouf next to the coffee table, her hands folded into a neat parcel in her lap. "About where Camilla came from, and about her being adopted."

"I don't know if adopted is the right word. She belonged to one of my grandmother's friends, who passed away. She ended up with the daughter, who hated dogs and was only too happy to give her up when my grandmother asked about her. Seems Camilla has a hard time connecting with people."

"Don't we all," Isla murmured.

"You, Little Miss Sunshine?" Theo scoffed. "Please."

He shifted on the couch, grunting from the pain in his ankle. It was blowing up like a balloon and while he could tell it wasn't broken, he'd be out of action for a few days. Great. At least he could work from home.

That means seeing more of Isla.

He shouldn't be excited about that prospect. He *wasn't*…at least, that's what he'd keep telling himself.

"I am *not* Little Miss Sunshine," she said, frowning. "That makes me sound vapid."

"Being positive and upbeat and caring is vapid?" Now wasn't *that* telling. And intriguing.

"It sounds like a woman who'd wander right into a dark forest and get eaten by the big bad wolf. TSTL, I think they call it. Too stupid to live."

"I find it interesting that you equate sunshine with being vapid and stupid." He looked at her, surprised that her feathers were ruffled by something so innocuous. Hell, he figured anything that was the opposite of him was a good thing…for other people.

"That's because it's a caricature. It's easy to think someone is happy and sunshiny when they're putting on a professional face." She folded her arms across her chest.

"So you're faking it for me?"

"Well, no. When you put it like that…" Isla shook her head. "I mean, isn't that how people *are* at work? You have to put on a certain front."

For some reason, knowing that she felt compelled to put on a front with him made him uneasy. Sure, Theo never expected honesty from people. He never expected trustworthiness or transparency or honor. Those things were precious and rare. But he'd felt as though Isla was different in that way—that maybe she *was* everything she appeared to be. An open book, perhaps, if nothing more.

"I don't," he said. "People can take me as I am. Or as I'd rather, not at all."

She tilted her head, eyes narrowing slightly like she was trying to figure him out. "Don't you get...lonely?"

"Loneliness is privilege."

"And letting people think you're horrible is the best defense," she muttered.

The room went so silent, Theo was sure he stopped breathing for a moment. He could even hear the soft in-and-out whoosh of Camilla's breath from her dog bed a few feet away.

"And where's the line between defense and reality, huh?" he replied coolly. "Perception is as good as the real thing."

"Perception doesn't make truth." Isla looked at him with her clear blue eyes, like she could see right into him. Like she could see the very core of who he was—a dark, empty space where no light had glowed for an age.

"Says the woman who's putting on a front."

She bristled. "I'm trying to be professional."

"And what part of being professional made you stand in my door watching me run when you should have been controlling my dog?"

Her eyes went wide. Oh yes, he'd seen her alright. His treadmill faced the big window overlooking Central Park and the reflection had been clear as day—wide eyes, lips slightly parted. It had filled him with a roaring, powerful energy the likes of which he hadn't experienced in years.

Maybe ever.

The want and desire in her face had set him ablaze. And now, seeing the pink heat rushing to fill her cheeks and the shock in her parted lips only fanned those flames. She wanted him.

And he wanted her.

Bad, bad idea. If anybody got word that you slept with an employee...

No. Not going to happen.

"I should get Camilla's dinner ready." She shot up like a rocket and hovered for a minute, hands wringing in front of her before she vanished from the living room, the sound of the refrigerator door telling him that she was fetching some leftover pasta for Camilla.

He turned on the couch to watch her coaxing the dog awake and encouraging her to eat with all the sunshine she tried so hard to deny.

There was nothing stupid or vapid about it.

But wanting her was dangerous. Even here, in his safe space, where he was certain nobody could find out, the risk was too great. He didn't trust Isla not to talk, not to sell the story to some media outlet in a bid to get her old career back. And yeah, he knew everything that happened to her before she came to work for him. It hadn't been hard to find. The internet had been awash with criticisms of her. Maybe that's why he felt like there was a kindred connection between them—they'd both been publicly lambasted. Used to sell advertising. Picked apart.

But if she wanted back in, wouldn't a story about him be great leverage?

And he couldn't allow himself to be used like that ever again.

10

Isla didn't see Theo the next morning. She knew he was home, because she could hear conversation coming from his office. It sounded like he was on a conference call, the sharp tone of his voice making her jump as she'd walked past to fetch Camilla's bits and bobs.

Maybe it was the pain in his ankle, or perhaps it was how Theo dealt with people—but she felt sorry for whoever was on the other end of the line. They were getting chewed out something terrible!

"Good morning, Miss Camilla," Isla singsonged as she walked into the living room, where the dog was curled up in her bed. She raised her pale gold head and looked at Isla for a moment before dropping her head back down. "Oh no, you don't. The itinerary says 9:00 a.m. walk in the park. Don't you want to hump a statue or terrorize a child or something fun like that?"

The dog made a snorting sound as if to say *been there, done that. What else you got?*

It was fun making up a voice for Camilla in her head. And Isla chose to one hundred percent ignore that it probably made her sound like she had a few screws loose. Didn't she deserve a little fun? A little playfulness in her otherwise serious life?

She imagined that the dog sounded like a cross between Katharine Hepburn and Meryl Streep in her role as Miranda Priestly in *The Devil Wears Prada*. It certainly fit her style.

"What if I let you chew on a shoe?" Isla offered, crouching in front of the dog's bed. Camilla raised her head and pulled her lips back, baring her teeth a little. "Yeah, yeah. So mean and nasty. I know you're more likely to pee on me than bite me."

She held her hand out to Camilla, not trying to pet her or disturb the dog's space, but letting her know she was there. Camilla kept her teeth on show for a second and then dropped the act when it was clear Isla wasn't going away.

"That's right, now who's boss."

Truthfully, Camilla was the boss. But Isla figured it was better for her self-esteem to pretend that she was in charge.

"Come on. Up, up, up." She reached out farther and gave the dog a scratch behind the ears. When Camilla's tail thumped against the side of the bed, Isla had to force herself not to squeal with joy. Progress. "I know this makes it clear I'm a sad person who's desperate for your approval, but whatever. That's between you and me."

Camilla pushed up from her bed and nailed Isla with a hard stare, as if to say *you're pathetic, human.* Then she trotted off toward her water bowl in the kitchen.

"Your tail complimented me, whether you like it or not."
Isla did a little happy dance. "The tail doesn't lie!"

That was the moment that Theo hobbled into the living
room, a crutch under each arm. Of *course* he caught her having a full-blown conversation with an animal, and gloating
over the fact that a dog did what dogs were known best for.

"Uh, hi." She straightened her spine in the hopes it would
make her look a little less ludicrous. "You got crutches."

"My doctor does house visits, luckily."

Theo looked delightfully disheveled and much closer to the
man she'd met in Central Park than any version of him she'd
seen since. His dark hair was rumpled, free of any attempt at
styling and his jaw was coated in a generous dusting of stub-
ble. Wow, the guy went from polished penthouse prince to
star of her dirty girl dreams in less than twenty-four hours.

She liked this version of him much, *much* better.

He wore a pair of dark gray sweatpants and a white T-shirt
that was fitted to his muscular chest—so fitted, in fact, that her
brain made the hop, skip and jump right back to the memory
of him running on his treadmill.

*Running…right until you were responsible for turning him into a
human cannonball.*

She still felt bad about that.

"Do you and Camilla usually have a nice talk in the morning?" His lip twitched.

Okay, so he'd heard it all. Great.

"Are you usually yelling at your employees in the morning?" she shot back, cringing the second the words left her
mouth. In addition to knowing she liked to talk to Camilla
as if she was human, now he also knew that she was listening
to his conversation.

Theo raised an eyebrow.

"I wasn't eavesdropping," she clarified, though whether it

was more to herself or to him she wasn't sure. "Your voice carries. It was hard to ignore."

"I don't tolerate people not performing in their jobs."

Her lips pressed into a thin line. Was that a threat? "Maybe you'd get more out of people if you were nicer to them."

"Isn't there a saying about that?" he drawled. "Nice guys finish last."

"What about you catch more flies with honey?"

"You should aim higher than flies, Isla." His amber eyes gleamed and he wore that impossibly sexy smirk that did terrible, tumbling things to her insides. "Flies aren't worth your time, nor mine."

"Are you trying to prove a point from our conversation yesterday?" She planted one hand on her hip. Camilla was standing between them, her head swinging back and forth like she was watching a tennis match. "The fine line between perception and reality, and all that."

"Are you asking me if I'm trying to prove I'm an asshole? I don't need to prove anything. I am what I am."

She wanted to growl in frustration at him. Because she really *didn't* think badly of him, even if there were quite a few signs pointing to the fact that Theo Garrison was the beast people claimed him to be. Only…she didn't believe it.

And regardless of whether Sylvana the psychic had *actual* powers or was ripping off Manhattan's rich and richer, her words had resonated with Isla. Theo lived a life that was all about protection, so why would his reputation be anything else?

His personal baggage is not *your problem.*

"Whatever. I'm taking Camilla out for her walk, go be a jerk if that makes you happy."

Theo's lip twitched. It irritated her how amused he was. His smirk was a thorn under her skin, because Isla had been laughed at more in the last few months than most people would be in their entire lifetimes.

It made her feel really freaking small.

"All I did was ask if you and the dog had a nice chat," he replied smoothly. Then he hobbled closer on his crutches, and Isla's eyes drifted to the way his biceps flexed as he shifted his weight to stay off his injured ankle. "You were the one who reacted defensively."

"It's hard not to around you," she said. "It feels like every time I come here I don't know which version of you I'm going to get. Nice Theo who smiles and makes jokes or Mr. Hyde who's got a barb for every conversation."

"You *did* cause me to fly off my treadmill into a wall," he said drily. "Don't I deserve to be annoyed about that, at least for a day or two?"

"Yes." Isla sighed. "I feel bad that it happened. Truly."

"I'm grumpy because relying on other people makes me uncomfortable."

Isla blinked. That felt like a real truth. A real part of him. Something honest and raw that maybe he wouldn't share with just anyone.

"I know that feeling. One time I got the flu so bad I couldn't even leave my bed, and my little sister had to do everything for me." She shuddered at the memory. "I *hated* it. Some people think if they won the lottery, they'd have people to cook and clean and do everything for them. No thank you, I would die."

"The sweet woman with the sunshine smile is a secret control freak," Theo mused. "Interesting."

Sweet? Sunshine smile? Was that what he thought of her?

"Not one of my better qualities," she admitted.

"I wouldn't say that. I appreciate a person who likes to keep everything in hand—it's a sign of self-assurance."

Isla wasn't so sure about that.

"Enjoy your walk with Camilla," he said, continuing to hobble past her. "I'll try to be on my best Nice Theo behavior when you get back."

Isla watched him move slowly into the kitchen, an offer to help hovering on the tip of her tongue. But much like Isla's canine charge, Camilla's owner required a deft touch and a slow approach. Get too close too soon, and Theo would bite. But if she was winning the dog over, then maybe she could win Theo over, too.

Isla had messaged Scout to see if she was free to meet them at Central Park. The company would be nice, since she'd spent most of the week either hanging out with the other dog sitters at doggy day care or speaking with the various pet professionals that Theo employed, and *that* made her feel disconnected from the real world.

Scout was always a shot of reality.

After hovering around their meeting point for a good fifteen minutes, Isla found Scout near the Hans Christian Andersen statue. Punctuality was not her friend's strong suit, but Isla had come to accept it over their years. Scout walked along the path, a pair of headphones lodged in her ears and her long, blond hair pulled back into a perky ponytail. The music was so loud, Isla could hear the tinny bass from a few feet away.

"Hey!" Scout shouted, not realizing how loud she'd spoken until Camilla startled at Isla's feet. The dog growled as if telling her off for the fright. "Oops, sorry 'bout that."

"She's a bit sensitive, this one." Isla nodded toward the dog. "Just like her dad."

"You knew the dog's parents?" Scout's mouth popped open. "That's cool."

"No, I mean Theo. Her owner and my very grouchy boss."

"That's right." Scout snapped her fingers. "Sparkly vampire magnetism guy."

"I did *not* call him that." Isla felt her cheeks grow hot.

"Sure you did. You may not have used those exact words, but you said it with your eyes." Scout grinned. "Shall we?"

The trio walked past the statue and along the path toward the boathouse. It was a beautiful day—blue skies, minimal clouds, shining sun. Isla looked over at Scout's outfit with some envy. Her friend was wearing a pair of slouchy ripped jeans, a boxy cropped T-shirt that showed off her taut stomach and Vans sneakers. She looked breezy and comfortable, and meanwhile Isla was already sweating in her sleek dark denim jeans, black ankle boots and silky blouse.

But she couldn't bring herself not to look her best for a day of work. Especially knowing that Theo was going to be home and that she would definitely see him.

Like he cares how you look.

But it wasn't about his opinion, really. More that Isla held herself to a high standard, and that included looking professional at her job...no matter what job it was.

"So, how's work?" Isla asked.

Scout made a groaning noise. "Don't ask."

"Too late, I already did. Now you have to tell me."

"I have parted ways with my employer." Scout pulled a pair of sunglasses out of the small cross-body bag at her hip and slipped them on. "It was regrettable, but necessary."

"Again?"

The funny thing was that when Isla got fired for The Incident it was the first time Scout had been able to comfort her rather than the other way around. Scout's employment history was shakier than an old house in the middle of an earthquake. The reasons were mixed—bad fit, unrealistic managerial expectations, shitty boss, poor working conditions—but the result was always the same.

"Don't *again* me. I was supportive when you were out on your ass," Scout grumbled.

"Sorry. I didn't mean to sound judgmental." Isla reached out and squeezed her best friend's arm. "I'm surprised, that's all. I thought you liked it there. You sounded happy."

"Getting a paycheck made me happy."

"Then what happened?"

They walked side by side, steps falling in time. Scout's demeanor seemed heavy, like she was carrying some stress around and Isla hated seeing her friend like that. Sure, she wasn't the most disciplined or punctual person. But she had a big heart and genuinely cared about the people around her, and Isla was convinced that mattered more than things like punctuality. Besides, Scout was usually late because she was helping one of her neighbors or stopping to be kind to someone in the street. Her employers didn't always see that as a good thing, however.

"Same old, same old." Scout shrugged. "I was late a few times because Mrs. Nelson asked me to drive her to a doctor's appointment and I couldn't say no. Her memory isn't great and she forgets to tell me things in advance, or she thinks she's told me but she hasn't. It's really sad."

The elderly lady who lived next to Scout was all alone—no kids or grandkids in the state. After her husband passed away a few years back, she really relied on Scout to get by.

"Is it worth losing your job over?" Isla asked.

"I'm supposed to ignore an old lady who's crying because she forgot to fill her prescription and she can't get to the drugstore on her own? Come on." Scout frowned. "Yeah, okay, I'm a freaking bleeding heart, I get it. But I couldn't leave her."

"I love that part of you, I really do. But when are you going to put *yourself* first? You won't be able to help Mrs. Nelson if you have to move out because you can't make rent."

This was the core difference between them; Scout was weighed down by a lot of things that happened in her past, so she lived in the moment. Isla, on the other hand, was convinced that the future was the only thing that mattered. Which meant being responsible now and always worrying about the consequences her actions would have on the next month or the next year.

"My mom put herself first her entire life, and look how *that* turned out." Scout snorted. "I know yours wasn't any better."

"We really lucked out on the maternal lottery, didn't we?" Isla shook her head. "But I see that as all the more reason to build a future for myself and for Dani. Stability is important."

"Kindness is important," Scout argued. "Besides, I don't think I'd know stability if it slapped me in the face with a soggy taco."

Isla laughed and her best friend grinned. "At least we can disagree about this stuff without it affecting our friendship. I really appreciate that."

"So you don't mind being BFFs with someone who can barely stay employed?" She framed the question as a joke, but Isla knew there was some real insecurity underneath it.

Isla had tried to reassure her countless times that they were friends no matter their differences. And, in plenty of instances, *because* of them.

"You know you don't need to ask me that," she said.

"Well, maybe I do."

Isla raised an eyebrow. "Why?"

"So..." Scout stopped dead in her tracks and Isla almost stumbled as her friend grabbed her arm. "I had an idea."

"Uh-oh," Isla teased. "We all know what happens when you've been noodling on some grand scheme."

"It's not a scheme. Think of it more as..." Scout tapped a finger to her chin. "A business suggestion."

"Suggestion? Okay, tell me."

"I think you should open a social media agency for animals."

Isla blinked. Usually Scout's ideas were a bit off the wall, but this wasn't crazy. Not by a long shot.

"Hear me out." Scout pulled her phone out of her pocket. "The Dachshund Wears Prada is currently heading toward five thousand followers."

"Are you serious? That's wild." Yesterday she'd been at fifteen hundred. How the heck had it grown so fast?

"Yeah, and you haven't even been trying." Scout held up her hands in defense. "Your words, not mine."

"It's true."

Isla had purposefully *not* been keeping tabs on the numbers, because she was convinced it would suck the joy out of things. And Lord knew she needed as much joy in her life as she could get. But maybe that wasn't entirely true.

She'd posted videos and reels in the last few days, knowing those things "fed" the algorithm and made it happy. She'd even filmed a few videos while waiting for Scout earlier, banking them to post next week. At the time, she'd told herself it was for her own amusement, but what if she'd subconsciously been trying to build something?

Going from zero to five thousand followers in a week was...a sign.

"So what if you *did* try? What if this is exactly the thing you've been looking for?" Scout said.

Isla's head swam. A pet social media agency? It made sense. What better combination was there than the internet and animals? Ever since the early days of online communication, animals had been the entertaining, wholesome beacon of pixel light. ICanHasCheezburger was around by the mid 2000s and by 2012 Grumpy Cat had taken the world by storm. Then there was Boo the Pomeranian, Doug the Pug, Tuna the Chihuahua with the overbite that spawned a thousand memes. Not to mention that black-and-white cat with the markings that made it look like he had a hipster moustache.

"You're good at this, Isla." Scout showed her the profile page of the account she'd created. There it was. Proof in the numbers. "You're *not* a dog sitter. You're a social media whiz and don't let any of those fuckers tell you otherwise."

Isla was touched by her friend's passionate declaration. "I love you."

"I love you, too." They started walking again and Camilla trotted happily in front of them, her shiny tail swishing back and forth. "You should do this."

Isla sucked in a big breath. "I don't know if I'm ready to strike out on my own. That's a huge step and I'm still licking my wounds and—"

"If you're not careful, you'll be licking your wounds forever. Trust me."

Isla frowned. "What do you mean?"

"I mean, one big hurt can go on a *really* long time if you let it. I don't want to see one mistake derail you from what should be a successful and fulfilling life." Scout looked over to her. "I have *always* admired how together you are, Isla. You're everything I wish I could be."

"Ha! A boring workaholic with no social life to speak of. Yeah, right." Isla threw her a disbelieving look. "I'd kill to have some of your zest and spontaneity. Men have literally fallen all over themselves for your attention ever since you hit puberty. And it's not just men, *everyone* loves you."

"Everyone except my employers," she quipped with a desert-dry tone.

"Maybe if we were mashed together, we'd make the perfect person."

"No such thing as perfect, right?" Scout sighed. "Think about my idea, okay? I know it probably grates on every sensible bone in your body but...what happens when dog sitting doesn't cut it anymore?"

Scout's question sucked the warmth out of Isla's body and a cold drip of realization slid down her spine. She was right, what *would* happen then? Were her old colleagues and industry contacts going to suddenly forget all about The Incident? Would they welcome her back with open arms after she essentially disappeared from the internet for several months?

Unlikely.

Working for Theo was a temporary thing. A Band-Aid. But Isla currently had no plans for what came next, and her future-protecting self hated that. Sure, the money Theo was paying her was covering the basics, but Dani always had more ballet expenses and those were currently coming out of their savings. Eventually it would whittle down the small nest egg Isla had built over the last few years until there was nothing left.

But starting her own business? That seemed risky as heck.

"I think it's a great idea, but..." Isla rolled the pros and cons around in her mind.

The most painful thing was that she'd always planned to strike out on her own one day. It *had* been the big ticket item in her ten-year plan—establish herself within a reputable agency, build up a client list and then start her own agency. But that was supposed to happen a certain way, from a point of stability. Not from rock bottom.

And it was supposed to happen in the future, with every proper step along the way neatly ticked off in her bullet journal. *After* Dani had finished high school and had gotten herself a scholarship for college.

"Let me guess, it doesn't fit with the plan," Scout said.

Isla huffed. It was annoying how well her friend could read her sometimes. "Maybe."

"Here's an idea. Why don't you challenge yourself to increase your Instagram followers? Say, get to twenty thousand. And when you do—"

"*If* I do," Isla corrected.

"*When* you do," Scout retorted with a hard look. "Then you'll consider what I've suggested."

"How did we end up talking about me?" Isla said as they paused to watch a group of cute guys jogging past.

"It'll lead to me eventually," Scout said. "Because when you start your agency, you'll need a loyal employee to do your bidding...and I may know someone. She's not so good at turning up on time, but she's great with people and she really wants you to succeed."

"I'll think about it," Isla said. "But I'm just thinking."

Yet even as she vowed not to turn this into a big deal, her mind was already whirring with ways she could increase the number of people following The Dachshund Wears Prada.

11

By Wednesday the following week, Theo was back on his feet…kind of. He was down to using one crutch and hobbling rather than hopping. He was also, however, still working from home. The last thing he needed was anyone trying to give him sympathy for his ankle or worse, trying to help him.

Unfortunately, one person who didn't quite get that memo was Isla.

He'd found her cooking him something to eat on Monday night before she finished her shift, and yesterday she'd bought him fresh bagels from the bodega around the corner. The *good* ones! Then he'd found her reorganizing his towels so they were easier to access.

His towels did not need reorganizing. He did not need bagels. And he most certainly didn't want to feel that warm little bubble in his chest whenever she did something nice for him.

He also didn't know why the hell, after spotting the spine of a fantasy book sticking out of her bag, he'd ordered one of his staff to deliver a special edition anniversary reprint from the same author to his house so he could give it to her.

"The quicker you sign these contracts, the quicker I will be out of your hair." Irina waved her papers at him, and Theo shook himself out of his strange thoughts. It was irritating how often his brain drifted to all things Isla in the middle of a workday. "I know you don't like people being in your home unnecessarily."

"You make me sound like a recluse." He reached for the contracts and picked up a vintage Mont Blanc pen that had once belonged to his grandfather. Each of the contracts were neatly labeled with colorful tabs in his preferred methods— yellow for a full signature and blue for initials.

"You *are* a recluse," Irina replied drily. "A young man like you should be out living in the world, not wasting away behind a curtain."

"I don't see any curtains in here." He didn't look up from the contracts. The sound of the pen scratching across paper filled the air.

"It would sadden your father to see you like this."

Theo's throat tightened. A memory flickered, a young man who looked very much like himself wearing a three-piece suit, and a woman in a glittering silver dress. His parents had been one of the most photogenic couples in the world, and yet nothing about the way his father looked at his mother had *anything* to do with being photographed.

As quickly as it came, the picture glitched and disappeared like someone had yanked the cord on the back of a television.

"Don't push it," he warned.

"Fine. But we still need to talk about the gala."

Theo put the signed contract to one side and started working on the second one. New hires, a big acquisition of three manuscripts from an author they'd lured over from another publishing house, a vendor agreement. It was never-ending.

"What about it?"

"Nia said you'd put a media blackout on the event."

Nia was his head of publicity and she had *not* been happy about that email. "That's right. Although I don't know why you're bringing it up, since it's not your job."

Irina's expression pinched. "*I'm* bringing it up, because every time you stonewall one of your people, they come to me."

"And you hold up your staff and say *you shall not pass*, right?"

She let out an annoyed huff. "Like it or not, Theo, publicity is part of life. Especially when you're talking about a charity organization."

"Nia was only planning the event off the side of her desk as a thank-you to my grandmother. It's not official company business. Besides, when the new people take over, they can do as much publicity as they like." Theo thumbed another contract, finding the tab and flipping it open so he could scrawl his name across the line. "This event is meant to pay an intimate tribute to my grandmother's hard work and accomplishments, and to introduce the new director. It's *not* meant to be a public spectacle."

Irina rubbed a hand over her face—not really for the sensation, because actually massaging her face would disturb the makeup she carefully applied each day—but to let her boss know exactly how irritating he was.

"You can rub your face as much as you want," he said drily. "Unless you're a genie lamp in disguise, it won't do anything to make me change my mind."

"I should quit," she said, folding her arms over the front of her silk blouse. "That might teach you a lesson. Maybe *then* you'd listen to the people around you."

"Unlikely." He scribbled his signature across the last contract and then slapped it on top of the pile and returned his pen to the silver holder on his desk. "You know I'm as incapable of change as I am of tolerating the press."

"What's the point of self-awareness if you're not striving to improve yourself?" she asked, rolling her eyes. "Change is necessary."

"Change is a risk." Theo leaned back in his chair and knotted his hands in his lap. "Any time you change things you allow a new set of variables to enter the equation. That means more opportunity for exploitation."

"I'm talking about improving your communication skills or your empathy, not redesigning your home security system." Irina shook her head. "Theo…you're a frustrating man. I see what a good heart you have in how you cared for you grandmother and how much you care about keeping your family's legacy going with this business, but you act like you don't need anybody or anything. No man is an island."

"Maybe I'm more of an archipelago." He grinned.

Irina rolled her eyes. "You'd be up to your ears if I quit, because no one else would put up with you."

"Good thing I pay you handsomely, then. That way we both get something out of this arrangement." He pushed back on his chair and stood gingerly, reaching for his crutch.

Irina saved him the effort and handed it to him, frowning. "How's the ankle?"

"It's fine. Doc says I should be off the crutches by next week, but no running for another month." He frowned. Running was his way of relieving stress. It was almost like sweating physically pushed the bad feelings out of his body and he never truly felt free of them until he'd had a punishing session on the treadmill. Therefore, not being able to run was leaving him feeling antsy and grouchy.

Well, grouchier than usual.

"You're really not going to budge on the publicity thing?" Irina asked with a sigh.

"No."

"Okay." Irina scooped up the contracts. "At least I can tell Nia I tried."

"Nia shouldn't be coming to you after I gave my final word, anyway. I won't be manipulated into giving people what they want."

"It's not that. You know Nia was a huge fan of your grandmother's work and she wants to do everything in her power to see that it continues on—that's all. I know this might be a shock to hear, Theo, but not everything is about you."

He snorted. "I wish it wasn't. My life would be a lot easier if everyone forgot who I was."

Too bad the more he hid away, the louder the questions got. Who *was* Theodore Garrison anyway? Businessman, mogul, misanthrope? Ugh. Some even speculated that he'd gone mad over the years, like someone locked away in solitary confinement. But his mind was perfectly sharp.

"Some people spend their whole lives trying to be somebody," Irina said quietly.

"Only because they don't understand what it costs. Trust me, I would trade all of this—" he waved his hand around "—if it meant being left the hell alone."

Irina nodded, clearly knowing she wasn't going to win this one. She opened a big black leather bag with a double-C clasp on the front—last year's Christmas gift. Theo even had it monogrammed for her. Despite their differences of opinion, he valued Irina. A lot.

He just didn't like it when she decided to poke into his personal life.

"Here," she said, pulling out a small stack of ivory pearlescent envelopes. "These are some invites to the gala. Everyone on the list has been covered off and they'll go into the mail this afternoon, but I figured I'd give you a few spares in case you had anyone else that you'd like to invite."

"Thank you."

"Are you bringing a date?" she asked, almost teasing.

"Why do you ask it like that?"

"Because you view dating much like publicity—a necessary evil for people other than yourself." She slid the contracts into the middle pocket of the bag and snapped the clasp shut before slipping it into the crook of her elbow. "I think the world would fall over if you brought a date to an event."

"I don't think dating is a necessary evil, I think it's an *optional* evil."

"You're telling me a young, handsome man like yourself is happy to go without a lover's touch?" She headed toward the door of his office, pausing at the threshold. "Humans are wired to belong to a group. I refuse to believe that you're happy locking yourself away here and never forming a connection with anyone."

A quippy reply leaped onto the tip of his tongue, but what was the point? Irina would never understand his need to protect himself. "Why do you care?"

"Because I've known you a long time, Theo. You might be my boss now but I remember when you were a boy. I knew your parents and your grandparents. I know how much love existed in your family and..." She sighed. "In some ways, you feel like family to me. If I had a son of my own, I would never want him to sit by while life drifted past him."

"I run a multibillion-dollar publishing house. How is life drifting past me?"

"What else do you have besides work, Theo?"

"Work is my life."

"Exactly." Irina shook her head, looking like she wanted to say more but then thought better of it. "Even your grandfather knew there was more to life than work. Even *he* would cook a meal on occasion to sit down with the people he loved and talk about the things that mattered to him. When was the last time you did that?"

Before he could respond, she walked out of his office, leaving her question hanging in the air like a cloud of perfume. It lingered, taunting him. A few seconds later he heard the ding of the elevator and the whoosh of the doors as they closed.

Even he would cook a meal on occasion to sit down with the people he loved and talk about the things that mattered to him.

The words circled in his head, like vultures. Damn Irina and her nosiness; he didn't want or need her mothering. Theo was happy with his life as it was. Perhaps he'd be happier on an island somewhere where nobody knew his name. But while the family business was still in his hands, then his life was here in Manhattan.

He simply had to make the best of things and that meant no goddamn press at a gala he was planning to attend. Nia had been pissed—but that was a hard line for Theo. If there was press at an event, he would decline an invite no matter *who* sent it to him. Even his grandmother had understood that. So why would he bring them in if he was the one organizing it? And perhaps the guests who were attending might also like a break from public attention.

The quicker he got this gala thing over with, the better.

Then the charity would be officially handed over to new management, and he could get on with his real job.

And why was cooking a meal a sign of living life? Theo hobbled slowly out of his office and into the main room. The sun was setting outside, rich red-and-gold light sparkling off the buildings on the other side of Central Park as well as the Hudson. This time of day was so vibrant, he could *almost* understand why his grandmother had loved the city as much as she did.

Another memory flickered—his mother cooking for him. She wasn't the best cook, especially since she'd spent many of her years on movie sets and living on location somewhere glamorous around the world. Cooking had never been part of her skill set...but she tried. Her specialty was a simple dish she'd picked up in Italy. Pasta tossed with a good quality olive oil, fresh herbs, toasted bread crumbs, chili and topped with a little parmesan.

When she made it for him, Theo felt like he was consuming pure love.

It couldn't be *that* hard to make.

He stood on the threshold of the kitchen, hating that Irina's words had gotten under his skin but knowing they would eat away at him until he proved her wrong. Maybe Isla would like something to eat when she got back from taking Camilla to her playdate.

He moved slowly through the kitchen, resting on his good leg and locking his crutch under his armpit so it didn't fall over. He had some spaghetti, thanks to Isla's recent shopping trip...and some oil that had been in his cupboard a while. But nothing else. No bread crumbs, no chili. Nothing with which he could make a meal.

This is ridiculous. You don't need to cook. You could buy a whole damn restaurant chain if you wanted to.

But something was needling at him and Theo's stubbornness ran deep. He grabbed his phone and downloaded an app that would allow him to order some groceries. Chili, bread crumbs, parmesan, herbs.

How hard could it be to cook a meal?

★ ★ ★

Turned out, cooking wasn't quite as easy as he'd thought, especially on one leg. Everything needed to happen at once. How did people do this every day? Water bubbled away in the big pot Isla had used to make pasta for Camilla and when it spilled over the edge it hissed on contact with the hot stove.

"Shit." He limped over and turned the heat down. The packet of pasta was sitting on the bench and when he opened it, he stared at the long, rod-straight noodles. How much was he supposed to put in? All of it?

Theo ground his back teeth together, trying to figure out what to do. Instead of using a recipe, he was trying to go from the memories hovering in the back of his mind. He knew that you boiled the water with a pinch of salt and then put the pasta in. His mother had always toasted the bread crumbs too and—

He sniffed. What was that smell? Shit! The bread crumbs. He glanced over at the pan where the bread crumbs were supposed to be "lightly" toasting and saw smoke coiling up. Using a wooden spoon, he moved the crumbs around only to find they were completely blackened on the bottom, and disturbing them lifted an acrid charred scent into the air.

Beep! Beep! Beep!

The smoke alarm pealed in protest, as if mocking his total lack of domestic skills.

"I know there's fucking smoke," he growled. Ugh, what a mess. Grabbing a hand towel, he waved it in the air trying to clear the smoke and get the alarm to stop. After flapping like a manic bird trying to take flight, Theo slumped back against the counter and let out a noise of frustration.

This was not going according to plan.

At that moment, right when he was wondering why in the hell he let his assistant get under his skin like this, Isla rounded the corner. He hadn't even heard the elevator ding over the alarm, so there was no chance of hiding any of the mess and attempting to save his dignity. Camilla trotted up beside her, already free of her harness. She took one derisive look around the kitchen and turned tail to head into the living room.

"What happened?" Isla asked, dropping her bag, along with Camilla's, onto one of the stools at the kitchen island. "Did you...try to cook?"

She looked so dumbfounded that Theo wasn't sure whether he should be insulted or amused. "Yes, I tried to cook."

"Oh." Isla peered into the pan sitting on the stove that contained the lumps of burned bread crumbs. Her nose twitched, like she wanted to sneeze.

Theo bit back his usual response in a scenario like this, which was to say something snappy and push the other person away with his words. He *hated* being vulnerable and showing that he was gloriously, wildly incapable of something as normal as cooking a meal was pretty damn vulnerable.

But he didn't want to push Isla away. Part of him worried that if he pushed too hard she might not come near him again, and...

Well, he wanted her near him.

You know why this is a bad idea. You know why letting anyone get close to you is dangerous.

"The first time I had to cook a meal for my sister the smoke I made was so bad my landlord almost called the fire brigade," she said, leaning against the counter and flicking her hand in the direction of the charred crumbs. "This is nothing. Rookie status. When you have someone pounding on your door because they think your life is in danger, *then* you can play in my league."

Theo couldn't help but laugh, one-hundred percent sure she was exaggerating for his benefit. "That's very sweet, but you don't need to make me feel better."

"Everybody should have someone to make them feel better." She reached for the pan and carried it over to where the trash was hidden away under the sink. When she dumped the crumbs into the plastic liner, a little plume of smoke wafted up and she wrinkled her nose again. "Hmm, looks like this will need to soak for a bit."

Theo reached across the stove top and turned off the burner that was boiling the water. "It's probably for the best. I didn't know how much pasta to put in anyway."

Isla bit down on her lower lip as if stifling her amusement. "Why the urge to be Martha Stewart all of a sudden?"

"Don't ask," he muttered.

"Too late." She smiled at him, her blue eyes glimmering with curiosity and amusement.

"I…" He scrubbed a hand over his face. What was this woman *doing* to him? Irina's comments had only gotten to him because they made him think about Isla and how it might feel to sit down for a meal with her.

How it might feel to do normal things like have a conversation with someone over a glass of wine and…connect.

Connect? Really? What happened last time you did that?

"I thought you might be hungry."

She blinked. "Oh."

"I mean, you get hungry, don't you? It's not a strange assumption." He could feel his walls starting to go up around him. This was an idiotic idea. A ridiculous, foolish, ill-advised—

"I believe all humans get hungry," she replied, her cheek forming a dent from her efforts not to laugh. But with Isla, her laughter didn't feel cruel or mocking. It felt…human. "Being a biological need and all."

"Right." He shook his head. "Well, this clearly isn't going to happen. I—"

"We could always order pizza," she suggested shyly. "I like pizza."

"I do, too."

The kitchen felt very quiet all of a sudden, like a blanket of hush had been thrown over them. There was a strange, delicate connection between them—like he'd extended a hand and so had she, even though they weren't quite touching yet.

"I'll order," he said gruffly, clearing his throat. "Any preferences?"

"I'm easy, so long as it's not Hawaiian. You don't like pineapple on your pizza, do you?" She looked at him like this might be some hard limit for her. Maybe that's how her dating choices were made, weeded out with a simple question of fruit on pizza.

"No, not really."

She looked relieved. "Good. I'll go feed Camilla her dinner."

Theo watched as Isla went to the fridge, where she'd started keeping batches of cold pasta to mix in with Camilla's dog food. Not much, but a few shells here and there so the dog would eat, and she was slowly weaning her off.

That was Isla in a nutshell—she worked at gaining someone's trust with small, consistent actions. Maybe that's why he felt drawn to her. Because there was a rhythm to her, a consistency and a reliability that he'd found to be sorely lacking in the general population. Isla was steady, calm, sweet.

Beautiful.

He swallowed when she bent down to retrieve the pasta container on the bottom shelf of the fridge. Her jeans stretched tight across her ass and after a second too long, he dragged his gaze away and started looking for the pizza joint on his food delivery app.

It wasn't like he'd never been around a beautiful woman

before. His ex had been like that—stunning. Smart as a whip, too. But as someone desperate to climb the ranks of the Upper East Side, there had also been a steely determination that overrode her sense of loyalty and trust.

She had betrayed him.

Everyone will betray you.

He tapped at his phone, wondering what he was getting himself into. Theo knew better than to play with fire and yet here he was, fingertips dancing over the top of the flames... and he had no desire to stop.

12

Isla wasn't exactly sure what was going on. Theo had tried to cook dinner because he thought she might be hungry. How was she supposed to read into that? *Was* she supposed to read into that?

It was incredibly sweet, especially since it was clear the man never cooked. Why would he? He could snap his fingers and have anything he wanted materialize right in front of him. And sure, he might not be a god, but he was so out of her league that he may as well be.

Not that Isla dated, but if she did it would be someone so *not* like Theo Garrison.

"Why are you even thinking about dating?" she muttered to herself as she scooped Camilla's food into her Tiffany bowl.

"One, he's your boss. Two, he's your boss. Three…he's your *boss*."

Camilla looked up at her as if to say *are you having a melt-down, woman?* But then she stuck her snout into the bowl before Isla even had a chance to finish dishing up. No complaints here. If Camilla was eating then Isla was happy.

"What do you think?" Isla asked the dog as she rinsed the can out in the sink and popped it into the recycling container. "You must have good taste in men, since you're so discerning about everything else in life."

The dog made a snorting sound and continued to hoover down her food.

"Fair enough." Isla sighed. "I'll let you finish your meal first."

It didn't take long. Now that Camilla's appetite had returned, she was getting hungry at dinnertime like she should be. Isla had noticed a change in the Dachshund—there was a little more spring to her step. A little more pep in her tail.

Isla crouched to grab the bowl, not realizing there was still one little morsel left because she was too far in her own head, and Camilla snapped at her. Her teeth narrowly missed Isla's knuckle but she was sure the dog could have made contact if she really wanted to.

"Jeez, just when I think we're getting along," she grumbled and Camilla continued to lick the bowl so clean she could use it as a mirror. "Are you done now?"

The dog sat her furry butt on the ground and looked up at Isla as if to say *now you may take my bowl, servant.*

"Thank you, kind master," Isla muttered to herself as she washed the bowl and then got the brush out to give Camilla her nightly grooming. "Come here."

The dog came freely now. In the first week it had been a struggle and Isla suspected one of the previous dog sitters was rough with her. Camilla's fur could get quite tangled, but Isla was gentle and took her time, and now Camilla seemed as though she'd started enjoying the brush-down.

The dog lay down on her side, legs stretched out and tongue lolling out of her mouth as Isla smoothed the brush over her. She did this cute little leg twitch and then let out a happy sigh.

"See, I'm not so bad," Isla said. "I'm making sure you're happy and healthy, so you get to do all the things your mom wanted you to do. But it would be nice if you kept your teeth and your growls to yourself. And peeing on Mrs. Tipton's monstera plant wasn't very nice either. Oh, and maybe don't hump your playdate, because that poor Chihuahua looked traumatized."

Isla would swear the dog smiled as if reliving the memory.

"You can hump stuffed animals *only*, okay? Not the real deal." Isla helped the dog flip over to her other side. "I wonder if stuffed toys are for dogs what sex dolls are for humans. Because there are a lot of similarities, I guess. Well, minus the orifices."

"That a fact?"

Isla was so startled she yelped and fell back on her ass, and the dog scrambled to her feet, barking at the sudden intrusion.

"Sorry, didn't mean to scare you." Theo stood in the doorway, his single crutch wedged under one arm and a wicked smile on his lips. "Pizza's here. But please continue your discussion on stuffed toys being the sex dolls of the animal kingdom, it was truly fascinating."

Camilla looked at both of them as if disgusted by their presence, and then she trotted past Theo and disappeared into the penthouse, no doubt to hide herself away.

"That was…a private conversation." Isla got to her feet and finished cleaning up, not daring to look at Theo for fear her face might actually burst into flames from the humiliation.

"You're quite chatty with the dog," he commented.

"Why not? All creatures need conversation."

"And sex dolls?" He raised an eyebrow.

She gritted her teeth. How unfair was it that she let him off the hook for the bread-crumb thing and yet he took any opportunity to tease her! "That's not polite dinner conversation."

"You're probably right." He chuckled and the sound was dark and delicious. It sent a tingle of awareness streaking through her body. "Although I'm not sure I'd classify myself as polite."

"You're not." She washed her hands in the sink and dried them on a hand towel. "What pizza did you order?"

"Pepperoni and *polpette*. Simple, but I figured you for a traditional kind of woman."

"Why do you say that?" She followed him out to the kitchen where two boxes were waiting, along with two empty wineglasses.

"Red?" he asked and she nodded. "The comment about the pineapple, for starters. But you also strike me as someone who likes to uphold tradition. You've got old-fashioned values and you like classic things."

Huh. Interesting. That *was* how Isla would describe herself. "I didn't realize you'd been paying such close attention."

Now it was Theo's turn to look away. He busied himself pouring the wine and flipping the pizza boxes open. He motioned for her to take a seat on one of the stools and then he came around to sit next to her.

"I'm observant," he said. "It's a necessary skill in my life."

He raised his glass to hers and she mimicked him, the chime of crystal on crystal ringing through the kitchen. They were so close, Isla's shoulder almost brushed Theo's arm as she reached for a slice of the pepperoni. There was an electrical current in the air, a zap and a zing and a vibration that made it feel like every nerve ending in her body was dialed into him. She was a radio turned to his frequency, a spring wound too tight.

"Well, you're right. I *am* a bit traditional."

"Looking for the husband and babies and white picket fence life?" he asked, biting into a slice. He made a little moaning sound that was so soft Isla almost didn't hear it. She *wished* she didn't hear it, because then her body wouldn't be hot enough to boil water and she wouldn't be wondering what other of life's pleasures made him moan like that.

"Maybe one day, but not yet." She shook her head. "I have enough responsibilities for now."

"Your sister, right? I remember you saying that when we met in the park."

"That's right." Isla bit into her own slice and made a twin noise to the one Theo had made. "Damn, this is *good.*"

He grinned as though proud that she approved of his choices. "The chef is a genius. Nothing too fancy, but they use quality fresh ingredients and some special herb mixture that was passed down from his great-grandmother. Best pizza in New York, if you ask me."

"If I died now, I would be a very happy woman."

"What's your sister like?" he asked. Isla looked over at him to see if he was being polite—despite his earlier declaration—but to her surprise, he seemed genuinely interested.

"She's fourteen going on twenty-four. Wants to be older and have more freedom, but she's also very responsible for a girl her age. We uh…had to grow up quickly." Isla took another bite and bought herself some time to think. She didn't like talking about their mother, mostly because other people didn't understand.

Mothers were revered, as they should be. But the simple fact was that not all people who became mothers were suited to the job, and hers was a case in point.

"My mom never wanted to be a mother, I don't think. She got pregnant with me by accident while she was young, and she wasn't well equipped. Mom was always dating, one guy after the next, looking for someone who'd make her happy." Isla shook her head. "Then when I was twenty and my sister was in elementary school, Mom took off with some guy she'd been dating a month. I went from being a big sister to parent overnight."

Theo frowned, his eyes narrowed in intense thought. "She just…left?"

"Yeah." Isla nodded and took a sip of her wine. "That was six years ago."

"Your sister is lucky to have you," he said.

"Absolutely." Isla laughed. "And I'm lucky to have her. We make a good team."

"It sucks having to grow up when you're still a kid, doesn't it?" He leaned his elbow on the counter and turned to her. God, they were close. His knee bumped the side of her leg and her breath hitched.

It was such a small thing, a touch with no more intention than someone walking too close on the street. But it felt monumental, somehow. Like she'd breached some barrier or passed through some gate. He was allowing her to be in his space, to be close, to be real.

"I honestly don't know what's worse," she said. "Losing your parents when they loved you or knowing that they chose to leave because they never loved you enough to stay."

He made a slow, thoughtful *hmm* sound and it rippled through Isla's body. The way he looked at her was like being trapped in light, being *seen* in a way she never had before. For so many years she'd worked and worked and worked, always a background figure—the person behind the scenes who made everything look good. She stood behind her clients and be-hind her sister, pushing them forward.

But in this moment with Theo, *she* was front and center. She was the star.

"I don't often meet people who make me think," he said. "But you do. You make me wonder about things."

"Why?"

"Because I find you interesting."

Isla laughed. "Sure, the man with a rich and storied family history who lives in the lap of luxury finds *me* interesting. I'm a workaholic with a failed career and the responsibilities of a single parent. What exactly about that is interesting to you?"

His lip lifted in that sexy half smile, half smirk. "You really want to know?"

"Indulge me."

"You have full-blown conversations with a dog in an effort to win her favor. You have this innate desire to help people, even those who don't encourage your affections. You're responsible and yet there's something ultimately free about you." He ticked the items off his fingers. "And in some strange paradox, I find you totally, wildly innocent and yet absolutely sinful."

Isla's breath hitched. Seeing him so close—watching the excitement and attraction flare in his usually remote eyes—filled her with a sense of feminine power. She wanted to explore him. Conquer him.

Energy crackled in the kitchen, zipping between them like fairies sprinkling magic dust. Theo had her under a spell, entranced…and she loved every second of it. "You're not what you let people believe. You're so much more."

The words, though quietly spoken, took whatever thread of restraint they were both clinging to and snapped it clean in half. Theo leaned forward, sliding his hand along Isla's jaw, his thumb brushing gently over her skin. He was close now. His cologne mingled with the fruitiness of the wine on his lips.

Yes.

Her whole body sang out for his kiss, her heart beating steadily and quickly in her chest as she willed it to happen. Their noses brushed and his lips parted, hers following in aching, anticipatory want. They were frozen in this moment, suspended in the air like a snowflake gliding on a breeze.

"Do it already," she whispered, letting her eyes flutter shut.

Theo's warm breath drifted across her skin, and then the soft, yet confident pressure of his mouth on hers was like being melted by the sun. And melt she did. Her fists closed around the soft fabric of his sweater, curling so she could tug him closer. He stepped down from his stool and pulled her with him. Then he wedged her against the kitchen island, one hand thrusting back into her hair and the other resting on her hip.

She tipped her head back, inviting him to kiss her more deeply. He tasted heavenly—*felt* heavenly. The hard press of the counter at her back was no match for the warm, hard man at her front. Theo's hand skated around her hip and to her lower back, pressing her against him. The waistband of his sweats brushed against her stomach as her top rode up a little, and the sensation was everything. It was the oxygen in her blood, the spark in her brain, the tingle in her skin. His body rubbed against hers as he delved deeper and she met him there, gasping at the brush of hardness at her stomach.

Her whole body pulsed and molten excitement gathered between her legs. Each breath came shallower, like dragging air into her lungs was a relegated priority, second to the feel of his palms traveling down her back to cup her ass. Second to the pressure of his lips. Second, even, to the gentle bump of his nose against hers as they changed angles.

A sigh rose up from deep inside her and she allowed herself

to explore his body. The broad expanse of his shoulders, the rounded muscles at his arms, the narrow waist and lean hips and...*oh*. Her fingertips brushed the ridge of his erection lining his inner thigh and Theo groaned in response.

The loud peal of Theo's phone broke them apart, and Isla clapped a hand to her chest in surprise. He canceled the call and placed his phone back on the marble countertop, but the moment was shattered. Then Isla caught the time on the display of his oven. 8:00 p.m. She scrambled for her own phone, heart thundering. She'd turned it off earlier to preserve what was left of the power, because she'd accidentally left her battery-pack at home. The phone blinked on. Ten messages.

"Shit, shit, shit."

Dani had started sending her increasingly frantic texts and left a few voice mails as well. Isla was supposed to be home by now, and she'd promised her sister they would hang out. She'd completely lost track of time.

"I have to go." She scooped up her purse, not daring to look at him.

"I'm sorry." His voice was tight. "We shouldn't—"

"I know, I know." Oh my *God*. Had she kissed her boss? What the hell was wrong with her? That was employment 101, don't mix business with pleasure...especially if you were going to be destitute without your job. "It didn't happen."

Only it *did* happen. It abso-freaking-lutely happened.

And Isla would be lying through her front teeth if she said she'd forget about it anytime soon. For a moment she wanted to scream. When she dragged her eyes back to him, Theo was leaning his weight on his good foot, hair a little mussed, amber eyes wild and fiery, lips delectably swollen from her kiss. Not to mention—

Do not *even think about looking at his crotch right now.*

They stood there for a moment and Isla wanted to say something more, but her throat was clogged with anger and frustration and...guilt. She'd left her sister panicking and alone, which was Dani's greatest fear. That was absolutely unforgivable.

"I have to go," she repeated, her cheeks filled with heat and her body still pulsing like she was heading right into Theo's bedroom instead of out his front door.

She turned and headed through his apartment, already dialing her sister back so she could apologize. But her body was still running on adrenaline from their kiss and her hands trembled as she navigated to her call log. She had to get herself together. *Now.*

When Dani answered, there were relieved tears and a few choice curse words that Isla would let slide since it was her own damn fault for freaking her sister out.

You will not *self-sabotage this thing. Theo Garrison is off-limits.*

Her priority was her sister, and that meant keeping her job was the only thing she should be focusing on right now. Not on her boss's incredibly sexy eyes, not on how addicted she was to chipping away at his stone-cold facade. And certainly not to the memory of his kiss, which was now branded deep into her brain.

Isla slunk through the front door to her apartment, feeling like the worst big sister in the world. The place was dead quiet—a rarity. Even when Dani was doing the right thing and blasting her music through headphones instead of speakers, there was *some* noise. The brush of pointe shoes across the floor, the squeak of floorboards as she pliéd or maybe the sound of fingers tapping at a keyboard. Something.

But now the apartment was shrouded in darkness and quiet as a tomb. Isla flicked the lights on and scanned the main room. "Dani?"

Her sister must have been studying. Two textbooks overlapped on the coffee table, along with a spiral-bound notebook featuring her sister's flowery handwriting and a half-consumed glass of juice.

But no Dani.

Her bedroom door was cracked open, but there was no light inside. Nor any shining under the bottom of the bathroom door. Isla's heart leaped into her throat. What if she'd taken off? What if...?

Then she heard it. The muffled sound of a sob. Not coming from Dani's room, but from Isla's.

She walked slowly across the apartment and peered into the darkness. A small lump in the middle of the bed moved and a head lifted, bleary-eyed and squinting into the light shining from the living room behind Isla.

"You forgot about me," she croaked. The words were a gut punch.

It might seem like an extreme reaction to some—perhaps a ploy for attention or a teenager's natural tendency for drama. But that wasn't the case.

She walked into the room and kicked off her shoes before climbing onto the bed and pulling her sister into her arms. Dani's slender frame resisted for only a second, before she curled into Isla's embrace, her shoulders shaking. For a moment, they lay there silently.

This was not the first time Isla had come home to find her sister in tears. Ever since she was little, when their mother had walked out and returned only to walk out again in a cruel and continual seesaw, Dani had a deep fear of being alone. There'd been stages of her life where nightmares and panic attacks were the norm, and when Isla's career had afforded her sister access to therapy, she'd done everything in her power to help Dani deal with those dark waves.

Most days she was better at coping now. But not *all* days.

"I'm sorry I'm late and that I didn't answer your calls," she said softly, stroking her sister's hair.

"You promised." Dani hiccupped. "You promised that we would hang out tonight and then when you didn't answer I got worried."

"I know." She let out a long breath. "But what have we talked about?"

"That you're not ever going to leave me the way Mom did."

"That's right. And what else?"

"That sometimes you get caught up and you will always call me back as soon as you can."

"And?" Isla prompted.

"I'm your number one priority."

"That's right. And sometimes putting you as number one means that I need to be away for a little bit because I'm work-ing or doing something important for our life."

If only that was why you were late tonight.

The fact was, Isla was being selfish. And stupid. What the heck was she thinking kissing her boss like that?

It wasn't like she had a safety net if things went south and he decided to fire her.

"I'm sorry I freaked out," Dani said in a small voice. "I know in my head you love me, but sometimes there's a voice telling me things that aren't true."

"Like what?"

"That it's my fault we got left behind. Maybe I didn't try hard enough to be a good dancer or to get good enough grades or…something."

"You know that's not true, right?"

"Yeah, it just feels true for a minute."

Isla sat up and pulled Dani with her so they could look at one another face-to-face. Light slanted into the bedroom from the living room, casting shadows across her sister's face.

Outside a siren wailed and blue-and-red lights flickered for a moment before disappearing. Dani was still hugging Isla's pillow and her cheeks were stained with tears.

Dani looked down. "I keep worrying you're going to get a boyfriend and then I'll have to live somewhere else."

"What do you mean?" Isla blinked. This was news to her.

"I saw a picture of a man on your computer and he was really handsome and I thought…" Dani sniffled. "Maybe you wanted to spend time with him instead of me."

Oof.

The girl had no idea how close to home she'd hit—and this was precisely why Isla didn't do relationships. The one time she *had* brought a guy home to meet Dani, her sister had freaked out so much that the mere mention of the guy's name brought on a panic spiral. After breaking things off, which had hurt because Isla really liked the guy, she'd made a promise to herself not to get involved with anyone else until Dani was older and better able to handle it.

"I wasn't snooping, I promise," she added hastily. "Your laptop was open."

"What was the guy's name?"

"Theo. He's your boss, right?"

"Yeah, he's my boss." Isla nodded. "And yes, I was at his place tonight when you called. We were…discussing work."

Great, now you're lying to her?

Isla wasn't sure what was better—be honest and admit that she *had* forgotten about her plans with Dani because she was in a lust-induced brain fog brought on by the most off-limits man possible. Or lie to save her feelings.

If only there was some kind of training manual for raising a teenager, because Isla felt like she got it wrong all the damn time. This wasn't the life she'd envisaged for herself. Sure, she wanted kids someday in the future. But being twenty-six and not able to date because she was trying to raise a fourteen-year-old with severe abandonment issues wasn't easy.

"Do you think she'll ever come back?" Dani asked, picking at a flaw on the duvet cover. "Mom, I mean."

Isla watched her little sister. Periodically she'd asked this question and Isla had always tried to skate around it. Sometimes she said positive things like "anything is possible" and "she's come back before" but now Isla found herself so weary and so emotionally drained that she didn't have it in herself to give Dani hope.

And really, what was the point of hope when it was false?

"I don't think so," she said softly.

"Really?" Dani's shoulders deflated.

"Is it possible? Yeah. But based on everything I know about her and how she operates… I don't think she will." Isla reached for her sister's hand. "Look, I know her not being here is hard, and I know that you harbor a secret desire that one day she'll come back and we'll all be a family. I had that same secret feeling for a long time, too."

"But not anymore?"

How honest was too honest when it came to a fourteen-year-old? "The way she has treated you, Dani, I'm not sure I could forgive her even if she did come back."

"She left you, too."

"Yes, but I was an adult." *Barely.* "You were still a little girl. It's different."

"Why do you think she doesn't care about us?"

"Some people are born selfish and they can only think about their own wants and their own needs. Because of that they end up hurting those around them. But the thing is, you and I are not like her. We're *not* selfish. We're a team and a family and when I promise I'll never leave you, I mean it with every piece of my heart."

Isla found herself blinking back tears. This kid meant the

world to her—even though it was hard, most days. Even though it made her tired and afraid and it meant missing out on a lot of "normal" things that other women her age got to do. It was worth it. Dani was worth it.

"You don't ever feel like I'm a…" Dani paused while she searched for the right word. "A burden?"

"No," Isla replied fiercely. "Never."

"Even when I freak out?" Dani's voice caught and Isla squeezed her hand.

"Especially not then. That's what family is. When one of us is hurting it's the other person's job to take care of them."

"But you're never hurting, so I don't get to take care of you." Dani frowned. Isla's eyes had adjusted to the dark now and she could see the blotchiness on her sister's skin, the tear tracks and the messy way her hair stuck out from a ponytail that was half falling out.

"Ah yes, but you see I'm going to get old before you, so I'll get my payback then. You'll have to help me wipe my butt."

"Ew! I mean, I'll do it because I love you, but that's disgusting."

"Love can be disgusting." Isla smiled when her sister giggled. "You're not a burden. Not even when you're having the worst freak-out possible."

"Promise?"

"I promise." Isla leaned in and hugged her sister tight and Dani hugged her right back. "I'm sorry I was late tonight. It's not cool for me to do that without letting you know."

"Do we still have time for a movie?" she asked in a hopeful voice.

"Are you going to give me a hard time in the morning when you have to get up for school?"

"Nope."

Isla narrowed her eyes and her sister looked back with an

innocent expression. "Okay fine, but you'd better get your ass up on time."

"I will." Dani grinned. "Can we have some dessert? I saw there was ice cream in the freezer."

"Sure. Go and scoop some out for both of us while I get changed."

"Thanks, Isla." She looked shy for a moment. "I love you."

"I love you, too. More than anything."

As Dani scampered away to get their dessert ready, Isla mulled on that thought. She really *did* love her sister more than anything—more than her career, more than her dreams, more than any man.

Protecting her and giving her a chance at a normal life was the *only* thing that mattered.

And you think being a dog sitter is going to do that? One, Theo won't need you forever and two, you have to build something for the future.

Otherwise how would she help Dani pay for college in a few years? And without getting back into her old career, what other choices did she have? Isla had no degree, no experience doing anything other than social media. Unless you counted menial office work, but those kinds of jobs would barely cover the basics.

Maybe Scout was right.

It felt risky to even think about striking out on her own, not knowing if it would work. But it also felt risky to be a sitting duck, hoping that the gatekeepers would suddenly forgive her indiscretion and let her back into her old life. She couldn't guarantee that would *ever* happen.

The answer wasn't clear. All she knew was that getting involved with Theo Garrison was a risk she couldn't afford.

13

On Sunday morning, Isla decided that she owed both Dani *and* Scout a treat. One, for being late and making Dani worry and two, because Isla should have been more supportive about Scout losing her job. So, she rounded up her little sister and her best friend bright and early for one of their favorite but not-often-indulged-in activities: brunch.

There was a place in the South Bronx with a rooftop terrace and little metal tables and chairs that did the *best* pastries. Not to mention their coffee tasted like liquid gold. It was a rare treat—partially because frequent brunch wasn't in Isla's budget and partially because she refused to line up for a meal. But going early had two benefits: no line and no rush to clear the table once you were done.

And right now, Isla was happy to do *anything* that took her mind off Theo.

"This was *such* a good idea," Scout said. She lowered herself into one of the metal seats as the server placed some menus on the table. Now that they were in the shade cast by an umbrella, she pushed her sunglasses onto her head and pulled her hair tie out, letting her gold hair tumble down her back. "Why don't we do this more often?"

"Uh, money, time, insert other adult responsibilities here." Isla laughed and took her own seat. Dani grabbed the last one and dropped down with so little grace it was hard to believe she'd ever studied ballet at all. Two white earbuds were lodged into her ears and the cord dangled down, attached to an old and rather beat-up tablet in her hand.

"What's she watching?" Scout asked, trying to peer over.

"Some ballet YouTube channel that she likes. Normally I'd tell her no screens at the table but..." Isla sighed and shrugged. "I don't have it in me to 'mom' today."

"Fair."

"Besides, that thing is a piece of crap anyway and she'll be lucky if she gets another half hour out of it before the battery dies. I've been meaning to buy her a new one."

"But time, money and insert other adult responsibilities here?" Scout repeated Isla's words with a laugh.

"Something like that." Isla tipped her face up, leaning back in her chair far enough that she caught some sun on her skin. The warmth felt good. For the first time in weeks, she felt the muscles in her shoulders and neck start to unwind. "Anyway, I wanted to treat you both. I felt bad for the 'again' comment I made the other day when you told me about your job. It's been weighing on me, so I wanted to say sorry the best way I know how."

"With butter and sugar?" Scout smiled.

"And caffeine."

"Thanks, but you don't need to do that."

"I do. I didn't mean it to sound harsh because I know what it's like being on the other end of it."

"Well, thanks. I appreciate it. Although one little 'again' pales in comparison to what my grandparents said." Scout's expression darkened. "Apparently I am irresponsible and immature, just like my mother was."

Isla frowned and shook her head. "You are *not* like your mother."

One of the things that Scout and Isla bonded over in high school was their turbulent family situations. Both had absentee fathers and less-than-stellar mothers. Isla's mom often disappeared on dates and would bring strange men back to their home, but Scout's mother was something else. She tended to disappear a lot, too, usually getting high or sobering up in lockup.

And like Isla, Scout had a younger sister. But they'd eventually been split up—with their ultra-strict grandparents kicking Scout out of their home in her late teens for being too rebellious. These days she only saw her younger sister with their permission.

To say it was a tense relationship was putting it lightly.

The server came past to take their orders—cappuccinos and *pains au chocolat* for Isla and Scout, and ice chocolate with whipped cream and a strawberry Danish for Dani, who popped her earbuds back in the second she'd voiced her desires.

"When did you see them?" Isla asked.

"Last night, so the wounds are still fresh." Scout sighed. "I don't at all want to dismiss how hard it's been for you raising Dani, but..."

Tears glimmered in her friend's eyes and a lump formed in the back of Isla's throat. She reached out and grabbed Scout's hand. "I know you'd give anything to be in my situation and have your sister live with you."

"Yeah, I would." She swallowed hard and then blinked her tears away, tension giving way to her usual sunny smile. "Anyway, we did *not* come here to talk about the sorry state of my family life."

"You know you can always vent to me, wherever or whenever. That's what friends are for." Isla nodded. "No judgment, my previous thoughtless comment notwithstanding."

"I'd rather talk about *your* work. How many followers are you at?"

Isla didn't even need to look this time. "Fifteen thousand."

"It's going up quick."

"I figured out how it grew so fast, too." Isla paused as their coffees and pastries were delivered to the table, and she reached straight for her drink, wrapping her hands around the mug and taking a tentative sip to test the temperature. Perfection. "I snapped a picture in front of the fancy pet salon that I take Camilla to once a week. They shared the picture and they have close to a million followers—seriously, whoever is doing their social media should get a raise. Someone left a comment on their picture asking who runs The Dachshund Wears Prada account and the salon replied with this really cryptic response about protecting their celebrity client's names."

"Huh, weird. Do you think they know it's you?"

"No way. I've seen at least five different Dachshunds in that place just in the time I've been taking Camilla. They must be a popular breed for the clientele." Isla bit into her pastry and hummed in delight. "Oh man, this is *good*."

"So why the cryptic response?"

"It's social media 101—always leave your audience wanting to know more."

"I would *suck* at that." Scout shook her head and tore off the corner of her pastry, popping it into her mouth and chewing thoughtfully. "I'm too much of an open book."

"Like I said, whoever is running their account is doing an

amazing job. A bunch of people started speculating in the comments on that post and my account has been growing steadily. I'm already starting to get DMs about promotional things," Isla said. "Nothing major because we're still talking micro-influencer numbers, but…"

"Go on, you can say it." Scout grinned. "I was right. You *should* open your own pet social media agency!"

"I'm not at twenty thousand yet, that was the deal. If I can do that then I'll consider it." She sipped her drink. "Terrifying as it might be."

"Maybe you could hit up your boss for a loan."

"No." The word shot out of her before she had time to consider the consequences of revealing such a strong reaction. "That would be inappropriate."

The corner of Scout's lip twitched. "Mr. Sparkly Vampire Energy's too tight with his cash?"

"Stop calling him that." Isla cringed. "And I have no idea how he spends his money."

Scout watched Isla over the rim of her coffee cup, clearly amused by winding her friend up. "Touchy."

"I'm not touchy." But the more she protested the more suspicious she looked. And it wasn't hot enough to blame her rapidly warming cheeks on the weather. "Look, if I'm going to do this then I'm going to do it properly by applying for a business loan."

"Wow, so you really *are* considering it." Scout blinked.

"Why do you sound surprised? It's a good idea."

"Oh, I know it's a good idea. It's more that…" She paused, her eyes tilting up to the sky as she thought about how to frame her answer. "Well, you're not one for taking risks."

"I took a job from a man I met in a park. How is that not taking a risk?"

"You were desperate. Desperation breeds uncharacteristic

behavior." Scout nodded wisely. "Now you're *not* as desperate, because you have a paying job even if it's not the one you want. Making a move from this point is different."

Isla frowned. Sometimes she didn't like how well her friend knew her. "I'd argue that I'm still a little desperate. A cushy dog-sitting job might be fine for now, but my brain will turn to mush if I have to do this forever. And it's not like any doors in my old industry are being opened back up to me. I emailed an old colleague the other day to see how things were going and she 'politely' asked me not to contact her via her work address in case anyone saw my name pop up in her inbox."

Scout pulled a face. "Ouch."

"People's memories are longer than we give them credit for," Isla grumbled. "So yeah, maybe the desperation thing still applies. But I won't go into any kind of business without crunching the numbers and making sure that I'm minimizing the risk as much as possible. I would never do *anything* to endanger Dani's future."

"But?" Scout asked teasingly.

"But," Isla replied with a sigh. "I have to admit that maybe this is exactly the solution I've been looking for. There's a market for it—especially for people who want to break into the social media space but don't understand how it all works, or for bigger accounts who want to offload some of the grunt work like dealing with sponsorship deals and managing the admin side of things. So many big brands are turning to influencers over models and even actors or singers these days. Why simply hire a pretty face when you can find someone with a built-in platform of millions? I *have* to imagine there's bleed over into the animal realm as well."

"You know your whole face lights up when you talk about this stuff," Scout said. "It's what you're passionate about."

"Passion doesn't pay the bills."

"Neither will dog sitting, eventually. Like you said, you can't do it forever." Scout stuffed another piece of *pain au chocolat* into her mouth. "And don't you think people find more success doing the things they love?"

"Debatable. But luckily it happens the thing I love is also something that could make money. Emphasis on the *could*, though. I still need to do more research."

"No rush," Scout said with a grin. "I'm here whenever you're ready to talk business."

Isla leaned back in her seat. It was a big decision, but she'd be lying if she said there wasn't a little voice in the back of her mind telling her to go for it. Her whole life she'd made the sensible decisions—sticking with an established agency and getting a steady paycheck while her colleagues broke away and built something for themselves. Was it possible for someone who was responsible and sensible to the core to *ever* strike out on their own? It was what she'd always wanted—to be her own boss.

But that dream had been swept under the carpet along with the rest of Isla's desires the second she had to play mom to her sister. And where had being sensible gotten her? Years and years of hard work and navigating company politics and putting up with being a lackey...all of it had been erased by *one* mistake.

Meanwhile, her friend from the early years of working at the Gateway Agency had said "screw this" three years in and started her own business. She'd made the Forbes 30 under 30 list for signing TikTok stars before the app blew up.

You'll never get there if you don't build something for yourself.

And what would she be teaching Dani if she never took risks to reach for something great? But on the flip side, what if it all came crashing down?

Isla had too many questions swimming in her head right now. She knew one thing for certain, however. Risks in business may become inevitable, but she would never take risks in love.

14

Theo had been on pins and needles all Monday long. Isla had been slipping in and out of his penthouse without a peep the past few work days, collecting Camilla and her things and exiting before he had a chance to speak with her. Part of him wondered if maybe that was for the best.

He'd kissed her last week like his life depended on it. Like it meant something.

And how could it possibly mean anything when he'd vowed long ago that no single person would mean something to him ever again.

And yet…

Theo narrowed his eyes on the signed book sitting on his desk and the crisp, pearlescent envelope atop it. A gift and an invitation told him that vow had been broken. He wanted Isla closer to him. He wanted to kiss her again even though he knew it was dangerous. At the very least, he wanted to clear the air.

Drumming his fingers on the edge of his desk, he carried the items out into the living room along with his laptop. He'd work there until she came back so she would *not* slip past him again.

He got into the zone, answering emails and working his way through an executive information pack for a new publishing imprint they were planning to launch in the fall. The hours melted away. This was the space he'd occupied for so long he wasn't sure he knew what else life had to offer beyond the numbing effects of being bone-tired at the end of a long day. It was hard to dwell when your brain was wrung out, hard to feel grief and loneliness when all you wanted was sleep.

Work had been his solace and his safe space for his entire adult life.

The *ding* of the elevator behind him pulled Theo into the present and he listened with senses on high alert. The *whoosh* of the doors opening was followed by the clack of block heels and the patter of paws. One step, two steps, three steps… freeze. The change in the air was like a ripple.

"Good afternoon," he said smoothly, without shifting position.

"Were you waiting for me?" She sounded a little defensive.

"A man can sit in his own living room, can't he?" He closed the laptop and placed it on the coffee table, then pushed up to a standing position, still careful not to put his full weight on his bad ankle. When he turned, he saw her crouching to free the dog from her harness. Camilla stuck her nose in the air and trotted off into the penthouse like she couldn't even bear the thought of his presence. Isla didn't look much warmer.

Why isn't there a manual for this stuff?

Isla bit down on her bottom lip, avoiding his eyes as she hoisted her bag higher onto one shoulder. "How's the ankle?"

"Getting there. I'm not using the crutches as much anymore, but I won't be running a marathon anytime soon." He frowned as she rummaged through her bag, no doubt trying to buy some time. "Can we talk?"

"We're already talking," she replied in barely more than a whisper.

Shit. She wasn't going to make this easy for him. Good thing he'd brought a peace offering. Well, he wasn't sure the invitation would be a peace offering—depending on whether she liked fancy parties with tiny food and pompous small talk.

Maybe don't phrase it like that.

"I, uh…about what happened last week," he started, but she held her hand up.

"Please, it's not necessary. I'm happy to forget all about it if you are."

Oof. It wasn't exactly a surprising reaction but it had been a damn long time since he'd kissed a woman, and a response of "I'm happy to forget it" didn't exactly stroke his ego.

"You trying to tell me I'm a bad kisser?" he asked with an awkward laugh, trying to insert some levity into the mood.

"Oh no," she said shaking her head and then catching herself. The answer had come quick and maybe it was a sad indication of Theo's life, but it stoked his pride. "I mean…"

"You mean it was great but I'm your employer which makes things a bit awkward."

The edge of her lip pulled up into a half smile. "That's about it."

"I didn't mean to put you in an uncomfortable position."

"It wasn't all you," she replied, shaking her head. "I encouraged it."

"I'm pretty sure I encouraged it, too."

They stared at one another for a long moment and Theo felt a ripple of wanting rush through him. Isla knotted her hands in front of her—today she was wearing a cute A-line dress in a royal blue with a paler blue cardigan over the top. It made her eyes look like twin chips of blue topaz and contrasted starkly against her dark brown hair.

He fought back the urge to tell her how pretty she looked. The last thing he wanted to do was make things worse.

"In any case, I wanted to assure you that it would have no bearing on your employment. And I, uh...brought you a peace offering." He reached for the book. He'd wedged the envelope inside, marking the title page where the author's signature was scrawled in black marker.

Isla's eyes narrowed in curiosity, then widened. "I *love* this series!"

"I know. You had a copy of it in your bag last week." He cleared his throat and thrust the book toward her. "The author happens to be one of the first people my grandfather ever signed when he started the publishing house, so he's very gracious about doing favors."

Isla's fingers brushed Theo's as she took the gift, her eyes holding his for a few heartbeats. Before she opened it, she ran her fingertips along the embossed design of the jacket. "It's a beautiful edition."

"We're celebrating the thirtieth anniversary of publication." Theo nodded. "We had a special edition designed and a limited number printed. They're for an event coming up, but I figured you might like one."

"That's so..." Isla shook her head, her cheeks flushed pink and a smile blossoming. "That's really sweet. Thank you."

"Open it."

He felt like a giddy boy, the way he used to on Christmas

morning. Not from opening his own gifts, but the special joy he'd long cherished from giving to others. It had been his job to hand out the luxuriously wrapped parcels, and he remembered with clarity the anticipation in waiting for his mother's smile. It was a special excitement he hadn't felt in a long time.

Not until this moment.

Her eyes flicked up to his and then back down to the book, and she caught the envelope sticking out the side with her thumb, using it to open up the title page. A delighted gasp shot through the air.

"It has my name on it!" Her mouth formed a surprised O. "You...you had him sign it for *me*?"

"Sure did."

Theo had ordered a staff member to take the book to the author's home in Soho so the man could personally sign it. Then it had been brought to Theo's apartment. No doubt the request had gotten tongues wagging because Theo never did stuff like this.

"I started reading these books when I was twelve and..." Something flickered across her face. "Well, I've actually never owned a copy before. I've always gotten them from the library."

She didn't have the money for books growing up. He caught the story underneath her words and it speared him in the heart. His life was far from perfect, but there were so many things he'd taken for granted.

"Well, anything you want from our catalog—name it. It's yours." He nodded stiffly, suddenly unsure of the point of this gesture. All he knew was that he'd felt compelled to do it, to give her something as a symbol of...

What, exactly?

Theo didn't know.

"Thank you. That's incredibly generous." Her smile was

suddenly shy, paired with eyes that were unguarded and expressive. "And what's this?"

Her thumb flicked the edge of the pearl envelope, as though she was unsure what to do with it. On reflection, it probably looked like a card of some kind. Maybe something *too* personal.

"It's, uh…" Theo cleared his throat. "An invitation."

Isla slipped the book into her bag and ran her nail under the seal of the envelope. "Looks fancy."

He watched for her reaction as she pulled the single sheet of thick, gleaming card stock out—a flicker of confusion in her eyes, the slight tilt of her head, her fingertip tracing the embossed edging.

"I don't understand," she said.

"I'm inviting you to my grandmother's gala. New management is taking over her charity, since I'm unable to do it myself, and we wanted to do a final send-off to honor her memory," he said. "I don't usually attend these kinds of things, to be honest. Gram knew I wasn't much for parties and she never pushed me. But I want to be there to support what she accomplished."

"And you want me to come?"

"I want you to come *with* me."

She blinked. "Oh."

Was that a good *oh* or a bad *oh*? The line seemed so fine he wasn't quite sure which side her reaction fell on.

"Like as a work thing?" she asked.

"Well, Camilla *isn't* invited since I'm pretty sure she'd ruin the entire thing by peeing on someone's foot." He let out a laugh and raked his hand through his hair. "So technically it wouldn't be a work thing as your dog-sitting duties would not be required."

Her lips parted, like a question was hovering on the tip of

her tongue. She wanted to know in what capacity he was inviting her—was it as a date? As a friend? As an...emotional support human? Theo wasn't sure what the answer to that question was. All he knew was that he wanted Isla by his side.

The thought of facing everyone alone and being forcibly reminded of the fact that his family was reduced to one made him want to barricade himself inside his apartment. He *knew* how alone he was. How alone he would be for the rest of his life. Nobody needed to remind him.

But if he had Isla's sunshine personality and her ready smile to accompany him, then maybe it would be that bit more bearable.

"I hate going to these things alone," he said, feeling like an absolute tool.

What kind of man was nervous about walking into a room full of people? He knew that was years of societal conditioning telling him that "being a man" meant never being vulnerable—a lesson that, for better or worse, he'd taken on and all but carved into stone—and the truth was, he *was* vulnerable in this situation.

He wanted her help and he was making a total hack job of asking for it.

"I tend to be a bit of a bastard when I'm nervous and I really don't want to dishonor my grandmother's memory," he admitted. "I'm comfortable around you, so I figured maybe if you came with me then I would be less likely to bite someone's head off if they ask the wrong question."

Isla's expression softened and she nodded. "I understand. Camilla is a bit the same way."

"You're not dog sitting me," he grumbled.

"But you want me to be your handler." Her lip twitched. "That's kind of a relief, because it felt like you were asking me on a date for a minute there."

Theo kept his face still and didn't show any reaction at all. Had she really disliked kissing him that much? It certainly hadn't felt like it. Oh no, at the time she'd melted into him like warm toffee. She'd kissed him back with excitement that matched his...at least he'd thought so.

He shook his head. "No, nothing like that."

"I'm happy to help so long as I can make sure my sister has someone to hang out with. She doesn't do so well being on her own at night."

Something tugged at Theo's heartstrings. The nights had always been the worst for him too, after he lost his parents.

"Let me know if you can make it," he said coolly, like he was no longer concerned with her answer. "I can always ask someone from the office if you can't."

She bit down on her lower lip and nodded. "I'll call Dani now and double-check."

With a nod, Theo reached for his laptop and tucked it under his arm so he could make his way back into the study. He was left with an uneasy feeling about the whole thing. On one hand, he was sure Isla would say yes and that she was only being a good sister by checking. Getting what he wanted always made Theo happy.

But on the other hand, he was annoyed by his own disappointed reaction to her comment about the date thing. Because disappointment meant he'd had expectations and expectations meant there was desire.

And desire was something that didn't have a place in his life.

For the remainder of the week Isla oscillated between being excited about the gala and feeling sick about it. She'd organized for Dani to have a sleepover with one of her friends from ballet and had found the perfect dress stuffed in the back of her closet with the tags still attached. Granted, they were consignment store tags because Isla couldn't have afforded to buy a dress like this new.

But the week after the Met Gala she was supposed to have attended an industry award night. Her team at the Gateway Agency had been nominated for Best Audience Engagement Campaign. It was a big deal—a *huge* recognition of their hard work—and she'd treated herself to something pretty in celebration.

Only, Isla had never made it to the event and the dress had never been worn.

The thought of glamming up and going someplace fancy was exciting. Not to mention that she'd be seeing Theo in a tux, which was sure to be the best visual of her entire life. When he'd confessed to feeling comfortable around her—implying a level of trust that she knew he didn't hand out easily—well, *that* warmed her heart.

And then the book... The sweet, personal gesture had made her feel special. Cared for. Appreciated.

But she shouldn't want those things from him.

"Whoa! You look *pretty*." Dani poked her head into the bathroom, her eyes widened in surprise.

"Because I'm such a cave troll normally. Gee, thanks." Isla laughed and continued to lean toward the mirror, combing a mascara wand through her lashes. Even doing her makeup, something that normally would feel natural as breathing for Isla, was fraught.

If she put too much on, was she trying to look appealing to Theo? If she did too little, would it look like she didn't care? Should she even be wearing something sexy to an event memorializing a dead woman?

Isla looked at her reflection. The emerald green dress had a somewhat plunging neckline and a slit from floor to midthigh, but the covered back and flutters of fabric gently resting on the tops of her shoulders stopped it from feeling *too* sexy. Although since she wasn't generously blessed in the chest area, Isla could easily forgo a bra and that *did* feel risqué.

Gah! Why was this all so confusing?

She didn't have butterflies in her stomach. Oh no. She had a goddamn army of dragons in there. Not to mention an echo in her head that said she was excited to see Theo's reaction to her, and *that* meant she wasn't simply dressing up for herself.

"I didn't mean it like that." Dani rolled her eyes and came over to wedge herself between Isla and the wall so she could watch. "I mean, it's not every day you wear a ball gown."

"That's very true."

"I thought you were working tonight." Dani watched her closely, eyes narrowed as if she was looking for anything that might hint at a lie.

"I am."

"You don't look like you're going to work."

Isla stuck her mascara wand back into the tube and tossed it into her makeup bag. All that was left was to apply some lipstick. She rummaged around for her fancy tube—the Dior one with the gold packaging that she'd scored at a press event earlier that year, which she saved for special occasions.

"What do you really want to know, Dani?" Isla pulled the cap off her lipstick and swiped the bullet across her lips. The color had a faint sheen and made her look a little poutier than what she had going on naturally. "Because it sounds like there's a question hiding you don't want to ask."

Dani scowled. "I'm just saying."

"I know you better than that." Isla turned to her little sister and placed a hand on her shoulder. "And I've always said you can ask me anything, right? No question is off-limits."

"Are you going on a date?" The worry in her voice caught in the back of Isla's throat. Dani's big blue eyes looked up at her unblinkingly, worry brimming so close to the surface it looked like it would spill over at any moment.

"No, sweet thing. I'm going to a stuffy, boring event with my boss because he asked for my help. Why would you think I'm going on a date?"

"Well, you're all dressed up and you look really pretty and you suggested that I have a sleepover at Lola's so I wondered if maybe you wanted me out of the house." Her eyes dropped to the floor. "If you want to have a boyfriend, you should have one."

Dani couldn't even look at her while she said the words. Isla figured her sister thought it was the right thing to say even though she didn't want it to happen—that was Dani in a nutshell, far too wise for her young years and caught between her own fear and her desire to be a good sister.

"Come here." Isla pulled Dani into a hug. "I know you're worried about me getting a boyfriend because you think I'll leave you like Mom did. One, that's not true. I will never leave you. And two, I *really* am going to a work thing. Cross my heart and hope to die."

"Stick a needle in your eye?"

"I'd rather not, but for you I would." Isla laughed. "Do you trust me?"

Dani looked up, a crease still between her brows. "Yes."

"Okay, then you can stop worrying. All your concerns have been dissolved." Isla bopped her on the head and Dani laughed, swatting at her. "You may now go on with your night, eat copious amounts of sugar and giggle over some boy who's far too young for me to know about."

"Lola's mom always makes us eat healthy." Dani pulled a face. "And not healthy like you do, where I can pick my vegetables. She makes us eat...kale."

Dani's expression of disgust was so visceral that Isla couldn't help but laugh. "Well, I appreciate that Mrs. Travers cares about your well-being, but I'm with you on the kale thing. It's gross."

"You have to chew it forever. It's like eating rubber leaves." Dani shuddered.

"Yes, but when you're in someone's home you have to respect their rules, okay?"

"I will. But I don't have to like it."

"And no sneaking it under the table to their dog, either." Isla narrowed her eyes at her sister. "I heard about that last time."

Dani rolled her eyes and flounced out of the bathroom with the drama that only a teenager could.

"I mean it!" Isla called after her. "And get your things together, we leave in five minutes."

Isla took one last glance at her reflection to check her makeup. She almost didn't recognize herself—this dolled-up, polished and primped version of herself was like a relic from another time. Even when she'd worked with the agency, getting dressed up was purely a practical thing, because they had to look the part for their clients.

The last time she'd dressed up because she wanted to look sexy and attractive had been years ago, back when she still thought she could juggle it all—her career, pseudo-motherhood, love. Back when she thought it was possible to be everything to everyone.

Now she knew better.

At the last minute she took off the necklace—a fine strand of faux-gold dangling toward her cleavage—leaving it on the bathroom counter. Then she wiped her lipstick off and replaced it with a boring clear balm.

Playing make-believe would only get her in trouble. She *wasn't* a woman who could have it all, and love and lust were too far down her list of priorities.

15

Theo had asked Irina to organize a limo for Isla, but for some unknown reason Isla had refused the offer. Given he needed to be at the venue early to meet with the new director and make sure everything was as his grandmother would have wanted it, he didn't want Isla being stuck hanging around until the party started—hence offering her the limo.

But she'd insisted on taking a cab and had even refused his offer to pay for it.

The past week had been a little awkward between them. He'd been ending his workday earlier than normal, hoping to catch a glimpse of her. And she was like a cat, wary and yet curious, padding through his house as though she didn't want him to notice she was there, but he'd caught her watching him a few times.

Despite all this, a line had been drawn in the sand and he would respect it—this wasn't a date. There would be no flirting, no touching. Certainly no kissing.

Would that stop him thinking about kissing her? Unlikely.

But he was a man of tremendous control. Of discipline and focus and a steel-like resolve that came from growing up fast in a fraught world. He never understood people who couldn't control their impulses, because what would life be like if one simply went around doing things because they felt like it? Chaos, that's what.

Isla was here as his employee tonight, and nothing more.

As the gala began, people poured into the warehouse event space. Theo's grandmother had always looked for unique venues for her charity events—turning her nose up at the pompous ballrooms at places like the Waldorf Astoria and The St. Regis New York. She would have loved this place. The red-brick factory facade housed a wide-open space inside, which had been transformed into an indoor garden. Theo was footing the bill for tonight's events, so he'd spared no expense to celebrate his grandmother's memory.

The room was filled with hanging baskets of heady gardenias and colorful hydrangeas, with big leafy plants and potted trees strung with fairy lights. Pathways had been created, dotted with standing tables and two bars where people could get drinks. There was even a swing draped with flowers. Old footage of Etna Francois-Garrison was projected onto the walls—black-and-white video of Gram when she was in her thirties, wearing a ball gown that seemed ultramodern for the time. Seeing her smile, which had never changed even as she'd aged, was like jabbing himself in the heart.

He caught Frank Ferretti watching the footage, lost in memories. For a moment he stood by the older man, in companionable and empathetic silence, before clamping a hand on his shoulder and thanking him for coming.

"Wouldn't miss it," Frank said gruffly, and Theo caught the slight sheen in his eyes.

They chatted for a moment and then he spotted Nia and excused himself to go talk to her. She was dressed in a sleek red dress, her curly black hair swept up in a way that showed off a pair of large gold earrings that glittered against her dark brown skin.

"You've done an outstanding job," Theo said. "Gram would be devastated to miss such a great party."

Nia smiled. "This would've looked amazing in the press photography."

"I appreciate that you respected my wishes."

"I was under the impression it was more of a command than a wish." Nia smirked.

Theo shot her a look. "Potato, po-tah-to."

Nia was another employee who'd been with the publishing house a long time, originally hired as a fresh-faced graduate by his father more than twenty years ago. She'd often volunteered her services to Etna, impressed by his grandmother's charity work and hungry to make a name for herself. As one of the most trusted and senior people in the whole company, she certainly had achieved that.

"I have to give credit to the event firm," Nia said. "They did the heavy lifting—both literally and metaphorically. I just rallied the troops."

"Rallying the troops is the important job."

"Don't you know it," she teased. Then her face turned serious, her dark eyes pinning him to the spot. "Are you still refusing to give a speech?"

"I only need to refuse once," he replied.

Nia rolled her eyes. "You're stubborn as a mule."

"I'm a man who knows what he wants. I won't be swayed no matter how persistent you are."

"I'll take that as a compliment," Nia replied. "And you owe me some time after this. My children have forgotten my name."

"Send me an email tomorrow. Whatever you want."

Nia bid him a good night as she headed off to check on the catering company. Theo hovered to the side of the room, positioning himself so he had a good vantage point of the main entrance. Two men in suits were checking invitations at the door, and people continued to trickle in and fill the room. It was a distinguished crowd—much like his grandmother's funeral had been. Senators, CEOs, blue bloods. There was even a prominent rapper who was covered in tattoos and wore a suit the same shade of gold as his front tooth. Etna had befriended the man a few years before she died, and while they made an unlikely pair she enjoyed his company very much and her keen eye had spotted his philanthropic spirit immediately.

People flocked to Theo, surprised to see him at a social gathering. It had been a long time. A *very* long time. And he tried his best not to let the tension of it all hike up his shoulders and make it look like he didn't want to speak to people, even though that was exactly how he felt. But he wasn't here for himself, tonight. He was here for his grandmother.

Out of the corner of his eye, Theo caught a flash of green. It was only when a hand raised tentatively, and he caught a familiar shy smile that he realized he was looking at Isla.

Holy shit. Maybe this was a giant mistake.

Theo walked away from the man who was talking to him without even excusing himself. It was almost like his feet were stuck to a magnetic track dragging him toward her. Isla's dark hair tumbled down her back and shoulders in glossy curls and her eyes were smoked with a deep green eye shadow. But her lips were bare, almost like her lipstick had been kissed away. For some reason, that contrast struck him as surprisingly erotic.

"Hi," she said. "This is quite a party."

"My grandmother was quite a woman." He held his hand out and she reached for him, her eyes coasting over his body. So, the appreciation was returned. "And that's quite a dress."

"You like?" Her eyes lit up.

He encouraged her to twirl around. The gleaming fabric rippled around her legs with the movement and the deeply cut neckline made his heart beat a little faster. "Although 'like' is putting it mildly."

What happened to no flirting?

"I'm glad I finally had a chance to wear it, actually." Isla's hand drifted to the front of the dress, almost like she was feeling a bit self-conscious. She needn't have, because she eclipsed every single person in the room. "I bought it for an award ceremony for work and…well, turns out you're no longer invited to those if you get fired."

Theo frowned. "Maybe I could talk to some people."

"Talk to some people?"

"My name means something around here, even if it's mostly driven by morbid curiosity. I know how to open doors." He cleared his throat. "Maybe I could help."

"Ah, but then I wouldn't be your dog sitter anymore, would I?" Isla pointed out.

Hmm, that was true. "I don't know why I have this protective urge when it comes to you."

Isla looked at him, her expression a mixture of curiosity and wonder and maybe a little bit of smugness. "I thought you didn't like me. Well, aside from the kiss thing."

The kiss *thing*. He scrubbed a hand over his jaw. "Don't feel bad, most people think I hate them. I have resting asshole face."

Isla burst out laughing and Theo couldn't help but grin. The sound was wonderful, pure and clear like a bell. When

Isla laughed, it was like the sun broke through the clouds even if it was completely dark outside.

"Resting asshole face, I like that." Her eyelashes lowered. "I happen to think your face is quite lovely."

Theo cleared his throat, aware that they were being watched. Irina was standing next to Nia and they were both looking in his direction, lips moving and heads slightly bowed. The last thing he needed was rumors flying around the office.

"Would you like a drink?" Theo asked, motioning toward the bar on the other side of the room. "I find it impossible to get through these things without an adult beverage."

Isla looked a little relieved. "Yes, please. I'm totally out of practice."

They headed toward the bar, which was a funky structure made of a live green wall strung with lights and dotted with flowers. The two women behind the bar were dressed in hot-pink dress shirts with black suspenders. The waiters carrying food around the venue were also in brightly colored shirts and suspenders.

"My grandmother had a rule about hosting parties," he said to Isla as they waited in line. He could easily have gone to the front to order their drinks, but Theo was more than happy to stand around chatting with Isla. "Never let people sit down."

"Really?" Isla laughed. "That sounds like hell for all the women here. I've seen heels that would double as murder weapons."

"People don't mingle if they're sitting down, and the whole point of a social gathering is to meet people...or so she said."

"You disagree."

"I mean, maybe she's right. I wouldn't know. I don't really attend parties."

"They're good for people watching," Isla said. "I was always that girl on the edge of the room, observing. I liked to guess what people's stories might be based on their behavior. It's fun."

"What would your story be for that guy?" He subtly pointed to a couple at a stand-up table. The man was in a traditional tuxedo and the woman wore a shimmery gold dress that barely reached her midthigh. They were younger than most of the crowd, and the guy was talking animatedly while the girl smiled on. "I'll tell you if you get it right."

Isla narrowed her eyes. "I'm going to guess that *he's* the plus-one."

"Good catch. How did you know that?"

"It seems like he's trying a bit too hard. Watch his mouth, he barely takes a breath. I'd put money on her being bored out of her skull but like a well-raised society woman, she's trying to be polite. The smile is fake, though. I'd say they were set up by someone—maybe her mother? She's regretting saying yes." Isla's blue eyes skated up to Theo and she raised her brows. "How'd I do?"

"I'm impressed." Theo nodded. "That young lady is Serena Vandoorne, daughter of Belgian diplomat and heir to a considerable family fortune. The guy I don't recognize, but I can tell he's from new money. I would say *no* to the setup. It's more likely she brought him here to irritate her mother. You nailed her regretting her actions, however."

"This is fun." They arrived at the bar and ordered some drinks—a champagne for Isla and a whisky neat for Theo. Then they perched at a table with a good view of the crowd. "Pick another one."

Theo nodded toward another couple, in their midforties. The woman wore a flowing black dress and a large, brightly colored necklace that sat like a plate across her collarbone. It was studded with vibrant jewels in yellow, pink and green.

"Hmm." Isla watched the couple for a few heartbeats. "She's pregnant."

He leaned closer so it looked like they were having a private conversation rather than speculating on the guests. The scent of Isla's perfume, something soft and warm and a little sweet, wound through his system, and it took everything in him not to turn his head and brush his lips across the smooth line of her jaw. Instead, he reached for his drink and took a healthy swig, relishing the smoothness and the warm glow that had started inside him.

"What makes you say that?" he asked.

"She hasn't touched her champagne and she keeps reaching for her water. Plus, that dress she's wearing is very loose." Isla nodded. "Most people wouldn't notice, because her necklace is a complete showstopper. That entire outfit is designed to be boring as hell on the bottom so that nobody looks too closely below the neckline."

"Fascinating."

"I don't think she's told him yet," Isla added.

"How do you know that?"

"She seems fidgety, excited. Maybe they've been trying for a long time and she finally fell pregnant. There's an anticipation to her." Isla nodded. "Close?"

"I have no idea. I was wondering whether you'd guess he's ex-military."

"Anybody can see that. Look at his hair." Isla took another sip of her champagne. "And you sure know a lot for someone who doesn't get out."

"My assistant loves to gossip. I absorb it by osmosis." He nodded to another couple, an older man and woman both with snowy white hair. The woman wore a navy pantsuit and her partner looked equally slick. They were dancing even though there was no dance floor and they looked at one another like there was nobody else in the room. "What about them?"

"Madly in love." Isla smiled dreamily. "I feel like you picked them to trick me. My first instinct would have been to say they've been married for decades but now I'm thinking maybe...recently married?"

"Damn." Theo shook his head in wonder. "They got married last June. He's eighty-one and she's seventy-nine."

"Friends of your grandmother?"

"Yeah, she was the maid of honor." He laughed. "I don't think I've seen someone so excited to be part of a bridal party."

"That's sweet." Isla watched the couple swaying for a moment, but then her glance cut back to Theo. "It's really lovely that you're here even though it's not your scene. Your grandmother would be very proud, I'm sure."

"Don't count on it." Theo swished his drink around the glass tumbler, watching the amber liquid catch the light. "They wanted me to give a speech tonight, but I don't do public speaking. Not anymore."

"Not anymore?" Isla frowned.

"Long story. But everybody is going to wonder whether I don't care enough to get up and say something."

"Anybody who's been in your presence for more than three seconds can see how much you care about her." Isla looked at him so intently, he wondered if she had some kind of X-ray vision. "Don't let anybody tell you otherwise."

"You're not going to attempt to convince me that I should do it?" Talk about a surprise reaction—Isla seemed like the uber-responsible type who would put herself out of her comfort zone to do the right thing. "I have to say, that's not what I expected."

"People show they care in different ways."

Like giving someone a signed book from their favorite author.

"You know," she said. "It's that whole love language thing. Corny as it sounds, I think there's some merit to it. Some people show love with big extravagant gifts or public declarations and grand gestures. But other people prefer more personal, meaningful things. Something that shows a person truly understands what their partner wants and needs."

"For example?"

"Well, this is going to sound ridiculous but…" Isla laughed. "I try to do a pizza night with my sister once a month. We share it, and I always order one with olives on it even though I hate olives."

"Because she likes them," he said with a nod. "Why don't you do half and half?"

"Because I give her all the olives I pick off. The kid is weird, she puts so many olives on I swear you can't even see the meat or the sauce anymore." Isla shuddered. "But it's not only about the olives. She likes the ritual of it. It shows that we balance one another out, in a way."

"I can see that."

"So no, I don't think you need to stand up in front of a room and publicly declare you love someone for that love to be real and meaningful. Given your history, I understand why you wouldn't want to."

"It's easier to be silent," he said, searching her face. "That way people can't use your words or emotions against you."

"So long as you say something when it matters," she replied with a nod.

He had. Before his grandmother passed, he told her that he wasn't sure he would have made it through his parents' deaths without her.

"Frankly, I think we could all stand to do a little less talking and a little more listening," Isla added.

She was so close that he could kiss her now if he leaned in

a little further. He could capture those lips with his own and plunder that sweet mouth and drag her gently curved frame against his. They could sneak out. Or hide in the trees while he devoured her.

Stop it. You know where the line is.

But the more time he spent with Isla, the more he understood why some people put everything on the line to get what they wanted, to get *who* they wanted. No other woman had ever made him feel so strongly. It was almost like he could feel the thread between them being fortified. She understood him, respected the way he was and wasn't trying to change him or mold him into the version of a man she *thought* he should be. She wasn't trying to exploit him or use him.

And that was a new experience.

Isla found herself relaxing into the evening as the champagne worked its magic on her coiled muscles and fear of not belonging. People flocked to Theo, and she helped him gracefully exit conversations by cutting in whenever they went on too long. He'd mouthed her a grateful "thank you" as they'd walked away from a particularly nosy conversation-starter. It was uncanny how in-tune they were, like they were dialed in to the same frequency and talking in their own private language.

She savored the warmth of his hand at her lower back and her body sang out whenever his hand accidentally brushed hers. God, it felt like she was in high school again! Lusting over a boy well out of her league and getting warm and fuzzies from silly little things like a secretly shared smile or look.

It means nothing.

And it should stay that way.

They found a spot to stand that wasn't in the main thoroughfare, so Theo could easily see who was approaching him.

"Hey," he said, touching her arm and sending another unnecessary shiver through her. "I need to check something with Irina, so I'm going to grab her for a minute. Do you want another champagne? I can get you one on the way back."

"No thanks." She'd already finished her third and her head was a little fuzzy. Not in a bad way, but in a way that told her if her lips got any looser then she might say something she'd regret in the morning.

Like how you wish we could get out of here and go somewhere private...like back to Theo's place.

Her mind brought on a rush of images—fantasies tinted with the memory of their kiss, which made them feel alive with color and taste and sound. She suppressed a delicious shiver and clenched her hands down by her sides, trying to distract herself from the desire pulsing through her.

Off-limits. Out of your league. A bad freaking idea.

"You sure?" His lips curved into a tempting smile and his rich, warm eyes made her want to melt into him.

"Uh-huh." She smiled brightly—maybe too bright, because his eyes narrowed in interest. "I'm a lightweight, I'm afraid. My dirty little secret is out."

His chuckle was dark and deadly. "I'm calling bullshit on that one. If you're hiding a dirty little secret, it's got nothing to do with your drinking fitness."

She sucked in a breath, the fitted waist of her dress constricting her. For a moment she felt everything—the brush of the faux-silk on her skin, the throb in her feet from her shoes, the dull ache between her legs where she hadn't felt anything but her own hand for years.

"Can I plead the Fifth?" she asked.

"Worried about self-incrimination, interesting." His gaze swept over her. "We're going to pick this conversation up the second I get back."

He headed into the crowd, disappearing into an area marked Staff Only, leaving Isla alone. The rest of the room rushed back into her attention—the clink of glasses, the soft beat of the music, laughter, whispers, hellos.

"Do you mind if I rest here for a moment?" A woman smiled at Isla as she juggled a half-empty champagne flute and a gold clutch. A stiletto dangled from the crook of her finger by one elegant strap. "I'm having a shoe emergency."

"Of course." Isla moved around to the side of the small, high table and motioned for the woman to take her spot. "Broken strap?"

"It's the damn clasp." She dumped her glass and clutch on the table and then brought the shoe up to her eye. "The pin pushes through to the wrong side and then I can't get it back on."

A man joined the woman a second later, his hand sliding seductively around her waist. His eyes were a little unfocused and he smiled at Isla in a way that made her back up a step. Drunk people were not her favorite.

"I saw you hanging off Theodore Garrison's arm," he said, nudging his date. The woman looked up with interest. "Who would have thought he finally brought a woman out in public."

"Oh, I'm…" She shook her head. "I work for Theo."

He'd been introducing her as such all evening, the line in the sand clear despite the buzz going on inside her body.

"Really?" The man raised his eyebrow suspiciously. "You two don't have a workplace vibe."

"Well, I *do* work for him," she replied stiffly.

"You look really familiar." He narrowed his eyes and Isla had to hold back a laugh.

The chances of them running in the same circles were pretty slim. Even when she'd been rubbing elbows with fa-

mous people, rich kids weren't in her orbit. Most of the people she'd worked with were actors, models or entertainment
personalities building their personal brands, and frequently
they had working-class backgrounds.

Growing up without much tended to be good motivation
for a strong work ethic.

"I get that a lot," Isla replied. "Friendly face."

"No." The man shook his head. "I've got a memory like
a steel trap."

He tapped the side of his head and the woman rolled her
eyes like she very much did *not* agree with that statement. But
then she looked at Isla again, eyes narrowing. "Yeah, actually
you *do* look familiar."

Something frigid slid down the back of Isla's spine. They
weren't looking at her in that generic "have we met before"
way that people did at social events. She scanned her memory, but neither registered. And she *was* good at remembering
faces and names—it had been an asset in her old line of work.

"Something tells me we didn't go to school together," she
quipped. Isla had grown up in Highbridge, and she doubted
very much that either of these two had ever ventured higher
than Ninety-Sixth Street, let alone crossed the Harlem River.

"What did you do before you worked for Garrison?" he
asked. Isla had the sense of being a goldfish in a glass bowl
with someone tapping on the outside and making ripples in
her world.

"Uh, I…" Her eyes skated in the direction of where Theo
had gone a few moments ago, hoping that he might be strid-
ing back and able to return the favor of extracting her from
this conversation. But no such luck. "I worked in marketing."

"For who?"

Shit. She could lie and excuse herself from the interroga-
tion, but what if they knew who she was. She opened her

mouth to respond, but the guy—who'd been tapping away at his phone—suddenly gasped.

"You're *her*!" He turned the phone around and Isla went cold all over.

On the small screen was the video that would haunt her for the rest of her life.

She was standing next to Amanda, worry streaked across her face. The camera captured the luxurious hotel room behind her.

"Pace yourself," Isla said, following the sentence with a nervous giggle. "You've got this, okay? Do your thing. Look beautiful, smile for the cameras, and then go and enjoy the rest of the night."

There was a pause for several heartbeats, then Amanda clamped a hand over her mouth and promptly vomited all down the front of her couture gown. The chunky fluid splattered the floor and there was a collective gasp in the room as everyone jumped back, out of the splash zone.

Isla could still smell it and her stomach rocked violently, threatening to bring up the champagne and canapés she'd consumed.

"Holy shit, I can't believe it!" The guy's laugh was like nails on a blackboard. Isla felt her face growing hotter and hotter, and her head started to swim.

Suddenly there were more people at the table, all laughing and pointing.

"We watched this in my office for *days* after it happened," the drunk guy said. "Thank you for the entertainment. Nothing like watching a Disney princess blow chunks."

Isla's breath came faster, her adrenaline system kicking in and making her feel shaky all over. "Please stop."

"Cut it out, Brodie." The girl who'd been fixing her shoe glared at her friend. "Don't be a jerk."

"It's just a bit of fun." Another guy leered at her. They all stunk like whisky and cigars. "I bet you got fired, huh? Can't imagine the boss would have been happy you broadcast *that* to the whole world."

"That moment where she says 'we can fix this'—oh my God, I laughed so hard. You can't fix that shit, honey." The first guy cackled and slapped his friend on the back. "We can fix this!"

"Did you know it's a sound on TikTok?" The second guy got out his phone. "You're famous, baby."

Isla wanted the ground to open up and swallow her whole. Tears pricked her eyes but she begged herself not to cry—that would only make things worse. Her mortification level had been well and truly reached. Grabbing her evening bag, she wedged it under one arm and pushed past the group, head down. One of the guys grabbed her arm, making her almost stumble.

"Oh, don't be like that. We're only joking." His eyes were more glazed than a Krispy Kreme. "Can't you see how funny it is?"

Out of the corner of her eye, Isla saw Theo approach, his face filled with thunder. He clamped a firm hand on the man's forearm and wrenched him back, causing him to yelp in surprise. The group appeared to be in their early twenties—possibly children of the people who were here to support the charity.

"Didn't your parents ever teach you not to grab a woman who doesn't want to be grabbed?" Theo said, his voice hard-edged and rough. He had a good few inches on the younger man, who tried unsuccessfully to wrestle out of Theo's grip. "Apologize."

"Fuck you." The guy tried to shove Theo off, but he couldn't get free.

Theo leaned in and whispered something in his ear and the

younger man's face drained of color. When he looked at Isla, his eyes were wide. "Sorry."

"Louder," Theo growled.

"I'm sorry." The younger man looked suitably humiliated and Theo released him.

"Now get the fuck out of here before I have security pat you down."

The group scattered like a flock of seagulls. Isla felt something wet on her cheeks, and brushed the back of her hand across her face in horror. Tears. "You shouldn't have done that."

"Why not?" Theo's eyes were almost glowing with anger. "Someone needs to teach them a lesson, since it's clear their parents don't."

"That's not your job."

"Why were they giving you a hard time?" he asked, coming closer. Isla hugged her bag to her stomach, like she needed the protection of something between them.

"You didn't hear?"

"All I saw was you trying to leave and some asshole laying a hand on you. Now, before you give me the 'I can take care of myself' speech, I *know* you can. Okay?" He took another step closer. "But you're here because of me and I'm responsible for that. Which makes it my job to do something if I see you're being mistreated."

Isla's shoulders relaxed a little. "What did you say to him that made him apologize?"

"I said he should do a better job hiding the drugs in his pocket."

Her eyes widened. "He had drugs on him?"

"I didn't know for sure, but it wasn't a wild leap. You can bet I'm going to have a chat with Nia about the guest list and how those assholes were let in." He shook his head. "It's the problem with people who've grown up with no troubles—it makes them entitled."

Isla nodded. Her stomach was churning up a storm. No matter how hard she tried, she'd never be able to undo her mistake. It was captured forever. She'd become a TikTok sound, for crying out loud! A perpetual joke. Something to be mocked.

"I have to go." Isla walked past Theo, avoiding his fiery gaze and hoping she'd be able to scrub the shame from her skin with a hot shower.

But to her surprise, Theo fell in step alongside her. "Good idea."

She looked up at him. "No, *I* have to go. You can stay without me, you'll be fine. You don't need me."

"No, but maybe I want you," he said simply.

She almost tripped over her own feet but managed to catch herself before she went A over T. "You don't want me."

The edge of his lip twitched like he was trying to suppress a smirk. "That a fact?"

"Yes." She nodded. "Trust me."

"I notice your response wasn't 'but I don't want you' by the way. I find that interesting."

They were in the middle of the gala—surrounded by pink-and-gold twinkling lights, leafy plants and the heady aroma of flowers. It was magical. Like something from *Alice in Wonderland*. He looked even more mysterious dressed in black and smelling like gentle wood smoke and something warm and rich.

"This is the part where you confirm whether I'm right or not," he said, leaning in and letting the warmth of his breath skate over her skin.

"You're right, I didn't give that response," she replied, her voice tight.

"But this isn't a date."

She *had* made that statement a week ago, when he'd given her the invitation. It had been solely a reminder for herself, like she'd needed to hear it said out loud in order for her brain to finally get the message. But right now, being in his space, smelling him, wanting him, she had no idea what this was anymore.

"It isn't a date *here*," she said softly.

What are you doing? This is exactly what happened last time. He opened the door and you walked right on through like a sucker.

But she wanted to get out of here...with him. Not because he'd come to her aid when she needed it, but because every time she learned more about him it only made her hungrier for him. For the next layer. The next secret detail.

She wanted to drown herself in the knowledge of him.

"I have an idea." His hand came to her lower back again and her body sang out at the touch, only this time he slipped his hand farther, curling around her waist and tugging her closer. "We leave now, because parties are dull and I'd much rather have you one-on-one than share you with anyone in this room. We go back to my place and have a drink and then, if you'd like to go home, I'll get my driver to take you."

She turned, her face a mere inch from his, heart beating wildly in her chest. Suddenly her dress felt too tight, too firm. She was hot all over, need creating a drumbeat in her bloodstream that was like fists pounding the earth.

"What do you say?" he asked, his nose almost brushing hers.

"Yes." The word hissed out of her like the last bit of control was leaving her body and evaporating into the heady, floral air. "Let's go."

16

The entire ride back to Theo's place was an exercise in restraint. Isla had slid her hand across the back of the private car to grab Theo's, slipping her fingers between his as the lights blurred past them in the window.

Neither one of them spoke a word the whole way home. When the driver pulled into the underground car park, he followed the lines toward an area with another security gate. *This* was how Theo got in and out of the building every morning without being seen. For a moment she wondered what the hell she was doing—stealing away with a man who did everything in his power to be a ghost.

They walked toward the private elevator entrance, hand-in-hand. It opened immediately and they stepped inside, his thumb brushing over her knuckles in a way that was gentle and reassuring. Tender even. When he gave a squeeze, some of her apprehension melted away.

Some, but not all. He was her boss. Her employer.

And while this situation didn't feel like a typical boss/employee relationship—because this *wasn't* her career, only a temporary measure and she wouldn't rely on Theo for important things such as reference checks—there was still a little part of her brain that flagged and cataloged risks.

This could go south. Fast.

She toyed with the idea of backing out, of calling the whole thing off and requesting to go home right now. It would be safer, that way. Safer for her bank account. Safer for her future. Safer for her heart.

What does your heart have to do with any of this?

As if he sensed retreat may be imminent, Theo turned to Isla and brought his hands up to cradle her face. He hovered there for a moment, as if giving her the chance to back out or pull away or tell him to stop. But she was molten and her eyes fluttered instinctively shut as he lowered his lips. There was a steady hum of anticipation in her bloodstream, a beat that found rhythm with her heart and made a tightness gather in her belly.

She could have backed away. Maybe she *should* have backed away. But Isla was as immovable as a stone monument, her lips parting and her head tipping slightly back so that when he kissed her, it was deep and penetrating. The brush of his lips over hers was sweet relief—because she'd been thinking about kissing him again, ever since that stolen moment in his kitchen. She'd been dreaming about what might have come next.

It was a dream she'd *never* harbored before, not about any man. Not about anything that wasn't aligned to her goal: creating stability for Dani. And this was anything but stable. It was shaking ground beneath her feet and a roaring wind scattering her hair and adrenaline making her heart thump faster than ever before.

"My God, you taste good." Theo's breath skated across her skin as he kissed along her jaw and down to her neck. Isla heard a moan before registering that it had come from her lips and her hands curled into the lapels of Theo's tuxedo. "You smell good too, what *is* that?"

Perfume. Something outrageously expensive in a bottle that looked fit for a museum. The gift had come from Amanda and Isla hadn't been able to bring herself to use it until tonight. Anything from her old life—luxury items she would never have been able to afford on her own—turned her stomach these days, like they carried the stench of her mistake. But she'd wanted to fit into Theo's world, even if it was only an illusion.

And it most definitely was an illusion.

"Maybe I wake up smelling like this," she said huskily.

"I hope I get to find out."

Her response was cut off by a soft *ping* as the elevator doors slid open. Despite the fact that she'd come into his apartment every morning for the last few weeks, there was an energy charging the air tonight that made everything look different.

"Ready?" he asked with a wicked smile as he stepped into his apartment.

Her breath hitched. "Of course."

He held his hand out to her, ever the perfect gentleman. There was something slightly old-fashioned about his manners, an ingrained politeness that made her feel safe, cared for. And, if she was being honest, it made her feel a little bit like Cinderella.

Allowing him to grasp her hand, Isla used her other to hold the length of her dress as she stepped out of the elevator. Her heels made soft clicking sounds against the floor and she released the fabric of her dress with a soft *whoosh*. The silk whispered over her skin in a way that felt deeply sensual.

Only one lamp remained on, which cast the room in a soft, intimate glow. Outside, Manhattan sparkled like she'd never seen before. They were high up and the city stretched out before them, lights glistening against an inky sky, winking at her as if they knew exactly what she was about to do.

Like they knew every single naughty thought swirling in her head.

"I knew the view was amazing," she said, walking to the window and pressing a palm against the glass. "But this is…"

"It's something else at night, isn't it?" He came up behind her, his presence warm at her back. He brushed her long hair to one side, exposing the cutouts at the back of her dress and pressing his lips to one little exposed area of skin. "Do you want that drink?"

She shook her head, unsure what to do, what to say. What the hell was *wrong* with her? She'd been on dates before. She'd come back to a man's house for "a drink" and knew what it meant. More importantly, she *wanted* to be here. God, how she wanted it.

Against every sensible thought in her head, Isla wasn't turning on her heel and walking away now. She couldn't. Because as risky as this was, she couldn't live with a lifetime of "what if" questions when it came to Theo Garrison.

She turned to face him and mentally pressed down on her doubts. If she was going to do this then she refused to let worries dampen her enjoyment. "I'm okay."

"Are you nervous?" He reached out to toy with a loose curl.

"What makes you ask that?" She looked up at him, willing herself to come across as confident and sure of herself and all those other things she wished she could be again. It was like life had taken a wrecking ball to her sense of self and she wasn't sure how long she'd have to sift through the ruins before she could put herself back together again.

"Maybe *I'm* a little nervous," he said. He couldn't seem to stop touching her—his fingertips playing with her hair, the delicate strap of her dress, the chain of her evening bag.

"You?" Isla scoffed. If Theo was nervous then she was John D. Rockefeller.

He looked like a god in his tuxedo. A broad-shouldered, dark-haired, smoldering-eyed god. Even without saying a word or moving a muscle, he radiated power. Authority. At the gala, she'd seen him in full form—the way people watched him and listened to him, curious and magnetically drawn even when he didn't want their attention.

And the way he'd fiercely defended her tonight like she meant something to him. Like he cared...

That man had nothing to be nervous about.

"What?" Theo stared at her. "You think men don't get nervous in these situations?"

"Men maybe, but not gods."

Now it was his turn to make a noise of derision. "I'm no god."

"Seems like you are." She trailed her fingertips along the buttons of his shirt, then over the silk of his lapels. "Tonight, people hung off your every word. They flocked to you."

"That's because I don't get out much. You have no idea how much of a rare occurrence this was." Something flickered across his face—like a shadow. But the light hadn't shifted around them. "I'm not..."

Isla watched him, curious. "What?"

"Normal."

No, he was far from normal. A prince up in his tower, locked away and obsessed with privacy. He was like nobody Isla had ever met before.

"What's normal anyway?" she asked, choosing to make light of the situation.

"Good point."

"So, *are* you nervous?"

He laughed and the sound was deliciously dark, utterly captivating. It rang through Isla's body like church bells, sending a shower of sparks over her. Yeah, Theo was *anything* but normal.

"Maybe a little," he admitted. "It's been a while since I had a woman in my home."

"I've been here every day," she whispered.

Theo smoothed his hands over her shoulders and down her arms, then he eased her backward. Cool glass hit her back and she shivered and goose bumps rippled across her skin as her breath quickened.

She wanted this. Badly.

"Not like this." His body crowded hers, his hands gliding back up and tracing the deep neckline of her dress. Her insides softened, the coil of tension slowly unwinding itself. She became liquid. "Not for *me*."

Lord, this man. This unusual, remote, wonderful man.

Isla didn't need to stretch up too far, since her heels gave her an extra few inches, and she wound her arms around his neck, lining her body to his. Her dress was thin, and she felt every bit of him through it.

"Well, you don't have anything to be nervous about." Her lips brushed over his skin. "I want to be here. I want...this."

And as soon as she spoke the words out loud, she knew there was no turning back. The truth was out there and Isla wasn't going to make it home tonight. Theo brushed his lips against her neck and she leaned her head farther to one side, encouraging him to keep kissing her there. Warm breath skated over her skin as he trailed a blazing path up to the sweet spot under her ear. He pressed against her, wedging her between his hard body and the thick glass.

"Good." He all but growled the word. "Because I've been thinking about this a lot. Too much."

"Me too." Perhaps it was risky to admit it—but Theo had been a daily feature in her thoughts. The permanent star of her dreams. The subject of her fantasies.

"Every day you come here looking like…" He broke off and swore under his breath. "Do you have any idea how maddening it's been to watch you? You're like sunshine and light and it's so beautiful I can't stand it."

Hot, pulsing need flowed through Isla, making her head feel light and a little dizzy. When had she *ever* been the subject of anyone's attention in a good way? People either looked at her like she was a colossal failure or they didn't look at her at all. There was no in between. She wasn't special. She wasn't lucky.

If Theo was worried about *not* being normal, then Isla was his opposite. Her life was relentlessly average. This dress, this perfume, this…everything, it wasn't her. Not the real her.

His hand ran down her waist, over her hip and to the spot where the fabric split at her right thigh. With a deft touch, he skated his palm through the gap and soon he was touching her skin to skin. There was fire in his eyes, a light in the dark depths that made her suck in a breath. Theo was a man with many layers and tonight she got the sense that she was peeling them back, one by one, trying to find out what was underneath.

As he skimmed his hand higher up her thigh, parting her dress further, his eyes never left hers. It was like they were watching to see who might break first. Who might blink.

But then Theo's hand shifted, skating around to the inside of her thigh, and Isla knew she'd lost. She shifted, opening her legs so that he could touch her more easily. When he pressed the heel of his hand against her sex, her knees almost buckled. There was something so languid about his movements. So decadent. He wasn't rushed. Wasn't following a well-worn pattern or trying to impress her with any moves.

The cool glass of the window was sweet relief against her back and she let her head loll against it. The room was silent, save for the thundering of her heart. Theo brushed his fingertips over her underwear, a pair of silky panties that she hadn't worn in so long they'd been shoved right to the back of her drawer. Her life didn't need lingerie. Not until tonight.

But the thought of him peeling that inky black scrap from her body was enough to have a moan clogging the back of her throat. Her body sparked as he slipped a finger beneath the elastic of her underwear, stroking her.

"Good?" he asked, his lips brushing her ear.

She nodded, curling her fingers into his hair and pressing her mouth to his. He kissed her like the end of the world was coming, deep and desperate and thorough. He was hard against her and, in a moment of lust, she reached out to touch him. Steel length met her fingertips as she ran her hand up and down, enjoying the way he expelled a silent breath against her neck.

It wasn't enough. She needed to feel the real him. Needed to feel him naked and hot in her palm. When she reached for his fly, he moved her hand away. "Not yet. I need to see all of you first. Turn around."

Isla sucked in a breath. The idea that Theo was nervous was total bullshit—the dark, commanding tone sung through the air like he was born to utter those exact words. And she was under his spell.

Isla turned to face the window, looking out over the glittering city in all its glorious detail. In the reflection of the glass, she caught Theo's eye. He was almost glowing with intensity and the second his hand brushed her back, she shivered. He didn't need any guidance to find the closure cleverly concealed by a piece of fabric.

The sound of her zipper being lowered cut through the silence and cool air hit Isla's back for a second before warm lips trailed the length of her spine. Theo released the fabric and her dress slithered to the ground, puddling at her feet. Underneath she wore only the black silky panties, which were trimmed with lace and had a cheeky cutout at the back.

There was a masculine sound—a gruff, pleasure-filled sound—behind her. "I'm never going to get this image out of my head, Isla."

She shifted her view to look at her own reflection—wide, blackened eyes, tousled hair, swollen lips. Her nipples were peaked from the cool air and excitement, and her hands fluttered by her sides.

"Show me," he said, his voice pure gravel. She turned again, moving to cross her arms over herself, but Theo caught her wrist in one hand. "*All* of you."

She felt like a gift being unwrapped and something told her Theo would be the type to take his time, carefully peeling tape and paper from a precious item and savoring the moment. Isla hooked her fingertips into the waistband of her underwear and slid it down her hips. It too whispered to the ground and then she stood—only in her barely worn high heels and cheap earrings, feeling so out of her element and yet perfectly safe that she wasn't sure she'd experience such a dichotomy ever again.

"Do you only want to look?" she asked.

"No." He lowered himself in front of her, bracing his palms against her thighs. "I want to do way more than just look."

"Good." Isla's throat was so tight she had to squeeze the word out, excitement drumming inside her. The sensation built, like a bolt being tightened. Or a bow being pulled taut.

He rubbed his palms up and down the front of her thighs until his thumbs brushed over the apex of her sex, teasing the tight bundle of nerves there. Isla gasped. Cool air brushed over her heated skin as Theo blew gently on her before planting a chaste kiss on her. Electricity galloped through her veins and Isla reached down for his head, to steady herself.

"Tell me how it feels."

"Intense." It had been a while—a *long* while—and sex was a luxury. Like most luxuries, it didn't feature prominently in her life. "I…it's been…"

"I know. Me too."

He ran his tongue between the folds of her sex, drawing a line to her clit. Her eyes clamped shut when his lips descended on her, his tongue moving in a way that turned her liquid. She was no longer a woman, no longer human. She was nothing but pleasure.

Pressing one palm against the glass behind her, the other threaded through his hair and held him in place, showing him what she wanted. His tongue swirled and darted, lapped and licked and flicked until her thighs quaked. She'd forgotten how good this could feel. A pressure built inside her, pinpricks of light dancing behind her shuttered eyelids and she chased the feeling.

"Yes!"

Suddenly she was tumbling, falling and crashing down into something wonderful and exhilarating, familiar and yet new at the same time. His name flew from her lips as pleasure ripped through her, buckling her knees so they sagged against his shoulders.

"I've got you." Theo threaded an arm behind the backs of her thighs and scooped her up, carrying her through his apartment.

She knew where his bedroom was, but her brain was addled. Foggy with lust. He pressed his lips down to hers as he walked and she lost herself in his kiss, knowing that she would never be able to look at him—or herself—the same ever again.

17

As Theo carried Isla through his house, the weight of her body a delight in his arms and her cries still echoing in his head, it occurred to him that tonight had contained a lot of firsts. The first time he'd appeared publicly—aside from his grandmother's funeral—in years. The first time he'd had the desire to draw attention to himself by stepping in to protect another person. And now he was carrying a beautiful woman to his bed as though he was a newlywed sweeping his bride over the threshold.

But that's what Isla did to him.

She gave him a glimpse into another world, a world where he wasn't willfully alone. A world where his heart hadn't been shattered into a million irreparable pieces so long ago that broken was the only way he knew how to be. A world where he might fall in love with the right woman and become whole again.

That's not what this is.

Sure, he could tell himself that. Whatever would help him sleep better at night.

He walked them into his bedroom and lowered Isla down onto the bed. She looked like an angel who'd fallen out of the sky, wings lost but the ethereal glow of her skin and the gleam of her dark hair proving she couldn't be merely mortal. Or maybe she was a lost goddess, a temptation sent to throw a spanner into his carefully controlled life.

"I like the way you're looking at me right now," she said. She was still wearing her strappy sandals, glittering gold strands crisscrossing in the most delicate way.

He lowered himself, knees sinking into the bed, as he brought his hand to her ankle. Cradling the joint with one hand, he unfastened the fiddly strap and unwound it so he could slide the sandal free from her foot.

"How am I looking at you?" he asked as he worked the second one free.

"A little wondrous."

"Is that what the kids are calling it these days?" He raised an eyebrow as he dropped the second shoe to the floor. Now she was completely naked, spread out like a gleaming gift under a Christmas tree.

She laughed. "It's not a code word."

"Well, I like the way you're looking at me, too."

And he meant it. Most people looked at Theo like he was either a zoo exhibit or a ghost, but Isla was different. When she looked at him it was like she saw him. The Theo who lived way, way under the layers of protection—both physical and emotional—all the way to the joyous boy who'd once had the world in front of him.

For a long time, Theo had thought that little boy died along with his parents. But Isla made him wonder...

Maybe that part of him had simply been asleep.

"If you've interpreted my look as 'hurry up and get undressed' then you're correct." She propped herself up on her forearms. "Because if you don't get out of that tux soon, I might lose my nerve."

He unwound the bow tie at his neck and shrugged out of his jacket, laying the items of clothing neatly over the back of a velvet reading chair. He toed off his shoes. Then removed his socks, taking his time and watching as Isla's eyes grew smoky and wide. They were beautiful eyes, a vibrant sky blue with flecks of stormy gray and navy.

He undid his tuxedo trousers and pulled the zip down, noting the way her eyes followed the movement. Each piece came away from him, like baggage being shed, and when he was done, Isla held her hand out as if inviting him to get lost in her.

And lost was exactly where he wanted to be.

He came down to the bed, wrapping her up in his arms and lowering his head down to hers. His nose brushed her cheek and then his lips coaxed hers open, tongue sliding as he tasted her deeply.

"How's that nerve doing?" he asked, planting one hand beside her head so he could look at her.

"Pretty good," she said softly, her hand toying with his hair. "I...I don't want this to affect things, you know. I like working with Camilla and I..."

For a moment he saw the worry streak across her face. Of course she was worried—he knew that her employment situation had been dire. God, what happened tonight was a prime example that people had long memories and failing empathy.

He knew that better than anyone.

"I give you my word that nothing that happens tonight will affect tomorrow." He brushed the hair from her face, catching her eyes so she knew he was serious. "This is now, and tomorrow is then and they have no bearing on one another."

"You should have been a writer," she said, softly. "You have a beautiful way with words."

Running his hands under the hollow of her back, he lifted her up to him and she wound her arms around his neck. If he didn't have her soon he was going to burst. But there was no way he was going to do anything else until he knew that she was all in.

"You can trust me, Isla."

She looked up at him, blue eyes flicking back and forth in a way that made it look like she was searching for something. Or maybe she was weighing the risks. There were so many reasons for them to *not* go down this path. But Theo couldn't seem to stay away from her. It was a strange feeling, foreign. He didn't gravitate to people. Ever.

"I *do* trust you," she said, nodding as if solidifying the thought in her head. "And now that I've made this supremely awkward, you should just kiss me until we both forget I said anything."

Pink spread across Isla's cheeks and it made Theo smile from so down deep the breath stilled in his lungs. This woman. This beautiful, sunshine woman.

He kissed her hard, pressing her into the bed and nudging her thighs apart with his knees. Theo skated one hand along her rib cage to cup her breast, and she moaned when he thumbed her nipple. Isla arched against him, gasping as he moved his hand back down, over her stomach and between her legs. She was slick, ready.

"Please," she whimpered.

"Tell me what you want." His lips moved across her neck, down her chest until he captured a hardened nipple with his mouth. Sucking gently, he continued sliding his finger in and out of her, and her hips rocked up to meet each thrust.

"I want you, Theo. All of you." Her fingernails scraped against his scalp. "Now."

He reached for his bedside drawer, where he was pretty sure there was a pack of condoms wedged way down at the back. When his fingertips brushed the cardboard corner of a box he almost sighed in relief.

"Hurry." Her lips brushed his ear.

She watched from the bed with hungry eyes as he tore a foil packet open and rolled the condom down his length. But despite her pleas, he wasn't about to be rushed. There was something utterly devastating about the insatiable look in her eyes—reservations wiped away like a wave smoothing the sand of a shoreline.

Trust.

It was like a precious glass bubble—something he suspected she didn't hand out freely. And he sure as hell didn't have it in high quantity. But together, there was a fragile bond connecting them. Something special. Fleeting, perhaps. Which was exactly why he wanted to savor it.

Savor *her.*

Her hand stretched out and he slid his cock into her palm. "Hmm, yes."

She worked her hand up and down, lips blazing a trail across his chest and shoulder. Passion burned brightly in her eyes, still smoky with makeup and the starlike glitters twinkling on her eyelids with each blink.

He was going to remember this forever.

The bed shifted as he knelt between her legs, spreading her thighs apart with his hands. The lust in her eyes urged him on, and he was desperate to hear her moan again. To feel her clench around him as he took her. His skin tingled. He felt so…alive. So present.

He opened his mouth and the words hovered there, right on the tip of his tongue. But saying something like that would make this real. Meaningful.

"Theo, enough." Her legs came around his waist, her ankles crossing behind his back. "Please don't make me wait anymore."

"So impatient," he said with a chuckle.

He pressed against the entrance to her sex and she moaned, shifting underneath him with anticipation. When he pushed into her, burying himself all the way, they both gasped. Her muscles clamped around him and he pressed his face into the side of her neck.

"Oh, Theo," she sighed. "Yes."

She urged him on by rolling her hips and meeting him thrust for thrust. Their bodies fused together, lips and tongues meeting, limbs tangling. He slid his arms under her, pressing her to him so that no air could get between them. He had to be as close to her as possible.

"I want you on top," he whispered. Then he rolled them so he was on his back and Isla was riding him, thighs straddling his hips. Her long dark curls hung over her shoulders and she tipped her head back, rocking her hips back and forth. Theo watched her through hooded eyes.

She was magnificent.

He could feel her orgasm gathering, tightening her, tensing her. The second she broke, it pushed him over and he clamped his eyes shut, until he found his release.

As their pleasure subsided, Isla slumped against him and she pressed her face to the base of his neck, lips against his skin.

He was incredibly at ease. Peaceful in a way that he hadn't known in decades.

Perhaps ever.

Isla had officially tipped his understanding of the world on its head.

Sometime later, Theo stirred with the feeling that he was being watched. Isla was bundled up in his arms, the duvet over the lower halves of their naked bodies, and her blue eyes fixed on him. She reached out a fingertip and traced a scar on his abdomen.

"Appendix removal," he confirmed, his voice still clouded with sleep and satisfaction. "I was seventeen."

"It's the only mark on you. No tattoos, no piercings, no other scars."

"You've looked everywhere, have you?" He chuckled.

She lifted up the duvet and peeked underneath with a cheeky grin. "Yep."

"I'm frightfully boring."

"You are not." She laid her head down on his chest, her fingertip continuing to trace the scar. "Was it painful?"

"I honestly don't remember." He squinted into the dim light. The room was lit by the glittering city outside, which created shifting shadows across the bed. It felt cozy and intimate. Maybe that was why he had the sudden urge to reveal himself to her. "All I remember was that I was disappointed when I woke up from the surgery."

"Why?"

"In my young mind I thought it was God's way of letting me be with my parents. I thought I was going to die and I welcomed it." They'd been dark days, back then. Bleak days. "I wanted a Get Out of Jail Free card."

Emotion gleamed in her eyes. "I want to give teenage Theo a hug."

"Gram made me talk to some professionals for a while, but..." He laughed. "I was about to say I don't like talking to people and then I realized that I'm volunteering everything to you without you even asking. So I guess I almost made a liar of myself."

"You trust me." It wasn't a question.

"I do."

The gentle, genuine smile that blossomed on her lips was like a fist to the heart. It hit him in a way that was raw and real and...perfect. "Why?"

"You're kind. It's not a quality I see very often." He pushed his fingers through her dark curls and brushed her hair away from her face. "Most people are nice when they want something or they use the illusion of kindness to get close enough to build trust, only to break it later. But you're not like that."

Something flickered across her face—like a hint of worry, or vulnerability or...something. "Sounds like you're putting me on a pedestal."

"I've only said things that were true. It's the reason Camilla hasn't taken your hand off yet, because you're the only person who's treated her like she's not a pain in the ass. You've taken things slow to earn her trust, keeping at it even when she snaps." He wrinkled his nose. "You've been doing the same thing with me."

"Treating you like a dog?" She laughed.

"Being patient and persistent."

"I feel like *you're* the one being persistent. You invited me out tonight and then back here..." Her lashes lowered. "It's been a long time since I went back to someone's house."

"I won't believe it's because you haven't had offers."

As his eyes adjusted to the dark, he could see the faint blush spread across her cheeks. "I've had a few, here and there. But my life doesn't really lend itself to pleasure and sex and relationships. My sister doesn't..."

"Tell me."

"We're actually half sisters," Isla said. "Although it doesn't make a difference to me."

"Oh?"

"My mom is...a love addict."

"A love addict?"

"Yeah. People think addiction is just for drugs and alcohol and that kind of stuff, but I think it's possible to be addicted to a feeling, too. She keeps chasing love, no matter how much it destroys her life. She's forgotten about her children, quit her job, left her whole life behind to chase another man across the globe. And for what? The pursuit of something that only seems to give her pain in return." Isla made a derisive sound and shook her head. "If that's not addiction, I don't know what is."

"And Dani has taken that very hard?"

"Yes. I try to make her feel loved and safe, but..." Isla bit down on her lip. "She has a deep-seated fear that I'm going to leave her one day, too. That if I fall in love like our mother did, that I'll forget all about her and she'll be alone in the world."

"So you don't date."

"Frankly, with trying to build my career and taking care of her—making sure she eats and does her homework and that we spend time together—it doesn't exactly leave a lot of room for dating."

"So this is an unusual thing for you."

"Very."

He ran his fingertip over the curve of her shoulder and down her arm, unsure how to feel about what she was saying. On one hand, knowing she'd bent her rules for him filled him with warm satisfaction. But on the other, he'd *also* bent his rules by allowing himself to feel something for her.

And there was no way he could label this as "just sex" and nothing more, because Theo didn't place importance on superficial things. Yes, he found Isla attractive. But Theo had met plenty of attractive women in his time and they'd barely registered on his radar. Why? Because physical need was something he could control. Easily. If it was simply a case of Isla being attractive, then his bed would be stone-cold tonight.

The reason he couldn't stop thinking about her had nothing to do with how she looked and everything to do with *who* she was.

"I don't..." She sighed. "My priorities are different than a lot of people my age. I don't necessarily want it to be this way, but life has dealt me a hand and I'm playing it as best I can."

"That's admirable."

"I'm not a saint. There are times where I wish that Dani could get over her issues and let me live my life a little bit more. Of course any time I think that I feel *horribly* guilty," she admitted. "I love my sister more than anything. She's worth whatever sacrifice I have to make. But do I wish some days that I could be like a normal twenty-something woman and have a night on the town and find a cute guy to fall in love with? Yeah, I do. No matter how hard I try to make her see that I'd never leave her, the fear has a strong hold."

"That's why you rushed out after we kissed." The penny dropped. "You checked your phone and she'd been trying to call you."

"Yep."

"And here I was thinking I was a terrible kisser," he teased.

"Maybe you are." She traced the edge of his mouth, a wicked smile curling her lips up. "Maybe you're like a big, slobbery animal."

"A big slobbery animal, huh?" He hauled Isla on top of him and she shrieked, the sharp sound dissolving into laughter and then into a moan as he slid his hands up her sides and cupped her breasts. "Well, I guess you must be done with me tonight."

Isla shook her head. "I'm not done with you, yet."

"Yet?"

"Morning is a long way away." She smoothed her palms up and down his chest. "We've only got one night, so why not enjoy it as long as possible?"

There it was, another line in the sand. Isla was good at doing that, drawing boundaries around herself. Setting rules and fence-lines.

It should be *everything* Theo wanted out of a sexual dalliance. All the fun, none of the strings. And yet Theo found some part of himself struggling against the idea of boundaries, like it might constrict him. Like it might stifle him. For a man who thrived on locks and walls and distance, this was not the norm.

"What do you say?" Isla leaned forward and whispered into his ear, her breasts pressing against his chest and her glossy hair falling in a sheet around them, blotting out the rest of the world.

"Stay the night," he murmured against her lips. "Who cares what your boss thinks anyway?"

She pressed her lips down to his, coaxing him open with a deep and delving kiss. The warmth of her body cradled in his arms was like nothing he'd experienced before.

It was like coming home.

18

The following morning, Isla snuck out of Theo's place at the crack of dawn to head home and change. Nothing like slinking around the city in a fancy gown around sunrise to make a woman feel like the whole world was judging her. The cab may as well have been blaring that Lonely Island song "I Just Had Sex" at full volume with the windows down.

Even Camilla had given her the stink-eye when she'd been caught creeping through the penthouse looking for her evening bag.

She'd had all Sunday to stew on her decision. When she'd returned on Monday morning to collect Camilla, Theo was already on a call in his office and Isla had been able to sneak in and out without him noticing.

"It's not a big deal unless you make it a big deal," she said to her reflection as she rode down the public elevator at Theo's penthouse. "Besides, what's wrong with two consenting adults doing the horizontal mambo?"

At her feet, Camilla made a snorting sound as if to say *you're disgusting, woman.*

"What, you don't like the term horizontal mambo? How about bumping uglies?" She couldn't help but laugh as the Dachshund stared straight ahead, pretending Isla wasn't even there. "Knocking boots? Getting jiggy with it? Rolling in the hay? The horizontal refreshment?"

At the sound of someone clearing their voice, Isla was horrified to realize that she'd reached the foyer and there were two well-dressed older women accompanied by a man of a similar age, and all three of them were staring at her.

She bowed her head and hurried past the group, ignoring the enthusiastic smile from the man and appalled stares from the women. "Excuse me."

Great. She officially had sex on the brain *more* now than she did before. This was not good. Sleeping with Theo was supposed to scratch the itch, not make it worse! Turns out her attraction to him was like a mosquito bite, the more she agitated it the stronger the feeling got.

"We are *not* going to think about this all day," Isla said as she turned right onto Fifth Avenue. "We've got work to do."

In fact, Isla wasn't the only one working today. Camilla herself had a job that involved playing model for a photo shoot. Oh, and not just any photo shoot either. No, this was for *Vogue.*

Like *the Vogue.*

Anna Wintour and the September Issue and every iconic model and celebrity ever, *Vogue.*

The photo shoot was taking place a few doors down, in an apartment that belonged to a famous artist. The building was old and grand, and Isla followed the instructions to sign in at the front desk. A security guard accompanied her, and Camilla did not approve. The second they stepped into the elevator, she bared her teeth at the man and growled.

"Feisty," the security guard commented, shooting Isla a look.

"She has trust issues."

"Don't we all," the man muttered.

The elevator opened and he led Isla to one of two doors. He knocked, and a few seconds later the door swung open. Inside, jazz music played and there had to be at least ten people bustling about.

"We've been waiting for you." A man in an outrageously bright shirt motioned for them to come in. The security guard bid them goodbye and Isla marveled at the interior of the apartment.

It had twelve-foot ceilings; every wall was painted a stark, almost-blinding white and huge canvases dotted the space. There was a single red sofa in the middle of the room, but it looked more like an art piece than a place where someone would want to sit at the end of a long day. The canvases were all bright colors—with slashes of stop-sign red, grass green, electric blue and an acid yellow.

"I'm Ansel. You must be Camilla."

"I'm Isla, actually. This is Camilla." She gestured down but the man rolled his eyes.

"Honey, as far as I am concerned you are one entity and I don't have time to learn another name."

Isla blinked. "Okay then."

"Now, we need Camilla to come through to the dog grooming area so we can get her shoot ready. Chop, chop!" He snapped his fingers and hurried into the apartment, with Isla tugging on Camilla's lead to get her to follow. No chance.

The dog planted her furry butt on the ground and stared stubbornly up at Isla. "Come on, don't do this now. Please."

But the dog wouldn't budge. Maybe it was something about all the strange people in the room, or perhaps it was the loud music or bright colors. Whatever the reason, Camilla was rooted to the spot.

"I said *chop, chop.*" Ansel planted his hands on his hips. "Are you deaf, woman?"

"Sorry, she's a little timid meeting new people." Timid sounded good. Much better than stubborn as a bull and twice as tough as an old boot. "Come on, girl. Let's not waste people's time. I'll give you a treat."

The dog's ears perked up at the word *treat*. Thankfully, Isla had been on her game enough that morning to shake a few of the gross dried jerky-looking things that Camilla loved into a plastic bag. She fished one out and held it in front of the dog's nose.

"You'll get this if you cooperate." When she took a step, Camilla followed. "That's a good girl."

Eventually she lured the dog to the grooming station, where a woman with red hair was waiting with a brush, some clippers and a pair of sharp-looking scissors. Thankfully, Camilla didn't snap at the poor woman. She set Camilla up on a table and Isla handed over the treat.

"You're a total sweetheart. Aren't you, girl?" The woman smiled and trimmed a little around Camilla's face. "You've got such lovely fur but we really want to see your pretty face as best we can today."

Camilla sat still, so relaxed that her eyes fluttered closed for a second. The rest of the room buzzed, and a willowy blonde walked out from behind a curtain, wearing a hot-pink ball gown with gauzy sleeves and layers of jewels around her neck. A makeup artist flittered around her, dusting powder over her forehead and nose while a man with a platinum-blond pony-tail fussed with the model's hair.

There was a photographer—a reedy man with thick glasses and a deep scowl—and a young woman who appeared to be his assistant, adjusting the lighting.

"Wow, you're really good with her," Isla said as she pulled her eyes back to the dog groomer and watched her work. She had a soft, soothing voice as she talked to Camilla. It was almost the antithesis of the rest of the room, which had a tensely energetic atmosphere.

"Thanks." The woman smiled. "I'm August."

"Isla. How'd you get into doing dog grooming for photo shoots?"

"Oh, the photographer is a client. He's got a beautiful Chow Chow named Severina and I've been grooming her for several years now. When this project got accepted, he recommended my services."

"So you're doing all the shoots?"

"Uh-huh." August moved Camilla's face to the side and snipped. "We're almost done. This is the second to last one. It was supposed to happen earlier but...well, you know."

Isla nodded. Apparently the shoot was originally supposed to be with both the dogs and their owners, but Etna had passed away before it could take place. The model was dressed in a replica of one of her most famous outfits, from the 1950s. Isla recognized it from a photo she'd seen while researching Theo and his family before turning up on her first day.

It was the kind of dress that stuck in your mind.

"Tragic, really. She was very philanthropic." August pulled a sad face. "But I'm glad they decided to go ahead. I think it's going to be one of the most magical photos in the whole series."

"You must see some things, grooming pets of people like this." Isla gestured to the room.

"Sure, I do. But some of my four-legged clients are more famous than the two-legged ones who technically pay the bills." August smiled. In addition to her red hair, she had a wide, genuine smile, full cheeks and freckles dusted across her nose. "In fact, one dog I used to groom went on to be named one of the top ten pet influencers by Forbes. I haven't worked with him for a long time, because they moved out to LA and I didn't want to go with them."

"Impressive. Pet social media sounds like big business," Isla said, curious to hear what else August might know. She wasn't about to spill her secrets or anything, but this was all feeding into her idea about the agency.

The more she thought about it, the more it felt like the right solution to her problems.

It was a way to use her major skill set, plus it was an area that had potential to grow, unlike if she bound herself to a basic entry-level office job. Plus, she'd be setting a good example for her sister about the importance of chasing your dreams.

And, she'd started to realize that maybe there would be a way to balance things out—perhaps going part-time working for Theo and spending the rest of her time setting the company up.

"It sure is. In fact, I stumbled across the *funniest* Instagram account the other day. The Dachshund Wears Prada, have you heard of it?" August was concentrating on Camilla, teasing out some of her hairs like they'd done with the model's hair and holding it all in place with a sticky-looking product, which was a good thing. That way she hadn't noticed Isla's shocked expression.

"Uh, yeah, I have actually."

"Whoever is behind it has got a *great* sense of humor. All

my friends in the industry have been trying to figure out who it is. It's like *Gossip Girl* for pets!" She laughed. "That story about the Chihuahua eating the lipstick was *hilarious.*"

Isla had introduced a gossip-like element to the posts, sharing funny stories that were borderline-true, although some were totally made up, to see if adding a storytelling element might drive interest. It did. The numbers were climbing steadily and Isla's DMs had been exploding with questions, speculations and partnership requests. Of course she hadn't posted anything that might identify Theo *or* Camilla, because she didn't want to bring them unwanted attention.

If she could replicate this success for a client base, then nobody would be able to laugh her out of the industry again. Isla would have control back, her career back, her reputation back. Most important, she would have security and Dani's future back.

But a guilty feeling niggled in the back of her mind.

Was she betraying Theo's trust by using his world as social media fodder? Last night, he'd opened up to her about something deeply personal. His pain, shame, grief. What more evidence did she need that this was *way* beyond casual sex? And not only did he open up, so did she. She'd admitted something that had made her feel like a bad person, she'd been vulnerable with him.

And now she was thinking about building a business off the back of something she created while earning his trust.

It's not like you're spilling his secrets to the world. It's just the dog, and he doesn't even seem to like her that much.

But no matter how she rationalized it, Isla couldn't deny the little lump that had settled in the pit of her stomach.

"Okay, she's all done!" August gave Camilla a little scratch under the chin and the dog closed her eyes to enjoy the attention. "What a sweetheart. You're going to steal the show."

"Please bring the dog over here," the photography assistant called out.

August carried Camilla over to the red couch, where the blonde model was draped across the cushions, surrounded by the stark white high-gloss floor tiles and white walls with the vibrant oversized canvases hanging on them. The skirt portion of the hot-pink dress spilled onto the floor and a pair of equally bright pink shoes were arranged to look as though they'd slipped off the model's feet, but Isla had seen the assistant fussing with their positioning for a good ten minutes.

"Here." The assistant pointed to a patch on the couch and August lowered Camilla down.

The dog looked over at the model, who appeared as disinterested in her as Camilla was in the model. August made some soft cooing noises and pulled something out of her pocket, a treat.

"Sit," she said in a surprisingly commanding voice and the dog plonked her furry butt right down. Then she held her right hand out. "Shake."

Camilla daintily lifted one paw and placed it in August's hand, earning herself the treat.

"Good girl! Drop." August snapped her fingers and pointed down and Camilla dropped. This time August scratched her under the chin instead of giving her a treat. "Okay, you're good to go."

She stepped back and the photographer started giving the model instructions, the camera snapping away.

"I spent some time working with a dog trainer," August explained to Isla. "My boss was amazing. He could get even the most aggressive animals to yield. I can't even tell you how many animals he prevented from being put up for adoption."

"That's incredible. You didn't want to stay in that field?"

"Grooming is a bit more my speed," she admitted. "I like

being able to spend happy time with the animals, getting to know them and their families. I found the training side of things quite stressful, but I learned a lot and it's really helped me grow my business."

"I don't suppose you have a card on you?" Isla asked.

"Sure. You know someone looking for a groomer?" She pulled a stylish gray-and-gold card from a holder that was tucked into the tool belt around her waist. It reminded Isla of the tool belts worn by makeup artists.

"I might," Isla replied, taking the card. "Thanks. If I didn't know any better, I would have thought you were some kind of dog whisperer."

"Not the first time I've heard it," August replied with a proud nod. "Even so, I didn't have a lot of support when I started my business."

Isla raised an eyebrow. In front of them, the photographer clicked away and the model moved and pouted. Camilla looked like she was about to fall asleep, thankfully. August really *was* a dog whisperer.

"How come?" Isla asked.

"My parents wanted me to follow in their footsteps, you know? Do something that required a billion years of schooling and a lifetime of debt so they could show off what a 'success' I was to their friends." She rolled her eyes. "I couldn't think of anything worse. I worked part-time in a pet store for a while and that's how my boss from the training place found me. He was the one who gave me the support to go out on my own."

"It's scary to think about leaving behind something stable," Isla replied.

"Yeah, but if that stable thing isn't making you happy, then what's the point? If we have to work, we may as well try to find something that we enjoy, right?" She shrugged. "I get not everybody is in a position to start their own business out of passion, but I had a feeling in my gut that told me it was the right thing. Like if I ignored that feeling then I would regret it later."

"I know *exactly* what you mean." Isla laughed. "I've been having this same mental battle myself, to be honest. I have a great idea and I know I have the skills to make it a success, but there's always part of me that's holding back out of fear."

"I say go for it." August nodded. "Be smart about it and always have a plan, but life's too short to be scared of making the leap."

The model moved suddenly, and Camilla leaped to her feet, barking and baring her teeth. But one quick lift of August's hand and the feisty little dog dropped back down into position and plopped her head onto her front paws.

Isla shook her head in wonder. If she decided to strike out on her own, she was going to make sure she kept in touch with August. Excitement bubbled up inside her, desire tugging at some place she'd tried to silence for some time. Ambition. Belief. Things that had been shattered so hard by her fall from grace that she assumed they were irreparable. But what if this was all leading her to a specific point. *This* point.

Something told Isla that maybe she could rise from the ashes.

The following morning, Theo was feeling edgy as hell. He wouldn't be seeing Isla that day, as she'd requested a day off since Camilla had nothing important on the schedule. Something to do with her sister, apparently. Of course he'd agreed, and they'd both continued to avoid talking about their night together. Not that he should have been surprised. She'd drawn her boundaries, after all.

But he was disappointed.

All of this left him plenty of time to take care of Camilla

and ponder why in the hell he thought it was a good idea to sleep with Isla. Not that he'd had a hope in hell of resisting the woman, but still.

Emotional entanglement was always a bad idea.

Shaking his head, he made his way into the living room where Camilla should have been asleep in her bed. He was walking much better now. His ankle and foot still sported an ugly yellow bruise but there wasn't much pain, thankfully. The doctor said in another week he may be able to do some light interval training, switching walking with a light jog. He needed exercise as a distraction. A distraction from Isla, from his feelings about her, from the niggling voice in the back of his head that said he was going to repeat the mistakes of the past.

But then Theo was presented with a more immediate problem. Camilla was not in her bed.

"Camilla?" he called out, but the penthouse was still and silent. No skitter of nails across tile, no barking or growling. Not even the swish of a long, silky tail against furniture.

Great. She'd probably snuck into his bedroom on a mission to demolish another one of his suits while he was having a coffee and catching up on work in his office. He made his way to the bedroom and frowned when he found the door closed. Peeking inside, he confirmed that the Dachshund was not in there. He checked the laundry, bathrooms, his home gym and the kitchen. Nada.

That left only one room. Theo made his way to the penthouse's guest room—though it was hardly ever used for the purpose which the name implied. Nobody ever stayed here. The room was mainly storage, containing boxes of things belonging to his grandmother that he hadn't found the strength to go through yet. Papers, photos, personal items. Every time he opened the door and stepped inside, it was like the words *not yet* echoed through his body.

The door was ajar and when he pushed it open, the sight made a lump stick in the back of his throat.

In the middle of the floor, surrounded by neat stacks of boxes, was Camilla. One box had been torn open, shreds of cardboard littering the ground, and items dragged out through the hole to make a nest. Silk scarves, a cashmere wrap and what appeared to be a lap blanket were all cradling the body of the small dog.

Yet not a single item appeared damaged. It was almost as if the dog had carefully taken them out one by one and placed them into a pile so she could lie in them. The scent of his grandmother's signature perfume—Guerlain Shalimar, which he'd bought for her on so many occasions—wafted into the air.

Camilla looked at him and let out a baleful sound of pure anguish.

"I know," he said. "I know."

He walked into the room and dropped down onto the floor next to her, fingering the edge of an Hermès scarf in vibrant green and pink.

"I bought her this scarf for her seventy-ninth birthday." He sucked in a long, deep breath. "Pink and green was her favorite color combination, which I'm sure you know. She said they were her happy colors, because it reminded her of the new growth and blossoms in spring. That was her favorite season, too. No matter how bleak things had been before, growth and renewal were always possible in the spring. Life moved on."

Camilla raised her head, ears twitching. He thought she might have growled at him for touching her nest, but she seemed almost happy to have him there. Maybe it was a shared understanding of what had been lost. Or maybe all that scratching and building had tuckered the dog out.

"Now I'm talking to you like Isla does. It's a good thing she's not here to catch me or else I'd never hear the end of it." He laughed and scrubbed a hand over his face. "Who even am I right now?"

He dropped his hand down and smoothed it over the cashmere stole, which was probably now embedded with dog hair. He'd gotten rid of ninety-nine percent of his grandmother's vast wardrobe, but there were a few pieces he couldn't let go—items he'd bought for her, or things that she'd had a very long time that she wore a lot. There was even a pin that had belonged to his mother, that his grandmother wore to his parents' funeral and on his mother's birthday every year after.

"They were really close," he said aloud, not sure if he was talking to the dog or himself or to nobody. "Even though my mom married into the family, Gram always treated her like blood."

He felt something wet at his hand and blinked in surprise. Camilla had licked him, something she *never* did—partially because he didn't let her get too close and partially because she never showed an interest in him. But she'd shuffled closer, almost army-crawling flat on her belly, although he supposed that wasn't too hard for a Dachshund since they barely had to lower themselves to touch the ground anyway.

"Do you…want something?" He looked at the dog and she stared back at him with her big black eyes. "You're actually pretty cute when you're not terrorizing people."

She nudged his hand with her nose as if trying to tell him something. Did she wanted to be petted? Was this a ploy so she could sink her teeth into him? He reached out tentatively, smoothing his hand gently over the top of her silky head, and she sighed, flopping her head down onto his thigh.

"You like that, huh?" He continued to stroke her, touching her floppy ears and smoothing his fingertip in the space between her eyes in a rhythmic, repetitive motion. She blinked sleepily and then her eyes shut properly. A few seconds later the sound of her deep, even breathing filled the room.

Theo looked at the pile of belongings on the floor, at the little dog by his side and listened to the vast quietness of his home. It was unsettling to have it feel so full and yet so empty at the same time. Much like he himself felt, so full and yet so empty.

Full of dangerous thoughts about Isla, full of memories of his grandmother, full of his usual worries about privacy and security. And yet there was undeniably something missing from his life. Not only the gaping hole where a family should have been, but something else. Something personal.

Maybe Irina was right about him watching the world pass by. His life didn't have much in it these days and the older he got the more it seemed his world shrank. He hadn't always been the Hermit of Fifth Avenue. For a time, he'd tried to live and to love, but it had come back to bite him. He'd closed the walls in around himself, fortified his heart and his home and promised himself no one would ever hurt him again.

And they hadn't, because for someone to hurt him they'd need to be part of his life and Theo didn't do relationships of any kind. No friendships to speak of, certainly no romantic entanglements. And beyond the mutual respect he had with his assistant at work, there was literally no one else in his life.

You're going to die alone.

Was that the worst thing in the world? Better to be alone than to be betrayed, right?

Theo was no longer sure.

19

Isla sat in her usual spot at the doggy day care, watching the chaos in front of her. She'd come to enjoy the cast of characters here. There were "twin" Yorkies—Maxine and Paulette—who had tons of personality and more than a little attitude. The Maltese Terrier, Dolly, who turned up every day with a different colorful set of matching hair clips and collar. Then there was Beaux the Frenchie who barreled through the group with his infectious, happy energy and his big brother, Ace, a sweet Cavalier King Charles Spaniel.

There was something about dogs that Isla loved. Maybe it was the fact that they were honest with their emotions—if they were happy or sad or grumpy or excited, you knew it. There were no emotional games or tricky politics to navigate.

And if they wanted to hump something, they went on humping without feeling guilty about it.

You did not *just wish that you could hump like a dog.*

Okay, maybe she did. So what? It had been a week since Isla had slept with Theo and over a month since she started working for him. Now they were tiptoeing around one another like the marble floor of his penthouse was littered with eggshells and broken glass. Did she regret that night? Hell no. Would she do it again if the situation didn't have too many risk factors associated with it? Abso-freaking-lutely.

But unfortunately for her, there *were* too many risk factors. Her brain knew it. Her heart knew it. The part below her belt...well, that bit wasn't quite on the same page yet, but it would have to get on board.

Isla swiped her thumb across the screen of her phone and scrolled through some photos she'd taken on her day off last Tuesday. Dani had a doctor's appointment and had taken the day off school. As a treat, they'd walked the High Line and gotten ice cream. Isla had taken the opportunity to plan some posts for The Dachshund Wears Prada, including an adorable shot of a Corgi with the fluffiest butt Isla had ever seen.

She selected it from within the Instagram app and added some Sir Mix-a-Lot "I Like Big Butts" lyrics, along with a funny story about how difficult it would be to sniff a Corgi's butt without getting hair in your nose. The activity section on her account was jam-packed with hearts, comments and tags of people talking about her content. When she noticed the name of a prominent beauty influencer in the list, her eyes widened. The woman had over two million followers and she'd reposted one of Isla's pictures.

Swiping across to her account page, she had to stop herself from gasping. Thirty thousand followers. Three. Zero. *Whoa.*

But just as Isla was about to text Scout and tell her that she'd well and truly smashed the 20K challenge, her phone started ringing. It was Dani's school.

"Hello?" Isla stood and walked out of the playdate room and into the company's foyer. A woman walked past her with an Afghan hound on a leash, and went into the direction of the large dogs' room.

"Isla Thompson?" asked a clipped voice on the other end of the line.

"Yes."

"We need you to come and collect Danielle from school. She was involved in an altercation and—"

"Altercation? Oh my God, is she okay?" Isla pressed a hand to her chest. "Is she hurt?"

"She's not hurt, but the other girl may have a broken nose. She's been taken to hospital to have it checked out." There was a clicking sound in the background, like long nails over a keyboard. "Danielle has been suspended effective immediately. We need you to come and sign some paperwork, and take Danielle home."

Isla shook her head. "I can't believe..."

"Believe it, Ms. Thompson. Now, if you could be here as soon as possible, that would be appreciated."

"Of course, of course." Isla hung up the phone. "Shit, shit, shit."

Since when was Dani involved in any "altercations" at school? She was strong from all her ballet training, but the girl had a heart of pure marshmallow. She was a lover, not a fighter.

What was Isla going to do? Camilla was supposed to have an appointment with the salon that afternoon to get her toenails clipped, but otherwise the day was pretty clear. In fact, her schedule was getting clearer and clearer once all the wild things Theo's grandmother had booked started to slow down.

Obviously Theo himself hadn't lined anything additional up, other than keeping the regular, ongoing grooming type things.

Did she have time to go back to Theo's place and drop Camilla off? It would easily add another twenty minutes to her journey. The school administrator had sounded angry and Dani was probably freaking out. Given Isla hadn't received any texts or calls, she must have had her phone confiscated.

She had to get there now. Which meant Camilla was going to come for a ride.

Isla got to the school in less than forty minutes, opting to go for the subway because the traffic looked horrendous as always. Camilla had appeared unsurprisingly horrified, probably never having set foot in the subway before. If Isla hadn't been so worried about her sister, it would have made for some hilarious Instagram content.

They walked onto the school grounds and headed straight to the administration office. Was she even allowed to take pets in there? No clue.

Isla spotted Dani immediately, face red and splotchy, sitting in one of the plastic chairs lining the office. Not wanting to waste any time, Isla went through the motions as quickly as possible, listening to the lecture from the vice principal and signing the forms required to acknowledge Dani's suspension. Three days. Nothing they couldn't manage, but Isla wanted to get her sister out of there as quickly as possible so she could hear her side of the story.

Only once they were all in the back of a cab, with Isla promising the driver a good tip if he'd let them in with Camilla, did she finally turn to her sister. "Spill. Now."

"I don't want to talk about it," Dani said sullenly.

"Yeah, I got that from the way you refused to answer Vice

Principal Henderson's questions back there." She narrowed her eyes. "You *punched* someone. What were you thinking?"

"Her nose isn't broken, she's only saying that to get out of trouble." Dani rolled her eyes. She slunk down against the seat, arms folded over her chest and her chin tucked down. Her long, brown hair was falling out of its ponytail.

"I don't care if you don't want to talk about it." Isla shot her sister a stern look. "This is very out of character and I know you wouldn't hurt someone without a reason. That doesn't excuse what you did, but I want to know why."

Dani let out a long sigh. "She made a comment about Mom."

The girl in question had given Dani a hard time on and off over the years. She lived in the same apartment building and they'd been at the same elementary school. Now they shared a homeroom in high school. But she was a standard mean girl—mouth too big for her own good, but not a lot of substance behind it. Had a couple of yes-girls who followed her around. But usually it was like water off a duck's back to Dani, because she had her eye on the future and high school was a necessary evil between now and then.

"What did she say about Mom?" Isla asked gently.

"She said that Mom was a ho." Dani's lip quivered. "She said that she left us because prostitutes make more money in Europe."

"That's it?" Isla raised an eyebrow. Sure, it wasn't a pleasant thing for someone to say but it was a baseless comment and Dani would know that. "One bitchy comment from a girl whose only defining quality is that she's mean to people and you throw a punch? I don't believe it."

"Then she said that I would have to become a ho too, because I would never make it as a ballerina. She said only people with money can become ballerinas and that even though you try to act fancy, we're just poor people pretending to be better than we are."

Isla's jaw clenched. Okay, so now the punch made a lot more sense. "You know that's not true."

"Maybe it *is* true," Dani mumbled. "I'm not stupid, I know most of our money goes to my ballet. What if we run out of money? Then I can't be a ballerina, right?"

Well, shit. "We're not going to run out of money. Yes, we have to make sacrifices to be able to afford your tuition. And yes, it's expensive and we'd probably live someplace nicer if we didn't have to pay for it."

Dani's eyes watered.

"But you know what," Isla said. "It's worth it to me. I don't care that we can't go on vacation. I don't care that we can't go to fancy restaurants. I don't care that I have to shop at Goodwill or that I have to patch our clothes sometimes. All of that is worth it to me so that you can do what you are meant to do with your life."

Dani's hand reached out to pet Camilla, who was sitting between them. The dog licked her hand as if trying to offer her own brand of comfort, and a smile flickered on Dani's lips.

"Dani, look at me." Isla waited until her little sister dragged her eyes up. "We are *not* pretending to be better than we are, because life isn't a competition. You and I are doing the best we can with what God has given us, okay? I support your dreams like you support mine."

"I do support you." Dani nodded, sniffling. "That's what made me mad, like she thought less of you."

"I know, baby." Isla cupped Dani's face with her palm. "But here's the thing, people who are too afraid to try achieving something for themselves often hide that by criticizing others."

"Why?"

"Because it's easy to hide on the sidelines and never put yourself out there. What's the risk in doing nothing and being nothing?" Isla paused to watch it sink in. "But you *are* something. You're creating something, and you're going to inspire other people instead of bringing them down."

"Really?"

"Yes, really." Isla shook her head. "Do you think I'd be sacrificing all this if you were just some shrub with no potential?"

Dani giggled. "I'm not a shrub."

"No, you are not. You're talented and kind and dedicated. You're not the kind of young woman who lets people push you to the point of physicality, are you?"

"No." Dani lowered her eyes. "I shouldn't have done that."

"No, you absolutely should *not* have. It's never okay to hit someone." Isla held up a hand when Dani opened her mouth. "I know she provoked you. Vice Principal Henderson told me another student had come forward to vouch for you, saying that she raised her fist first. But here's the thing, you're still going to write a letter of apology to the school for not upholding the values our family holds high and we're not going to fight your suspension, either. It's important that actions have consequences."

"Yes, Isla." Dani sighed.

"And these three days are *not* going to be a vacation. You're going to get ahead on your schoolwork and I'm going to check it." She raised both eyebrows, asking for Dani's compliance. Her sister nodded quietly. "Good. Now I'm going to drop you home so I can get back to looking after this little mite."

Dani's eyes widened. "Wait? You're not coming home with me?"

"I can't skip out on work, you know that." Isla frowned. "Especially not since I took a day off last week. You're perfectly capable of doing your homework at home by yourself."

"But..." Her lip quivered. "Can't you bring Camilla back to our place? I'll even help! She likes me, see?"

Dani held her hand out and Camilla pressed the top of her head into the girl's palm. Tongue lolling out of her mouth, she looked happy as a pig in mud while Dani scratched her behind the ears.

"I can't do that." Isla shook her head. "One, our place is not dog-proofed. Two, I have to get back and rearrange some appointments over the next few days so I can be home with you."

"Please, Isla. I don't want to be there on my own." She looked like she was about to burst into tears. Dani got like this when she was stressed—clingy, emotional. Isla knew she should probably be a bit harder on her, but it tugged at her heartstrings every time. Maybe it was time for her to have another session with the psychologist. Whatever it cost, Isla would figure it out. But that wasn't going to help right now, unfortunately.

Crap. What about Theo's rule? She wasn't supposed to bring anyone into his house without him first vetting them. Sucking in a breath, she rationalized that he would understand... hopefully.

Besides, he wasn't due home for several hours. Isla could slip in, fix some dinner for Camilla, reschedule the appointments and finish off some of the things on her to-do list, like washing Camilla's bedding, all without Theo knowing that Dani was ever there.

"Tell you what, you can come back to Theo's place with me while I get everything organized, *if* you promise to do your homework quietly while I work."

"I promise." She nodded. "I won't say a word."

The last thing Isla needed was the fantasy of Theo colliding with the reality of her real life.

Theo was having a shit of a day. After his grandmother's gala, an article citing an "anonymous source" spoke about how he'd neglected to give a speech and had even left early. Clearly that must mean he didn't give a crap about all her hard work.

Why was boasting and externalizing the only way someone could show support?

Theo had done countless things to help his grandmother's numerous philanthropic activities over the years, from providing business advice to being the bad guy when she needed to pull someone in line but didn't want to do it herself. He'd brainstormed with her and helped her problem solve. In fact, some of his favorite memories of the two of them were the times they'd sat on her couch, drinking tea and bouncing ideas back and forth.

She had a sharp mind, as well as a big heart. But the spotlight had been *her* pastime, not his. And now one of his guests was talking behind his back to reporters. He knew he shouldn't care—people who focused so much on criticizing others usually had little in their own life to be interested with. But it got under his skin.

And after snapping at Irina unnecessarily, he decided to work the rest of the day from home. He had to review a bunch of documents for the new imprint launch, including a partial manuscript from a much-talked-about debut author that was currently at auction for a potentially eye-watering amount thanks to him having a very prominent mentor.

When Theo walked into his penthouse, brain swirling with all the things he needed to do, he almost didn't notice the figure sitting at his kitchen island. "Uh…"

The girl's head snapped up and her eyes widened in shock, like she'd been caught doing something far worse than what appeared to be algebra homework. But there was no mistaking who she was. She had Isla's eyes.

"You must be Dani," he said.

"How do you know my name?"

"Well, I can only assume you're Isla's sister. But if you're here to rob my house, you're doing a pretty terrible job of it." He smiled. "Also, I met you that day at Central Park. You're the ballerina girl, right?"

"Yeah." She looked around, as if hoping her big sister would materialize, but Isla must have been in the depths of the apartment somewhere. He could hear a faint drumming in the background that sounded like water running. "Isla said you wouldn't be home until later."

"Work sucks."

She rolled her eyes. "Everything sucks."

Ah, teenagers. From the dawn of time they were all the same. "Why does everything suck?"

"I'm in trouble." She looked guilty about it too, so whatever she'd done she knew it was wrong. "I got suspended from school."

"That's not good." He dumped his things onto one of the empty chairs next to Dani. "Do you want a hot chocolate? I think I have some of the fancy stuff laying around here. No marshmallows, though."

"Sure." Her face lit up. "Thanks."

He went hunting in his mostly bare cupboards for the remnants of a gift basket that a literary agency had sent a few weeks back. He'd taken out the yummy things, including a container of drink mix made with Valrhona chocolate, and tossed the rest. So, he set about making her a mug, frothing the milk using his espresso machine. When he was done, he handed the mug over and Dani eagerly took a sip.

"Wow, that's *good*," she said.

"Why did you get suspended?" He leaned against the countertop.

"I was involved in an 'altercation' with someone from my homeroom." She lowered her eyes. "She's not a very nice person but I should have more control over my actions."

It sounded a heck of a lot like she was using someone else's words there. "I got suspended from school a couple times, myself."

"Really?"

"Sure did."

"What did you do?"

What *hadn't* he done? After his parents' death, Theo had been on a sharp and dizzying downward spiral. He'd had verbal outbursts, thrown things, broken windows…worse.

"I stole my teacher's car."

Dani's mouth dropped open. "Seriously?"

"Yep. He was a mean old man and he said something insensitive about my mother, so I snuck out of another class later that day, hot-wired his car and took it for a joyride." Theo chuckled. "My grandmother was *livid*."

"How long were you suspended for?"

"Oh, I can't remember. That was a long time ago. But I returned the car in one piece…well, a few wires were hanging out, but they were able to put it back together."

His grandmother had forced him to volunteer at a soup kitchen for a year after it happened. But the teacher never made a comment about his mother ever again.

"Isla was real mad at me," she said.

"Was she right to be mad at you?"

"Yeah." She nodded.

"If you know that, then you'll be alright. It's the people who do bad things and can't admit their wrongdoings who are a problem." He reached out and patted her awkwardly on the shoulder. "If you're anything like your sister, then I know you're a good person."

She gave a small and fleeting smile, but it disappeared behind the giant mug he'd given her. Despite them being half sisters, he could see a lot of Isla in her. Not just the big blue eyes or the dark brown shade of her hair, but the sincerity that radiated from her. The genuine spirit and authenticity.

"How are you going to make it up to her?" Theo asked.

"What do you mean?"

"Well, Isla takes care of you and you did something bad.

Usually it's a good idea to get back in the good books," he suggested with a wink. "Maybe a little gift?"

"Like what?" Dani seemed to like the idea.

"Flowers? That usually works. Do you know what kind she likes?"

"Uh, hmm." Her nose screwed up as she thought about it. "Oh, she brought home these pink flowers once. They were from an event and the person let her take some home. She really liked them."

"Pink flowers, got it." He pulled out his phone and brought up the website for a local florist. "How about these?"

He showed Dani a picture of a bouquet with lush pink roses and carnations and something white and frilly-looking that he couldn't identify.

"They're like $200!" Dani gaped at him.

"Don't worry about the price. You just tell me what to put on the card and where to send them, okay?" He asked Dani to type in their address and to put a message saying sorry to be written onto a card to go with the flowers. "There we go, they'll be delivered tomorrow. I'm guessing she's going to be home with you if you're suspended, right?"

"She said she has to work."

"We'll see about that."

Dani nodded. When she looked up at him, her gaze was soft and open. "Thanks. I think she'll really like the flowers."

"I think so, too." He nodded to the book open in front of her. "How's the homework?"

"Stupid." Dani spat the word out as if it tasted bad. "I hate math."

"Do you want some help? I happen to be pretty good with numbers."

"You can try, but even the teacher couldn't make me understand it." She frowned. "I'm just not good at it."

"Or maybe your teacher hasn't explained it to you in the right way." He came around to the other side of the island and took the seat next to her. "Okay, so show me what you're up to."

Isla was almost finished with everything on her list. Camilla's bedding had been washed and thrown into the dryer, she'd been fed and was now playing with a plushie toy that was in the shape of a slice of pizza. Isla had put in an order for some more dog food, booked her annual vet checkup and had rescheduled the next few days so she could work reduced hours and be home earlier to check on Dani.

Turning the laundry taps off, Isla was surprised to hear voices coming from the other room. She frowned, listening and then caught the familiar sound of a deep, sexy baritone that had been circling in her head all day.

Theo was home early.

"Crap, crap, crap." Isla dried her hands and hurried into the kitchen, where she found her sister sipping something out of a mug that was almost as big as her head, while Theo— still dressed in a sleek, well-fitted navy suit—sat next to her as they both leaned over an open textbook.

He was explaining an algebra equation, speaking slowly and patiently and making Dani laugh when she got defensive for not understanding. For a moment, Isla watched them, transfixed. Her sister *hated* math and no matter how many times Isla had tried to help her with the homework, it usually ended in Dani getting frustrated. Didn't help that her teacher was a crotchety old man with the patience of a gnat.

But Theo's voice was calm and soothing, and he nudged Dani toward the solution. When she got it right, her head snapped up and she looked at him with awe. Then her gaze shifted to Isla and her private viewing was over.

"Theo, hi," Isla said, walking over to the bench. "Uh…"

"Yes, I'm home early," he said, anticipating her next comment. His warm gaze swept over her, curious but not judging. "And yes, it's okay that you brought Dani here."

The tension in her neck and shoulders immediately eased. "Thanks. It was quite the afternoon."

"I told him what happened at school." Dani sipped from the mug and Isla could see now that it was a hot chocolate. Had he made it for her?

Her body was full of emotions and questions, and it felt like a big, messy tangle inside her. Something about seeing Theo with her sister, helping her and making her feel safe and welcome...well, that was like a big shot of glittery pink energy to her soul. On the few occasions she *had* dated before giving up on having any semblance of a love life, guys her age weren't too keen on the whole "pseudo-mom" thing.

Her situation meant sacrifices, responsibility and hard choices. *Not* the kind of thing a young professional in his twenties was typically looking for. She couldn't pack her bags and head off for a weekend in the Finger Lakes on a moment's notice. She couldn't go on club crawls and slink back into bed at 4:00 a.m., sleeping until midafternoon the next day. She couldn't have passionate, noisy sex in her bedroom without making prior arrangements.

Spontaneity was not an option. Selfishness was not an option.

But something told her that Theo understood all that. For the man who'd craved nothing but family his whole life, he would understand that it was *worth* letting all those things go.

"Did you tell him that you're going to be home for the next three days?" Isla asked.

"Uh-huh." Dani nodded.

"I've already told her you can have the time off," Theo said. "I was planning to work from home tomorrow anyway, so I'll make sure Camilla doesn't eat any more of my suits."

"She did that?" Dani gasped. "Why?"

"Because grief makes us do strange things," he replied, and Isla cocked her head. It sounded like there was a story in there. "But I'm a grown man capable of handling a small furry loaf of bread."

Dani giggled. "She's not a loaf of bread."

"I should get you home. It's dinner and then early to bed for you," Isla said sternly. "Suspended people don't get Netflix."

"Okay," Dani replied, her shoulders drooping.

"And I don't need tomorrow off," she said to Theo. "But I've moved some of Camilla's appointments so I could do a half day if that works?"

He slid off his stool and walked over to her, his sexy swagger almost melting her on the spot. When he placed a hand on her shoulder it was like she'd been run through with electric energy—her whole body tingled with it.

"Take the day," he said softly. "She needs you."

"Are you sure?"

"Family comes first, always." With a nod and a brief wave of his hand in Dani's direction, Theo disappeared into the penthouse, leaving Isla feeling as though her legs were made of jelly.

Who was this man? The beast, on first glance, who turned out to be complicated and layered and wonderful. A family man with no family. A lover with no one to love. Her heart ached in the most bittersweet way possible.

Deal with the pressing things first, and you can moon over Theo later.

"Come on, troublemaker. Let's get you home," Isla said, gesturing for Dani to grab her things.

There was one thing that she and Theo could absolutely agree on: family *did* come first.

20

ISLA: I know what you did.

THEO: What? *angel face emoji*

ISLA: The flowers. They're beautiful.

...

ISLA: Don't deny it. Dani told me everything.

THEO: It's nothing.

ISLA: It's not nothing.

THEO: It seemed like you were having a rough day yesterday.

ISLA: I was.

THEO: Plans for tonight?

ISLA: Dani has a ballet technique workshop. I thought about making her stay home as part of her punishment, but those things cost a fortune.

THEO: I asked what YOU were doing.

ISLA: I have a blissful three hours free of parental responsibility and nothing planned.

THEO: Dinner? I promise I won't try to cook again.

...

THEO: No pressure.

ISLA: I'd love that, actually.

THEO: Me too.

ISLA: I'll text you when I'm on my way over.

There was something so delightfully *normal* about a text exchange for making dinner plans. There were no gilded invitations, no requirement for an executive assistant to find time in his calendar. No sense of dread or obligation. In fact, while Theo would never admit it aloud even under threat of death, he had butterflies in his stomach at the thought of see-ing Isla. Butterflies. Pathetic, right?

But he'd been thinking about her all day. About what a good big sister she was and how holding her in his arms had made him feel like the man he was supposed to become, in-stead of the hermit loner he *had* become. About how when she looked at him, a smile hovering on her lips and no walls between them it felt like he could change.

That he could trust.

After he got Isla's text saying that she was on her way over, Theo paced around the house, his anxiousness wearing grooves into the floor. His eye hovered on the private elevator, but a knock came at the front door.

When he pulled it open, she stood there smiling sweetly at him. Her hair was loose around her shoulders and she wore the same blue dress from the day he'd met her at Central Park, along with a pair of wedge heels that brought her a little closer to his height. No more sensible pants and ballet flats.

"Hi," she said almost shyly.

"Why are you knocking?" he asked, stepping back to hold the door open.

"I figured since I wasn't turning up for work, I'd do what a proper guest should and knock."

A line in the sand. Only this time, the line wasn't between them. It wasn't a barrier or a wall.

It was an invitation.

"Did you order already? Something smells amazing." She stuck her nose in the air and sniffed. "Oh my gosh, whatever that is I need it right now."

"Pasta, garlic bread, red wine and tiramisu for dessert. I figured everyone likes Italian food."

She shook her head. "First the flowers, now this. It feels like I'm on a date."

How was he supposed to respond to that? She was right. These *were* markers of a date. He was rusty, doing the steps out of order. Fumbling. Being unsure of how much was too much.

Relationships were never his forte.

"Forget I said that," she said quickly, shaking her head. That pretty pink flush spread across her cheeks. "I've got a big mouth."

"I'm glad you came," he replied, figuring honesty was the best policy.

"Me too."

He motioned for her to follow him into the dining room, where he'd set the table with their food. It was still hot, since it had only arrived a moment before she did, and the wine was airing in two glasses.

Camilla trotted into the room, tail swishing with each stumpy-legged step. She went straight over to Isla and sat, looking up at her with shiny black eyes. He'd taken one of his grandmother's old scarves and wrapped it around Camilla's collar as a decorative touch. Perhaps that was sacrilege for a designer silk scarf, but he figured after she tore his grandmother's box open that maybe the smell might make her happy. She'd been in a good mood all day long.

"Look at you, sweet girl." Isla bent down and stroked the top of Camilla's head. "Don't you look fancy."

"She got into my grandmother's silk scarves, so I figured we may as well use them." He shrugged one shoulder.

"I thought you said her clothing was donated to a museum."

"Most of it was, and some sentimental pieces went to close friends. But the scarves still smelled like her and..." He turned away. "I wasn't really sure the museum would want such small things. They seemed more interested in the ball gowns and bags and jewelry."

"Well, I think Camilla looks lovely. That green is such a

nice color." Camilla wagged her tail and stuck her paw up onto Isla's wrist the second she stopped scratching her head. "Okay, okay. Look who's being needy."

"She's like a different dog, now," he said, watching them. Isla was so gentle with her and Camilla was relaxed and happy. "I swear, some days I wonder if you secretly switched her out when I wasn't looking."

"She needed to be loved." Isla stood. "I'm sure your grand-mother showered her with affection and when that was gone, the world probably felt like a very strange and lonely place."

The words socked Theo hard in the chest. Boy, did he un-derstand that sentiment.

By the end of dinner, Theo and Isla were chatting like old friends. She regaled him with stories from her life in social media and he traded tales of what it was like going to Cannes with his actress mother and sitting on the sidelines of her film sets as a child. When they transitioned to dessert, they moved into the kitchen, sipping espresso and eating the decadent Ital-ian confection with small spoons and moans catching in the backs of their throats.

Isla sat on his kitchen counter, scraping the glass bowl with her spoon to get every last little bit. "I have to admit, tiramisu was never my go-to dessert but this has totally converted me."

Theo held his hand out for her bowl and she handed it over so he could stack them in the dishwasher. "What did you nor-mally order?"

"Lemon and chocolate gelato. Not exactly sophisticated," she replied with a laugh. "But eating out is a rare treat, so I don't have a lot of data to work with."

"No?"

She shook her head. "Dani is only now becoming indepen-dent. When I started working in the industry, she was still a little kid and I had to get home to give her dinner and put her to bed. My work required me to do nights sometimes, especially during awards season, so I'd never go on a night out for fun when I'd already neglected her for work."

"You've done a good job raising her."

"She punched another student." Isla made a groaning sound and rubbed her hands over her face. "I have no idea what she was thinking."

"She wasn't. The prefrontal cortex isn't fully matured until we hit our midtwenties. She's acting on hormones and instinct."

"Don't stick up for her." Isla laughed. "She knows better than that."

"What do you think pushed her over the edge?"

"The girl made a comment about us acting like we're better than we are." Isla's bare feet knocked gently against the cupboard doors below the counter. "Like because we're not rich that we shouldn't dare dream for more out of life."

"That's some bullshit if I ever heard it." He snorted.

"Right? I was so mortified when I had to face the vice principal—he still remembers me from when I was a student and it was like having my lack of parenting experience shoved in my face." The muscle in her jaw pulsed like she was grinding her back teeth together. "I know I'm not perfect, but I really am trying my best."

"Fuck that guy."

She laughed. "Yeah, fuck that guy. What right does he have to judge me?"

"None. And you're doing more than trying," he said. "That girl is going to grow up to be strong and courageous and hardworking because of you."

He detected a change in the air, a shift in the connection between them. Sitting on his kitchen counter, Isla looked like a fantasy. Like a fantasy he hadn't allowed himself to indulge in, an alternate version of his life, with a glossy filter and perfect lighting and a woman who loved him heart and soul.

Maybe this was the path he could've taken if life hadn't taught him to keep his heart under lock and key.

A ring on her finger. Sex. Connection. Emotion that didn't send him running. Having Isla touch him was like being a block of ice set in front of a roaring fireplace—his sharp edges were rendered ineffective. His coldness melted away. He became something else entirely.

"You really understand, don't you?" she said.

He stood in front of her, exposed. Because as much as he understood her, she understood him. That comment earlier, about the world being strange and lonely after his grandmother's death...that wasn't for Camilla. That was for him.

"Yeah." He nodded. "I do."

She held out her hand and he took it, running his thumbs over her knuckles. There was a deep sadness in her eyes that called to him, like her wounds wanted to be one with his.

"Is everything okay?" he asked.

Something flickered in the blue depths of her eyes, but she brought her hand to his face, cupping his jaw. "When I'm with you it feels like everything is okay."

He leaned forward, drawing her to the edge of the kitchen counter so he could stand between her legs with one palm on either side of her. Penning her in. Claiming her.

"And when I'm with you it feels like everything is nothing. Like there's nothing else at all."

Isla leaned forward and wrapped her arms around his neck, kissing him deeply. She tasted of coffee liqueur and wine and cream, and her fingers drove through his hair. He placed one hand on her thigh, sliding up under the hem of her dress, feeling the warmth of her skin against his palm.

"You can't live your life in a bubble, Theo," she whispered.

"This bubble is looking pretty damn good to me." He fingered the tie at her waist. Would the whole thing come open if he undid the delicate little bow holding her dress closed?

"There's a whole wide world out there."

"I only care about the world in here." He brushed his lips along the edge of her jaw, feeling her loose waves tickle his neck. "How long until you need to leave?"

"Hour and a half," she said, her voice breathy.

His eyes searched hers, silently asking if she wanted to keep going, and she nodded, the "yes" leaving her lips so soft it was no more than the puff of warm breath fogging up on a brisk morning. He slipped one hand inside her dress and palmed her, rubbing her breast in slow circles while he kissed down the side of her neck. A soft *thump* sounded as her head lolled back against the kitchen cabinet. The way she gave in to him—so easily, so freely—made him feel like a god standing on the edge of a cliff, looking down on all he owned.

And it was because she was strong, that when she chose to let him lead it *meant* something.

A gentle hum rippled through the air as he flicked his thumb across her hardened nipple. "You're very persuasive," she said, her voice soft and breathy. "It's easy to forget about everything else here."

"Good. When you're with me I don't want you thinking about anything but how good you feel." He untied the dress and pushed the fabric open with both hands, watching it slide off her rounded shoulders and then helping her remove her arms one by one.

She was almost naked—a stark beauty against the white marble countertop and cupboards. A feast for the senses.

"You really do make me feel like I'm an ordinary girl who's found out she's a princess. It's a tempting tale."

"Why do you think it's a tale?"

"Because I *am* ordinary." She wrapped her arms around his neck and pulled him close. Theo's whole body was wound tight with anticipation and he pressed his hardness between her legs, wishing he'd already divested her of that scrap of lace masquerading as underwear. "I'm a working-class woman with no formal education, a dwindling savings account and one hell of a black mark against her name. I'm categorically not the caliber of woman you should be with."

Okay, well *that* pissed Theo off. "And why do you think that's your determination to make?"

She laughed. "I get that you're terrible at being told what to do, but I'm stating the obvious. This…" She gestured with one hand. "Isn't real. This is a virtual reality of the kind of fantasy I had in my head as a teenager."

"Dirty mind for a teenager," he said with a raised eyebrow.

"You know what I mean. This is the subject of a whole genre of fan fiction—ordinary girl gets plucked out of obscurity by the famous guy."

"Will you stop calling yourself *ordinary*. Isla, you're majestic. In all my years of being around the kind of people you think I 'should' be with, I have never met anyone who makes me feel the way you do. This might be a fantasy to you but it's fucking real to me."

The silence that followed his outburst was almost oppressive, like he could choke on it if he wasn't careful. He hadn't meant to spill these feelings to her, because he didn't know how this was supposed to work. He had *zero* experience in how to be in a relationship. Zero experience in caring for someone other than himself.

Hell, even when it came to sex he was less experienced than most, a few one-night stands peppered through his adulthood amounting to much less than the average man. Much less than people expected of him.

But all he knew was that when he was with Isla, it felt like maybe his life would turn out okay.

"I'm sorry," she whispered, tracing her fingertip along the edge of his jaw. "I didn't mean to say that I was only here for kicks."

"Then why *are* you here?"

Maybe he needed to hear her say it—that all this talk about who he "should" be with wasn't her planning an escape route. Because despite all his huffing and puffing and all his promises to not get attached, Theo's walls were crumbling. Isla could see him. She knew him in a way nobody else did. He'd shared things with her that he thought he'd take to his grave.

He needed to know that this wasn't just screwing around to her.

"I…" Her lip quivered and her big, blue eyes stared into his. "Every time I tell myself I shouldn't be doing this, that I don't have room in my life for anything more than the bare necessities, I end up here. In your arms. Touching you. Kissing you."

The waver in her voice was like a fist around his heart. He leaned forward, capturing her mouth with his, sliding his tongue against hers. Her arms tightened around him, clutching him close like he was her last tether to earth. The only thing keeping her in place. He thrust his fingers into her hair, easing her head back so he could kiss her more deeply.

When she pulled away, her eyes glittered. When a tear squeezed out of one corner, he caught it with his thumb before it even had the chance to fall.

"I'm scared by how right this feels." She shook her head. "And I'm scared I'm going to mess it up because I have a habit of doing that with important things."

"You don't think I worry about the same thing? I don't

know how any of this is supposed to work. All I know is that when you're here, all that nasty stuff in my head is quieter and I forget that I want to be alone."

"I make you forget that?" She swallowed, and he traced the line of her neck with his thumb.

"You make me forget a lot of things, Isla. Things I thought would haunt me until the day I died."

She grabbed his face and pulled him close, kissing him hard. He could taste the saltiness of an escaped tear and the sweet earthiness that was unique to her. He sucked in every sensation—the insistent pressure of her lips, the possessive loop of her arms around his neck and the scent of vanilla on her skin. She was warm, wanting. Honest.

He unwound her arms from his neck and pulled them above her head, pinning her wrists in place with one hand. "I want you like I have never wanted anything."

"That's a lot coming from a man who wants for nothing."

"Material possessions, maybe. But I have wanted for so much more." Theo used his free hand to palm her breast, then further down over her stomach and between her legs. The soft moan she rewarded him with was golden. "And you are at the top of the list."

"Then have me," she whispered. "Take me to bed."

He hoisted her from the countertop and she grabbed his hand, pulling him close so that her body lined his. They stumbled together, legs bumping and feet tripping. She held on to him the whole time, lips at his jaw and neck and cheek as though she needed to cover every part of him. When they reached his bedroom, he laid her down on the bed and stood back, admiring her.

Every part of her was magnificent—from her full, hard-tipped breasts to the dip at her waist and her soulful, blue eyes.

A wicked smile crossed her lips as her hands went to the edge of her underwear, thumbs hooking underneath the elastic.

"Are you going to put on a show for me?" he asked, excitement and lust swirling up inside him. It blotted out those softer emotions for a moment, allowing him to focus on the more primal instincts. Baser needs.

"Do you want that?"

"Yes."

She levered her hips up and slid her panties down over her hips and thighs. The lacy fabric tangled at her ankles and she wriggled one foot free and then the other. As she scooted back farther up the bed, her eyes were locked on his.

"More?" she asked.

"Hell yes," he rasped. He was so hard it was torture not to reach down and grasp himself—but he wanted to string this moment out. Make it last.

"What do you want me to do?" she asked coyly.

"Touch yourself." The words stuck in his throat, almost drowned out by the quickened thumping of his heart. "I want to watch you."

She looked up at him with smoldering eyes, her hand skating down over her belly, fingertips fluttering over her skin. But she didn't rush into it—oh no, Isla was a master of anticipation. She ran her hands up and down her thighs, dragging her nails so that faint pink marks were left behind on her fair skin. They disappeared within an instant, but the visual sent a shudder of delight through Theo's body.

He was a statue, rooted to the plush carpet underneath his bare feet. Sucking on her lower lip, Isla sank back against the cloudlike pillows and let her hand wander farther. She reached between her legs and clamped her thighs shut around her hand, not letting him see.

"You sure you want this?" she teased with a wicked glint in her eye.

"Please," he said, his voice hoarse now with wanting. "I'm not too proud to beg."

She laughed softly. "I like the sound of that."

"And I've never begged for anyone my whole life." He sunk his knees down onto the edge of the mattress. "But I'll beg for you."

Eyes wide and lips parted, Isla lowered her knees to the side, showing him everything. Her eyes fluttered shut and the sounds coming from her mouth were the soundtrack of his fantasies. Theo was hit with the full force of her power.

How could this woman call herself ordinary? How could she think that there was anyone better for him than her?

She was it.

Shock rippled through his system. He liked her, sure, but...

You know it's more than like. It's so much more.

For a moment, Theo recoiled, but at that instant—as though she knew he was about to retreat—Isla reached out and pulled him forward, fully clothed. Their mouths met and her hands roamed his body, thrusting his sweater up and then going to the waist of his pants. Her hand was in his underwear, around him, her lips at his ear, whispering all manner of dark and dirty things.

"I don't want this to be a one-woman show." Her voice was soft. But her gaze held him captive and he knew he'd never be able to say no to her. "It's better with you inside me."

Theo pushed back and finished undressing, only returning to Isla when he was naked and a condom was covering him. He came down to the bed, drawing her tightly into his arms. He wanted there to be nothing between them—no air, no hesitation.

Just them.

★ ★ ★

Isla reveled in the feeling of Theo's body covering hers, and in the feeling of being wanted and protected and appreciated.

"I want you so bad," he said, his voice thick. Rough. Seeing the perfectly polished Theo—a man always in control—come undone like this was better than any sparkling jewels or gold. "I've resisted wanting you every second of the way."

"Really?" The word was a mere whisper.

"Really. And not just because you were working for me, although perhaps that should have held me back more." He shook his head. "But I couldn't resist wanting you, even though I know I'm not an easy man to love. I'm not...made for this."

How could he say that?

The pain in his voice made her heart swell. He was broken, yes. But broken didn't mean wrong, it didn't mean bad and it most certainly didn't mean undeserving. For what was more human than being broken? She wound her arms tight around his neck, pulling him toward her with an instinctive need to have him as close as possible. Her body sank farther into the mattress.

"I think you're perfectly made for this," she whispered. "Because it feels right to me. *You* feel right to me."

Vulnerability flickered in his beautiful amber eyes, but it was quickly overshadowed by the swirling, gathering lust turning his eyes to smoke. "You tempt me, Isla. You tempt me with things that have never tempted me before."

"Tell me," she breathed, her body crying out for him to be inside her.

"This. Tomorrow. Next week." He brushed his lips over hers. "The future."

"Please," she begged. "I need... I need you. Not tomorrow, but right now."

With a rough sound and eyes like fire, he pushed inside her and her body gave in to him, melting and yielding and turning to liquid pleasure. The feeling was exquisite. Familiar. Whole. She felt...cherished.

He moaned against her neck, lips blazing a trail over her skin and hips moving back and forth in deep, fluid strokes. Cupping his face, she kissed him with everything she had. With every bit of hope and faith and desperation inside her. His lips probed hers, tongue delving into her mouth, and as their bodies fused together, they found a rhythm. *Their* rhythm.

Everything else evaporated. Her past pains and insecurities stripped away as if nothing existed but this present moment. No baggage, no worries, no fears. Only the glorious now.

"I'm close." She rocked her hips up to meet his, her body trembling.

Her hands fisted in the sheets and she arched, shattering with him inside her. Her cries echoed off the walls of his bedroom, and a second later Theo followed, his face pressed into her hair as he found release. As she lay there, heart full and body sated, she couldn't help but feel that she had been fundamentally changed.

There was no going back.

21

Over the next two weeks, Isla found a strange new rhythm with her life. Each day she would work for Theo, running Camilla to and fro. Then he would come home from the office early—they'd make love, talk about their lives and connect in a way Isla had never experienced before. Then she would either go home to have dinner with Dani or—if Dani had ballet—she'd linger in Theo's bed until it was time to leave.

Between all this, The Dachshund Wears Prada continued to explode.

Isla felt a shift in her confidence, and she wasn't sure exactly what had driven it. Was it seeing her work appreciated? Building something from nothing and seeing it take off? Or was it the man who crooned soft words into her ear, who told her she could do anything?

Isla wasn't sure she could even separate those things. It was entwined by fate.

"Isla!" Dani called. "Have you seen my wrap skirt?"

She was bent over a suitcase on her bed, packing for her ballet summer intensive camp. All her best leotards neatly folded, a new pair of pointe shoes tucked beside the gift Isla had hidden in there. It was a thin silver bracelet with a tiny charm of a ballet slipper. Isla had been holding onto it for almost six months, waiting to surprise her.

"It's here." Isla grabbed the gauzy burgundy skirt from the couch, where she'd painstakingly tried to repair a seam. But the fabric was fraying and it wouldn't hold for long. Hopefully, however, it would be enough to get her through the camp so the other girls wouldn't tease her. "And don't forget your toe pads."

"Got them." Dani was positively humming with energy.

"Gee, it looks like you won't even miss me at all," Isla said with a doting smile. Every day since Dani had finished up the school year, she was like a different person. Happy, buoyant, cheerful.

"Puh-lease." Dani shot her a look. "You're happy to get rid of me."

Isla laughed. "Since when?"

"Since you got yourself a boyfriend." When Isla opened her mouth to protest, Dani held up her hand and rolled her eyes with extra sass. "Don't try to deny it. I know you and Theo are boyfriend and girlfriend."

"We haven't actually put a label on it, if you must know." Isla folded her arms across her chest, feeling a little defensive.

"Why? I thought you liked him." Dani folded up her skirt and stuffed it down the side of her suitcase.

"How do you know that?"

"Because of how you look at him, *duh*. Plus, I know you stay at his house until you come and pick me up from ballet." Dani shrugged. "You always have this big smile on your face and you smell like boys' perfume."

"Am I supposed to call you Detective Pikachu now, huh?"

"Pika! Pika!"

"Very funny."

Dani looked pleased with herself. "I'm just saying, don't think I'm stupid and that I don't notice things, okay?"

"I don't think that."

Dani fussed with her suitcase, making sure everything was in its right place. "I don't mind, you know."

"What?"

"That you're dating Theo." She looked up. "He's nice."

Isla looked at her younger sister, wondering how the heck she grew up so fast. Standing there now, Dani wasn't a little girl but a young woman on the verge of coming into her own. She was growing tall and willowy, her face losing the child-like roundness she'd had as little as six months ago. Her eyes gleamed with intelligence and her movements were becoming more confident and graceful.

"Whatever happens, you'll always be my number one, okay?" Isla said.

"Promise?"

"Of course I promise." Isla held her arms out and Dani came to her, pressing her cheek against Isla's chest. Isla stroked her hair and hugged her sister tight. "We're a team."

"But you want Theo to be part of our team?"

She sucked in a breath. How was she supposed to answer that?

You know exactly *how to answer if you're being honest.*

"I like him a lot, but..." She stepped away, keeping her hands on Dani's shoulders. "Dating is complicated."

"Tell me about it." Dani snorted. "Maria Fernanda from school was dating Alexander for like five whole weeks and then she found out he kissed Natalia at some party and there was a *big* fight."

"That's a lot of drama," Isla said, amused.

"Too much for me." Dani shook her head. "But I don't think you and Theo will have drama."

"Why's that?"

"Because..." She thought about it for a moment. "He doesn't seem like a drama llama."

Isla laughed. "No, he certainly is not."

"And I don't want you to be lonely while I'm away at camp," Dani said. "Maybe he can come here and watch Netflix with you."

"That's a good idea."

Dani looked up at her, face totally serious. "Will you be okay without me?"

The nerve on this kid. Isla couldn't help but laugh, her sister was such a character. "I'll be just fine, thank you very much."

"Good, because I don't want to have to worry about you while I'm doing my classes, you know," she replied with a cheeky grin. "It will mess with my zen."

"You are so full of it, girl."

"But seriously, if you like him then you should date him." Dani nodded.

"Won't it make you worry?" She'd never really thought about needing her sister's permission to date, but having her blessing actually meant a lot to Isla. Because they *were* a team. "That I'll be like Mom?"

"You're not like Mom." She shook her head. "Mr. Minelli asked me to think about what my life might look like if Mom never came back and I think it would be the same as it is now. I like how things are now."

"You do?" That warmed Isla's heart.

"Yep." She nodded. "Sometimes I worry that you will leave, but Mr. Minelli pointed out that you have never once left. And past behavior is a good indication of future behavior."

Isla's chest clenched as her sister repeated her school counsellor's words. She was maturing, growing up before her very eyes.

"I trust you," Dani said. "Even if I get scared sometimes."

"Thank you, baby. I trust you, too." Isla blinked as tears pricked the backs of her eyes. "Now, you didn't look in the zip pocket of your suitcase."

"Why would I?" Dani asked, but her face morphed as she realized there was something hidden in there. She bounded over to it and shoved her hand into the small pocket, pulling out the tiny black box inside.

"Open it."

Dani pulled the bracelet out, gasping at the little ballet slipper charm. "I love it!"

Isla went over to help her put it on, her fingers fumbling a little with the delicate clasp. It was just like her sister—dainty, sweet, stronger than it looked. She slipped it over her wrist and secured the clasp, letting the charm dangle in the air.

"I want you to know how much I believe in you, Dani. You can do anything, you know that? Just work hard and be brave and keep going when things are rough."

"Just like you did."

"Yeah, just like I did."

As Isla helped Dani with the rest of her preparations, her mind lingered on her sister's unsuspectingly wise words. She *had* worked hard. She *had* been brave. She *had* kept going when things were rough.

Launching her own business was the next logical step. All

she had to do was believe in herself enough to take the leap. The Dachshund Wears Prada was the universe telling her to keep going, to keep pushing, to keep trying.

She could do this.

And as for Theo…she wanted him without the boundaries that she'd been so carefully putting into place. That meant they needed to be equal and he could no longer be her boss. Starting her own agency would fix both problems—give her dreams back *and* allow her to be with Theo without any power imbalances.

Worries and risks swirled in her mind, but Isla knew deep down this was the right move. She'd crunched the numbers. It could work. All she had to do was be sensible, probably working for someone else part-time while she got things off the ground. But with her research and careful planning and social proof…

It could really work.

Besides, if she announced that she was the wizard behind The Dachshund Wears Prada account then what more social proof did she need to convince people to give her their business?

The only thing that stood in her way now was telling Theo. Because she wouldn't start a relationship *or* a business with skeletons in her closet.

It was time to come clean.

Theo felt himself zoning out, the presentation projected onto the wall in front of him growing blurrier by the minute. The drone of the presenter's voice faded until it was nothing more than a buzz in his ears. At one point—in fact, at *most* points—in his life, this was the stuff he lived for. Work, building on his family's legacy, the day-to-day sameness of the four walls of his office.

But right now all he could think about was the fact that Isla was coming over…and staying the night.

Dani was off to ballet camp and would be gone for two

weeks. That meant two whole weeks of not having to linger at the door while he kissed Isla, silently begging her to stay just a moment longer. Two whole weeks of waking up with her warm body entwined with his. Two whole weeks of doing whatever the hell they wanted…including a little vacation.

He'd booked a luxury cabin upstate with one of those big sunken tubs and a bedroom that overlooked a lake. There was already champagne chilling in the fridge there and dinner would be cooked by a world-class chef. Oh, and the place was dog friendly so Camilla could come along, too.

He'd already packed his things and was planning to surprise Isla that afternoon. He had everything planned—they'd have a snack, get dirty in the shower, then he'd whisk her away.

"Mr. Garrison?"

"Huh." He shook his head, trying to bring his attention back to the present. "Sorry, what was that?"

"I wanted to know if you signed off on the packaging approach for the new imprint? We need to share mock-ups with the retail reps. Walmart was very interested."

"I'll take another look at it before I head home." He nodded. "Are we done?"

His leadership team exchanged glances, as if they sensed something was up. Nobody said a word.

"I have somewhere to be." Theo pushed back on his chair and walked out of the boardroom, needing to be in his own office for a while. He couldn't concentrate. This was *highly* unusual, since he had a stamina for work that would make most people's eyes bleed.

But not today.

He couldn't quite believe how fast he'd slipped down this slope. But, if he looked back, Isla had been chipping away his barriers from the moment he met her. That very first day in Central Park, he'd given up his real name. If *that* wasn't a sign that he was different with her, he didn't know what was.

And he'd started to wonder, for the first time *ever*, if he could have the life he'd always assumed was out of reach. She didn't want anything from him, she wasn't interested in using him to climb the social ladder, she wasn't looking to exploit his story. With her he could just…be.

But as he was about to enter his office, he noticed something out of the corner of his eye that alerted his intuition. Irina was sitting at her desk, with the executive assistant to his head of finance standing next to her. The two women laughed at something on Irina's phone.

"What's going on?" He wandered over to her desk.

"Oh, don't mind us." Irina pulled her glasses off and gently dabbed at her eyes with a tissue. "I think I had too much sugar from those cupcakes that Trident Media sent over."

"It's my fault." The other assistant shook her head. "A friend forwarded me this Instagram account about a Dachshund that gossips about all the pets of famous people in Manhattan. It's very clever."

Dachshund? A strange feeling settled in Theo's gut. "Show me."

"I really don't think it would be your thing," Irina said. "You hate social media."

"Humor me."

With a shrug, Irina handed her phone over. Theo looked at the picture—a shot of a dog, almost entirely out of frame in front of the Tiffany's on Fifth Avenue. The caption read: *Tiffany's is so 1961. You can't even have breakfast here. You lied to me, Audrey! Doesn't stop the pet of a celebrity you love to hate stopping here every morning, though. xoxo C.*

There was something about the picture that prevented him from handing the phone back. While it all seemed benign, a little flash of color at the edge of the photo made him look closer. There was a faint green blur that looked a hell of a lot like the edge of a piece of silk fluttering in the wind. After a few wrong taps, he found his way to the profile page.

The Dachshund Wears Prada
Canine. Heiress. Fashion icon. Will pee on your Chanel.
For business inquiries, DM me.
xoxo C

There were photos of Manhattan scenery, lots of different dogs playing in Central Park or walking along the sidewalk. There were also shots with the dog mostly out of the frame, so only a little bit of tail or a paw showed. It was clear this was C, the protagonist of the account.

But one photo made his heart almost stop. A pair of gold high-heeled sandals were in the shot, one standing and another toppled over, nestled by plush white carpet. In the background, was a dog bed. The focus was on the shoes, so you couldn't really see if there was even an animal in the bed.

The caption read: *Big night last night. Let's just say the after-party was the highlight of the evening, if you know what I mean. xoxo C.*

Theo's blood ran cold. It couldn't be…

Except too many things lined up. The date of that post was the day after his grandmother's gala and the gold shoes looked a hell of a lot like the ones Isla had worn. He couldn't say he remembered them in great detail, since her feet had not been the focus of his attention, but they seemed to match his fuzzy memory.

And the flicker of green in that other photo was the same shade as the silk scarf he'd tied around Camilla's collar.

Theo handed the phone back, stone-faced. Irina rolled her

eyes. "I knew you wouldn't find it funny. I know your taste well enough to predict that."

"You didn't notice anything about this account?" he asked.

She looked at him strangely. "Should I have noticed something?"

"No."

Before she could ask any more questions, he turned on his heel and went into his office, pulling the door closed. On his laptop, he Googled *The Dachshund Wears Prada* and several listings popped up. There were a few posts from a pet forum, a post on Reddit and a couple of gossip-type articles that pointed to the Instagram account. Lots of speculation, but no real detail.

Until he came across a Twitter thread of people talking about it. Someone had asked who people thought was behind the account and names were being tossed about—a socialite and daughter of a prominent New York senator, a former Hollywood actress who'd gone into animal-based philanthropy, a Wall Street hedge fund bro who had a public Instagram for his Dachshund, Flick. Some even speculated it was Netflix making a publicity stunt to promote an unconfirmed *Devil Wears Prada* reboot.

But one tweet made the breath catch in the back of his throat:

@Sohocialite89 didn't I read something about Etna Francois-Garrison having a Dachshund? Maybe she left it to her grandson in her will. Crazy rich people would do that.

That's when Theo remembered that Camilla had taken part in a photo shoot recently. His grandmother was supposed to do it, but she'd become too sick in her final days. So they'd moved it and found a model to take her place. But the article itself that would appear in *Vogue* alongside the photos would talk about the relationship she had with her dog. It would refer to Camilla by name.

Camilla the Dachshund. C.

For a moment, Theo could only stare into space, a hollow yawn of nothingness growing inside him.

Isla wanted back into her old job. He'd been hoping to hang on to her as long as possible, but Theo wasn't naive. He'd been preparing himself for the inevitable day when she'd leave for the kind of work she really wanted. In some ways, he'd been looking forward to it.

If he wanted something longer term with her, she couldn't remain his employee. And so he'd planned to talk to Isla about it while they were away. He was going to broach the topic of how he could help her find a job so that he was no longer her boss—no rush, no deadline. However, it was important to him that she knew he wanted to do things the right way. That he wanted to support and respect her.

That he wanted for this wonderful thing to continue.

And now…

Now he'd found out that Isla was using Camilla to get what she wanted. And that meant she was using *him*. How long had she planned to let it go before announcing who C was? Before drawing on his name and notoriety for her own gain? How much longer until she betrayed him?

"She's already betrayed you." Anger rippled through his body like a shock of electricity.

She *knew* how he felt about publicity. She *knew* how he felt about people prying into his private life. She *knew* that he'd let her get closer than anyone else ever before.

And that had been a giant mistake.

22

Isla let herself into Theo's place after she dropped Dani off at a friend's house. She and another ballet student were going to the camp together and the girl's mother had kindly offered to drive them both. Which meant Isla could get to Theo's early and surprise him. They'd talked about her staying over while Dani was at the camp, so she'd brought some clothes and had planned to freshen up before he got home from work. His shower was a billion times better than the crappy one in her apartment.

But before she got sexy with him, she was going to come clean about The Dachshund Wears Prada and her plans to start her own agency. They'd talked a little here and there about her career dreams so the agency idea wouldn't come as a huge shock. But as for the other bit…

She tried to shake off her nerves as she walked through the penthouse. Camilla was curled up and sleeping like a good girl in front of one of the windows, where the sunlight was streaming in and warming her small body. Isla didn't disturb her.

Shower first, then deal with everything else.

She carried her overnight bag into Theo's bedroom, stopping short when she saw something sitting on his bed. It was a bag, very similar in shape to her own, but instead of practical black polyester, his was made of a cognac leather. It had some initials embossed into the leather—EFG. His grandmother's. It was open at the top, and Theo's clothes were neatly folded inside.

There was a piece of paper on the bed next to it and when she peeked, she could see it was for a booking. Theo's handwriting was scrawled in black ink: *8:00 p.m. Chef Dubois $1,500.*

Isla scratched her head. What in the world…?

"You're early." Theo's voice made her jump.

She placed her bag on the floor and turned around. He stood in the doorway, dressed in a gray three-piece suit and a crisp white shirt. His hair was mussed. Must have been a long day at work.

"So are you," she said, walking toward him. But she stopped short when Theo didn't reach for her the way he usually did. In fact, his coolness was reminiscent of her first days of working for him, where he was remote and removed. Where she felt an anger simmering below the surface.

"You spoiled my surprise." He nodded toward the bed. "I had grand plans for the next few days."

"You were going to surprise me with a trip away?" Warmth kindled inside her—maybe that was why he seemed a bit distant. He'd wanted to surprise her. "That's so sweet. But what's with the chef?"

"He's a renowned private chef."

"You were going to pay $1,500 for a private chef to cook for us while we were away?" Her eyes almost bugged out of her head.

"That was for dinner tonight."

"Are you serious? That's..." She shook her head, but then something cold struck her in the chest. She'd almost missed the most important part of his statement. "Wait. Was or is?"

"You tell me."

The air around him was so frigid, Isla actually shivered. Something was wrong, *very* wrong. "What are you talking about?"

"I came across something interesting today," he said, walking past her and into the room. He raked a hand through his hair, following the wave that he'd created by repeating that action over and over. "An Instagram account."

Isla's stomach dropped. "The Dachshund Wears Prada."

"You're not going to deny it?"

The absolute nothingness in his expression was what worried Isla the most—because she'd expected him to be disappointed. Mad, even. Heck, she would have taken him being furious because at least then it would show he was feeling something. But this blankness meant he'd already started shutting her out.

"I was going to tell you," she said, cringing at how she sounded like a terrible cliché. "Tonight."

He seemed to look right through her. "Right."

"I know it sounds like a lie, but..." She closed her eyes for a second to draw on the strength inside her. "I swear it's true. I was going to tell you about it and I was going to tell you that I'm planning to start my own social media agency."

Something flickered in his expression, but it was gone in an instant. Extinguished like a birthday candle.

"I should have said something sooner." She pressed her hand to her chest and her heart was beating a million miles a minute. "The last thing I want is for you to feel like I betrayed your trust."

"Too late."

"Theo." She stepped toward him and he flinched. The movement was so small and so subtle she almost missed it, but that tiny visceral reaction felt as strong as if he'd slapped her across the face. The rejection resonated through her in haunting waves. "I never shared anything personal on the account. I never mentioned you or your family by name, and I most certainly never took any pictures that people could link to you. That was a line I was never going to cross."

"You used Camilla as internet fodder."

"I used a *persona* for internet fodder. Nothing in those posts can come back to bite you or your company—most of the stories I told on there were either amped-up versions of real life or they were completely fabricated. It's more fiction than fact."

"You don't think people will take it as fact? You don't think once they find out it's my world propping up that account that they will analyze every single word to speculate about my life?" His voice was dead calm. Dead cold. "I know how this goes, Isla."

"I understand why you're paranoid about—"

"I am *not* paranoid. I have the history to back up my concerns. I have a lifetime of proof why it's smart to fiercely protect my privacy." He turned to face the window, pushing her out of his view. "And I should have been smarter than to let someone in."

"Someone like me?" Panic fluttered in her chest, like a hummingbird trapped between two hands.

"Not someone like you, Isla. Someone, period." He turned,

jaw hard as steel and shoulders set broad like a blockade. "I knew better than to let someone—*anyone*—get close to me."

"What are you so afraid of? That people out in the world know your dog sitter posted some funny, made-up things online?"

"Made-up, like that post insinuating we slept together the night of my grandmother's gala?" Now she saw the crack in his facade. There was a fissure, a sliver showing the real Theo hurt and roaring behind his walls of ice. "Am I worried about people finding out that I slept with you? Yeah, I fucking am."

Isla reeled. "Why?"

"Because you work for me."

"So? It was consensual. I *wanted* to be here and I have no issues with telling people that."

"Do you really think it matters what either one of us says? Once people get wind of a story like that, the only thing that matters is what's going to generate clicks and ad revenue. If you really think there's more to it than that, then you're even more naive than I first thought."

"I am *not* naive." She clenched her back teeth together.

"For someone who's worked in that space, you of all people should know gossip grows like a weed."

Her breath came out in a rush. "Were you really never going to tell people about me?"

He blinked. "Of course not."

"Even if I no longer worked for you?" She shook her head, trying to understand whether he was serious or whether he was simply lashing out because he was hurt.

"Yes, even then."

Isla's mouth dropped open. Sure, they'd never explicitly talked about what might happen if she stopped working for him and no, they hadn't set any boundaries or rules or anything like that. But she'd assumed that things were progressing in a way that might mean something longer term. After all she…

It hit her with a force of a battering ram.

You love him.

No, that couldn't be right. Love? So quickly? She was *not* her mother, falling for a man she barely knew and wishing for things that only existed in fairy tales. Chasing a dream while the real world crumbled around her.

This wasn't love. It couldn't be.

"I'm not some dirty little secret," Isla said, scrubbing her hands over her face while she tried desperately to unthink that nasty, dangerous thought. "I deserve more than to be shamefully tucked away in a drawer."

"You think I wanted to hide you because I'm *ashamed*?" The crack had grown wider, splintering and racing through his protective shell. "I wanted to protect you."

"I can protect myself."

"No, you can't," he said with a snort. "You have no idea what's out there. If you're even asking me these questions, it tells me you really *are* naive. Not that any of this matters, because it turns out you're not the person I thought you were anyway."

Isla let out a shaky breath, emotions swirling like a tornado inside her. "I know why you're doing this."

He said nothing, but he stripped his jacket off and threw it on the bed. His long, strong fingers began to work the buttons on his vest, popping them one by one. It was like he needed to do something with his hands, something to keep himself busy.

"I know you're doing this because you're hurt," she continued. "And I'm sorry I hurt you, Theo. I swear I was going to tell you about the account and what my plans were. For what it's worth, it only started as a joke between myself and a friend. I was still hurting after getting fired and taking this job…"

Was this going to make her sound like an ungrateful bitch? Possibly. But she figured the only way she could get out of this mess was to be honest. Rather than running away and hiding like the last time she screwed everything up, this time she was going to stand her ground and fight. Fight for herself, fight for what she cared about, fight for her future.

And that wasn't only the future of her work, but the future of her life with Theo, too. Because that's what she wanted.

She'd never let a man into her life before because she had too many boundaries. Even when she'd dated that other guy, she'd had one foot out the door. Ready to leave at a moment's notice because she had no greater fear than being irresponsible and driven by primal impulse, like her mother. She had never let her base wants rule her life.

"I'm so grateful you hired me, because I was in a deep, dark hole. But this isn't what I want to do with my life." Tears pricked the backs of her eyes, but she blinked them away. Could he possibly understand her position? "I worked *so* hard to get to where I was, and one slipup took it all away. It was like my progress had been wiped out. I was given a clean slate that I didn't want. So I made a silly Instagram account."

"A silly Instagram account mocking what my grandmother wanted for her pet."

"I can see how it looks like that. I promise I can." She nodded. "But none of this was ever supposed to be more than me blowing off steam. That's it. I never meant to hurt you or disrespect your grandmother. I…"

Was she going to say it? Was she going to stop putting barriers around herself and instead lay herself on the line, even when it was likely she'd get slashed in two?

Yes. Because she might not feel comfortable labeling her

feelings, but she couldn't deny their existence. She *felt* something for Theo. Something strong and real. Something worth risking her heart for.

"I want to be with you and I don't care if the world knows it."

Theo wanted to believe her. He wanted to believe like he'd never wanted anything for a long, *long* time.

She stood in front of him, dressed casually in a pink T-shirt, jeans with a rip across one thigh and cute pink socks with slices of watermelon on them. Her dark hair was swept back into a ponytail and her face was bare—leaving her big, blue eyes to take all his attention. She looked fresh and innocent and…believable.

But how could he believe her when all signs pointed to what history had already taught him? People would use him.

"Of course you'd want the world to know it, because that would help your cause, wouldn't it?" he said, fighting the hot, fiery feeling crawling up his sternum. "That would help you launch a successful agency with publicity from being attached to the Hermit of Fifth Avenue. What a story it would create! The misanthropic recluse and the social media whiz."

Her lower lip trembled. "You really think I would date you to further my career?"

"Maybe it's not the only reason, I'm sure my money would help."

"How dare you." Tears glittered in her eyes. "Just because I don't come from much doesn't mean money is the only thing that matters to me."

She seemed genuinely hurt and for a hot second, Theo wanted nothing more than to bundle her up in his arms and whisper apologies in her ear all night long. What an awful thing to say.

But she was the one who lied. She was the one who de-

ceived. She was the one who risked bringing more attention
to him when he'd spent his whole adult life trying to get
away from it.

His accusations made sense, logically. But there was a bit-
ter taste on his tongue, because deep down he didn't know
what to believe. From the moment he'd met Isla, she'd seemed
genuine. She'd seemed *real*.

That's why her secret had hurt him so badly.

"I should have known better," he said, more to himself than
her. "You were trying to get closer to me from the second you
started working here. Putting things in my cupboard, taking
care of me when I was injured."

"Theo, the *only* thing that points to is how barren your life
has been if you take someone showing you the most basic of
human decencies as a sign of them trying to get close to you
for their own gain."

The woman knew how to land a punch, that was for damn
sure. "My life is barren for a reason. *This* is the reason, because when I get close to someone they prove that I should
never have let them in."

"I haven't proven anything besides some bad judgment." She
folded her arms across her chest. That was when Theo realized
that Camilla had come to the door and was looking at them
both with her glossy black eyes. Her head made slight movements, flicking back and forth between him and Isla, and he
got the feeling of a kid watching their parents fight. "I should
have told you what I was doing. I take full responsibility for
that. But you're blowing this *way* out of proportion."

"You have no idea what I've been through," he seethed.

"I have some idea."

"You don't."

"I know the media ate you for breakfast after your parents died." Her nostrils flared like she was trying to keep her

tears at bay, the sympathy rolling off her in noxious waves. He didn't want her to look at him like that, like how people had looked at him for *years*. "I know that video of you crying was circulated for a long, *long* time."

Shame swept over him. He'd been so weak back then—just a boy trying and failing to be a man. He'd crumbled when he should have been strong and the world never let him forget it.

"Did you know they called me a pussy at school? Did you know I got beaten up by a bunch of douche bros and had to go to my parents' funeral with a black eye where *everyone* could see? I never wanted to do that interview." He almost spat the words out, the anger rising up in him so hard and so fast he was struggling to control it. "But apparently it would have been 'bad form' for our family not to speak about it. Never mind what I needed."

"That should never have happened." A tear splashed onto her cheek and she whisked it away with the back of her hand. "I'm sorry you were put through that."

"Did you know I *had* a girlfriend once?" He laughed bitterly at the shock on her face. "While I was in college, I met this woman at a party. Leah. I fell hard for her because she was sweet and unpretentious and she didn't know anything about the world I came from."

Isla bit down on her lip and her eyes lowered to the floor.

"I wanted to give her my mother's ring as a promise, but Gram wouldn't let me have it. I argued with her, because I thought I knew better. And then I found out Leah had been in touch with a reporter and that she was going to give an interview about what it was like to date me." He let out a sound of disgust. "She was going to tell *my* story without my permission."

"I don't know what to say." Isla shook her head. "That's terrible, but this isn't the same. I'm not looking to tell your story. I want to create *my* story. I want to build something to show my sister how important it is to be tenacious and resilient and hard-working. Your story is *yours*, Theo."

"So you're going to delete the Instagram account?"

Isla's eyes widened and he could see the shock rippling through her. "It doesn't have anything to do with you. I'm not going to use your name to advance my agency. I wouldn't do that."

"But people will know. Once you announce your agency and, I assume, that you were behind this account, people will put two and two together."

"And I will release a statement saying you have nothing to do with the business." She frowned. "Do you really think I need to rely on deception tactics to be successful?"

"It's not exactly a leap."

"I built this from *nothing*. I built it from so little, in fact, it was never meant to grow the way it did. But that proves I have talent, that I can build a business and make it work. But I'd be stupid *not* to leverage The Dachshund Wears Prada to launch my agency—I might be confident in myself, but I still need to put food on the table for my sister. I still have to make sure she has security. And that means I need to launch from the best position I possibly can."

He understood the need for survival, he really did. Not in the same way that Isla had experienced it—not for things like rent money and food. He was fortunate to never have worried about those things. But he understood the need to protect himself the way she did.

"I know these two things seem in contradiction, but they're not. The last seven weeks…" Isla shook her head. "I had no idea how I was going to get back on my feet. You offered me a job and you helped me to see how strong I was. How I could keep going."

"Don't." He held up a hand. "Don't try and turn this into something sweet that we shared, because I did *not* buy into having my life used for a story."

Isla's eyes searched his face. He could see the desperation setting in, that she was grasping for straws. "I'm sorry. I understand completely why you're upset. But this doesn't have to be a big explosion. I want to be with you and I know you want to be with me."

"You're so confident of that?"

She faltered, but then she drew her shoulders back. "I am. I don't date, Theo, and neither do you. So the fact that both of us went against how we normally behave says something. It means that we pushed one another out of our comfort zones, we *grew* together. We've changed for one another."

"I haven't changed. I won't change."

"You are *not* the same man who scolded me for buying him groceries. You let me in and I did the same for you. That's not a throwaway thing." She reached for him, but he backed up and she sucked on her lower lip. "We don't have to end this."

"It's already over, Isla. It was over the second I figured out you were behind the account." He looked down to the floor, avoiding her pleading stare and the judgment from Camilla in the doorway. "There's no fixing this."

"If you keep pushing people away, eventually they'll stop trying," she said quietly.

"Then I will finally feel like people are listening to what I want," he said coldly. "Get your things. You're fired."

She released a shaky breath, but like the dignified woman she was, Isla scooped up her bag and headed out of his bedroom, pausing to pat Camilla on top of her furry head. Her footsteps echoed off the high ceilings and eventually he heard the front door close.

Camilla looked at him, snorting as if disgusted with his

actions. He wasn't sure he could blame her. Nothing about what had happened felt right. He *knew* he was overreacting on some level, but at the same time...

It was never going to work. Her job involves being seen and you want to stay hidden—it's a recipe for failure.

That didn't make him feel any better as he stared at the leather bag on his bed or the printout of his accommodation booking. It didn't make him feel any better when Camilla turned on her paws and trotted out of his room, pausing to throw him a look of disdain over one shoulder. It didn't make him feel any better when the penthouse became so silent the only thing he could hear was the dull thump of his own heartbeat.

"It's for the best," he said to himself.

But Theo wasn't sure he could believe it.

23

ONE MONTH LATER...

Isla pushed back from her desk and leaned her head from one side to the other, trying to stretch out the tightness in her neck and shoulders. She'd finished up work for the day and had everything neat and organized for her counterpart to come in the following morning. She'd even left a little Post-it wishing her a good day.

Sliding her chair under the desk, she dropped her heels into a shopping tote and stuffed her feet into a pair of sneakers. Her poor feet were already crying out for a rest. But working as the receptionist at a high-end pet salon required her to look presentable at all times, even if running from the desk to the treatment rooms in stilettos was likely to give her a bunion.

Yep, that's right. Isla was a receptionist, but only part-time.

Three days a week, to be exact, *and* she got to see Camilla whenever Theo's assistant brought her in for a haircut. The rest of the time Isla was working on building her pet social media agency, Paws in the City. Which was exactly what she was working on tonight…by going to look at an office space.

Isla walked out with the groomer who'd taken the last appointment and locked up behind them. Scout was waiting on the sidewalk, dressed in her usual attire of ripped jeans, a band T-shirt knotted at her navel and her hair in blond Princess Leia buns.

"Ready?" She bounced on her feet and clapped her hands together. "I have a good feeling about this one."

Isla sighed. "Just like you had a good feeling about the other fifty-something places we looked at?"

It was ridiculously hard to find an office space to rent in Manhattan that wasn't either A, *stupidly* expensive or B, a rat-infested shoebox masquerading as an office. Isla knew those things going in, but the real estate agent had assured them they would find something. After all, if Isla wanted to look legit then she needed a place for her clients to come see her…a place that wasn't her no-animals-allowed apartment.

"You have to stay positive—we only need to find one place." Scout patted her on the back as they walked.

"I'm starting to think what we want doesn't exist."

Isla had crunched the numbers over and over. Between what little she had in savings, the income from her part-time reception job, plus the freelance social media work she'd picked up through a gig website—using a pseudonym so people would actually hire her—she knew *exactly* how much she could afford to spend on a place. To the cent.

And that would only last her six months. So that was how long she had to make her business work. Given loads of businesses took years to become profitable, it was a tall order.

But Isla was confident in her abilities *and* she'd set aside the money for Dani's ballet classes for next semester so she knew that wouldn't be affected. Yeah, it was kind of like trying to balance on a knife's edge. And if one thing went wrong the whole lot could come tumbling down like a house of cards.

But what choice did she have?

The reception job was little more than minimum wage, and Isla was still seeing rejection emails from job applications she'd put out months ago. Paying for a college course to re-educate herself would put her in the hole as much as it would to set her business up. So she could either stick with her low-paying job and struggle forever, or take a risk. A calculated, well-thought-out risk.

"Here it is." Scout pointed at a tiny sliver of a building, sandwiched between a coffee shop on one side and one of those touristy places that sold plastic Statue of Liberty replicas on the other.

"Ladies, hello." Their real estate agent came forward with a wave. She was a sharp woman usually dressed in all black, although sometimes she splashed out with a little gray or navy. A pair of thick-rimmed glasses sat on her nose. "Let's take a look."

They went through the single-door entrance and walked up the stairs to the second floor. There were two offices.

"There's an accounting firm here," the real estate agent said, gesturing to a frosted glass door with the firm name printed in simple block letters. "They've been leasing for over a year and seem stable."

"And they'll be okay with animals coming and going?" Isla asked.

"The partner's wife works at an animal hospital, actually. They're dog people, from what I understand, so no issues there." The agent pulled out a set of keys and opened the other door.

Isla and Scout followed her inside. It was *tiny*. But it appeared relatively clean, and there was even a reception desk in place.

"Used to be a spiritual healing clinic of some kind." The woman scrunched her nose up. "Some crystals and aromatherapy bullshit, no offense if you're into that. Place has been clear less than a week and it'll go fast at this price."

Isla looked around. She didn't notice any rats, which was a plus. Or cockroaches.

"There's one appointment room," the agent said as she showed them through a door. While compact, it would be enough to fit a small table and chairs for meetings. Then they went to the last door off the reception area. "And this 'office' space was more commonly used as a supply cupboard, I believe."

No kidding. "I can see why you used air quotes."

The office space would barely fit a desk, let alone a chair. There had been shelving built-in, obviously to convert the room into a storage space, but it *did* have a thin, rectangular window. If Isla bought one of those micro desks from IKEA, she could wedge it against the window-side and have enough space to get in and out. She could hang a hook on the wall for her coat in winter.

"You can't swing a cat in here, but it's clean," the agent said. "And it's in your budget."

At the top end, admittedly. Right on the line of being too much. But it was the best they'd seen for the money.

"Can you give us a few minutes?" Scout asked with a smile.

"Of course. I'll leave you to it." The agent walked out to the landing outside and closed the door.

"What do you think?" Scout asked.

"It's perfect, actually. Tiny, but perfect." Isla let out a long breath, feeling more anxious about her life choices than she had in weeks. Now that it was becoming real, the weight of the pressure had come bearing down on her.

"Great." Scout blinked. "So why do you look like you're about to lose your lunch?"

"I don't know, it's…" Her chest felt heavy and tight. "Would a normal person just get a job and do their nine-to-five instead of putting everything on the line hoping for a moonshot?"

"You *know* what you're doing." Scout slung an arm around her shoulders. "And you don't need a moonshot, not right away. You've crunched the numbers and you have a *ton* of contacts from the companies who've reached out to The Dachshund Wears Prada, so you're not going in cold. I mean, I'm not sure why you haven't done the grand reveal yet…"

Why *hadn't* she outed herself as the mastermind behind The Dachshund Wears Prada? People were still reaching out to her, speculating or wanting to do business, the followers were still going up. And yet she hadn't been able to bring herself to pull the trigger.

Theo.

It had been a month since he'd fired her and she'd left his penthouse in tears—angry at him and angry at herself. Angry at the world because it felt like every time she took a step forward, the universe shoved her back with two hands.

"I don't know if I can," Isla said, admitting aloud for the first time what had been in her head for the last four weeks.

"What do you mean?"

"Theo was right, I…" She sighed. "I betrayed his trust. I intruded on his privacy when he asked me not to and outing myself will blow back on him."

No matter how many scenarios she rolled around in her head, she couldn't figure out a way to out herself without also outing him. Too many people knew who she was—the other dog sitters at the play group, the people who'd seen her at the gala, the concierge staff in his building. They would all recognize her if it went to the media.

"It doesn't matter how it started and that I never intended to hurt him. It matters how it *finished*." Weariness crept through her body, winding like vines around her limbs. "I can't do that to him."

"He fired you, Isla. You don't owe him anything." Scout shook her head, confused. "Unless…"

"Unless I love him." Saying it out loud didn't feel as good as it should have. It didn't lift the weight from her shoulders or unclog the back of her throat. "He's been hurt by people his whole life. I don't want to be one more person who uses him."

"Whoa." Scout bobbed her head slowly. "Sparkly vampire energy guy, who would have thought?"

Despite her regret, Isla laughed. "Stop it."

"What are you going to do?"

There was only one solution. "I have to shut down the account."

"You're a good person, Isla. But you *need* this to work, don't you? Wouldn't shutting the account down, like, shoot you in the foot?"

Maybe. Probably. "Yeah, it would."

But what would she be teaching Dani if she climbed over others to get ahead? What would she be teaching her sister about the world if she said that success was worth more than treating people with dignity and respect?

She tipped her face up to the ceiling, hoping she might find answers there. Instead she found an ugly light fixture. "I'll make note of all the contacts of the companies who got in touch before I delete it. That way I have their information and hopefully their interest means they're looking for people to work with."

"I want to help," Scout said with a firm nod. "I appreciate that you're trying to do the right thing and I believe you can make this a success."

"You've already helped, Scout. You've been here the whole time pushing me and supporting me and being the best friend a woman could have." Isla hugged her. "That's more than I could possibly ask for."

"I'm serious, though."

"So am I." Isla wrinkled her brow in confusion.

"I have some money." She nodded and Isla raised an eyebrow. Scout was not exactly super regular with her work, so how did she have savings? "It's legal, I promise."

Isla rolled her eyes. "I know you're not a criminal, girl. Please don't lump me in the same group as your family thinking bad of you."

"That's my demons talking, not yours. I get it." She chewed on her bottom lip. "You know my grandparents are well-off, right? You're the only person I've ever told."

Isla blinked. "Yeah, but I thought you had nothing to do with them."

"Only when I get 'visitation' with Lizzie, but I basically pretend they're not there and they do the same with me." She sighed. "They gave me ten thousand dollars."

Isla gaped. "But why would they give you money if they disapprove of you?"

"It was so I'd stop asking about getting custody of Lizzie."

"Oh, Scout." Isla hugged her friend again. "They really did that?"

"I didn't want to take it, because I won't stay away. But they knew my bank account details and they transferred it right in so they could show Lizzie I'd taken money from them." She scrubbed a hand over her face. "I've tried to give it back, but they won't take it."

"That's so...cruel."

"The money has been sitting there for ages. They let me see her once a month, at most, but if I push for more they've threatened to put a stop to the visits altogether." Her face crumpled. "It's dirty money, as far as I'm concerned. But I'd like you to have it, for the business."

"No." Isla shook her head. "I can't take that."

"Please. Let me feel like I'm contributing to something good for once in my life." Scout placed a hand on each one of her shoulders. "You've got the best chance of both of us in being successful and I want to buy a ticket, okay? I want to be part of this."

"Scout…" Isla's heart ached for her best friend. "You don't have to *buy* your way in to being part of this. I want you here."

"Look, I have money and you need it. It's sitting in my bank account doing nothing and I feel sick every time I see it. I'm *not* going to spend it on me." She looked stricken. "I can't stand the thought of proving them right about who I am."

"I can't just take money from you."

"Then maybe I can be an investor? Businesses have those, right? Maybe it can be a loan with some generous repayment terms and then once you've paid it all back to me, I'll donate it to an animal welfare charity. Or maybe I can be a business partner?"

"You really want to do this?" Isla asked. The money would make a world of difference.

"Of course I do. I want to see you succeed and I respect that you're doing the right thing by Theo even though he was a grade-A dick-face to you."

"We were dick-faces to each other," she said with a sigh. "But I care about him, a hell of a lot. And even though I know there's no going back and fixing things, I want to be able to hold my head high, ya know?"

"I do."

"So we're doing this?" Excitement filtered through Isla's veins, making her jittery and a little unsteady on her feet. "I can't believe it."

"Believe it, Isla. Paws in the City is going to open its doors once we give this place a fresh coat of paint and find some furniture." Scout grinned. "And I assume you're going to need a receptionist extraordinaire, right? Or an assistant maybe? I know someone who comes pretty cheap."

Isla gave her a playful shove. "Don't undersell yourself. I *know* how good you are with people. You'll be an asset to this business."

The two women walked out of the office and shared the exciting news with the real estate agent. As all three of them traipsed back down the stairs and out onto the street, Isla was filled with mixed emotions. But one thing she knew above all else, was that deleting The Dachshund Wears Prada account was the right thing to do. For Theo and for herself, because Isla *wasn't* the kind of person who was happy to climb toward success using others as stepping-stones.

Every day that had passed in the past month felt longer than the last. Without him, there was a gaping hole in her life. But starting her business would keep her busy and she hoped that eventually the pain would fade. Wasn't there an old saying that it was better to have loved and lost? She wasn't so sure about that.

But she *had* loved Theo, even if it had seemed too scary to acknowledge at the time. Maybe, if she was lucky, she'd find a love like that again in the future.

24

Theo leaned back against the plush leather seating of the private car as it drove through the streets of Brooklyn. Outside, the sky was impossibly blue and the clouds were so fluffy it looked as though they'd been painted. Eventually, the cemetery's main entrance appeared and the car followed the winding road to where his grandmother was buried.

It was the first time Theo had been to visit since the funeral.

"Ready to see Gram?" he asked Camilla, who was sitting in a special dog seat. She seemed more than happy to shove her nose toward the small gap in the window and sniff the world outside.

In the last month they'd formed a bond like Theo could never have expected. He'd decided not to hire another dog sitter—partially because no one could ever take her place, and partially because he felt like he could manage Camilla himself now. He'd scaled back her appointments to the essentials and donned his disguise to take her out every night for a walk around Central Park. Irina helped him out on occasion, too, by taking Camilla to her grooming appointments.

She hadn't shredded a single suit *and* she even liked to curl up in his lap at night while he caught up on work after dinner. Dare he say it…they were friends.

The car rolled to a stop and Theo unclipped Camilla from the seat's safety mechanism so he could attach her leash. He didn't know if dogs were allowed in the cemetery. Better to ask forgiveness than permission, right? He wasn't even sure why he'd brought her, but he needed some support and Camilla was it.

They walked across the springy grass and Camilla's tail bounced happily with each step. His grandmother's gravesite was neatly tended, with fresh flowers bursting from a vase. Theo had brought another bunch with him along with a small vase.

"Here we are." He paused and crouched, brushing away a single leaf that had fluttered down onto the plaque.

Camilla sniffed the air and looked at Theo, then at the ground. She pawed at the ground gently, so as not to disturb the earth, almost like she was saying hello.

"I brought Camilla here to see you, Gram," he said, setting the flowers down. "You wouldn't believe that we've become buddies. I'll be honest, I was really pissed at you for hiding her in the will. But…"

He shook his head. Now he was talking to dogs *and* dead people?

Well, who else are you going to talk to? You've pushed away every living person who tries to get close to you.

"You always knew what I needed, even though I resisted it at every turn." He laughed and shook his head. "I'm pretty good at that self-sabotage thing, huh?"

Camilla barked her agreement.

"No need to kick a man while he's down," Theo grumbled. "It's just how I am. I'm not meant to be the person who connects. It's too hard."

But wasn't it equally hard being alone? Because he was now, truly and utterly alone. No family, no friends. The closest he had was his assistant, but that was a working relationship and he couldn't confide personal things to her.

With every day that passed he waited for it to get easier. To get less lonely. And with every day that passed the gaping hole in his life grew bigger. It didn't help that Camilla *still* waited by the door each morning, hoping Isla would show up. One day she sat there and cried pitifully, causing Theo to crank up some music to drown it out.

Isla betrayed his trust. Used him.

But the more times he circled on that thought, the less anger it held and the less sense it all made. Did she *really* betray him? Or was he so conditioned to anticipate betrayal that he assigned blame to her actions without giving her a chance to tell her side of the story?

"Anyway, I wanted to talk to you. You were the person I used to go to when I was stuck and…" He placed a palm on the plaque. "I'm stuck now."

He wanted to change. Hell, when he was with Isla he *had* changed. Not completely and maybe not in all the ways he needed to, but she'd helped him open up. She'd helped him trust. She'd helped him *live*.

And not once had she judged him for being the way he was.

"I don't know why I'm looking for help here," he said to himself, scrubbing a hand over his face.

He wasn't sure exactly what he hoped to get out of this trip. A message from the heavens? But there was nothing more than the scent of roses and grass and the warmth of relentless sunshine. Theo hovered by the grave for a moment longer and then tugged on Camilla's leash. "Come on, girl. Time to go. There's nothing but ghosts here."

He walked back to the car and slid into the back seat feeling less than satisfied. On the way back home, as his driver took them through the city, Theo distracted himself by looking at his phone. He'd set up an alert for Isla's name, waiting for the hammer to drop about The Dachshund Wears Prada.

So far, nothing. But today there was an article that caught his attention.

From Disney princesses to Instapooches, Isla Thompson is determined to overcome her mistakes... (by Peta McKinnis, Spill The Tea Society and Culture reporter)

Who remembers the video of former Disney princess, Amanda Harte, puking down the front of her couture gown right before the Met Gala? Two careers hit a hurdle that day. Not only was Amanda dropped from a lucrative cosmetics campaign with industry giant Maybelline, but her box office debut released to less than stellar results. Critics claimed the performance was flat, but we have to wonder how much the star's fall from grace impacted her reputation.

Yet Amanda wasn't the only casualty. Career social media guru Isla Thompson—who thought she had stopped the Instagram Live video from recording—was fired from her role as senior consultant with the Gateway Agency. Since then she dropped off the map, turning her own social profiles to private and disappearing out of the public eye altogether.

Until now.

Yesterday, Thompson announced she was starting a brand new venture in the social media world by launching her own animal social media agency, Paws in the City. Here's what she has to say:

"Who doesn't love seeing a cute dog or cat on their social feed? With the online landscape becoming increasingly divided, animals are the one thing we all want on our screens. Paws in the City is a specialist influencer and modeling agency for our four (or six) legged friends and we represent clients with engaged fans across all social media platforms.

"At Paws in the City, we find the perfect animal for each advertiser's needs and work with our clients to create uplifting, engaging and inspiring digital content. Our mission is to make social media a happier, furrier place."

The article went on to provide more detail about Isla's plans and to give an update on Amanda Harte and how she was rebuilding her reputation. There wasn't a single mention of The Dachshund Wears Prada *or* Theo *or* the Garrison family. The only thing that was mentioned was that Isla had been working in the pet space while taking a break from being online in the past few months.

Theo clicked through to the Paws in the City website.

It was simple and clean, with a white, hot pink and gray color scheme. A professional photo of Isla holding an adorable floppy-eared bunny put a smile on Theo's face. It said "coming soon" and there was news of an office space in the works. Interested parties were directed to contact the company. She was really doing it—striking out on her own.

A surge of pride rushed through him. There wasn't a doubt in his mind that she would make it.

He looked through her website and the accompanying social accounts and there was still no mention of The Dachshund Wears Prada. Strange. Yet things became even more odd when he searched for the account on Instagram—and couldn't find it. More digging revealed that he wasn't the only one confused about why the account had been deleted.

The person behind The Dachshund Wears Prada remained a mystery.

Theo shoved his phone into his pocket and leaned back in his seat, perplexed. If Isla was starting her own business, why had she deleted the account? Wasn't that what their whole fight was about?

Not really.

Their fight had been about so much more. He was angry that she'd kept the account from him and then he'd done his usual thing where he slammed the door in her face, metaphorically speaking. In some ways, he'd felt a sense of relief in confronting her because then he could point to a specific reason for walking away. Then he'd fired her, knowing she needed her job. Knowing that she supported her sister. Knowing that she would have quit anyway and all he'd done was take decision-making power away from her.

He'd been an asshole of epic proportions.

Something had shifted inside him—something set in motion by Isla from the moment he met her. He'd thought after Isla left that he could simply go back to how things were before—work, work and more work. But it no longer held any satisfaction for him. She was a torchlight and he was a darkened attic, and she'd highlighted the shadows and cobwebs inside him.

The things she'd shown him...well, he couldn't ignore them any longer.

★ ★ ★

Several days later, Theo was sitting at his desk, staring blankly at his computer screen. He was so far behind in his work that his grandkid's grandkids would be playing catch-up.

That would require you to first find someone not to piss off long enough to have children.

He grunted at himself and swiveled his chair around to look out of the window. Camilla was snoozing lightly in the corner of his office. He'd started bringing her in to work, hating the idea that she was home alone all day. Plus it gave him an excuse to go for a walk at lunch. Everyone in the office thought he'd been replaced by a doppelganger, because surely that was the only excuse for him suddenly turning into a doting dog dad.

"Theo?" Irina poked her head into Theo's office.

"Yeah." He turned back around and scrubbed a hand over his face. He could feel the tiredness dragging his limbs down, and the lack of a decent meal in the last few days zapping his energy.

"There's a young girl at the reception desk claiming she needs to speak with you. I have no idea who she is." Irina pulled a face. "But she's very insistent. Darla told her you weren't available but she won't leave. I really don't want to have to get security involved, but…"

Theo's ears pricked up. "What's her name?"

"Danielle Thompson."

"Let me handle it." He pushed back on his chair and headed through the office, noticing the way people skittered out of his path like frightened chickens. God, he must have been even more of a beast of late than usual. Shaking his head, he made a mental note to do something nice for the office. A big lunch, perhaps. Or maybe a company-wide vacation day. It wasn't their fault he was messed up.

When he got to the reception desk, he saw Dani sitting in one of the plush, navy leather chairs, pointing and flexing her sneakered feet like she was in ballet class. He couldn't help but smile. "I hear there's a Danielle Thompson being rather insistent about speaking with me."

Her head snapped up and her blue eyes sparkled with mischief. "I was told you were busy."

"And I was told you didn't know how to take no for an answer." He motioned for her to follow him. "You want a drink or something? We can chat downstairs."

"Sure." She got to her feet and slung her backpack over one shoulder. "Do they have those frappé things? I like the ones with whipped cream."

"We can get you whatever you like."

Theo ignored the shocked expressions on both Irina and the receptionist's faces as he got into the public elevator with Dani. He could only imagine what stories they were making up in their heads right now—secret child, long-lost cousin.

"Why is everyone staring at you?" Dani asked quietly as they rode down to the ground floor.

"I don't get out much," he replied, stifling a smirk.

Once they got to the bottom and the elevator cleared out, he led Dani toward the coffee shop. There was a line, but by the time they'd ordered—an espresso for him and some sugary monstrosity frappé thing for her—there was a table free in one corner.

"So, what's the nature of your visit, Miss Thompson?" he asked as they sat down with their drinks.

"I want to know why you and Isla broke up," she said. When she sucked on her straw, her cheeks hollowed out from trying to get the fudge through the thin tube.

"How do you know we broke up?"

"It's obvious. She's sad, you're sad and no one is telling me a damn thing." She rolled her eyes.

"I'm pretty sure you're not supposed to say *damn*," he scolded gently.

Dani lifted one shoulder into a shrug. "Desperate times call for desperate measures."

"And why is it desperate?"

Dani waded her straw back and forth through the whipped cream, trying to mix the fudge into her drink. For a moment, she wouldn't meet his eye. "When I say sad, I mean *real* sad."

That socked him in the chest. "Is she okay?"

"Yeah. But like..." She sighed. "When you were dating, she seemed excited all the time, you know? And now it's gone."

"I understand," he replied quietly. He felt it down to his bones.

"I mean, she's excited about her business and all, but I notice things when she thinks I'm not looking. She just stares into space. It's freaky."

"You should talk to Isla about this," he suggested.

"But she won't talk back to me. She's all 'when you're a grown-up you'll understand' and blah, blah, blah..." Dani looked at him as if to say *ugh, sisters*. "Anyway, I figured fixing it was better than talking."

Theo raised an eyebrow. "And how do you think you can fix things?"

"You can get back together." Dani nodded like it was the simplest thing in the world. If only adult life was as easy as teenagers thought it was.

"I don't think that's going to happen."

"Why?" Dani looked at him with big, luminous blue eyes— eyes that were so much like her sister's, full of heart and hope.

"Because…" Lord. How did he explain this to a fourteen-year-old? "It's complicated."

"I never meant to break you up—it was an accident." Tears glimmered in her eyes now and Theo's heart was almost sliced clean in two.

"What are you talking about? You didn't break us up."

"But Isla knows sometimes I get…" She bit down on her lip. "Worried about her leaving me. And I told her that it was okay if you two dated, that I would try really hard not to be worried anymore. And then I had a bad night and I was crying and then she stopped going to your house and then you broke up!"

She seemed so genuinely distressed that he had to comfort her. Theo reached out to pat her hand and it was about the most awkward thing ever. But he was trying.

"You didn't break us up, Dani. It happened while you were away at ballet camp."

She blinked with watery eyes. "Oh."

"It had nothing to do with you. Your sister loves you very much and I know that she would have spoken with you if your being upset had something to do with it."

Dani looked confused. "But then why?"

"Are you going to throw something at me if I say you'll understand when you're older?" he ventured and she glared at him.

"Yes."

"It's not nice to throw things at people."

"It's not nice to assume I don't know anything because I'm younger than you. I'm very mature for my age, you know."

He tried to hide the smile twitching on his lips because he didn't want her to mistakenly think he was laughing *at* her. "I can see that."

"I don't want her to be sad anymore. When she's sad, *I'm* sad. And I don't like being sad." Dani pouted. "It sucks."

"Yeah, it does suck." A thought struck him. "How's Isla's business going?"

"Good." Dani's face turned sunny again. "She's working a lot and she has some clients. A cute Pomeranian and French Bulldog. Oh, and a bunny! She and Scout are working on the offices at the moment. I'm helping them paint."

"You're a good sister."

"Not that good if I can't fix this." Dani sucked up some more of her frappé.

"Don't drink it too fast or you'll get brain freeze." He frowned. Was this what it was like to have a family? Where you worried about little things like brain freeze.

"This is *not* my first frappé." She shot him a haughty look, but it turned softer. More curious. "Do you not love Isla anymore?"

The question almost made him choke on his own spit. "Love?"

"Yeah, I assume you loved her if you were boyfriend and girlfriend, right? And don't try to treat me like a kid—I know what I saw."

He chuckled. "Love is…"

"Let me guess, complicated?" She made an *ugh* sound of pure disgust. "Algebra is complicated."

"I'd take algebra any day," he admitted.

"Ew." She wrinkled her nose. "No way. I want a boy to fall in love with me and it will be awesome and not even a little bit complicated."

"I thought you wanted to be a ballerina."

"And aren't all ballets about love? Besides, most of them don't go so well, so I know what to avoid." She nodded.

"No black swans, huh?"

She opened her mouth as if to explain why he was wrong, but then waved her hand like she'd thought better of it. "Whatever. Isla is sad and I can tell you're sad because you have those puffy things under your eyes, but you're both so stubborn."

He blinked. Nothing like being dressed down by a fourteen-year-old to make you evaluate your life choices. That's when Theo noticed he hadn't even touched his espresso. He brought the small cup to his lips and it was already getting cold.

"Dani," he started, using the voice his father had used when Theo was a kid. "I like your sister a lot. She's a wonderful person and I wish her a lot of success. But we're not getting back together."

"You're too scared?" she asked and there wasn't a hint of judgment in her voice.

"I'm not scared." Except he was. He was fucking terrified.

Because Isla had gotten closer than any other person and the second things had been a little rocky, he'd hidden behind his defenses. Behind his hardness and his sharp edges and his walls. The real question was, *why* was he scared?

What if I let myself love her and I lose her like I lost the rest of my family?

There it was. The truth.

It wasn't that she betrayed him, it was that he could see himself loving her. That he could see himself falling so head over heels that losing her might completely destroy him.

But haven't you already been destroyed? You live alone and lock yourself away, and it will be that way until you die unless you do something about it.

"Here's the thing." He leaned forward and braced his forearms against his knees, cradling the little espresso cup between his hands. "Your sister deserves someone who's easy to love, who doesn't have a million hang-ups like I do. I've been through a lot and it makes me…difficult."

"But I'm difficult to love and she still loves me."

Dani's words were like taking a sledgehammer to his walls. He was showered in crushed pieces of brick, almost buried by the barriers he'd spent a lifetime building.

"You're not difficult to love, Dani. Isla told me what happened with your mom and I think it's totally understandable that you'd be worried." He nodded.

"And I know what happened with your parents," she argued, her brows knitted above her pert nose. "It was really bad. So I guess that means that I understand why you're worried, too."

Checkmate. "Woe to anyone who underestimates you, Dani."

She grinned. "I've been told I would make a good lawyer."

"I think you would."

She sucked on her drink and he finished the last of his mostly cold espresso, enjoying her company as he asked her questions about her ballet camp and what she was doing on her summer break. He could listen to her chatter for hours. There was something soothing about it—the youthful energy, her insight and lack of cynicism. For a moment he wondered if this was what it was like to have a real family, with siblings and every-day talk about which YouTubers she was currently obsessed with. Or maybe what it was like to have a child, someone young that you could inspire and support and watch grow into a wonderful, complicated human themselves.

Theo's phone rang and he canceled the call. But a text popped up a second later, Irina scolding him because he was about to miss an important meeting with the CEO of a major book chain who'd flown in from the UK.

"I have to go," he said reluctantly. "Duty calls."

Dani nodded, her shoulders a little slumped. "Okay."

"I promise it was nothing you did." He rose from his chair and held out a hand to help her up.

"Thanks." She nodded. "I still don't get it, though. I overheard her telling Scout that she needed to be the right inspiration for me and so that's why she couldn't do the Dachshund thing anymore. I thought that was why she wasn't seeing you and Camilla."

Theo shut his eyes for a moment. That was the confirmation he'd been looking for—Isla had deleted the Instagram account.

"She said it made her feel like a bad person." Dani frowned. "And I know that's because I freaked out the last time she had a boyfriend. I made her feel guilty."

"Dani, we're all entitled to our scars. But the best thing we can do is see them as a reminder of how strong we are, rather than a barrier for living our lives."

She bobbed her head. "That makes sense."

"You're not weak for being worried about the future. You're strong for still striving for your dreams in spite of that worry."

The teenager blinked, as if something had landed in an impactful way. "That's true. I keep dancing even though I'm worried I won't make it into the company I want."

"That's called resilience." He pulled her in for a quick hug, which surprised her as much as it did him. "I really do have to go now. But any time you want someone to talk to, you can call me, okay?"

He handed her a business card and she looked at it, as if a little confused by the gesture. Business cards were pretty old-school—maybe she didn't really understand the point of it.

"That's my email and phone number. Any time you need something, call."

He waved his hand in farewell and headed out of the café, taking brisk strides toward the elevator. Revelations were swirling in his head. Isla *had* deleted the account. Even after he fired her. Even after he used it as a shield to protect himself. Even after she had no possible reason to do something that would benefit him, especially to the detriment of her own goals.

A person's words meant little if their actions didn't uphold the values they espoused. And Isla's actions showed everything. She was a good person, heart and soul. He missed her like hell. Missed her smile, missed her joy, missed her tenacity and kindness and the way she held him like he was a real live person with something to offer.

As he rode the elevator back up to his company's floor, Theo couldn't shake the feeling that the ball was in his court. He had two options—go on like he had, miserable and alone. He could double down on building his walls and miss out on the woman who'd turned his world upside down. Or he could change. He could be resilient and forge ahead in spite of his worries.

As he walked into the reception area, ignoring Irina's scolding, he knew only one of those options had the chance to give him the life he never thought he could have. One with love and family and belonging. One with a future.

And that meant he needed to show Isla how he felt, rather than simply telling her.

25

ONE WEEK LATER...

Isla stood in the middle of the Paws in the City office and she could hardly believe her eyes. In record time and with the help of her best friend and her sister, she had turned this shell into a stylish, modern place of business.

Yes, her personal office was basically a glorified cupboard. But it was a *pretty* glorified cupboard, with a window that got some nice afternoon sunlight and furniture in shades of pale pink and a soft dove gray with gold accents. They'd given the walls a bright coat of white paint and hung a mirror to make the space feel bigger.

The Paws in the City reception area had pink seats with gold metal legs and on the wall was a large canvas with an abstract painting of a dog. Isla wasn't going to tell anyone that she'd found it for ten dollars on Craigslist. The meeting room was designed to look comfortable and creative, with big artfully decorated bookshelves serving as a backdrop for any animal headshots they needed to take. A small glass table was flanked by three comfy sofa chairs that Isla had found for a steal at Target.

Everything had been done on an extreme budget—second-hand items, DIYs and thrift-store finds. They'd done much of the work themselves, sanding and painting and putting together IKEA furniture while pop music blasted from whoever's cell phone still had battery power.

And now it was done.

"It looks incredible." Scout squealed and clapped her hands together. "Now, I know you want to get right into work but I will *not* let this moment pass without a celebration."

Isla laughed as her friend went to the bar fridge they kept behind the reception desk to store their lunches and bottled water for clients. Only this time, Scout had hidden away a bottle of champagne.

"It's 9:00 a.m.," Isla said with a laugh.

"Slow your roll, girl. I brought some OJ too and mimosas are totally a breakfast drink." She'd also stashed some champagne flutes for the occasion.

"You're the best."

There was a knock at the front door and Isla walked over, wondering who the heck was coming by. Perhaps it was their accounting firm neighbors wanting a sneak peek. But when she pulled the door open, Isla gasped to see her sister standing there with a big box in her hands.

"I thought you were going to the museum today," Isla said, letting her in.

Dani grinned. "I am…later. Scout wanted to surprise you."

"Oh my gosh. You guys." Isla's eyes brimmed with happy

tears, but there was no denying the persistent ache inside her. As excited and motivated as she was, the Theo-shaped hole in her heart didn't seem to be healing. All she wanted was to have him by her side, celebrating what could be.

"No tears." Scout thrust a mimosa into her hand and then handed a glass to Dani. "Sorry, girl, it's plain OJ. No bubbles for you."

Dani pouted and Isla laughed. "I've learned my lesson about teenagers and champagne, that's for damn sure."

"That moment led you here," Scout said, pouring a drink for herself. "Without The Incident, you might still be working as an underling rather than striking out on your own."

"Maybe everything *does* happen for a reason."

Dani opened the box. Inside were half a dozen perfectly frosted pink-and-white cupcakes with paw prints on top.

"They're adorable! We have to get a shot for the Instagram account." Isla set up the camera and got the girls to pose with her while they used the self-timer to take a photo of the three of them. "I couldn't do this without you two."

With Dani on one side and Scout on the other, Isla knew she was never going to risk losing the people she loved ever again. She'd learned her lesson from lying to Theo. From now on she would be honest, always.

Maybe you should call him…

The temptation was there, just below the surface. Constant. Unrelenting. But she'd told him how she felt at the time and it wasn't enough.

This circular thinking wasn't new. In fact, it was almost a daily occurrence. So Isla shook it off and decided to focus on celebrating her business. Earlier that morning she'd "opened" the website for new clients to contact her, although they already had a few people lined up. *And* she'd reached out to some old brand contacts and started rebuilding those relationships.

As Dani was retrieving a cupcake for herself, the phone on the reception desk rang. Scout shot them both a look.

"I'll get it," she said, swiping the phone from the cradle. "Hello, Paws in the City…yes, that's us. Wonderful. Actually, we have a few spots available tomorrow if you like?"

Isla couldn't wipe the grin off her face as Scout took down their first booking. Dani jumped up and down, squealing. The second the phone was back in the cradle, it rang again. "Hello, Paws in the City…yes, absolutely. When would you like to come in?"

Isla's mouth dropped open. Of course she'd used her contacts and skills to build interest before the launch, but she hadn't exactly been expecting a flood of calls the day they opened. Yet as Scout put the phone down, looking a little shell-shocked, it rang again. And again. And again.

"What is going on?" Isla looked on, bewildered. She hadn't even taken a bite out of her cupcake because she was so stunned.

Scout opened her mouth to answer, but the phone rang again. "Hello, Paws in the City…"

"Isla, look." Dani held her phone out. On it was a video of Theo from his publishing company's Twitter account.

At first, she couldn't believe what she was seeing. But it was him, sitting in what must be his office at work, with a beautiful view of the city behind him. He was wearing a suit and holding Camilla on his lap. Isla cringed at how much dog hair was going to end up on all that expensive tailoring.

"For a long time I haven't spoken publicly about my life or my relationships," he said, his intense amber stare penetrating right through the phone screen. "The death of my grandmother was a blow and, as many of you know without me having to say it, she was a wonderful woman with a huge heart. Some of you may also know her dog—this little critter, Camilla.

"But what many of you probably don't know, is that she was the mysterious voice of The Dachshund Wears Prada. Or rather, Camilla was the character created by a wonderful and creative woman by the name of Isla Thompson. She has since deleted the account out of respect for my privacy but…"

Theo paused, as though gathering himself. Camilla shifted on his lap, looking up at him with utter love and adoration.

"I've put my privacy first for so long, I no longer knew how to connect with people. I know people call me the Hermit of Fifth Avenue and I know that I have become more urban legend than man. So I'm making a public statement today. Isla Thompson is behind The Dachshund Wears Prada and she has gone on to create an exciting business called Paws in the City. I ask that you support her. Isla is the kind of person who brings light to darkness. She is the kind of person who picks herself back up when she stumbles and she's a wonderful influence on those around her."

Isla felt a tear splash onto her cheek and she brushed it away with a trembling hand.

"I could not be more grateful to have had someone like her in my life to show me how shuttered I had become."

The video continued on for a little while longer, but Isla couldn't concentrate on anything but the look of relief on Theo's face. He looked like a man reborn. A man who'd discovered that there was more than one path in life.

"It's gone viral," Dani said, snatching her phone back. "Look how many retweets it's had!"

The reception phone continued to ring and Isla drew her sister in for a hug, her mind a blur and her heart full. Theo had given her a great gift, and if this interest was anything to go on, she wouldn't need to worry about her six-month deadline.

★ ★ ★

Theo climbed the steps to Isla's new office. The building was small. So small, in fact, he'd walked right past it and ended up at the next intersection before realizing he'd gone too far. But now he could hear her voice floating into the stairwell, along with two others.

So many times on the way over he'd thought about chickening out. Isla might not have seen the video and him turning up could seem overbearing. But he'd believed Dani when she told him that Isla had been missing him. And Lord knew he'd been missing her.

Did the outcome of all this even matter? Well, yes, of course it did. But the outcome wasn't the *reason* he was here. He needed to bare himself to Isla, whether she accepted his apology or not. He needed her to know that she'd pulled him out of the darkest depths in which a man could find himself.

She'd changed him. Changed the course of his life.

When Theo got to the top of the steps, his heart was pounding. Not from exertion, but from the feeling that he was taking a bold step he'd never taken before. Being honest and open and vulnerable—these were not his skills. Not his abilities.

The door for the Paws in the City office was frosted, so you couldn't see inside. The company logo—expertly designed with a paw print and feminine flourish—was printed in gold. It looked polished and professional and enticing, like Isla herself. Sucking in a breath, he pushed the door open.

The three women in the office jumped at his entry. It seemed they weren't expecting anyone.

"Theo?" Isla's eyes grew wide and next to her, Dani's mouth popped open.

"Hi."

"Hi." Her breath stuttered. She shifted awkwardly on the

spot, her hands fluttering over the waist of her floral blue-and-yellow skirt. "What are you doing here?"

"I was hoping we could talk...unless you're too busy?"

The phone rang and a blonde woman picked it up, answering in a professional tone. Dani was halfway through eating a cupcake, a smear of frosting on her chin.

"No, I'm not too busy. I mean, the phone is ringing off the hook, but Scout has that taken care of," she said, glancing at Dani.

"Don't worry about me," the younger girl said with a shrug. "I'll keep watch over the cupcakes."

"I don't think so." Isla plucked one out of the box and narrowed her eyes at her sister. "I know what you're like."

Dani stuffed the rest of her cupcake into her mouth in one go and her cheeks puffed out as she tried to chew. "Myphhs umf mrphfrnh."

Shaking her head, Isla motioned for Theo to follow her. "We can talk in here."

She led him into the meeting room and closed the door, placing the cupcake on top of a glass table. The space was compact, but well laid-out, and all the light colors, glass and the big window made it feel warm and welcoming. "You've done a wonderful job with the space."

"Thank you," she said softly. "And you've done a wonderful job outing me as the person behind The Dachshund Wears Prada."

So she *had* seen the video. "It was the least I could do."

"How did you know I wanted to be outed?" she asked. Her hands curled around the back of one of the chairs, as if she needed something to keep her tethered.

"Because you were proud of what you built," he replied simply.

"I built something that hurt people."

"Not people, just me."

Her expression softened. "You're people, Theo. And I count Camilla in there too, even though calling her 'people' might be a stretch."

"Here's the thing, you didn't hurt me. Not in the way you think." He let out a long breath. "You were right—the account revealed nothing about my life and I could see that you'd been very careful to hide my identity. But when I found out, I was angry because I'd been used before. I tarred you with that brush without giving you the chance to voice your intentions."

"I swear I never meant for you to find out like that."

"I know," he said. "But at that stage I was falling for you so hard that I had no idea what to do about it. Your secret, in a way, became my life raft. I clung to it when I was scared about how you made me feel and I used it as a way to protect myself, to push you away."

She lowered her gaze. "You were right to do that."

"No, I wasn't. Because it was a betrayal of what we shared."

Say it, man. Stop hiding behind your walls and say it.

Isla was watching him, her eyes wide and sincere. Her fingernails bit into the soft-looking fabric of the chair in front of her and the light filtering into the room made her look like an angel.

Tell her. Now.

"Every single person I've ever loved is gone," he said, hating the way his voice sounded raw and rough. "Every. Single. One. You have no idea how terrified I was to realize that I felt something for you."

"I have some idea," she replied with a sad smile.

"I'm wired to assume the only outcome for love is pain. It's what history has taught me. It's what *life* has taught me. But there you were all sparkly and hopeful and so full of goodness and joy it was like staring into the sun. How was I supposed to come back from that?"

"You weren't." Her eyes glimmered and she shook her head. "You're not supposed to come back from that."

"And I haven't. Isla…" He stepped forward. "I'm sorry I was a complete and utter asshole."

"You don't get to carry all the blame, Theo. I played my part, too." She bit down on her lip. "I'm sorry I took so long to come clean."

The air was thick between them. They were both wounded, both guarded, both wary of love. But that's what it was—love. And Theo knew that love wasn't how they sold it in the movies. It was never that grand sweeping perfect thing. It wasn't a filtered Instagram picture or a carefully curated profile. It was *im*perfect, messy and inconsistent and gloriously, wonderfully complicated.

The old Theo shunned those things. But now, he'd seen what could be gained from opening up. From sharing yourself with another person.

Was there risk? Yes. Could he get hurt? Absolutely. But was being with Isla worth all that and more? One hundred percent.

Isla's head was almost swimming from the roller coaster of emotions. Her business was blossoming right before her eyes and this man had played a huge part in that. Now he was here, reaching out. Opening doors instead of closing them.

They'd both made mistakes. They'd both had barriers. Could they get past it all, together?

"Dani came to see me, you know," Theo said, laughing and shaking his head. There was almost something shy about him, which was the most endearing thing Isla had ever seen.

While there had been a certain appeal in Theo's brutish and brooding side, there was more to him than that. And yes, in bed he was forward, take-charge and relentless. In his work he was ambitious and persistent and motivated.

But there was also a hidden softness to him, a quietness. A goodness.

"She did?"

Theo nodded and stuffed his hands into his pockets. "She came to my office."

"Why on earth would she do that?"

"She thought she was responsible for us breaking up."

Isla closed her eyes for a second. "Oh, Dani."

"I set her straight. Told her that it had nothing to do with her and that you would have been honest with her if that was the case."

"Exactly. I would have!"

"I also told her it was complicated, which got me the eye roll to end all eye rolls," he said and Isla laughed, her eyes glimmering. "But she had a point. Adults tend to over-complicate simple things because we heap all our own baggage onto other people and get in our own heads. When really, relationships are as simple as can be."

Her heart fluttered with hope. "You think?"

"I do." Theo reached out and took Isla's hand in his, bringing it to his chest. His heart thumped under her palm, mimicking the same hastened beat as hers. He had hummingbirds, too. "The simple fact is I love you. Everything else is noise."

"Everything else is noise," she echoed. His words rang so true and she felt the love for him sweep through her body. It was so right she had no hope of denying it.

"I wanted to come here because I couldn't stand the thought of another day passing without me telling you, Isla. I don't know how to be a good boyfriend. I don't know how to be in a relationship. I don't know how to be a good influence on others or when to speak or when to listen." His warm amber eyes bored into hers, sincerity and love shining bright. "But I want to try."

"You *do* know, Theo. You know so much more than you give yourself credit for." Isla smiled up at him. "Do you think my sister, Little Miss Attitude, would have come to you if she didn't think you were good for me? That girl has a bullshit radar like I have never seen before. You passed with flying colors."

"It was the hot chocolate," he joked.

"You think you're the beast locked away in a castle, but you're just a man. A scarred, wonderful, giving man." She raised her hand to cup his jaw. "And I know what it's like to hide behind walls. I've done it for a long time, too scared that I would turn into my mother. Too scared that I wouldn't know how to be with someone *and* give Dani what she needs. I've doubted myself forever."

Her hands were almost trembling now, but it wasn't fear pumping adrenaline through her body. It was excitement. Anticipation. The thrill of knowing good things were on the horizon.

"But I also know that I would regret not kissing you now for the rest of my life," she whispered. "Because I love you, too."

He was in front of her in an instant, strong arms crushing her body to his. She buried her face in his shirt, melting against the soft cotton and breathing in the smell of soap and woodsy aftershave and him. Being touched by him—held by him—felt so right she almost wanted to cry. He brought his lips down to hers. Energy crackled around them and Isla was sure there were fireworks behind her eyelids as they shuttered. Theo's kiss was soft and deep and it hinted at more. So much more.

His tongue danced with hers, coaxing her to open to him. To melt into him. To be his, wholly and completely.

"Can you forgive me?" he asked.

"Can you forgive *me*? I won't let you take all the blame on this," she said. "I'll be honest, there was part of me that knew you'd be hurt by what I'd done and it was pure selfishness that held me back from telling you. I knew I'd never find another man who excited me the way you do, who'd be as good with Dani as you are. You were built to be part of a family."

"You have no idea how long I have wanted that." He pressed his lips to her forehead. "To not be alone anymore…"

"We can build one together." Her lips grazed his. "You, me, Dani, Camilla."

"And more to come?" His eyes were wide and hopeful. This man, this wonderful, courageous man.

"Yes."

He shook his head, a lock of dark hair flopping over his forehead. Strong fingers raked it back and Isla was struck by how much she wanted to feel those fingers dance across her skin again. "You're everything I could have hoped for. My parents would have loved you."

"I'm sorry I never got to meet them."

He cupped her face. Up close, she could see all the shades of warmth in his eyes—the burnt gold and fiery amber and the ring of espresso brown and flecks that were almost green. They were an endless, bottomless kind of beautiful.

"The second you stepped into my life I realized what I'd been missing," he said. "What I'd keep missing if I continued along the same path."

She searched his face, her eyes tracking over the details she'd come to adore—the proud thrust of his nose and the heavy row of lashes around his eyes and the full lips made for kissing. The softness of his skin and the sharpness of his teeth when he dragged them across her skin.

"We'll make this work, Isla. I want to be there for you and Dani, not just now but forever."

"You have no idea what you're promising," she said, shaking her head. "Offering to take care of a type-A teenager and her ambitious big sister is not for the weak of heart."

"Good thing my heart's a lot stronger than I ever gave it credit for."

"I love you so much." The words burst out of her as she looked up at him, arms around his neck and body lining his.

"I love you, too." He kissed her long and deep. "I want to take you out tonight. Dani and Scout, too. My treat. I want to celebrate all you've accomplished and all you're going to accomplish."

"And after dinner?"

"Dessert." He pressed his lips to her neck. "But no one else is invited to that."

"I'm sure we can make some arrangements."

Theo's husky laugh sent goose bumps rippling across her skin. "You're a woman who knows how to get shit done. I admire that."

"You do?"

"Absolutely." His hand skimmed over her hip and he was about to kiss her again when Isla's eyes caught movement at the meeting room door.

"Someone's peeking," she said. Then she pointed at the culprit, crooking her finger and calling them forward. "Come here, spy."

The door opened wider and Dani's face was revealed. "Are you done making up yet?"

"Are we?" Isla looked to Theo and his returning expression was wicked and sinful.

"That might take a while, yet," he said, whispering right into her ear in a way that made her shiver.

"Yes, we are," Isla said, shooting him a look. Then she looked at Dani. "Why? Are you invested in the outcome of this?"

She shrugged and scuffed her toe against the ground. "Maybe."

"Come here." She motioned for Dani to join them. She came over quickly and tucked in against her sister's side. "My favorite people in the world."

"Say cheese!" Scout was in the doorway with her phone up, ready to snap a picture of Isla's budding family. "Now everybody scoot, because we've got our first appointment arriving in five minutes. Game faces on."

Dani squealed and Isla's stomach pitched. This was *it*, it was really happening.

"You've got this," Theo said, grabbing her hand and squeezing. "Everything you ever wanted is right in front of you."

"It sure is," she said, leaning in to kiss him once more. Dani made a noise of disgust and headed toward the door, pausing only to throw a wink over her shoulder before she skipped into the reception area, a cupcake in one hand.

"Did she…?" Isla looked at the table. "She totally stole my cupcake."

Theo laughed and the sound was so free and bright Isla was sure she'd never forget it. "Ah, family, can't live with 'em, can't live without 'em."

They walked out of the meeting room, hand-in-hand. Who would have known that she *could* have everything she'd ever dreamed of? Mistakes would come and she would deal with them, but the lesson she'd learned remained: bet on yourself and those around you. Trust that everything that happens is moving you to where you want to be.

And right now, with love in her heart and a sexy, perfect man about to take her into his bed, Isla was exactly where she wanted to be.

Epilogue

ONE MONTH LATER...

Isla took in a long, deep breath and smoothed her hands down the front of her dress. She'd chosen this one because its rich berry color made her eyes pop and contrasted nicely with her skin. She checked her lipstick in the mirror to make sure none had gotten on her teeth and then she slid her feet into a pair of shiny black stiletto pumps, relying on the way they made her stand a little taller and straighter to help boost her confidence.

"You can do this," she said to her reflection.

Today was a big day. The *biggest* day, possibly.

A prominent New York journalist had taken an interest in Isla's story—how she came to kill her career with a single mistake only to bounce back by opening a business that had everyone talking. Today Isla was being interviewed about it and it was like her moment of redemption had come. The world would see that she *was* a successful businesswoman. That she wasn't a joke or a failure or a career-killer.

Isla's reputation would finally be restored.

A knock at the door made her suck in a breath, and a second later Scout poked her head in. "Showtime."

Nodding, Isla pulled her shoulders back and walked out into the reception area.

"Melanie Miller will be here in a minute with her crew," Scout said.

Her blond hair was pulled back into a chic low bun and she wore a pair of skin-tight black jeans with a hot-pink silky shirt. For the last few months, she'd worked as Isla's right-hand woman—doing everything from answering calls, to managing the company calendar, handling media inquiries and keeping the office supplies stocked. Having her best friend working by her side made everything feel less daunting, because aside from Theo and Dani, Scout was her biggest cheerleader.

"Get settled in the meeting room and I'll greet them when they come up," Scout added. "I put a jug of water and some glasses in there, plus some of our branded cookies."

"You're a gem." Isla pulled Scout in for a quick hug. "Seriously, I don't think I could handle all this without you."

"Thanks for taking a chance on me when you already know all my bad habits," Scout said.

"Hey, you've only been late once that I can think of and I don't expect you *not* to be human. In fact, I think your record is better than mine."

"Hmm, maybe that's because I don't have a sexy man luring me back to bed in the morning." Scout winked.

Isla opened her mouth to fire off a retort, but the front door suddenly swung open. At first, all she could see was a big bouquet of pink-and-white flowers and a set of long legs in black dress pants walking through the door. But then Theo poked his head around the side of the arrangement.

"What are you doing here?" Isla pressed a hand to her chest.

He knew today was the big day. Melanie Miller had tried to beg, borrow and steal her way into having Theo attend the interview, but Isla had stood firm.

Theo didn't give interviews, period.

The video he'd released before they reconciled was pre-recorded, not live. And he'd written the script. It was also the *only* public statement he'd made in years and Isla wasn't going to ask him to change that simply because a journalist dangled some juicy publicity in front of her.

Isla hadn't even asked him to take part, because there was no way she wanted him to think she'd use his name to further her business. His trust was far too important to risk.

"I heard there was some kind of interview going on today. I figured you might want some pretty flowers for the background." He grinned and Isla almost melted into a puddle. He could smile at her all day every day and the effect would *never* be less potent.

"That is so sweet, thank you." She leaned up onto her tiptoes and pressed a kiss to the corner of his mouth. Scout swooped in and rescued the flowers from Theo's hand and went into the meeting room to give them a moment of privacy. "I love you."

"I love you, too, Isla. I'm proud of you," he said, kissing her more deeply now that they were alone. His hand cupped her jaw and he ran his thumb along her cheek. "So damn proud."

"Let's see how the interview goes before you say that." Isla laughed nervously, her stomach swishing with the anticipation.

"When were you going to tell me that Ms. Miller requested to interview me as well?" He nailed her with a hard stare.

"I wasn't," Isla admitted. "I didn't want you to feel pressured and you know I respect your limits. You've done so much for me and for Paws in the City already."

Theo's video had brought them a flood of interest. So much, that Isla was already considering hiring someone else on. As it was, she'd contacted August the dog whispering groomer about using her services. *And* Dani came in after school on the nights when she didn't have ballet class. She was great with helping to keep the place organized and clean.

"I will *always* help you, Isla."

"I know. And that means I will only ask when I feel it's something that won't be painful." Isla smoothed her hands over Theo's shoulders. "Having you in my life isn't something I'm ever going to compromise or take for granted. Yes, Melanie Miller wanted you here for this interview, but I said if having you here was a requirement then I would have to politely decline her request."

Theo blinked. "You were going to walk away?"

"Absolutely."

"Even though you'd be featured on national television?"

"Yes, Theo." Isla laughed. "Luckily she still agreed to come. But I wasn't lying. If she had pushed the issue then I would have called it off. Nearly losing you last time taught me an important lesson—dreams aren't worth a damn if you don't have the right people by your side."

At that moment, Scout reappeared with an excited expression on her face. "They're coming! I was watching out the window and they've entered the building."

"Thank you for the flowers," Isla said, plucking a tissue from the reception desk and handing it to Theo. "Here, I think we both need one of these."

She managed to get her lipstick reapplied in time for Melanie Miller and her team to walk into the office. Isla had been trying to get Theo to leave before she came, but he was dragging his heels. The journalist and former news anchor extended her hand to Isla first, then Theo.

"What a pleasure to meet you both." Her cropped silver hair was sleekly styled, and she wore a royal blue dress with matching earrings. "I didn't think you were going to be involved in today's interview, Mr. Garrison."

"I've had a policy about not doing interviews for a very long time," he replied with a guarded smile. "And Isla thought she was protecting me by not even telling me about your request."

Isla looked at Theo, confused. Why was he telling a stranger this? It was very unlike him.

"However," he continued. "There's something that I've learned recently—letting people in can lead to some wonderful things. So, if it will help Isla's business, I'm happy to take part today."

Isla's jaw was hanging so low, she almost had to collect it from the floor. "But…"

"No buts." He took her hand and squeezed. "I'm not afraid of questions anymore."

"Please don't ask about Theo's parents," Isla said to Ms. Miller, shaking her head. A protective urge swelled inside her. She would fight anyone to take care of this man, as he would for her. "I'll never use his pain to sell myself or my business."

"You have my word." Ms. Miller smiled, clearly delighted at the turn of events. And Scout came over to invite them into the meeting room so the camera crew could set up.

"You really want to do this?" Isla asked as they were left alone in the reception area. "I would never expect you to put yourself on the line for me."

"Well, you should. Because being in love with someone means putting yourself on the line every single day. I'm all in, Isla. With you, with Dani, with the family we're going to build."

"Furbabies included?" Isla blinked back tears. She loved this man so much that it always made her emotions run riot.

"I don't know how Camilla will feel about that," he said with a laugh. "But hey, maybe she's changed too. I left the bedroom door open yesterday and she didn't destroy a single thing. Not even a tie!"

"Wow, maybe you *can* teach an old dog new tricks."

"You certainly can." Theo leaned in to kiss Isla and then paused at the last second. "I can't ruin your lipstick right before going on camera."

"As soon as this is over, you can ruin it all you want," she whispered. "In fact, I'm pretty sure our appointments are all done for the day. Scout can manage things for the last hour and Dani has ballet class right after school."

"You want to play hooky with me?" A wicked smile blossomed on his lips.

"Dirty hooky." She grinned. "The best kind."

Hand-in-hand they walked toward the meeting room, where cameras and lights were pointed toward two empty chairs. Isla looked up at Theo, pausing to give him one last chance to back out. But he stood tall, proud. Brave.

Isla had never known that love could change a person for the better. Yet now she knew that love had irrevocably and positively changed them both. All her dreams were aloft and the future in front of her was brighter than ever.

★ ★ ★ ★ ★

Acknowledgments

No writer is an island and there are so many people who've made this story possible. Firstly, I have to thank my husband for his constant support. Justin, I couldn't do any of this without you. Thank you for always keeping me going while I'm on deadline crunch, for reminding me that I hit the point where it feels too hard with every book, and for going on brainstorming walks with me. You're the reason I write about love.

Thank you to Taryn, my dear friend and writing world colleague. Your friendship means the absolute world to me. Thank you for always being available to jump on Skype and talk through a problem, for always being thoughtful, kind and generous with your time and ideas. Having you in my corner, and being in yours, makes this dream job even better.

Thank you to Dana Grimaldi, Kathleen Scheibling and the

rest of the Harlequin team for supporting and championing my stories. I'm beyond thrilled to be writing for HQN, and to be working with such an encouraging and professional team. This is absolutely a dream come true.

Thank you to my agent, Jill Marsal, for always being able to help me pick out the diamond in the rough of my ideas. Thank you for supporting me through the ups and downs, and for always encouraging me to believe in my abilities.

To my writer friends, Amy, Tara, Jen, Heidi and Samantha, our chats always lift me up and make me inspired to dive into my projects. Thank you for making this job less lonely! And thank you to Becca Syme and the folks in the Strengths for Writers group. This is my happy place on the internet. I love being around people who are working so hard on personal development.

Thank you to my family for supporting my career, and always being excited to see what I'm working on next. The reason family always plays such a prominent role in my stories is because of you all. I love you guys.

Most importantly, thank you to my readers. I am continually awed by the passion you show for my stories and the enthusiasm with which you embrace my words. It's more than I could ever have hoped for. With every book I write, I pour into the pages my hope that it brings you joy.

Lastly, to my coffee machine...you're the true MVP.